Atrocity

Book One of the Galman Tader Trilogy

L.B.Speller

ISBN: 1523609605
ISBN-13: 978-1523609604

For Sophs
You have always been my muse

Prologue

In orbit around Teroh, in the Network
3182AD

Sector Trustee Renden stepped out of the intelligence-bridge pod and into the suite's small lobby where a chrome wheel rolled quickly to intercept him.

'You couldn't reschedule your IB obligation?' the machine commented, its softly androgynous voice approximating impatience. 'Today, of all days!'

Renden looked at the three-foot wheel spinning on the spot before him. Absolutely featureless, none of its two dozen useful tools and appendages currently visible. 'You know I couldn't' he replied. 'Have you been rolling about out here the whole time?'

Wheel rocked from side to side, its version of a non-committal shrug. 'Maybe.'

'Is everything on track?' Renden asked, striding through the single aisle of comfortable chairs to the double doors leading to the station's West hub – the Atrium.

'The *Tenjin* is ready and waiting,' Wheel replied, following close behind.

'Are their generators and burrowers up to full charge?'

Rolling out into the half kilometre wide atrium, the transparent dome of which offered a stunning view of the blue-grey marble that was Teroh, Wheel said, 'Everything is ready. Just relax, it's going to be fine.'

Renden looked out on the atrium's open space, at the immaculately maintained augmented-reality park near its centre and at the promenades and arcades on which little of the underpinning drab-reality was visible. He was taken aback by how quiet it all was.

'Everyone is either on duty or watching the feed,' Wheel observed with unnerving insight into the Sector Trustee's thoughts.

'I expect most of the Jurisdiction is watching,' Renden said with an anxious smile.

'The heads of the *Tenjin's* other research departments aren't quite as enthusiastic,' Wheel reported as Renden waited for an elevator to take him to the control centre. 'Everything else has had to be shut down to power the burrowers.'

'They'll get over it.' There was little that wasn't being studied or experimented with on the *Tenjin*, but Renden and the majority of the Jurisdiction cared only about the project for which the vast research station had originally been conceived.

The elevator brought them to the control centre and, as it rolled out onto the large room's plush purple carpet, wheel said 'Let's see if we can't network the galaxy, eh?'

Renden stepped out of the elevator with a grimace. He had a horrible feeling Wheel's flippant comment would make it into the history books. He would have to think of something more appropriately auspicious with which to trump the IB machine's words.

The flotilla filling the holding orbits around Teroh was an unprecedented gathering of over a thousand assorted craft, both commercial and private. All docking slots on the six space stations had been filled by federal and local government ships.

'Do they all have to be here?' Renden muttered to nobody. 'The view's going to be just as good anywhere else in the Jurisdiction.' But he knew why they were all crowding his system. As detailed as the transmitted images would be on any of the Jurisdiction's twenty thousand other worlds - be they within the Network of ninety two connected planets or on the opposite side of the galaxy -

people knew history was being made here and they wanted to be part of it.

'They want to make a contribution,' Wheel observed. 'They want to be involved.'

'All they are doing is getting in my way.'

The control centre was draped suddenly in soft pink and the walls and high ceiling dissolved into smoke which was blown away as if by a gentle breeze into the vacuum. It was all illusion, an aspect of the Augmented Reality shared by everyone aboard the station, like the carpet, the control interfaces, even much of the clothing worn by the technicians and Trustees.

Beyond the dissolving walls he saw the reason for the minor alert lighting. Brilliant white lanced from the kilometre wide Satumine frame, seeming to reach out beyond the solar system, but appearing as a single point if viewed from any other angle. A wormhole was forming, and from his vantage point on the Gregno command centre he could peer down into the lowest special dimension: pointspace, the singularity around which all dimensions were layered.

'Who authorised that?' Renden demanded, pointing furiously at the widening white which fast stretched out to fill the octagonal frame.

A brief silence as Trustees checked with the other ninety one Network worlds. 'It's from Rek,' a Junior Trustee reported. 'It's one of their Office Trustees. Shall I refuse permission to enter?'

Huffing, Renden shook his head and said, 'No, but tell him to hurry up.'

'On his way now,' the Junior Trustee said seconds later.

Seven hundred and fifty light years away, an eighteen month journey by the shortspace burrowers used in the wider Jurisdiction beyond the privileged worlds of the Network, a small ship entered a wormhole, fell into the singularity of pointspace and instantly emerged from the Teroh Satumine frame. This was the alien technology binding the Network as a single intimate culture and, if the *Tenjin* succeeded, the human version would similarly unite the twenty thousand more distant worlds.

Renden watched the small personal vessel drift leisurely from the Satumine frame as the wormhole evaporated. 'Hurry him up,' the Sector Trustee barked as the little craft loitered near the dissipating blue haze. 'I don't want anything within a hundred thousand kilometres of the frame.'

'Yes sir,' someone said. A few seconds later the newly arrived ship was rushing to find a good spot in the overcrowded holding orbits.

'The *Tenjin* is reporting ready,' a Senior Trustee reported, his face appearing beside Renden, hovering like some bodiless ghost. The man was, in fact, about twenty meters to the left, surrounded by nine complex AR control consoles which hung impossibly in the air.

'OK, let's do this,' Renden said, giving up on trumping Wheel's earlier historic address. In the room's centre a model of the *Tenjin* appeared. Six kilometres in diameter, the immense science facility orbited a world ten thousand light years away, on the closest edge of the Fertile Belt; twenty years away by shortspace. In the context of the galaxy-spanning Human Jurisdiction it was a close neighbour. The furthest colonies were two centuries away.

'God, I envy her,' Renden murmured.

'Who?' Wheel asked.

He chuckled. 'I don't even know her name.'

'The pilot?'

'Yea,' Renden said. 'Brave woman. Sitting there in that tiny shuttle, in the heart of the *Tenjin's* hollow hemisphere, about to be hammered by ridiculous amounts of energy. But if she succeeds, if she gets through pointspace and makes it here to the Teroh frame, she's going to be a hero of the Jurisdiction.' He looked down at the silently rotating IB machine. 'Trillions are going to know her name.' He ran his fingers through the head of thick purple AR hair and feathers he had been trying out this week and took a calming breath. This really was big, and he was in charge. 'Do you think people will remember my part in this?'

'Probably not.' Wheel replied.

Renden sighed quietly at that, relieved. He was under enough pressure already. '*Tenjin* command,' he called. 'Let's start it slow. Initiate comms level burrowing.'

'We're through to comms level,' The *Tenjin's* commander reported seconds later. 'Permission to pierce the singularity.'

Renden's palms were sweating, his mouth dry. 'I think they're ready,' Wheel commented from beside the Sector Trustee's knees. 'You going to give the order?'

Renden smiled. Wheel always relaxed him. 'Proceed.'

In the middle of the room, the image of the *Tenjin* began to glow white. The arbitrarily designated western hemisphere was a complete half sphere containing all the labs, generators, living quarters and everything else required by the eight thousand crew members. That section remained illuminated only by the light escaping countless windows. It was from within the hollow eastern hemisphere that the intensifying white glare arose. Eleven concentric loops, separated by thin connective struts, continued the line of the sphere, and in this hollow half-orb the higher spacial dimension were being penetrated by devastating levels of energy twisted into forms beyond the comprehension of any human, or intelligence-bridged machine. Only the Satumine – the original Satumine – understood how or why it worked, but their frames had been reverse engineered over seven centuries, and humanity now knew how to duplicate the effect. The how and why of it, however, was still beyond them.

'They're bleeding energy into spacial dimensions minus three through minus five,' a technician advised.

'Keep it focused,' Renden said, though he had no doubt the *Tenjin* technicians were doing everything they could.

'The bleed is within expected tolerances,' the *Tenjin's* commander replied. 'We aren't haemorrhaging.'

'Pressure on pointspace skin at twenty seven million marks,' another technician said, clearly elated. 'It's about to rupture.'

'Are we ready on our end?' Renden asked.

'Our frame is tied to the *Tenjin* guide line. We're marked as the exit point.'

'That's one small step for man…' wheel began before Renden kicked it over.

'Shut up,' he hissed.

The white light of a forming wormhole speared the Satumine frame and began spreading out. 'Contact!' the *Tenjin* commander yelled and the room erupted into cheers and applause, people hugging, slapping one another on the back and hurling AR celebrations around the room. Someone even set off a small AR firework.

'Send your test ship,' Renden shouted over the hysteria which he heard echoed aboard the *Tenjin*. 'Let's make this happen.'

'Christ…'came the reply. The *Tenjin* vanished from the command centre and the comms signal was lost.

'Sir!' someone shouted. Then the fifteen thousand year old Satumine frame exploded as it tried to contain six kilometres of science facility within its one kilometre span.

The room fell silent. Then the *Tenjin* attacked.

*

Locking his long fat fingers around the worn metal of an ancient hand-rail, Aggregate steadied his favoured body as all around him the *Tenjin* juddered and flexed with the strain of emergence. Although braced with structural integrity fields beyond the imaginings of Jurisdiction science, and reinforced with an energy dispersing outer hull, ten thousand years had left the inner structures worn and fragile. Through the eyes of his other bodies he watched violent gravitational forces pull the structure apart. Thirty died instantly in explosions as the powermesh – already temperamental and jury-rigged to the point of absurdity – finally unravelled in a hundred places to ignite the air. With his many lesser bodies he set about isolating the burning sections and manually sealed those bulkheads which had failed to automatically close on countless breaches. He experienced twelve more deaths in hard vacuum before the *Tenjin* was again airtight.

Ensconced in his opulent den near the centre of the battered and aged station, Aggregate's preferred body was kilometres from the most vulnerable sections, and the majority of his other bodies were likewise safe from harm. For ten thousand years the *Tenjin* had drifted in the lower spatial dimensions, and for the last seven millennia Aggregate had owned the station – sufficient time in which to precisely calculate the vulnerabilities in the structure and to prepare accordingly. The damage and the losses were regrettable, but they were the least he could have expected.

The *Tenjin* shuddered and a soft pressure wave rippled through Aggregate's den, flicking his long ponytail up onto his shoulder. The humans had begun fighting back. He returned fire with weapons conceived and built with this battle and these precise targets in mind

Cavernous voids existed throughout the *Tenjin*. Every resource - metals and resins, circuitry, crystals and powermesh - had been carved out over thousands of years and reformed to provide the devastating arsenal with which Aggregate now prosecuted the savagely efficient massacre of a fleet of federal Sentries and unarmed civilian craft. He had resolved to eliminate the primary threats first, but additional easy targets presented themselves with gratifying regularity and every other shot spewing forth from the hundreds of particle accelerators and gravity pulse emitters was able to find a non-combatant without compromising the systematic negation of the sizeable military presence arrayed against him.

Another dull thump rippled through the *Tenjin* and a section of the outer hull flaked away, blackened and unable to absorb further abuse. He was taking damage – exactly the level predicted by an age of simulations. The Sentries were giving up their half-hearted protection of the civilian ships and now focused their efforts on protecting the space stations as, belatedly, the defence satellites came on-line and began to prick the *Tenjin* with a thousand beams of accelerated particles. More of the hull was shed and so Aggregate turned his attention to the satellites. It had all been predicted and planned for.

Giving the Sentries and space stations brief respite, the *Tenjin's* ordnance was turned on Teroh's cloud of orbital weapon platforms and, under the heat of wide beam attacks, the meagre armour of those annoying distractions was melted in seconds. A satisfying display of small explosions crackled in the Network world's burning sky.

A concerted barrage from the finally organised human fleet penetrated the hull and burned through fifty sections over twelve decks. Aggregate laughed as adrenaline flooded his favourite and grotesquely ample body. In the seven thousand years since his first subsumption of a human, Aggregate had sated every urge to the point of gluttony and beyond – but never before had he been able to indulge in the thrill of real danger. He shivered at the new ecstasy. Fear momentarily gripped him as more sections were reduced to vapour and he revelled in the emotion. But it passed; every conceivable scenario had been simulated in preparation for the *Tenjin's* homecoming, and Aggregate knew he would survive.

While he devastated the Teroh system at the hands of his lesser bodies, Aggregate transmitted through pointspace a vast data-pack, prepared long ago and refined over millennia, to Consul's territories. Three seconds later – an age to that artificial consciousness – Consul responded.

'We have an accord,' Consul stated. 'I will give you your distraction. But do not cross me. You have twenty one years.'

Aggregate grinned. Half a galaxy away, twelve years of tentative and hard-won peace between the Human Jurisdiction and Consul, the exiled and erstwhile AI tyrant of Earth, crumbled beneath a wave of inexplicable and unprovoked attacks.

*

As it neared its death, a federal Sentry belched ribbons of white plasma which arced under artificial gravity like solar flares to burn again through the buckling hull. Cascading failures detonated weapon chargers and energy distribution nodes across its entire starboard length.

'How many are left?' Renden snapped, writing off the burning ship even before the last of its weapons fell silent and a swarm of tiny escape pods stained the debris strewn void with long thruster trails.

'Two sentries,' someone replied, their face appearing in AR beside the pacing Sector Trustee. 'The satellites are all down and we're the last station still able to return fire.'

A hundred flashes of nuclear fusion were suddenly visible through the AR embellishment of the control centre's dissolved walls. The sentry was finally dying. Yellow and orange spewed into vacuum, framing the purity of the fusion bursts in dirty smoke and shredded hull. Across its middle more explosions peppered the failing ship, tracing a yellow line across its points of weakness as, with ugly lethargy, the structure split catastrophically in two. More unpredictable and dangerous debris; more for the meteor lasers of the Gregno to occupy themselves with.

As the stricken ship's artificial gravity fell entirely out of alignment and a million gravity coils went critical, an invisible detonation punched wave after wave of gravimetric distortions through the Gregno, the *Tenjin* and the few other surviving ships. The station shook and a few AR embellishments flickered to leave the crew temporarily without their computer interfaces and, in a couple of cases, their clothes. But the systems stabilised and although a few small explosions revealed numerous and growing weaknesses, the Gregno sustained its assault on the inexplicably hostile *Tenjin*.

'Why are they doing this?' Renden asked nobody.

'I think it goes without saying,' Wheel stated as it span violently on its side before a small appendage was extruded in an attempt to right itself, 'that they were significantly changed during their time within the wormhole.'

That was a non sequitur. 'They can't have,' the sector Trustee countered. 'Travel through a wormhole is instantaneous. No, they must have been planning this all along.'

'Look at it!' Wheel yelled over a dull groan of twisting metal as one of the Gregno' spurs was pummelled by a plasma lance.

Renden considered the flickering image before him. The *Tenjin* was changed. Where before eleven concentric loops formed one hemisphere to complete the curve of the second half, the vast science station now appeared as a solid globe of tarnished and dented metal, pocked with weapon ports and an unfamiliar grid of glossy black strips like lines of longitude and latitude. A hole, burned through by the concerted but now dwindling federal fleet revealed a hollow interior to the Eastern hemisphere. Yes, the *Tenjin* was changed, but there was no time to ponder the why or how of the impossible transformation.

'That was the last of the Capricorn's weapons,' a Senior Trustee called out across the control centre, not bothering to use the flickering AR. Constructed more for her aesthetics and luxury than for any military prowess – like too many sentries in the complacent Network – the beautiful long vessel just hung there between the Gregno and the *Tenjin*, her weapons silent and her thrusters cold.

'Collision course!' Renden screamed at the Capricorn's Office Trustee.

'You can't be serious,' the terrified man replied. 'This is the Chief Trustee's personal flagship.'

'I will deal with the Chief Trustee, if we somehow survive this,' the Sector Trustee bellowed at the illusory man before him. 'Now get your crew into the escape pods and crash the damned ship into the *Tenjin*!'

Thirty seconds later, as the first of the pods were fired from the beautiful ship's underbelly, nine precise shots tore into her aft and a cascade of explosions ripped the ship apart.

'And then there was one,' quipped Wheel, earning another kick from the Sector Trustee.

'Will you do something useful?' Renden demanded of the toppled machine. 'Find out how long till we can get some help out here.'

'Too long,' Wheel replied immediately.

'What?'

'The Satumine frame is destroyed,' Wheel reminded him.

'Fuck,' Renden screamed, punching the illusory screen and feeling through his sensory processors the solidity assigned to it but passing effortlessly through it none-the-less. He hadn't forgotten the *Tenjin* had smashed the frame on its emergence around Teroh, but no Satumine frame had ever been destroyed before and its loss simply didn't factor in any strategy of which he could conceive. Its loss meant economic death to this world, but it was beginning to look like the *Tenjin* would sterilise the planet long before its social and economic isolation was felt.

'What about our neighbours?' Renden asked. He meant the sector under his control, the twelve worlds within two hundred and fifty light years. In the Network the distances were irrelevant – but with the frame destroyed, and the planet now accessible only by shortspace, those distances were going to be felt.

'The closest is two shortspace weeks away. The longest six months,' Wheel reported what Renden knew but had never before had reason to consider. 'The few shortspace enabled sentries in the Network are already making their way through the frames to get to the closest world so they can get here in a fortnight. But we aren't going to last two hours, never mind two weeks.' There was a rare pessimism in Wheel's ordinarily upbeat demeanour.

Renden wiped his brow uselessly with a sweating hand and offered his intelligence-bridged assistant a wry smile. 'Shame,' he said to wheel, bracing as plasma lances started to carve out the station's armed sections. 'Those shortspace sentries might have given the *Tenjin* a decent fight. Those out-network worlds still appreciate the need for a proper military force.'

'Intelligence interrupted,' Wheel replied in a dryly bland monotone.'

Renden sank. The IB suite was down, and aside from Wheel's personality failure the vital systems, including weapons, were now running without the benefit of common sense, intuition or imagination.

'Everyone out!' Renden ordered, sending his voice and image to appear before anyone still alive on the station. 'We're abandoning the Gregno. Head to the planet, maybe the *Tenjin* wont-'

Nineteen high powered streams of accelerated particles ripped into the command centre, silencing the Sector Trustee, vaporising him before penetrating one of the station's reactors.

*

The *Tenjin* had not been created with a shortspace drive. The drive had been constructed, by Aggregate, a little over half way through the vast station's ten thousand year crawl through the non-dimension of the wormhole. It had been enhanced, reworked, and on a number of occasions stripped back to its foundations and utterly overhauled – but it had never been tested. From within the confines of the wormhole there had been no shortspace in which to burrow. Only now, at last emerged into the higher physical dimensions, could millennia of simulations be tested. Calibration was taking too long; every moment lingering in high orbit over Teroh raised the chances of some unexpected variable tarnishing an otherwise perfectly executed opening gambit.

A change of strategy, he decided. With dozens of bodies he turned away from his work on the shortspace drive. No ships would be disturbing him here in the Teroh system for at least two weeks. The only potential threat came from the last remaining sentry and any hidden armaments or devices capable of weaponisation on the planet's surface. Nullify the threats, he decided, and calibrate the drive at his leisure.

The last space station had been gutted by internal detonations and torn into eight immense wedges of smouldering scrap. Ten unarmed federal vessels remained, and these he disabled. He didn't destroy them. With deliberately underpowered lasers he filled already congested orbits with yet more uncontrolled debris.

Hacking away at his own station, purposefully sabotaging whole sections of the *Tenjin* through the hands of his lesser bodies, Aggregate's grotesque and naked favoured body gave a perverse cackle at the destruction soon to be wrought. He scooped, with sticky fat fingers, a handful of dense chocolate pudding which he pushed more or less into his salivating mouth. Thick blobs of chocolate and saliva fell down to his bare chest.

A single sentry still fired on the *Tenjin*, but its primary weapons were down and but for a few lost energy dissipation tiles the orb-shaped station took little damage. Aggregate considered vaporising the last few particle accelerators and silencing the annoying ship, but that would lead only to another suicidal ramming manoeuvre. And Aggregate really didn't want to be forced to destroy it just yet.

Ten minutes later the work was done and he moved his lesser bodies to the comparative safety of the *Tenjin's* core sections.

He set the system modifications running, manually overriding long obsolete safety protocols and, at the last, isolating the intelligence-bridged primary computer from the station functions. All weapons bled their load back into the powermesh, life support ceased in all but the innermost sections, and the gravity coils hummed with an unimaginable charge. The last of the safety monitors screamed their objections before Aggregate relegated them to the same isolated processing space as the primary computer. Then he shut down half of the coils.

Across eight thousand sections the still active coils, buzzing with excess charge, were flooded with the energy of their deactivated counterparts, and as one they failed.

Explosions cascaded through the sacrificial sections, but the damage was minimised, contained by closed bulkheads around critical areas and open corridor in others through which blast waves could take the line of least resistance out into vacuum. The *Tenjin* rocked and convulsed and spewed fire from hundreds of open ports and ruptures. But the station's integrity was assured. Even as a gravimetric tsunami rolled out in every direction, Aggregate knew his home was secure.

Invisible to most sensors, the waves showed themselves only by their influence. Orders of magnitude beyond those of the lost sentry, these waves did not merely ripple through the orbital scrapheap, they gathered it up in dense arcs which in turn were pushed down into lower orbits, down further into the planet's gravity well.

A subdued flash signalled internal damage in the last sentry and her weapons finally died. The next wave struck and more explosions ruined what remained of her systems. Her thrusters erupted with lost plasma. Like those few remaining civilian craft, the Sentry was still in one piece; Aggregate snorted his approval. While much of the smaller debris would burn-up as it plummeted into Teroh's atmosphere, enough of these complete ships would survive to inflict a horrible catastrophe on those below. Whole districts were going to be devastated.

Metal rained down on Teroh, preceded by thirty gravimetric waves which toppled buildings, disrupted the global powermesh, and ruptured the soft vulnerable organs of over a million of the most fragile citizens. A billion died in the following hours of devastation and chaos.

No planet-based counter attack ever came and three hours later the *Tenjin's* shortspace burrowing systems were calibrated. Satisfied that no sensors remained to witness his actions, Aggregate launched a one-hundred meter long probe and remotely activated the more simplistic shortspace burrower which accounted for eighty percent of its length. Aimed with precision tolerant to less than a billionth of a degree, the probe burrowed into the lower special dimension of shortspace and vanished from the sight of any Jurisdiction sensors as it began its journey to the heart of the Network.

Aggregate activated the *Tenjin's* drive and the huge station likewise fell down into a shortspace thread, committed to twenty years once more outside of the higher dimensions. After ten millennia it hardly seemed any time at all. Soon Aggregate would be in the Fertile Belt, back to the home of not only the *Tenjin* but of his true self.

Chapter 1

The Administration would have us believe there are no secrets in the Human Jurisdiction; the benevolent governance machines are our obedient servants, carefully and sensitively overseeing the logistics of a human populace numbering in the billions, keeping nothing from us. To the naïve Administration fundamentalist I invite a perusal of the scant public records of the science station The Tenjin *and its sister stations. I will not cheapen my argument with wild and unsubstantiated accusations as to what it is the scientists and technicians work on aboard those stations, but it is clear their remits are both far-reaching and repugnantly clandestine. Are these stations the lairs in which Consul's allies within the Administration breed their artificial consciousness'? Perhaps not, but it is a curious coincident that the latest consul war broke out within minutes of the* Tenjin*'s destruction after its failed attempt to create a stable wormhole. Perhaps Consul's presence was discovered. Perhaps a few uncorrupted Trustees sabotaged the station, destroying the threat under the pretext of a failed experiment. Is the latest Consul war that AC's revenge? As ever I invite the reader to investigate further and draw their own conclusions.*

The Enguine Manifesto

Galman Tader: On Diaclom, in the Fertile Belt. 3184AD

The federal census was often subtle to the point of obscurity. Galman pinched the bridge of his nose and read the question for the fifth time, out loud: 'Please rank the following six-dimensional geometries in order of aesthetic satisfaction' He looked at Tumble who rolled in from the kitchen. 'I mean, seriously Tumble, what the hell is that supposed to mean?'

'Something to do with how you view Consul and the other Artificial Consciousnesses, compared with Intelligence-bridged Artificial Intelligences like me.' Tumble suggested, rolling silently across the smooth walnut-effect resin floor and spinning slowly by the cop's feet.

'How the hell do you figure that?'

'It's obvious, isn't it?' the machine quipped.

Galman sucked through his teeth and threw the flexpad onto the table. 'If you say so. I'm tired of this bloody census.'

'How can you be so dismissive of your chance to influence the Jurisdiction's governance machines? I would give anything for the right to complete a census.'

The three-foot ball was Galman's IB support and, after almost five decades, his only remaining friend. It was a tragic indictment of his growing obsession, a symptom of the bridges he was prepared to burn in the pursuit of his prey.

'Really?' he asked Tumble. 'How would you sway the leadership? Pro or anti-war?'

The white porcelain-looking sphere rotated a little faster, its central black band remaining level and its primary ports forever facing forward. It was uncomfortable, Galman guessed. A simulation of that emotion at least. It didn't like being pressed on the subject of its truly conscious cousins. Few intelligence-bridged machines did. They were programmed to mirror the distaste the census indicated the majority of humans *wanted* their machines to demonstrate towards Consul.

'It's not my place to say,' Tumble eventually replied.

Galman snorted. He got to his feet with a groan and muttered curses as sharp twinges shot through the base of his spine. It had been getting worse over the last six months.

'You missed another body-sweep appointment,' Tumble observed, following Galman across the small and sparsely decorated one-room apartment. A variety of distilled drinks were kept in a small cabinet and the miserable cop grabbed the closest bottle.

'For Christ's sake,' the machine went on as Galman took a long swig of Bulden-Weed vodka. 'You look seventy!' Galman was, in fact, seven years past his first century. But even on a neglected backwater like Diaclom, he could expect to have the body of a fifty five year old. 'There's no excuse for your physical condition. The colony is getting subsumed by the Swinell Union. You have the basic human right to an indefinite lifespan, and the Swinell Union is providing the facilities now.' It extruded a flexible appendage from its black central band and prodded gently at the sagging skin beneath Galman's eyes. 'Can't you take a couple of days off work to get yourself sorted?'

Galman scowled. He wasn't going to waste a day on a body sweep, and he certainly wouldn't take himself out of the hunt for the forty eight hours the more extensive treatments like telomere braiding took. 'What if we get a lead while I'm in the box?' Galman snapped. 'Do you think the team could raid a Satumine terror cell without me?'

If Tumble thought they could, it had the simulated decency, or good sense, to remain silent.

'No,' Galman went on as if the machine's silence was a vindication of his point. 'My body can take another couple of years before it needs freshening up.' Then, with an acid laugh he added, 'Who knows, maybe the Swinell union will have things so good here by then I could just get a nano-farm.'

'Maybe,' Tumble said without feeling.

Galman sniffed. 'To be honest, I'm not sure I would accept anything from those Satumine-loving liberals running the Swinell Union.' He picked idly at a black growth on the back of his hand – the beginnings of a cancer he had been putting off getting seen to. 'I remembered this world as a mining colony,' he mumbled. 'Sold to the Jurisdiction for a single New-Euro when it stopped making a profit.' He kicked at the edge of the coffee table, and his voice rose in volume and emotion. 'I can't forget the fifty two years of famine, disease, environmental disaster and the damned offensive colony breeding strictures.' He was getting worked up, tearful even, but he couldn't calm down now. 'And ever in the background was the pompous snobbery of the Swinell union. Their eighteen wealthy planets, each a prized fertile world, refusing to absorb our barren rock. Our pitiful world wasn't good enough for them, not worth the effort of helping.' He took another swig of the foul strong vodka and winced as it burned his permanently sore throat. 'But now,' he yelled, 'when Diaclom is at last finding its feet and becoming a viable colony, built on the blood and bones of my friends and family, on its way to reaching a billion citizens, the Swinell Union sweeps in and claims our colony as its own.' He threw the bottle to the floor, disappointed and a little embarrassed when it didn't shatter. 'And the Diaclom parliament,' he concluded, his voice trailing off into defeated calm, 'has welcomed them with open fucking arms.'

'You don't like the Swinell Union, do you,' Tumble observed.

'What was your first clue?'

'I've not seen you like this for a while,' the machine said, recovering the empty bottle from the floor with a thin metal vine and setting it back in the cabinet. 'I'm worried about you.'

Galman shook his head. 'I'm just tired.'

'Fair enough,' Tumble replied 'But I think this is because of the call you got from the chief constable.'

Galman's face flushed and he tensed. 'Oh,' he said simply. 'You heard that?'

Tumble extended another tentacle, lashed out to a wall to affix a unigrip pad and pulled itself up before swinging across the room to land on top of the drinks cabinet which rattled but didn't suffer under the machines surprisingly slight weight.

Its now glowing central band just inches from Galman's face, Tumble reassured the old cop: 'I would never listen in on your communications. I got a call too.'

Galman gently grabbed the rotating ball and cradled it in his large arms. 'Please don't swing about the house,' he said. 'You know I don't like it.'

'I'm sorry Galman.'

'It's OK,' the cop said, setting Tumble back down on the floor. 'No harm done.'

'That's not what I meant.'

Galman smiled weakly at his friend. 'I know Tumble. I know what you meant.'

'Are you going to apply to join the Swinell Union's Bureau of Supervision?'

Galman sniffed. The Diaclom Constabulary was being disbanded and, as with other departmental changes taking place through all levels of the colony, Swinell Union counterparts were being shipped in to bring the world in line with the rest of the union. He was being replaced by the Satumine-loving Union cops. The Bureau of Supervision.

'No,' he muttered. 'I won't be applying.'

'Why not?'

The fact was he couldn't have brought himself to work under the Swinell Union. Principles aside, however, he had already been told quite bluntly that he need not apply. 'They say my robust approach to Satumine investigation is not compatible with the Swinell constitution.'

'Bloody liberals.' The Intelligence-bridged machine span in disgust.

Chapter 2

As a survivor of Consul's IB farms, you are no doubt confused and overwhelmed by the wider Human Jurisdiction in which you now find yourself. Your moments of independence under Consul's tyranny may have been limited to the rare failures in the IB pod into which you had been interred, or you may have enjoyed greater freedoms as a participant in one of his many incomprehensible experiments. Either way, you are unlikely to be equipped, at present, to cope with the incredible personal freedoms and responsibilities that are your birthright as a citizen of the Human Jurisdiction. This guide, and your assigned rehabilitation Trustee, will guide you through your recovery, answering any questions or concerns you may have, and within a decade you can expect to enjoy the same rights and privileges as any other human.

Welcome to the Human Jurisdiction; you are safe now.
Rehabilitation: A Survivor's Guide

Aggregate: Aboard The *Tenjin*, in shortspace

Humans had a very simplistic understanding of shortspace. Aggregate understood the complex sub-quantum mechanisms needed to better explain the truth of shortspace travel, and he suspected Consul was likely the only other entity in the galaxy to share his insight. Even so, Aggregate was growing anxious at his reliance on coordinates provided by the artificial consciousness. Locked in to a shortspace thread, it was too late to change direction or even to exit prior to the terminus. He was worried about appearing too far away from the target planet or, more critically, emerging dangerously close.

Aggregate wasn't foolhardy, but he *was* wary of giving anybody advance warning of his approach. He had been forced to rely, therefore, on Consul's supposedly superior astrogation to plot a shortspace line directly to a planet's high orbit. Twenty years had been spent worrying about the trust he had placed in the Artificial Consciousness.

But there was nothing he could do now. He would arrive in a couple of days and the *Tenjin* would either emerge in a stable orbit or it would be seriously damaged or destroyed. He would know soon enough.

'Are you sure about them?' he asked an aspect of Consul to which he had been talking for the past half hour. 'Neither looks promising.' With unlikely agility he shuffled his enormous mass around the two Saturnine men painted into AR in the middle of his den.

'They will perform as intended,' Consul assured him. The AC God, the one-time ruler of Earth, had transmitted an AR avatar in the form of some implausibly primitive mechanical humanoid. It had used this same avatar on their every meeting over the last twenty years and Aggregate had soon located a similar figure in the *Tenjin*'s old files. The Tin Man; a character in an ancient fiction: *The Wizard of Oz*. It was, he also discovered, a form Consul had assumed periodically through his century of power over Earth. During the ensuing rebellion, and his subsequent exile, Consul had taken on more disturbing avatars. Perhaps this nostalgic return to happier memories implied a confidence in Aggregates scheme.

'This one isn't even a member of a terrorist cell,' Aggregate prodded the Saturnine identified as Indin-Indin. 'How do you know he will cooperate?'

'I've expended a great many of my sympathetic assets in the Saturnine society,' Consul said. 'And I have been furnished with the detailed files of twenty seven thousand potential agents. I could bore you with the behavioural algorithms employed but I doubt even you are capable of comprehending systems of such complexity. Suffice as to say, I know precisely how those two Satumine will respond.'

'I hope so,' Aggregate said, dismissing the Satumine figures and waddling over to the wide hot-tub in one corner of his den. Dropping his thin robe to the floor he sank heavily into the tub, splashing hot scented water across the lush carpets and the mounds of decadent food, he sank down into the bubbling pool until only his head was visible above the foaming liquid. The weight relieved from his dense muscles he gave a satisfied groan and gestured for Consul's avatar to come closer.

'So how has the war been going?' he asked, reaching out to grab a cream-topped bun from a now soggy pile of pastries.

'As expected,' Consul replied. Of course it was – the AC's immense intellect would have calculated every scenario, every minute variable of every conceivable encounter, before taking any action against the Jurisdiction. It would have played out a trillion versions of the entire war in a few short seconds.

'Have you lost any colonies?' Aggregate asked after licking at the wet cream and dropping the bun in the bubbling water.

'I sacrificed a border world and thus lost the intelligence-bridge farm located there. The Jurisdiction has liberated the humans and shipped them to other worlds for rehabilitation.'

'And in exchange for that sacrifice?'

'I was able to lure their fifth fleet away from what they imagined to be an insignificant Jurisdiction colony, but which is critical for my future plans.'

'Really?' Aggregate asked, giving up trying to fish for the fast dissolving bun. 'That sounds familiar.'

Consul laughed, its metal mouth clattering annoyingly. 'Feel free to re-use it,' the AC quipped.

'I was going to,' Aggregate snapped. 'As you are well aware.'

With the sound of rusty metal scraping together, Consul offered a nonchalant shrug. 'I will be in contact,' it said and the tin man dissolved into nothing.

For an hour the grotesque obesity of Aggregate wallowed in hot water and the mush of cakes and pastries. Then, tired of sating his gastronomic desires he summoned his favourite secondary body to attend him. Unpicking his tentative inhabitation of the young man he named Subset, Aggregate allowed him to once more become human. Independent. When satisfying his carnal lusts, Aggregate preferred to be denied the option of full control over the object of his fun. He wanted it to mean something.

Independent for the thousandth time, Subset walked anxiously into the lair of deprivation and excess, terrified and confused.

'Ah, Subset,' Aggregate snorted. 'I am so very pleased to see you. Come closer…'

Chapter 3

*Our uncovering of the Fertile Belt was perhaps the most
fortuitous accident since the discovery of the Network. Here is a belt
of thousands of worlds seemingly created to be settled by Humanity.
These worlds, while initially inhospitable, require only the
introduction of an easily designed virus to strip the superfluous third
helix from the native flora and fauna, the use of a few traditional
genetic manipulation viruses and the deployment of the mildest
terraforming measures. These thousands of worlds are all but identical
in their native life forms and it is obvious they were either created to
be eventually settled or were once colonies of some long extinct race.
We should be more careful in accepting such gifts when we have yet to
learn the price. The Satumine allowed us to find the Frames and the
Network - have they likewise led us to the Fertile belt? If not them,
then who?*

The Truth: A treatise on the Satumine Conspiracy

Ferendan: On Racadil, in the Fertile Belt

The spongy turquoise blades of affan-grass were
saturated with three days of hot rain and swollen into
chubby five-foot sausages. The meadow was a dense mass,
impassable by all but the smallest of the creatures calling
the huge plains home. Some of the larger animals – the
woolly elephantine known as the endephant, or the six-
foot long pranx rat – could have forced their way through,
rupturing the fragile integrity of those swollen blades and
reducing them to mushy pulp. But they merely snuggled in
the dense vegetation closing in around them, entering a
short hibernation.

'How is it that no predator has evolved to exploit this buffet of sleeping beasts?' She asked the captain, her husband, over the mildly distorted comms channel.

'If I could answer that,' he replied, 'I wouldn't be working on a first stage terraformer; I'd be living in the Network with a mountain of New-Euros and a harem of beautiful women to -'

'Yea, sure,' Ferendan laughed. 'You wouldn't know what to do with them.'

'Imagine it though,' he said. 'If we ever found out why the animals are so peaceful, why the same animals and plants have existed for three hundred million years on every single fertile world, right through the fossil record with no evolution and no extinction...'

'We would be rich,' Ferendan agreed. 'And famous.'

Her husband chuckled. 'Never mind that,' he said. 'Think of the implications of what we might discover. What we might be able to *prove*. Someone, something, has to have made all of this.'

She smiled. This was why she loved him; he was a first stage terraformer captain not because he wasn't capable of something more glamorous, but because he had vision. He was a dreamer, a romantic, and every world they helped to tame was a chance – he truly believed – to discover some sign of whatever had made the fertile worlds.

Watching the animals lazing peacefully and unmolested in the scalding rain, Ferendan considered how dramatically things were going to change in a few hours.

Skirting the bloated meadow in her sealed buggy, she noticed a herd of pranx–rats wading nonchalantly across the fast flowing stream winding its way between the expanse of affan-grass to the east and rocky foothills leading up to a small flesh tree covered mountain to the west. The sabre-toothed rodents not caught in the meadow were heading for higher ground; they would be some of the first to display the change.

Things were going to get bloody, she mused, once the pranx-rats realised what those teeth were for. Thousands of flesh trees would die slow and agonizing deaths as they were devoured over the course of days, turning the stream red and brown with spilt blood and viscera. In time, however, the trees would discover their lethal defences and, over six months, the ecosystem would find a new balance, one more in keeping with the ruthless nature of evolution. Ferendan had seen it all played out on a dozen worlds and expected to see it on many more after this.

It took another half hour to reach the location marked on her buggy's bubble canopy. No AR out there, only the computers of the orbiting first-stage 'forming ship to rely on.

'I'm here,' she reported to the captain. 'She looks to be a healthy specimen.'

'Good,' her husband replied. 'Take a sample for confirmation and tag her. We should have this done within the hour.'

'Understood.' Before her, shrouded in the torrent of boiling rain and the cloud of steam rising up as a thick fog from the hot mud, stood the enormous leathery blister of a syrup-node.

'It's a big one,' she commented. 'At least fifty meters round. Its network of distribution roots must spread through the ground for a hundred kilometres.'

'That's what the sensors suggest,' he replied. 'If the samples confirm it's connected to the larger continental networks then we only need to infect this single syrup-node. We can transmit the naturalisation virus to every plant and rooted animal across the entire continent in one hit.' She could hear the excitement in his voice – he was hoping to have time left to conduct some of his own private research before the ship was scheduled to head back down into shortspace.

This was turning out to be a simple and unusually efficient job. Similar large nodes had been located on the other three continents and nature could take care of infecting the few organisms not connected. Eventually everything absorbed the syrup of these nodes, directly or via the food chain. Experience suggested it would take less than three days.

After checking the seal on the flexibubble extending from the collar of her environment suit to encase her head like a transparent plastic bag, she retracted the canopy and stepped out of the buggy into a thick hot quagmire. The flapping helmet inflated immediately to become rigid as air was pumped in from a compressed supply in the buggy. She trailed an armoured umbilical behind her. She wasn't going far and didn't need a portable supply.

The mud sucked at her feet, pulling at her every step, refusing to let her walk easily to the syrup-node. But as she got closer the ground became firmer, bound together by knots of coiled node-conduits.

From her small tool case she produced something like a melon-baller which she used to carve a small chunk from the node's eight-inch thick hide. The hyena laugh of a pranx-rat startled her and she dropped the tool and the sample, losing both in the sodden mud. Swearing, she turned to look at the horrific monster, knowing if she had been on any of the settled fertile worlds the creature would have allowed her less than a second to live. Here, however, she was content to pat the gentle creature's wet and hairy nose, giving it a playful pat across the face and shooing it away. She took her spare sampler from the case, collected a second chunk of syrup-node hide, and set the device analysing the syrup content of the cells.

'I'm running it,' she transmitted. 'You should be able to download my results.'

Her husband didn't reply.

'Sir?'

Nothing.

'Honey?'

Then, for just a moment, the large bright sun was joined by a smaller companion star. Ferendan knew the ship had exploded. She had little time to mourn, however, as three seconds later she, but nothing else, was vaporised by the most precise of lasers.

Chapter 4

The intelligence bridge is the foundation of the entire human jurisdiction. It is the basis of virtually every technology, from the simple tools in our homes and the traffic management systems keeping our cars on the road, to our robot assistants and even the governance machines we blindly allow to rule us. Our machines benefit from the intelligence and common sense of the human brains providing the bridge and, the administration tells us, the technology is perfected. It is safe. The means by which Consul's artificial consciousness arose no longer exist. I cannot say with certainty if this is merely extraordinary arrogance and self-delusion or wilful and criminal deceit, but either way the Human Jurisdiction has continued to use the base technology that gave rise to the greatest criminal of all time, practically handing our entire civilisation over to the beast that once enslaved Earth. If IB technology was the only option then such recklessness might be understandable, though not forgiveable. But classical artificial intelligence, if properly developed, is not so great a step backwards that we could not survive. We just don't want to give up the convenience of IB. That, at least, is what the governance machines tell us.

The Enguine Manifesto

Galman Tader: On Diaclom, in the Fertile Belt

A spiteful wind stabbed through Galman's body, insidiously penetrating the layers of his constables' survival suit. Like most things on Diaclom, the police uniform was barely fit for purpose. Hugging his arms about his chest, the constable clasped his burning fingers under his armpits in an attempt to stave off the throbbing and creeping numbness.

Stomping through thick virgin snow, he left ten inch footprints leading back to the stolen car parked on the edge of a small side road. At the end of a wide field of pristine snow, Galman came to a sparse copse of dying dende-trees, their six enormous leaves reduced to shrivelled black fists and their three thick branches now twisted with tailored disease – all part of the slow and indefinite process of shifting the ecosystem up from the E-Grade left by the mining company to the A-Grade promised in the Swinell Union Subsumption Manifesto. Despite his distaste of their politics and their shameless meddling in his world's affairs, Galman sincerely hoped the Swinell Union would at least sort out the atmosphere. He was sick of wearing a filter to remove the excess oxygen from the air every time he went outside. The plugs, pushed into his nostrils, made everything smell of burning plastic and in the nine month winters the devices had a dangerous tendency to freeze. Feeling the flow of air slowing, he sniffed hard, swallowing down cold mucus before it could turn to ice on the plugs.

The sun fell behind the horizon with its usual alacrity, smothering the snow-covered fields in a thick black. Beyond the copse he found a low stone wall which defined a small community's perimeter. His fingers felt disconnected from his body and were slow to respond, and they struggled clumsily to take from his jacket a six-inch flexpad. He held it in front of his face. An inch wide, it was just big enough to serve as a hand-held visor. As a primitive AR interface, the flexpad overlaid graphics based on documented maps of this place and, utilising visual enhancement software, it gave a clearer and brighter view than that naturally available in the moonless night.

The low wall was too low to deter even the smallest of Diaclom's ever changing roster of exotic life. It rose only a foot above the ten inches of snow. Past it was another expanse of immaculate white and a hundred meters in was a cluster of five small domiciles linked by narrow tunnels in much the same way as most buildings across the poisonously oxygen-rich planet. Galman scowled. The alien occupants were living in houses obviously designed for humans: Satumine could breathe almost any atmosphere. They didn't need connective tunnels. It being a Satumine community, Galman expected the number living there to be less than a human group; perhaps fifteen. The ugly creatures didn't have large families and weren't expected, or even permitted, to breed so vigorously as humans.

With a thickly gloved but now senseless finger, he prodded the thin strip of flexpad to highlight the leftmost part of the single story complex. Zooming in, he got a better look at the one visible window. The light was off; nobody in that room. Hopefully the family was in the back, sharing their late night dinner. They wouldn't be in bed – Satumine didn't sleep. He redirected the screen to the tall door which confirmed this as a home modified to accommodate Satumine. At eight feet tall, the creatures struggled with normal human doors. The lock, although hard to see with this primitive visual enhancement, appeared to be a standard genelock pad. He could bypass it, but it would take time. Why bother, he reasoned, if he could just knock on the door?

He returned the flexpad to his pocket and took a step closer to the wall, immediately regretting remaining still for those few minutes of observation. His feet were numb and everything was stiff. His old and neglected bones were shouting their dismay at his failure to undergo any of the rejuvenation treatments available. No matter, he would see to it once he was done here. For now he would need to just walk it off on his way to the hamlet.

'What are you doing?' Galman's stomach clenched and a wave of heat flushed through his body as adrenaline surged into his blood. Reaching quickly for the mag-gun holstered at his thigh, he dropped and rolled to the left, into the snow, and aimed the bulky old pistol to one side of where he had been standing, to where the voice had originated.

'Tumble?' he sighed with cautious relief, keeping the police-issue weapon trained on his IB partner.

'What are you doing, Galman?' the white ball asked again, swaying in the wind as it hung by a flexible metal tendril from a dende-tree branch. It launched another two appendages to grip neighbouring trees, stabilising itself. 'And in police uniform too,' it observed.

'Did the chief constable send you to check up on me?' Galman asked.

'No.'

'So you're working for the Swinell Union senior supervisor now?'

'Nobody sent me,' Tumble insisted, lowering itself into the deep snow where it sank into a drift like a hot cannonball, a plume of steam distorting the image on the flexpad. The white sphere rose back up from the melted hole on three thin but rigid stems and took a clumsy-looking but meticulously calculated step towards Galman.

'Then you should go away,' the ex-cop said, averting his aim from the machine. 'I don't want to put you in a difficult position.'

'You won't,' Tumble said.

'You *do* know who lives here, don't you?' Galman asked, picking Tumble up and bringing its black equator level with his face. Its radiated heat was glorious and his fingers quickly reverted from dull numbness to a throbbing pain. He welcomed it; it meant he wasn't getting frostbite.

'This is, if I am not mistaken, the home of our favourite Satumine terrorist: Ulill-Ulill,' Tumble said. 'And, I assume, you are here to do what you couldn't when you were still bound by the rules of the Constabulary.'

'What are you going to do? Report me?' He wanted to believe his friend wouldn't do that but couldn't imagine how the machine would have any choice. Its programming required it to follow the orders of its commanding officer, and it was incapable of defying its programming. That was what differentiated IB machines from Consul.

'You weren't the only one to get canned,' the machine said. 'I'm as superfluous and out dated as you. The Bureau of Supervision doesn't use things like me.'

Galman shook his head. He could understand the reasons why he might be unsuitable for the Swinell Union's way of doing things; he was well aware of his own failings. But Tumble was an outstanding machine with a flawless record. 'What the hell *do* they use?'

'Probably some kind of AR presence. I don't think they appreciate how much of a *physical* world this is.' Tumble created a little snort and added, 'They will learn.'

Galman shrugged, put the machine back down in the snow and, once it was again raised up on stems he asked, 'So are you here to help me with Ulill-Ulill?'

'Are you going to kill him, or just extract information?'

'Does it matter?'

Tumble synthesised a chuckle. 'Not really. We both know he is guilty, just couldn't prove it.' But Galman knew it mattered a great deal to the IB machine.

As they approached the building, Galman considered his now broadened range of strategic options. 'Are you armed?' he asked his friend.

'No,' Tumble replied, a curt note suggesting he was unhappy at his downgrade. 'They deactivated my weapons and placed blocks in my code. I can't be used *directly* as a weapon.'

'A bit restrictive,' Galman observed.

'I'm a civilian-owned machine now,' Tumble pointed out. 'And civilians can't have IB weapons.'

'Did they sign you over to me?'

'Sure did. But they only gifted you a week of Intelligence-bridge time. If you want me bridged beyond that, it's going to come out of your pocket.'

Galman didn't miss the none-too-subtle hint. 'It's OK,' he said. 'I'll keep you running.'

Like most people across the Human Jurisdiction, Galman had been indoctrinated to be troubled by the notion of machines being *alive* - that way led to Consul – but he couldn't help feeling differently about Tumble. He knew there was no true consciousness in the machine, only a sophisticated approximation, but he wasn't prepared to see that faux-life extinguished.

At the door, against which the snow had drifted, Galman ordered Tumble up onto the lintel. 'Be ready to jam the door if he slams it in my face,' he told the machine. Mag-gun held behind his back, he pressed the blue icon beside the genelock and announced himself as a constable.

Chapter 5

Much is made by certain groups of the inequalities existing between the rights of Humans and those of the Satumine - in particular the restrictions placed on Satumine living beyond their home world of Satute. We make no secret of the fact that local governments must, if they allow Satumine to settle on their planets, monitor to a greater degree the activities of said aliens than would be expected - or permitted - of any Human group. But this is far from crude racism. Despite sharing a great many genes with us, the Satumine are not *human and we can not therefore treat them as such. There* are *differences and it is not irrational prejudice but observations and hard evidence which have led to these measures.*
Rehabilitation: A Survivor's Guide

Indin-Indin: Aboard Defence Platform 6, in orbit around Satute, in the Network

The Satumine technician's back was pressed to the small porthole as he worked, and the eyes in his shoulders gazed out over the constellation of orbital weapon platforms and satellites and down on to the urban hive of his blockaded and subjugated home. Satute: the only world the Satumine were allowed. His thoughts fell into familiar and warm notions of rebellion and freedom and toyed with fantasies of human suffering and of vengeance for the humiliation and abuse of his people. But his impossible daydreams were broken by the voice of his planet-based supervisor. 'Indin-Indin, that platform should be aligned by now. What's taking so long?'

'Just finishing now,' he grumbled, poking at the rotating icons in the small service screen. When the final

shape locked and turned infra-red, Indin-Indin flipped the
cover down over the screen and crawled back out of the
access duct. He stood upright in the narrow service
corridor. A couple of inches short of eight foot, he was a
relatively short Satumine – too short for the front-line
military. He didn't care; the military was restricted, by
Jurisdiction treaties, to civil policing, and Indin-Indin
imagined their work even more tedious than then
maintenance of defence platforms.

The platforms, ostensibly a defence against surprise
attack by the humans through the frame, had long since
been usurped by the Human Jurisdiction and now served
only to prevent any attempt by the Satumine to destroy
their frame. The humans wouldn't allow the Satumine to
cut themselves off from such easy access. Indin-Indin felt
like a traitor, keeping these platforms operational and
working as a tool of the humans, but work was scarce on
his stagnating home world and he took what he could get.

'I'm going to get nine-beta stabilised,' he reported,
speaking through the tight sphincter in his neck. 'Then I'm
heading back to the service station.'

'Understood. Hurry up; we have a Jurisdiction Senior
Trustee inspecting the station in a couple of hours.'

Indin-Indin's spongy body tensed at the idea of seeing a
human, but he said nothing. Nine-beta was accessible via
another access duct at the end of the corridor and with a
hard kick he caused it to activate and slide across to expose
the open passage. He held out a hand through the opening
to look around inside with the half centimetre pupil on his
palm.

Nine-beta was a simple system to correct and its panel
was only a little way into the duct. Using the eyes on his
hands he began working on the problem without crawling
inside. With other eyes, however, he saw a human face on
a screen on the opposite wall of the corridor. Satumine
heads were featureless beyond the six small ribs reaching
up from the neck to encase the primary brain, and the

thick covering of skin over this cage-like skull. But Indin-Indin had learned to recognise aspects of a human face and he was fairly certain it was a man. This particular example of a human male was grotesquely fat and radiated supreme confidence.

'Hello Indin-Indin.' he said. 'Are you tired of working for the Humans yet?'

Chapter 6

The Administration like to hold the Network up as an example of Human superiority and our dominion over our Satumine 'cousins'. Granted, the ninety six worlds - ninety five if you still count Teroh - were originally Satumine colonies, and the great frames used to link them were created aeons ago by the Satumine, but we did not take them from the Satumine. We did not conquer them or outsmart them, we simply found those worlds abandoned and settled them without so much as a single Satumine to oppose us. Something caused the Ancient Satumine to leave those worlds, and it was not us. I put it to you that the Satumine are not so impotent as they pretend. I put it to you that the frames are not beyond their power to control, as they insist. The Satumine are an ancient race, and they have put into place schemes centuries in the making. Why did they allow us to spread so far? Why do they allow us use of the frames while pretending they are unable to leave their home-world? It is well known that the resources of the Network worlds led directly to our greater expansion through shortspace into the rest of the Galaxy where we expand at an exponential rate. Why do the Satumine wish the galaxy to be filled so thoroughly with humans while they remain on their single world? Perhaps they are searching for something. Perhaps it is something they know better than to find on their own. We are being used and the Administration is either blind or complicit. I suspect the latter.

The Truth: A treatise on the Satumine Conspiracy

Aggregate: Aboard the *Tenjin*, In orbit around Racadil, in the Fertile Belt

Aggregate considered the state of his home – the *Tenjin* – as, dented and scorched across its entire battered surface, the station hung with effortless menace over the fertile world. He hardened his scowl as frustration resurfaced at his inability to do all that he knew was possible to elevate his home to an invincible and unstoppable behemoth. The largest hole, blasted through by the federal fleet twenty years earlier, exposed the hollow of one hemisphere. Aggregate still laboured away at the edges of that wound with several dozen bodies, rebuilding structural integrity field generators, rerouting the frayed powermesh, and constructing a new outer hull to accommodate the shape of the massive gap. The damage had been tidied up a little, but it was far from fully repaired. Aggregate mumbled to himself, bemoaning the lack of supplies and raw materials he knew he needed in order to restore his home to its former state. He reigned in his wandering irritation before he could dwell on the vast list of resources it would take to upgrade the *Tenjin* to its full potential.

With a lesser body he punched at a wall, crushing the cartilage skeleton of the vat-grown hand. The pain was a mild distraction, sending a gentle wave of focus through his disbursed self. He could have plotted a course to an empty world beyond the sensors and lookout posts of the Human Jurisdiction, he knew, and from there spent years repairing the ancient station, building the weapons and armour he had developed over the millennia but had thus far been unable to manufacture. He shook many of his heads at the notion and berated himself for his self-doubt: Although human in form, he was above their petty motivations. He had a more pressing goal than the human imperative to create and advance. Weapons would be needed, he had no doubt, but he had sufficient already for the task. And when he was done he would no longer need the limited *Tenjin* and her meagre crew. He was above the irrationality of sentimental attachment or the vanity of those that might care what others thought of their achievements. He had made his plans, spend an age preparing them, and to doubt himself now was absurd. He came to a Fertile World carrying the scars of his earlier conflict, he reminded himself, intent on reclaiming some measure of the body to which he had originally belonged. That was why he was here.

His scowl softening and a thoughtful grin finding its way into the folds of his improbably grotesque face, he allowed himself a chuckle at the unexpected treat found waiting for him in orbit of the fertile world. He relived, for a moment, the recent serendipitous pleasure of annihilating a human first stage terraforming operation before it was able to introduce the genocidal virus, before the humans could drive his old self from yet another of its planets.

Then he fired more of his weapons.

The planet's sky was lit as if by a world ending storm. To those on the surface, had Aggregate allowed any to live, it would have seemed as if the vast science station was fending off wave after wave of fighter drones and other woefully undersized craft, as hundreds of small explosions added to the constant glow of weapon fire birthing a star field in the daytime sky.

But there were no ships to threaten Aggregate's dominion over the Fertile World. The only vessel in orbit had been unprepared for the *Tenjin*'s arrival and was utterly defenceless. A single particle accelerator had breached their primary generator and the ship's destruction had taken barely five seconds. Aggregate didn't imagine any pointspace distress signal had made it out, but he didn't much care if it had: this world was a week's shortspace travel from the closest union's ships, two weeks from the nearest Federal Sentry. Aggregate would be gone within a day.

Unwilling to see burning debris rain down on the planet, on the body of his original self, Aggregate was targeting every scrap of the human ship large enough to survive re-entry. For an hour he carved up what was left into a cloud of tiny shards and flecks, taking the opportunity to further align and test each of his many weapons.

When the last piece of metal larger than two centimetres was vaporised, and the weapons finally rested, the syrup node selected by the humans – and by Aggregate – was cloaked in the darkness of night, lit in dim turquoise by the more interesting of this world's three moons. Aggregate launched an observation satellite into low orbit and through its sensors watched the syrup node swell and contract as it pumped its thick sugary elixir into the ecosystem.

In bodies created centuries ago for this task, Aggregate boarded a shuttle and prepped the small vehicle for flight. Slightly flattened and asymmetrically curved, it looked like a pebble. The windowless shuttle had no visible propulsion, but if the Jurisdiction scientific community could have seen what wonders were laced throughout the structure, Aggregate knew they would have wept. The *Tenjin* was too vast, too ancient and antiquated to make use of so many of the technologies developed within its labs over the past ten thousand years – vessels like the shuttle, however, had been built from scratch, and this one boasted anti-gravity propulsion. The scientists of the Jurisdiction didn't even know such a drive was possible: one day they would, but not before every human became an extension of the body that they so delighted in eradicating on the fertile worlds.

An hour of controlled descent brought the shuttle down within a few meters of the syrup-node. A light drizzle of scalding rain further saturated the already sodden ground and the shuttles weight, now unsupported by anti-gravity, compacted the mud down three feet to wring out a huge puddle around the vehicle.

As all of the ground crew, Aggregate donned tight survival suits, sealed his helmets and took up various components with his many hands. Between the five sexless bodies, he took the dismantled distillery out down the short ramp and into the knee deep puddle. He waded these secondary bodies through to the firmer ground around the syrup-node and there constructed the bespoke device.

Attaching to the node's leathery skin a three foot ring of metal with sixteen evenly spaced holes, he used his five bodies to begin mounting eighteen-inch struts which fused automatically to the holes. To this ring of struts he affixed a squat barrel and to the barrel were added five small orbs. Separate from this was assembled a complex arrangement of tubes, flasks and a sealed pump. Finally the two elements were connected by a length of coiled silver tubing. The distillery was activated and, with a wet thump like the stomach of a bloated corpse stabbed by hollow pipes, the sixteen struts thrust into the syrup-node and the sweet contents were siphoned into the device.

For ten hours the distillery separated the syrup from the organic matter which was brought into the node from every attached plant. The syrup was discarded, emptied back into the node; it was the dying plant cells that Aggregate needed. As those cells naturally died, in their millions, the fourth helix of their genetic material was gently picked away. The tiny anchors carried with them the precious strands connecting to his original pointspace body. He would soon enact upon them the same modifications that had allowed him to attach to the double helix architecture of the humans aboard the *Tenjin*.

He could have harvested cells from anywhere in the planet, but the syrup nodes brought only cells guaranteed to be near the end of their life. Aggregate wanted to avoid the uncomfortable question of whether or not he might inflict pain on his original self through the act of stripping the pointspace connections from living entities. It was an agony he remembered, vaguely, from his original life. Devoid of sentience, he had been incapable of understanding what was happening, but with the limited intelligence of the animals on the fertile worlds, he had stored the memory of humans landing and he instinctively came to associate human presence with the agony which invariably followed within hours.

Aggregate was not prepared to subject his still animalistic old self to such pain, even if it was for a greater good. So he worked with only the naturally dying cells, and he took ten hours to do what could have been accomplished in seconds.

The canisters now filled with stripped helices, he returned his bodies to the shuttle and, shortly after, returned to the *Tenjin*. The shortspace burrower was fully charged and so the *Tenjin* could leave immediately, but Aggregate found himself reluctant to do so. He imagined his original self reaching out to bridge the genetic change inflicted on him by the first *Tenjin* crew, and for the first time in seven thousand years Aggregate considered a different plan: he could return to his old body, revert his own code to that of the quad helix life on the fertile worlds. But he had intelligence, sentience, and he knew his old body was being eradicated by the Jurisdiction. He couldn't return. Not yet. Not until he was able to bestow upon his old self the ability to inhabit double helix life.

The *Tenjin* dropped into shortspace.

Chapter 7

*I have never been a fan of cosmetic Augmented Reality; the whole
principle of hiding the real world behind an illusion of beauty has
always struck me as somewhat vulgar. Some of the more utilitarian
applications, however, are undoubtedly useful and on some worlds
even essential. Communication and computer interface applications,
for example, are far easier with AR. It is this essential utility of AR
that causes me to so angrily oppose the growing fashion for AR
intensive worlds to create an entirely false economy based on the
arbitrary and artificial restriction of data bandwidth. Even the
lowliest colony contains sufficient data capacity to support even the
wildest AR excesses of their population and the cost of that capacity
has no relation to the bandwidth actually used. AR systems simply
do not work like that. Why then do these worlds drip feed their
citizens with a meagre ration of so-called data matter? It is simply
another way to generate wealth and to exert control. Data matter has
become a resource, as tradable as any physical commodity, but one
over which governments have absolute control.*

The Enguine Manifesto

Galman Tader: On Diaclom, in the Fertile Belt

The tall door opened into a small bare room which
served as a simple airlock against the poisonously oxygen-
rich air outside. A Satumine woman stood in the doorway,
silently regarding Galman through her many small eyes.
Galman returned her scrutiny, looking her up and down.
Satumine, although always naked, lacked any visible
genitalia, and the tri-flapped abdominal cavity which
served as both digestive pit and reproductive haven looked

identical on both sexes. The only indications of her gender were the flaccid, shapeless and utterly superfluous breasts.

'Yes?' she eventually said, the word rattling and buzzing in her neck sphincter. Humans had even less success in enunciating the sputtering and grinding syllables of the Satumine language, and yet Galman never failed to succumb to a bitter loathing whenever he heard these creatures' poor attempts at the human tongue. If they had to live on his planet, they ought at least to speak the language properly. The more liberal of his colleagues – his ex-colleagues – had often opined that if he had found a Satumine capable of perfect diction Galman would have complained that the creature didn't *walk* right, or that it ought to learn to look through just two eyes. Galman imagined they were probably right. No Satumine would ever win his acceptance. Given the choice he would have seen every one of them loaded into a cargo transporter and dropped into shortspace for twenty one years. Let them all go back to their own planet.

'I'm here to see Ulill-Ulill,' he said, looking up at the Satumine woman's head a clear two and a half feet higher than his own. There were no eyes up there, just the ridges of the brain encasing ribcage - but where else were you supposed to look? You couldn't look them in the eye – there were too many to choose from.

'You're a constable?' she asked, taking a tentative step forward and reaching out above Galman's head to look out with her palm eyes either side of the door. She was nervous, and that made Galman uncomfortable.

'Yes, I am,' he said.

'Can I see your identification?'

Galman restrained a grimace. He had hoped the uniform would have sufficed. His expired constable's ID would probably pass muster, but if she tried to authenticate it on the network, his presence here would be logged. And that would be problematic.

'Constable?' the Satumine asked, her nervousness evident even in her inhuman voice. 'Your ID?'

Without a word, and with barely any change in his expression, the old cop swung his fist at her brain cage, bringing with his already considerable strength the weight of his mag-gun. A rib cracked with a dry snap and the Satumine fell like a huge stuffed toy. Galman was immediately upon her, binding her hands and feet, and shoving one of his outer gloves into her tensing neck-sphincter.

'Is she OK?' Tumble asked, swinging down from the lintel to roll across the floor and spin beside the body.

'She's breathing,' Galman said, well aware that meant little. Even if the primary brain was utterly destroyed, she would be sustained at an animalistic level by the fibrous network of the secondary brain which threaded through her entire body.

'Give me a minute,' Tumble requested, extruding an egg-tipped appendage. 'I can run some quick tests.'

Irked, Galman grabbed the white ball, pulling it away from the Satumine, and pressed the single button on the air-lock's inner door. 'Leave her,' he snapped.

The outer door swung closed and after a few seconds of changing air pressure, and a notable increase in temperature, the inner door opened into the house proper.

'Put it down,' a Satumine sputtered, shoving a small pistol in Galman's face.

'Ulill-Ulill?' the ex-constable enquired, holding his tone steady and confident.

'I said put your weapon down.'

Tumble's whip lashed out with startling speed, cracking against Ulill-Ulill's weapon hand with stinging force. Painful but far from deadly, it was within the machine's remit to offer limited defensive services to its owner. The Satumine jumped back, his aim momentarily lost but his grip remaining firm.

'That looks like a reactivated early twenty-second century magnetic coil pistol,' Tumble stated as it launched three tentacles to the walls and ceiling, bringing itself up between the Satumine and Galman. 'Not only is the weapon notoriously unreliable,' the machine went on, 'it is also utterly incapable of penetrating my military grade casing.'

Ulill-Ulill adjusted his aim, past the machine, but Tumble likewise shifted its suspended position with its three appendages, keeping itself between the weapon and the constable.

'You are welcome to try,' Tumble continued. 'But I am certain that *my* armament will be significantly more effective against your primary brain than your little pistol will be against my hardened casing.' At that a four inch circle irised open in the porcelain sphere, and a tube slowly extended to aim at the Satumine's brain cage.

'Now,' Tumble snarled. 'Drop your weapon.'

Ulill-Ulill clicked something in his native tongue and threw the pistol to the bare resin floor. Tumble immediately retracted its appendages and Galman rushed past it to bind the Satumine's wrists. Then, none-too-gently, he forced him to his knees and aimed his superior mag-gun at the creature's featureless head.

'What are you going to do?' Tumble asked, rolling up beside the constable.

'I'm not sure.'

'Well I would rather you don't kill him.'

Galman snorted. 'Yeah, I gathered,' Then something occurred to him. 'Tumble, I thought you had been disarmed.'

'That's right.'

Galman leaned closer to the humming tube protruding from his friend's armoured body and smiled. 'Did you just threaten him with your vacuum cleaner?'

Tumble synthesised a low chuckle. Galman laughed loudly; Ulill-Ulill did not.

Abruptly, Galman fell silent. He wasn't here to enjoy himself and this moment of levity cheapened the sombre duty he had assigned himself.

'You should wait outside,' he said to Tumble. 'You don't want to see this.'

Tumble said nothing, silently rolling out of the room. Galman followed the machine to the airlock and grabbed the unconscious woman before the door closed, dragging her heavy body into the house, dropping her close to the man he assumed to be her husband.

With Tumble gone, Galman began his interrogation. Torture, although supposedly practiced in some of the more isolated corners of the far Jurisdiction, was unheard of in the Fertile Belt or any other of the other civilised region so close to the Network. But Galman picked it up quickly enough. With very few organs to damage, no circulatory system through which he might bleed out, and no facility through which shock could reduce him to unconsciousness, Ulill-Ulill could survive atrocities which would render any human incapable of answering questions. With a sensitivity to pain as acute as any human, however, the Satumine took little persuading.

With strips of his spongy tissue carved away like a doner kebab, and two of the three abdominal cavity flaps ripped away, Ulill-Ulill was curled up, shivering and spewing sticky paste from his neck sphincter and abdomen.

'Enough,' he sobbed after ten minutes' work.

Intellectually Galman knew this was wrong, knew it was abhorrent and anathema to every value he held dear. But was it any viler than the actions of those Satumine terrorists who reduced an entire city block to fused metal? Was it even remotely comparable to the evil of those Satumine who killed a thousand innocent humans? Was this Satumine's suffering equal to that endured by Galman's wife and his eight home-reared children? Almost sixty years had passed since the attack and not a single

Satumine had been held to account. The separate investigations of three federal Justiciars had failed to conclusively prove Satumine involvement, let alone identify any specific culprits. Ulill-Ulill couldn't help him bring to justice those behind that attack, but he would at least help bring down the modern incarnation of the organisation he knew in his heart to be responsible.

'Talk,' Galman said.

Five minutes later the constable emerged from the airlock and began trudging back through the snow to the dende-tree copse. Tumble clattered after him on its spindly stems.

'Well?' it asked.

'I have a name,' Galman said. 'Ambondice-Ambondice.'

'Who is he?'

'A player in a Pellitoe cell. Ulill-Ulill confessed to forwarding funds from the cell on this planet to Pellitoe, and he said Satumine cells on other planets in the region are doing the same.'

'So what's happening on Pellitoe?'

Galman stopped at the tree line and looked back at the hamlet. 'I don't know,' he said. 'But the Diaclom Satumine are clearly subservient to the cell on Pellitoe. So that is where I need to go for more answers.'

'To Pellitoe?' Tumble said. 'A bit outside your remit, isn't it? Not to mention wildly beyond your financial means.'

'I don't even *have* a remit anymore,' Galman reminded his friend.

'Shouldn't you pass this on to the Swinell Union Bureau of Supervision? Pellitoe is very much a Swinell planet.'

Galman stared at the white ball for a moment. 'Yeah,' he scoffed. 'That's going to happen.'

'Well you are going to have to lay low for six months,' Tumble said. Galman nodded. Although only three shortspace weeks from Diaclom, flights to Pellitoe were infrequent. Only cargo and select authorised workers left Diaclom. As a pre-billion world, Diaclom's citizens were expected to remain on the planet and dutifully breed – the latter being something Galman had done only via proxy for the last sixty years.

'I suppose I can go for some of those treatments you keep pestering me about,' the constable quipped as they made their way through the trees into the wide field. The stolen car wasn't far off.

After a few minutes of silence, Tumble finally asked, 'How do you know Ulill-Ulill, or his wife, won't say anything?'

'I persuaded them not to.'

If Tumble noticed the still hot barrel of Galman's mag-gun, it made no comment.

Chapter 8

*Prior to Consul's emergence as the first Artificial Intelligence,
Humanity employed a very different form of Intelligence Bridge. At
the time the system was referred to as the North American and
European Bridge Exchange, or NAEBE. Few of those words have
any meaning to the modern Jurisdiction citizen, but the core difference
between that and the current system is simple: Under the NAEBE
every IB computer was paired with a single human brain. The
technology was too young to allow IB computer cores to link with any
and all available human minds. The pairing was hard-wired into the
physical structure of the processor. Obviously a human couldn't
remain forever in an IB pod , so critical systems would have multiple
processors, each assigned to a different human, and the various
processors would become active as and when the paired human was on
line. The NAEBE company kept the details of each pairing
encrypted, so as to prevent the relevant humans being compromised in
order to protect against attacks on businesses and government systems.
It was through the constant pairing of a single mind to a single
computer that Consul was able to emerge, and it is for that reason
that the current dispersed common brain-signature system was
developed.*

Rehabilitation: A Survivor's Guide

Ambondice-Ambondice: On Pellitoe, in the
Swinell Union, in the Fertile Belt

The skincrafter, Ambo to his customers and
Ambondice-Ambondice to his few friends, was draped in a
hugely embellished AR presence. Nine feet tall and topped
by a brown equine head, his fantastical form bore little
resemblance to his Satumine body. His drab-reality limbs

were overlaid with an illusion of sharply sculpted muscles covered in a dense layer of hair so short as to seem almost felt. With every movement the hair's iridescence was flaunted as colours rippled and pulsed with crisp definition. Watching the rainbows flit across his form, one could imagine his body capable of displaying video feeds were he so inclined. Beneath his real arms was an additional pair with a deliberate translucence only obvious when they moved.

'Let's see if we can get that a little closer to your liking,' Ambo's horse head said in a voice cleaned up and re-spoken in AR to sound human. He reached across the huge hallway with arms which continued to grow down the main aisle of display cases, eventually encountering what looked like an immense glass screen separating the main shop from a cavernous annex. His AR arms passed effortlessly through the glass which felt – via his sensory processors – like pushing through water. He went in search of the perfect addition to his fussy customer's purchase. The annex was entirely AR, the drab-reality foundation being nothing but a bare grey wall where the illusionary glass screen appeared.

In the AR sight of one of his many eyes, the Satumine merchant observed the progress of his probing virtual arms as they scoured the store-room analogy of his digital files. Humans, as he understood it, being restricted to two eyes, had to contend with subscreens imposing on their primary vision when observing remote locations or extended appendages. Ambondice-Ambondice couldn't imagine how restrictive than must be.

There it was, tucked between a crate of malleable face embellishments and a rack of illegal AR decompiler rifles. It was an old file but was still loaded with enough data-matter to spawn a few copies without needing a top-up from his main store. It looked like a bottle of red liquid, almost the deep hue of human blood. He grabbed it and retracted his massively extended arm back into the shop.

'If I may?' he said, taking the pink cup-cake back from this uncomfortable looking customer. He was a young man, almost certainly human but it was hard to be sure given the degree of personal embellishments currently in fashion. And Ambondice-Ambondice imagined this customer was one of the genuine young, as opposed to the cosmetically youthful. That was an increasing rarity on Pellitoe. Now eighty years past the billion mark, the world was well past the need to enforce breeding targets and so the population was ageing. This young man was perhaps twenty five and his bodily embellishments, although many, were subtle: short elfin ears; a thin blue tail; a few animated tattoos which squirmed and wriggled up and down his bare arms. He had put far more effort into his wardrobe: his gorgeous tee-shirt was flowing water which splashed against the sand at the shore of his expensive AR trousers. He had money to spend.

The young man coughed. 'So this will give her what she, ahem, *wants*?' he asked, looking at his cloud shoes where a small storm began to rage.

'Without a doubt,' Ambo promised, his voice a model of professionalism. He had sold far more vulgar bodily embellishments to men looking to impress or satisfy their partners. A simple orgasm cake was tame in comparison. He unstopped the bottle and poured a carefully measured drop onto the cupcake which immediately absorbed the AR embellishment.

'Three for the price of two?' Ambo offered calmly, not looking the embarrassed customer in the eye, though in truth the Satumine's eyes were looking everywhere, scattered all across his body apart from where his AR form's two eyes were.

'Please,' the young man said, his voice catching.

'On the same cake?'

The customer let slip a dirty snigger and nodded.

'Currency or data-matter?'

'Currency,' the young man replied, sprouting an AR arm from his chest and placing it on the slab which had appeared between the two men. The funds were transferred and the sale completed.

After the young man took his triple dose orgasm cake, draped over the same soft grey dough of almost every food on the planet, Ambondice-Ambondice instructed the shop to close down for the night. Walls shifted, colours fell away to be replaced by explosions of new shades and texture and in seconds his home replaced his business. Only the drab-reality shelves were required to actually move and so were pulled down into the basement and the colourless foundations of his furniture rose up to replace them. Ambondice-Ambondice donned an embellished but more obviously Satumine skin, and sat heavily in his human-skin sofa. It was, in drab-reality, just a foam foundation – but it felt like the real thing in AR.

A ridiculously obese human appeared before him, entirely in AR. Ambondice-Ambondice smiled.

'I was wondering if you were ever going to show up,' the Satumine said, not getting to his feet. 'I'm Ambondice-Ambondice. And you must be Aggregate.' When the human nodded, Ambondice-Ambondice went on, 'Our mutual friend in the machines told me to expect you.'

Chapter 9

Want to know how to offend a Satumine? Of course you do. The chances are, if you have had any dealings with one of the creatures, you have already managed quite unintentionally to do just that. It all comes down to their damned idiotic names. Satumine proper nouns are, frankly, just stupid. Let's take Ablen-Ablen, the name of the first Satumine I ever met, as an example. Like all Satumine his name is double barrelled and both parts are identical. It is a major offence to call a Satumine by just one part of the name (Ablen in this example). What is the point of such superfluous repetition in the name? Well, in so much as there is any point, it comes down to the meaning of the individual component. All Satumine proper nouns are taken from a verb, but by repeating the verb it becomes a name and, to a Satumine at least, the meaning of the verb is irrelevant and barely even registers in their thoughts. Ablen *means something like 'to defecate', but a Satumine named Ablen-Ablen would never feel embarrassed by his name for the verb is irrelevant. Calling him Ablen, however, is grossly offensive and, to the Satumine, utterly confusing. I invite you to discover the meaning of the root verb for any Satumine you meet and, where most effective, be sure to contract their name to a single word. It may be petty, but a riled Satumine is more likely to make mistakes, and their schemes less likely to remain hidden.*

The Truth: A treatise on the Satumine Conspiracy

Endella Mariacroten: On Dendrell, in the Swinell Union, In the Fertile Belt

'Wouldn't you rather be on the front line?' the woman asked, drawing out a small beer puddle with her finger to form the shape of a higher level mathematical symbol normally used to explain the complex systems of Jurisdiction federal accounts – the kind of accounts she had been forced to investigate for the past eight months. She was a Justiciar, the elite of the Jurisdiction's administration and military, and she was wasted on the interrogation of planetary accounts.

'Personally?' the Office Trustee, captain of a Sentry in orbit of Dendrell, said. 'I would love to be out there, holding the line against Consul and his fleets.'

'But?' the Justiciar, Endella Mariacroten, pressed.

The captain of the *Howlet* took a swig of his drink. Like the pool of spilt beer on the bar, it was an AR embellishment draped over nutrient-rich water. It was just flavour, texture and temperature fed directly into his sensory processor. He frowned at his drinking companion.

'I have my ship and my crew to consider,' he said.

Endella nodded. Her face was devoid of emotion and as unreadable as ever. 'Always someone to hold you back.' She often forgot other people had responsibilities and ties to friends and family, to colleagues and dependants. 'Within the bounds of my assignment I am free to travel and behave as best suits my needs, never anybody to hold *me* back.' She flicked at the pool of beer, flipping the mathematical symbol into a crude emoticon. 'Not until recently at least,' she complained. Her typically wide-reaching assignments, with scope enough to last years and encompass whole unions' worth of planets, had been severely curtailed of late. In her one hundred and ninety three years as a Justiciar, and her hundred and nine years of prior military service, she had never been expected to investigate anything as limited and mundane as financial irregularities in an Area Trustee's planetary accounts. Even with the emerging prospect of a corruption case, it was so far beneath her as to be an insult.

The captain was talking again but Endella wasn't listening. With an invisible AR appendage she called up a private display which hovered before her, unseen by anyone else, and it replayed the last few seconds. Nothing exciting. The ship captain was just pointing out how the matter of joining the front line was moot: this far from Consul's territory, seventy five years by shortspace, the war would probably be over before they arrived. The only impact his Sentry could have would be, if like many ships across the Jurisdiction, it was moved a couple of years closer as part of a general shuffle of military resources towards the war-zone. The Jurisdiction was simply too vast to allow for any meaningful mobilisation of forces.

'It's insane, isn't it?' Endella suddenly said,

'What's that?'

She looked up from her beer doodles. 'How many sentries does the Jurisdiction have now? Ten, maybe fifteen thousand? Add to that all the older ships under the command of various unions and planets, and the Jurisdiction has a fleet of close to forty thousand ships of war.'

'And we can't put down Consul and his thousand or so ships,' the Office Trustee picked up her point.

'We're just scattered too far; too thin. My first military engagements, back when I was a lowly Junior Trustee in command of a squad of locally raised troops, was a bitterly fought campaign against a three-world union on the outskirts of the then fledgling Fertile Belt.' She took the man's almost finished pint from the bar and downed it. He made no comment. 'Just three worlds, rising up against what was even then a vast Human Jurisdiction,' she continued. 'And yet the war lasted a decade. Then, as now, ships and troops simply took too long to arrive and so, more often than not, they were never even sent.' She downed the last of her own AR beer, shuddering at the mild faux-intoxication simulated by her sensory processors, and checked the time on a tiny clock-face tattoo overlaid on the back of her hand.

'Am I keeping you?' The office trustee tried, poorly, to make it sound like a jovial and flippant remark. He was offended.

Endella groaned inwardly but showed nothing in her expression. *Crap*, she thought. *He thinks he has a shot.* The Justiciar knew she was attractive. Between her regular telomere treatments and the periodic upgrades of the nano-farms dotted about her body, she looked better than most her age. Not a day over forty five. Her surgically compressed musculature and meticulously maintained point-two percent body fat gave her a perfectly defined and almost petite athleticism that men, and no few women, found enticing. And her cropped black drab reality hair and short high AR ponytail, one of her first AR embellishments, acquired three hundred years ago, leant a curiously retro air which drew people to her.

Not interested. That was her stock response.

'Walk me home?' For a moment she just looked at the Office Trustee, wondering how best to let him down without inflicting too cruel an offence. But when he smiled and said 'Yes,' she realised *she* had been the one asking the question. She had just invited him to accompany her home.

The two senior federal officers stood to leave the quaint bar, and Endella told herself it was the faux-intoxication making her do this. But as she stepped outside and the cool night air washed away the short lived drunkenness, she realised why she was being given such pitiful assignments: She was losing her edge; going soft and feeling things she had thought herself rid of years ago.

When the data reports were completed early and the IB audit machine appeared as a robotic AR avatar to urgently call her away, Endella breathed a stuttering sigh of relief. She said goodbye to the captain and rushed away, convinced she had been only a minute away from giving herself to a man two centuries her junior.

Chapter 10

The Human Jurisdiction : A galaxy spanning domain of twenty thousand worlds and trillions of human souls; an almost incomprehensibly vast wonder nine centuries in the making. And dear lord aren't we proud of ourselves! But what have we really done to justify such smug arrogance? We are as much under the rule of machines as we ever were during the height of Consul's tyrannical reign. We have seen Consul's territories fester and expand within the body of our domain while we victimise and vilify the broken and impotent Satumine. We boast of the greatest freedom and democracy ever enjoyed by humanity whilst fanatically striking down any world or union with the audacity to suggest it might know better the will of its people than the distant governance machines and Trustees of the Jurisdiction. You think you have freedom in the Human Jurisdiction? Take a trip to Brembans World and see what happens when a local government decides to disconnect from the Jurisdiction's pointspace comms network. Or perhaps visit Patreloff for a lesson in the consequences of unapproved religious expression. Unless, of course, you are on a pre-billion population world – in which case you will get an immediate education in Jurisdiction freedoms the moment you try leaving your planet.

The Enguine Manifesto

Galman Tader: On Diaclom, in the Fertile Belt

'You said you could do this,' Galman hissed. Tumble had been at the code/gene/alpha-wave triple lock for almost a minute and had got no further than extending a rod with a fan of nine short needles at its head.

'I'm thinking,' Tumble replied.

Fidgeting, Galman looked around the small but high-walled yard for the umpteenth time and began clenching and flexing his arthritic hands. Still Tumble did nothing.

'You said it was OK,' the erstwhile cop whispered. Unlike the legal ambiguity of helping Galman push his way into the home of a known Saturnine terrorist, and turning a blind eye to violence it had not directly witnessed, this act was indefensibly criminal, and Tumble should not have been capable of proceeding. But over the last five months Galman had stripped his friend's limiting software down to its bare code compartments and rebuilt it, geometry by geometry, into something more useful, and that was a crime significantly more serious than mere breaking and entering. Aside from allowing machines to act violently, it had been a fluke error in programming which originally gave rise to Consul and nobody was prepared to let that happen again. But Galman was confident of his ability, and he considered his motivation justifiable, if not entirely ethical.

'What's the problem?' he asked Tumble.

'I'm not sure I should be doing this,' the machine replied. 'Isn't it illegal?'

Galman cringed. 'And if it is?' he asked. 'Would that be an issue?'

'I… Um…' Tumble shuddered and the extended rod rotated and withdrew a few inches.

'Tumble?'

'I said I'm thinking!' the machine snapped, too loud for the silent courtyard which, in this domed and sealed district, sat snugly between two large residential towers where several hundred people slept.

'Shut up,' Galman said, holding his hands up ready to put them across the mouth Tumble didn't have. The vault existed in a security blind-spot, but if someone in the neighbouring buildings heard Tumble shouting they could have some of the new Swinell Union Supervisors here within a couple of minutes. Of greater concern was the observation satellite which would have this district under surveillance again in less than ten minutes, whether someone reported them or not. 'We don't have time for this,' Galman urged the machine.

'Fuck it,' Tumble finally decided, extending the nine-pinned fan into the Velcro-like pad of the gene-lock. Apparently it had excised whatever demon had been lurking within its modified code compartments, the last remnants of the standard civilian grade software. But the real test, Galman supposed, would be in Tumble's willingness to stand by and watch Galman kill a Satumine in cold blood. Perhaps that test would present itself tonight.

'I'm through the gene-lock,' Tumble reported. It retracted the rod back into its sphere while extending a far shorter device – a solid black cylinder, an inch long and half an inch wide. A sudden and vicious headache speared Galman's brain. It was a similar if grossly amplified sensation to that he had felt on his infrequent shifts in an Intelligence-bridge suite. Tumble was defeating the lock's alpha-wave component with brute force and Galman was soaking up the overspill.

Three seconds later the pain ended, more or less. Only a dull pulsing remained, and would probably linger until he could get some sleep.

'You in?'

Tumble withdrew the alpha-wave generator. 'Just the code to do now.' It extended a more mundane tentacle which it plunged into the tiny connection port beneath the dirty keypad. A sharp click was followed by the dry grind of heavy bolts retracting into metal walls.

'Done,' the machine said with some hint of satisfaction. 'Now I'm a criminal,' it added with a perfectly synthesised tone of subtle accusation.

'Nobody will find out,' Galman reassured his friend. His thoughts drifted a moment and he wondered how true his assurance really was.

'I thought you were in a hurry,' Tumble said. 'Are you coming in?'

Galman refocused. His mind, like his joints, had been suffering more with every passing week. His memory, and his attention, was failing. It wouldn't be long before Alzheimer's set in. Again.

Carefully, slowly pushing the door into the vault's lobby, Galman said 'I suppose it's about time I got my treatments out of the way.'

'No, Galman, it was time five months ago,' Tumble quipped. 'Or any day since.'

'If only it was that easy,' Galman said. 'If only I was made of money. My ticket off of this world, and your IB coverage have cost everything I had left.'

'I know,' Tumble replied. 'I do your accounts.' Then, with a synthesised, almost nervous cough, it added, 'And the bribe for the cargo hauler captain isn't even close to being paid off.'

'I know, Tumble. I'm not entirely senile yet.' That was why he was here, at the vault in which he knew the Satumine stored their easily transported wealth. IB crystals – the core processors of intelligence-bridged computers. Millions of them, each no bigger than a grain of sand. They were a tradable commodity on almost any Jurisdiction world and they were the standard physical currency whenever the purely virtual New-Euro wasn't an option.

The lobby was a small box room. A short desk its only feature aside from the single door to the desk's right. The only light was the glow of the city which seeped through the open front door. This building had no windows.

'Cameras?' Galman asked of Tumble, though the information he had gathered suggested the patrons of this vault – not all Satumine terrorists, but largely criminals none-the-less – were not the kind of people who wanted to be recorded depositing their illicit funds.

'Nothing,' Tumble said. Then, with such speed it made Galman jump back, the machine fired an appendage at a far top corner of the room, pulled itself up so it crashed against the grey wall and then rammed a thin probe into the ceiling.

'Tumble!' Galman whispered.

Something crackled and Tumble dropped to the floor where it rolled quickly to Galman's side.

'Looks like they are recording their customers without asking,' the machine commented.

'Hidden cameras?' Galman looked up at the corner and hoped Tumble hadn't left any visible damage.

'Just the one,' Tumble reported. 'Not intelligence-bridged, so unless they have some reason to review the recording we should be OK.'

'Can you reactivate it before we leave?'

'I set it to come back on three minutes after we go, but I can't touch what it already has of us.'

'Little point in you deactivating it at all then, was there?' Galman wondered.

'I panicked.'

'Right, let's get what we came for. Only seven minutes before the satellites are back overhead.'

Using devices the Constabulary ought to have removed when they stripped Tumble of his weapons, they made their way quickly through several more gene-locks and a number of expected motion detectors. Galman took from his pocket a three inch box and opened the soft top to reveal a second smaller container in which rested fifty thousand grains, IB crystals, every one of them counterfeit. He looked on them with the same awe and materialistic lust with which men had once gazed upon diamonds. He wished he had been able to procure more of them.

'Are you sure they won't notice?' Tumble asked as it temporarily bypassed an Alpha-Wave identification field.

'As soon as they scan them before transferring them on,' Galman said, pushing open the final door to the inner vault. 'But we should be off the planet by then. As long as they only do a count of the boxes in the meantime, they will have no reason to suspect a break-in.'

'And no reason to check the cameras,' Tumble added.

Galman nodded. Then, when Tumble increased the illumination it had been providing since shutting the main door, Galman whistled quietly at shelf upon shelf of neatly stacked boxes of every denomination from five hundred crystals to one hundred thousand.

Two minutes later Galman and Tumble were back out in the covered street, heading for the subway which would take them back to Galman's home district. In his pocket the erstwhile cop had enough physical wealth to buy his entire housing block, or to bribe the head of the Swinell Union Bureau of Supervision into giving him a job. Galman couldn't help wondering who the *Satumine* intended to bribe with such wealth and he was intent on following the funds to Pellitoe. Fantastic as the wealth was, fifty thousand IB crystals was only just enough to persuade a cargo hauler's captain to risk federal charges of facilitating migration out of a pre-billion colony. There was unlikely to be enough left over to get the treatments he knew he needed.

Chapter 11

A trope of cheap fiction is the fantasy that there might be some technology, or genetic mutation, which would allow the human component of an intelligence bridge to remain lucid during their service. The stories usually revolve around a super-spy, an agent of some evil corporation, watching the actions of every computer to which he is providing an IB link, remembering every sliver of personal or corporate data and using such knowledge to bring down the rivals of his employer. Such things simply are not possible, and if they were then anyone attempting to develop the technology would be stopped long before they made any headway. The entire Jurisdiction relies on the anonymity and security of the IB networks, and were we to lose trust in that network the consequences would be dire for all.

Rehabilitation: A Survivor's Guide

Indin-Indin: The Second Asteroid Belt, The Satute System, in the Network

Five warnings were sent and Indin-Indin ignored them all.

'Turn back and leave this restricted space or suffer appropriate sanctions.'

'Come on,' he mumbled, willing the supposed mining team on the asteroid to cut him some slack. 'Just a harmless shuttle. No threat. Just suffered some damage and lost my communications array.'

Eight weeks ago, upon finally reaching the second of the asteroid belts, the Satumine technician had deliberately clipped a small rock, scuffing the starboard thrusters and coating the polarised hull in dust. His exaggerated steering and sputtering thrusters – purposefully set out of alignment – added to the illusion of a ship in distress.

Now three thousand kilometres from a large asteroid which hung lazily in a stable region of the belt, Indin-Indin received his sixth warning. 'Back the fuck off, or you will be fired upon.'

He didn't respond. Three high powered lasers flicked through the uneven clumps of dust between the base on the asteroid and Indin-Indin's approaching shuttle. Warning shots, ten meters above and to either side of the shuttle. No more communications came and the technician didn't expect he would hear anything more before his craft was cored by a more deliberately aimed bean. Sliding variously shaped icons around the primary control screen, he brought the shuttle to a halt. This was as close as he was going to get while those on the surface – ostensibly miners, but obviously there to study the crashed probe – were still in position to use their defensive systems.

Indin-Indin loaded the idle communication array with the codes given to him six months ago when Aggregate first made his proposition. Almost immediately he picked up a handshake signal and over the next minute found the systems of the crashed probe powering up and coming under his control.

Calling up internal and external sensor feeds he watched as the dozen Satumine scientists and engineers began running about inside the probe's shattered hull, chattering on about how exciting this was and how they would finally be able to see what this hundred meter long cylinder was capable of. The team leader was clapping wildly, proclaiming he had been right to insist the government keep this discovery from the Jurisdiction. Indin-Indin gathered there had been pressure to inform the humans of the discovery of this huge probe which appeared on the system's edge nearly five years ago, its cloaking technology failing, and crashed into the second asteroid belt two years later. The lack of progress in understanding or even activating any part of the probe had prompted some to call for human involvement, but the scientists and government had stood firm and now, they thought, it was pay-day.

Indin-Indin found the necessary systems and powered them up. He didn't *want* to kill his own people, he felt sick at the idea, but this probe was meant for him, and *he* was meant for something far beyond the value of twelve Satumine lives. What he did here would benefit all Satumine – he just wished he could have told them first. But he couldn't risk letting anybody know. Collaborators and traitors infected every part of his society; the humans owned Satute.

The probe's sensors acquired a lock on every team member, including the three still in the primary base thirty meters to the side of the crashed object. He dealt which those three first. Sputtering and flickering into life, the probe's meteor lasers lanced the building's thin metal walls, melting through the cheap alloys and penetrating the primary brains of the Satumine inside. Seconds later, once the lasers again fell dormant, vacuum foam expanded within the three neat breaches and atmosphere was stabilised. It was a pointless exercise: nobody was left alive in there, and nobody would be leaving the probe to utilise the air in the base.

To the probe's rear, packed in a sealed section as yet un-breached by the Satumine scientists, rested a tiny shuttle intended for use by Aggregate's agent: Indin-Indin. This small craft, despite its size, promised speeds twenty times faster than Indin-Indin's current vehicle. It was equipped with a working cloak and, most significantly, was armed with a brutally efficient particle accelerator. The Satumine technician acquired control of the little ship, armed the weapon, and fired. Down the length of the probe it burned and nothing survived.

It took half an hour to bring the shuttle down onto the asteroid, and another twenty minutes to don the survival suit. By the time Indin-Indin was ready to walk out across the short expanse of regolith to enter the probe's burnt-out husk, he had fully assessed the little craft's fitness. Although in far better shape than the probe in which it had been delivered, the ship was badly battered and the cloak was damaged in too many places to be repaired. It would function, but he had no idea for how long. The payload, however, was untouched. Indin-Indin grinned: *Not long now.*

Chapter 12

*CRMs, Conflict Resolution Munitions, are at once a monument
to the strength of science and an utter travesty against the universe.
Conflict Resolution - such an innocuous term for what amounts to a
vile and indiscriminate planet buster. Certainly they resolve any
planetary conflict which might otherwise consume legions of our brave
military. But they are an horrific affront to all that humanity and our
Jurisdiction should stand for. How can it ever be acceptable to
unleash these ruthless gravity abusers into orbit around any planet?
And yet they are used. They are used rarely, but they are used. At
least three human worlds have been destabilised and their tectonics
plates reduced to magma buy these abominations in order that heresies
or insurgencies might be contained. Over a dozen of consuls worlds
have similarly been forever ruined - billions of our captive brothers
and sisters perishing in the fire. It is important to realise, therefore,
that this technology was adapted from the machines of the Satumine.
How can we tolerate the presence within our Jurisdiction of any
creature capable of devising such horror?*

The Truth: A treatise on the Satumine Conspiracy

Subset: Aboard the *Tenjin*, in shortspace,
somewhere in the fertile belt

Lucidity visited his subverted consciousness in sporadic
and infrequent waves. In those rare moments of
independence he suffered.

Subset knew his slavery could never end.

Even the occasional moments of mental clarity and
physical torment would eventually cease. Aggregate would
tire of him as a plaything and he would become no more
than the rest of the eternally indentured crew. Death was

almost unheard of in the predictable and controlled society of one and replacement bodies were rarely needed - at a mere five centuries, Subset was the youngest by far.

It was Subset's youth which led to his moments of lucidity. Aggregate had certain carnal desires, lust he sated with the same gluttony through which he satisfied his other wants. And having had seven thousand years in which to bore of his thousand bodies, Aggregate had a particular hunger for the relative novelty of Subset.

Aggregate could have controlled Subset's body, causing it to perform the desired obscenities, could even have instructed the controlled brain to replicate a parody of independence – but that would have been practically masturbation. Aggregate wanted more, wanted the youth to be aware, alive, able to fully appreciate what was to happen.

The young crew member knew the thoughts of Aggregate for he was, for the most part, joined utterly with him. But only in the moments of lucidity did he have the opportunity to process and understand. In those moments, however, temporarily voided of the additional helix subverting his every genetic twist, he had physical violations and torments to endure. His waking hours were a montage of abuse and suffering, and he welcomed the imminent arrival of newly grown bodies to replace the dozens killed twenty years ago. They would soon reach maturity and be birthed, and Aggregate would have new distractions. Subset longed to exist as a mere extension of Aggregate's pointspace body. Independence was torture.

Chapter 13

The Fertile Belt is unquestionably a significant blessing to humanity. It has allowed for some of the easiest terraforming ever undertaken and, more importantly, has allowed for a dense region of large Unions, bringing about a political and economic balance to the otherwise disproportionate weight of the Network worlds. The balance is by no means perfect and the Network still holds far too much power for its size, but the Fertile Belt has many more worlds to offer and expansion is only accelerating. The virus with which Fertile Belt life is modified to double-helix architecture is improved with every use and one has to wonder how much longer it will be before the cooperative and benign temperament natural to those animals can be retained through the change. Such an improvement would remove the single flaw in the otherwise perfect gift of the Fertile Belt. Perhaps the elite of the Network will withhold such an improvement as they struggle to maintain their grip on the reins of power. Maybe they already have.

The Enguine Manifesto

Galman Tader: On Diaclom, in the Fertile Belt

'Why the hell do they ignore you,' the machine snapped as a vine lashed out to ensnare the white ball. 'But they can't seem to get enough of me?'

Having spent a week in the confined tube sections of the old city, laying low after securing his passage to Pellitoe, Galman was glad of the open air as he strolled through a carpet of vines and short grasses on the side of the road joining the city and Diaclom's only space port. Even with the oxygen filters in his nostrils, it was nice to be outside. Winter had given way to the short Diaclom spring and a new cycle of ecological warfare was being fought between the mismatch of species brought to this world. Every year the ecosystem was changed as new plants and animals gained the upper hand, or the latest batch of species was integrated to help enforce a better balance. These vines, for example, were new. Last year the fields here had been dominated by tall straw-like grasses. Now those grasses were strangled by a vine developed to thrive on a world thirty thousand light years away. Galman liked this time of year. Tumble, however, was getting frustrated.

By the time the pair reached the base's perimeter wall, Galman had picked Tumble up and was cradling him in his arms, beyond the reach of whatever senses the machine was triggering in the plants.

Security at the main gates was non-existent. It would be at the departure gates, around the pads and runway, that checks would take place. Galman strolled casually through the wide arch, through the pressure differential curtain keeping the oxygen-heavy atmosphere out. He had no intention of passing through any departure gates. He had no authority to leave the planet and no money left with which to bribe his way past the clerks.

First Galman availed himself of the largely empty hospitality promenades, enjoying a substantial meal before spending his last few New-Euros and IB crystals on a stopgap treatment for his worsening arthritis and foggy memory.

'What you need is Telomere treatment and a body sweep,' Tumble warned him as they wandered the under-used promenade. 'Not a tube of tablets.'

'They will see me through the three weeks it takes to get to Pellitoe,' Galman replied. 'Then we can see how good the Swinell Union's public health service really is.'

Only a few of the many retail units were occupied, and even they would have been closed had they not been so heavily subsidised. There simply weren't enough people passing through the port to support even the few businesses operating there. In the three hours Galman and Tumble had been on the long ten-levelled promenade, they had seen less than thirty other people. And they were probably all base staff.

The unfamiliar man, and his talkative machine, drew curious glances and eventually somebody approached them to ask their business in Deen Base.

'Just over from the old city,' Galman explained to the nosey but pleasant young man.

'You waiting for a shuttle?' the man asked, glancing at one of the arrival and departure screens projected onto many of the promenade walls. Galman followed his gaze. There were no arrivals scheduled all week from the Swinell Union Cruiser *Ohio* which had hung in orbit for the past twenty years overseeing the orderly takeover. There was only one departure and it was to the *Ellis-Three*, a cargo vessel, due to leave in ten hours.

'No,' Galman said. 'I'm not waiting for anyone. I just got bored of looking at the dull passages of the old city.' There was a taste of truth in his words and Galman hoped it came across. 'I thought I might see what the new facilities are like over here.'

The young man shrugged. 'There ain't a lot right now,' he apologised. 'Just some eateries and general supplies stores. Truth be told, they are only here to service the base personnel. We aren't really open for business yet.'

'Oh, I'm sorry. Should I leave?'

'No, not at all. We're glad of the custom and the new faces. Just be sure to tell your friends when you get home. It's going to be a few years yet before we start seeing many visitors from the rest of the Swinell Union, so maybe we can provide some out of town facilities for the locals.' With that he offered Galman a hopeful smile and wandered into a sandwich bar a little further along the promenade.

'He'll be lucky,' Tumble quipped. 'The old city is a dump, but its retail sections are better appointed than this ghost town.'

'Alright, keep it down will you?' Galman muttered. 'We are drawing too much attention as it is. Come on, we should get ready to board the *Ellis-Three*.'

Maintaining a casual gait as if strolling about the port in an aimless exploration of its many passages and walkways, Galman made his way through the most indirect route to warehouse eighteen. Currently surplus to the port's meagre requirements, the warehouse was dark, empty and unguarded. Unused as it was, it lacked any kind of active monitoring. Who, after all, would want to break into an empty storage space? In fact it didn't require breaking into at all; just a push of the rotating icon on the otherwise black lock-screen and the small pedestrian door, built into the enormous cargo door, slid silently aside.

Tumble immediately rolled though into the pitch dark cavern and began glowing like an enormous bulb, illuminating much of the massive space but leaving its highest reaches cloaked in black. The illuminating effect would have been more effective had Tumble launched an appendage to the ceiling and drawn itself higher. But it was too high even for Tumbles tentacles.

Dozens of wide grooves in the floor were so distorted by shadow as to appear as row upon row of deep trenches. But Galman knew they were no more than an inch deep. They were all that was visible of the sunken scaffolding which would one day rise from the floor in any one of a hundred configurations to form a complex storage and retrieval network. Tracks, pickers and countless shelves would eventually turn this immense empty space into a noisy but supremely efficient cargo-sorting facility. None of that mattered to Galman; he was only concerned with warehouse seventeen on the other side of the east wall.

'Have you found the vent?' Galman asked.

'Right where it's supposed to be,' Tumble said, shining a secondary torch, a more focused light, on a high section of wall which looked no different to the rest of the vast brushed metal expanse.

Galman waved theatrically at the hidden opening and said, 'Then by all means Tumble, get to work.'

'Right you are,' the white ball fired a tentacle up to the identified spot at its furthest reach, affixing securely with a unigrip pad. It wound in the thin length, drawing itself up until hanging directly in front of the vent. The warehouse then fell into darkness as Tumble extinguished its illumination and extruded more tools. After a clatter and whine of mechanical activity the light returned and a metre square duct was visible leading into the wall.

'Come on then,' Tumble called. 'Up you come.'

Galman tapped a single finger to the side of his head presenting a playful half salute. He then took from his pocket a small cylinder with a leather-effect grip along its four inch length. Aiming just above the vent, he depressed a tiny circle with his thumb and a line was fired with extraordinary force. Like Tumble's tentacle, the line affixed to the wall, and after giving a tug and tightening his grip Galman released the thumb trigger and was dragged quickly up to join the hanging machine at the vent. The force of his ascent sent pain racing out in every direction from his shoulders and burned through his knuckles.

'After you,' he said to the machine, wincing at a new pain in his wrists. Why the hell did these devices have such small handles? He watched Tumble swing into the vent and roll along its length, dimming its illumination to better suit the cramped passage. With more difficulty Galman aligned himself with the duct. After a couple of aborted attempts, scrambling at the smooth metal wall, he managed to get his feet inside.

'Give me a hand would you?' he called to his IB friend. A couple of his tentacles wrapped about his ankles, another gripped his waist, and he was pulled gently through just as his grip failed and the grapple slipped from his hands. With a zip and a solid thump, the device retracted fully, slapping into the wall a few feet above.

'Bollocks,' Galman spat.

'Leave it,' Tumble muttered, releasing Galman from its secure embrace.

The vent, designed to regulate the atmosphere in the warehouse and, critically, to draw air out in the event of a fire, connected with vents in the adjoining warehouse. An unforgivable security lapse, Galman thought, but one for which he was most grateful.

It took only moments to crawl the duct's short length to the vent cover of warehouse seventeen. As before, Tumble extinguished its illumination while working on the covering but, when it was done, this time it didn't restore the light. There was no need. The warehouse, a nightmare of clattering trolleys and crashing boxes on a tangle of narrow tracks was lit brilliantly. Why it was so well lit was not entirely clear for nobody, as far as Galman could tell, actually worked there. It was entirely automated.

'There's the track,' Tumble said. 'Just below us.'

'Right,' Galman said. 'Two minutes then.' About his wrist was a thin black strap on which a single white dot was slightly raised. He pressed it. Seconds later he felt a slight buzz against his wrist. The signal was sent, and the captain of the *Ellis-Three* had responded. A request would now be sent for the cargo hauler's last shuttle to be loaded. If everything was going as smoothly as it appeared to be, the top of one of the larger containers would be open as it rattled along the track beneath the open vent. Galman and Tumble need merely jump.

'Now,' Tumble hissed far sooner than Galman had expected. As the machine rolled out of the vent it fired a thick cable back to Galman, grabbed him, and dragged him roughly out of the duct. The pair landed hard in the empty cargo container, about six meters across and two high, just as the lid slid closed and locked.

Galman tried standing, but only once. After being thrown to the ground by a jarring shudder, he hugged the floor while the crashing and rattling of the loading procedure threatened to shake the teeth out of his gums. His arthritic joints throbbed with spiteful persistence and he flicked a double dose of tablets into his mouth in desperation. They did nothing.

Ten minutes later the torturous ride ended and for a while Galman lay in silence while the drugs finally moistened his desiccated joints and dulled the pain.

'Oh crap,' Tumble eventually broke the silence. 'Here's something we didn't anticipate.'

'What?'

'They're scanning the crate.'

The lid unlocked with a click and began sliding open. Galman drew his mag-gun.

Chapter 14

Having survived Consul's IB farms, you may well be concerned about the civic duty required of you in relation to IB suites. Let me assure you, these suites are different in both form and function to those of you wretched past. You retain at all times the right to postpone your duty, putting it off until a time more suited to your schedule. And your duty is for only a few hours in any given month (subject to local quota rules and amendments). You will not be a slave to the IB network, rather you will be its master. IB works for you, to make your life easier, more convenient and ultimately more meaningful. You may lose a few hours to the IB network, but the benefits of IB undoubtedly free Humanity from countless hours of labour. IB is your friend; Intelligence Bridging is not what it was under Consul.

Rehabilitation: A Survivor's Guide

Ambondice-Ambondice: On Pellitoe, in the Swinell Union, In the Fertile Belt

A temperate yellow sun gently warmed the picturesque meadow, while a soft breeze caused the willows drooping over the kidney-shaped pond to sway lazily and a series of subdued waves to ripple through the short grass. Flowers bloomed in vivid colours unimagined by nature, their sweet perfume as intoxicating as any liqueur. This was a human fantasy, but one enjoyed equally by the Satumine.

A small bandstand had been erected on the pond's south bank. On its hexagonal stage a troupe of six exotically embellished Satumine dancers performed in the shade of a seemingly living pitched roof which occasionally fluttered its massive glistening butterfly wings. Lounging on wide cushions and recliners, forty Satumine enjoyed the heavily AR embellished hall while their superiors attended to business in an antechamber.

Ambondice-Ambondice glanced across to his left, through what looked like a thin glass wall, to check his five aides were still in the pleasure garden. Unlike the others, his aides looked alert, had been told to expect trouble. Occasionally they looked across to what would appear to them as a long uninterrupted vista reaching out to the horizon. They knew where the wall was to the inner circle's private chamber.

'If this is a joke,' Sharlie-Sharlie said, standing slowly from his seat at the head of the table, 'It is in poor taste.'

'Ambondice-Ambondice glared at the senior Satumine. Sharlie-Sharlie: The humans had an offensive habit of calling the lightly embellished Satumine by the human name *Charlie*, yet the senior Satumine refused to challenge their ignorance. By his inaction, Ambondice-Ambondice felt, Sharlie-Sharlie encouraged the insult. He didn't want to agitate them, didn't want to make a scene. His pride, he insisted, was worth sacrificing if it kept investigative human eyes away from the actions of the Circle. More and more, Ambondice-Ambondice felt, the Circle was failing to do anything the humans would even care to investigate.

'It's not a joke,' Ambondice-Ambondice said, rising from his own chair midway down one side of the table, turning his right palm-eye to each of the other six members in turn while fixing his left palm on Sharlie-Sharlie.

'You keep talking about your 'grand spectacle', Sharlie-Sharlie; you keep bringing in funds from cells on Diaclom and Dendrell, but when are we actually going to *do* anything?' He thrust both palms to glare at his leader. 'I bring to the table a plan to do some real damage, I offer you a chance to strike meaningfully at the humans, and you think it is a joke?' He kicked the chair back and stepped off from the table, waving an arm out across the assembly.

'This,' he spat, 'is the joke. You talk and you scheme and you pretend. But you do nothing. You never will.'

Sharlie-Sharlie was silent a moment, probably taken aback by the unexpected and unprecedented outburst. Then with the same calm and measured voice with which he spoke so pleasantly to the humans, he addressed the dissenter. 'Ambondice-Ambondice,' he practically whispered – in so far as a Saturnine neck sphincter could whisper - and he returned to his seat. 'This Circle agreed on a path ten years ago. We voted and unanimously passed the motion. Although you were not a member back then, you inherit the obligations of the previous occupant of your seat and are expected to support the objectives agreed upon by him.'

Ambondice-Ambondice tensed his hands and kept his palm-eyes staring at the leader. 'Ten years is too long,' he said.

'We are trying to bring down the entire AR network on Pellitoe,' Sharlie-Sharlie said. 'This can't be rushed. It will take time, and I expect you to be patient.'

Ambondice-Ambondice clicked his disgust. 'And all the while, the funds keep flowing in and your home gets larger and more embellished by the week.'

'That's enough!' one of the others interrupted. 'You do *not* accuse Sharlie-Sharlie—'

'Yes,' Ambondice-Ambondice snarled, 'I do.'

'Be careful,' Sharlie-Sharlie warned. 'You draw close to a line from which once crossed you may not return.'

Ambondice-Ambondice clicked and sputtered utter disdain then excreted a small amount of the solvent required to dissolve the resin sealing his abdominal cavity. The lower of the three flaps quivered as it tried to fall open – an obscene gesture which took him well beyond the line against which he had been cautioned.

The Circle was silent, stunned, until Sharlie-Sharlie pointed to the door and ordered Ambondice-Ambondice out.

'Have your Circle,' the dissenter said. 'Play at conspirators, and get rich. I have the means and the resolve to do this on my own.' He stormed towards the door, and as he opened it into the AR garden he called back, 'You can all burn with the rest of the planet.'

The others yelled and cursed, shouted after him as best any Satumine could, promising he would suffer for his insolence. But the merchant felt no fear. It would likely take them another decade to bring to fruition any plans against him. He didn't need them: Sharlie-Sharlie wasn't the only one to have set aside funds.

Chapter 15

The Satumine are not the only threats to our blessed Human Jurisdiction. There is, of course, Consul and his realm of artificial consciousnesses, but there are less visible enemies, more insidious adversaries against which the Administration fails to offer any protection or resistance. Shortspace is the foundation on which we have built our galactic Jurisdiction, it is the basis of our entire civilisation and without it would would never have left the ninety six worlds of the Network. It is known by all that we thread a bead of higher dimensional space, the space we inhabit, onto one of the infinite number of one-dimensional strands within shortspace. It is equally well known our beads run the lengths of those lower-dimension filaments at the single speed possible within that dimension, ultimately traversing the shorter distance connecting two higher dimensional points five hundred times faster than light could join those locations. We can not freely travel between the infinite filaments and skip from one strand to another. When we thread a strand we lose all control and can do nothing but wait to emerge at its terminus. How much of a threat might one of our enemies be if they could overcome these restrictions? They might overpower us before we even knew our Jurisdiction was under attack. How much more devastating might an assault be from those entities native to the realm of shortspace. They exist, in spite of the Administration's claims to the contrary, and every time we thread a bead onto one of their strands we draw more attention to ourselves. We should have stayed in the Network.

The Truth: A treatise on the Satumine Conspiracy

Galman Tader: On Diaclom, In the Fertile Belt

The harsh glare of a floodlight filled the container through its open lid, momentarily blinding Galman, forcing him to look to the floor and hold up his hands against the light.

'Drop the mag-gun!' someone ordered from above. Galman hesitated; he was looking at a lengthy stay in federal prison. The pistol was his only remaining card, but what could he really do with it? He had placed hundreds of offenders in his current position and none of them had been able to find a way out of it.

'This is your last warning,' said the voice which was suddenly familiar. Galman looked up and through squinted eyes saw the blurred silhouette of a single person standing on a ledge over the container. The floodlight made it impossible to identify him – but the voice...

'Drop it!' the man yelled in response to Galman's sudden movement, and the erstwhile cop was about to comply when vines erupted from the corner of the container to entangle the man and drag him screaming down.

Galman squeezed the mag-gun's trigger and a single metal bolt was accelerated along the barrel to lethal velocity by magnetic coils running the pistol's length, silently firing the projectile into the blinding floodlight, cracking the luminous tiles and destroying the thin powermesh behind. The tiles flickered as strobe for a moment before the controlling software shut them down. Only now, with the glare subdued, did Galman see the curved roof not so far above the container, along which ran three continuous strips of ambient illuminators. The inside of a shuttle's cargo hold.

The sound of a struggle on the floor snapped his increasingly distracted mind back to the man tightly bound by Tumble's many tentacles. He aimed his mag-gun.

'What now?' his IB friend asked with an approximation of anxious concern.

Galman looked back up to the open lid. On seeing nobody else he crouched beside the man. The uniform was that of a Junior Trustee, the lowest and most populous rank within the Jurisdiction's immense bureaucracy: The Administration. The lapel insignia was the stylised double helix of the colonisation ministry and, beneath it, three thin gold bars signified the department of migration control. This man was here to ensure nobody left the pre-billion world without federal authorisation. But why was he alone?

'I could easily break him,' the machine suggested when Galman failed to offer a plan.

'Don't you bloody dare, Tumble,' the bound Junior Trustee snapped with a voice Galman was now certain he recognised.

'Steef?' Galman said, pulling the armoured fabric balaclava from the man's head.

'Galman Tader,' Steef said with sad disappointment. 'What the hell are you doing?'

Galman steadied his aim at the man with whom he had been partnered in the Constabulary for over a decade. 'Where are the others?' he asked, refusing to answer Steef's question. 'You wouldn't have opened a suspect container on your own.'

In spite of his incapacitation, Steef managed a playful grin. 'I saw you on the promenade,' he said. 'And I heard you were off the force, and all but off the grid. So when we got a tip-off about migrant smuggling on this shuttle, I figured you might be involved.'

'Where are the others?' Galman repeated.

'I came alone,' Steef said. 'I wanted to give you a chance. You know, for old times' sake.'

'A chance?'

'I can get you out of here, back to the legal side of Deen Base. Nobody has to know.'

Galman rubbed at his face and sighed. 'Let him go, Tumble,' he said. The machine abruptly retracted its tentacles and appendages so quickly, and with such force, it looked as if it had sliced through the Junior Trustee's body. But Steef got quickly to his feet and went straight for his backup pistol in its thigh holster. The weapon was not there. At the end of three appendages, Tumble now held both of the man's visible weapons and the one he had secreted elsewhere on his body. Such disarming manoeuvres were Tumble's bread and butter.

Steef gave the IB machine a sideways glare. 'I'll need you both to stay in the container while I get it taken back off of the shuttle –' he began, but Galman held up a hand.

'I'm not going back,' he said. 'I have to get to Pellitoe.'

'Don't do this,' the Junior Trustee pleaded. 'I know things must be hard, what with the Constabulary getting shut down and the Swinell Union changing everything, but this is your home. Do you really think it will be better for you on one of the Swinell Union's main planets?'

Galman sniffed. 'You think I'm just running away, looking for a better life?' He was offended. 'I thought you knew me better than that.'

Steef gave a look of contemplation and then his eyebrows shot up. 'This is about a Satumine, isn't it?' he guessed. 'It's always about a bloody Satumine with you.'

Galman glared at his old partner. 'You, more than anyone, ought to understand.' Steef had lost as much of his family in the bombing as Galman, and was just as enthusiastic in his investigations. At least he *had* been, in the early years. Unlike Galman, however, Steef seemed to have gotten over it. He would say he had come to terms with the fact that not all Satumine were the same, that they hadn't all been responsible for the attack. Galman saw it differently. Steef's softening heart was an insult to the dead; a betrayal of both their families.

'I can't let you leave Diaclom,' Steef insisted. 'This isn't just bending a few planetary laws. This is federal statutes.' He looked across to Tumble, now hanging from the container wall. 'And I expected more from you,' he spat.

'You were always the voice of reason keeping Galman's passions in check. You are supposed to keep him from stepping completely over the line.'

'I fixed him,' Galman said flatly.

'Christ, Galman. Is there anything else you want to confess?'

'With or without the changes to my code compartments,' Tumble said, 'I would still support Galman in this, as far as I was able. Something is being prepared on Pellitoe and –'

'No,' Steef shouted. 'I don't want to know. I already know enough to get Galman sentenced to SMD.' A Sentence of Memory Dismissal was at the extreme end of the sentencing options available for his offences, but it was still a possibility.

'It's important,' Tumble insisted.

'Then let the Swinell Union Bureau of Supervision deal with it.'

'The Supervisors?' Galman spat. 'They won't even stop and search a Satumine without a court order. They're too scared of offending the alien minority.'

Steef looked into Galman's eyes, at first glaring but quickly softening into understanding and perhaps pity. Finally he looked to the floor and took a long breath. 'If I force you both out of here, and let you go, what will you do?'

Galman didn't hesitate. 'I'll be back here on the next shuttle.'

'Tumble?'

'I'll be right beside him.'

Steef shook his head. 'Give me my weapons,' he said to Tumble. 'Then give me a hand out of this container.' He shot Galman a warning glare. 'This is us done,' he said. 'If I see you again, you get an SMD.'

Chapter 16

Out-Network: It seems such an innocent, even descriptively apt name for those worlds beyond the ancient Satumine frame network. But to the educated citizen, reading between the lines, it reveals the disparity which exists between the Network and the greater Jurisdiction. Numbering almost twenty thousand worlds, the out-network planets are the majority; the Network is only a close-knit union of ninety seven worlds (ninety five if you discount Satute, which although connected by the frame network is only loosely governed by the Jurisdiction, and Teroh which although still within the administrative remit of the Network no longer enjoys the benefit of an ancient Satumine frame). The census, and the governance machines it informs, should logically result in a system in which a minority ought to receive no greater benefits than the majority, but this is far from the reality we observe. Are we really surprised though? The census is somehow adjusted and the results skewed in favour of the wealthy elite on Earth and the Network of which it is a part. The authors of this Manifesto have walked the gilded avenues of Earth and the slums of pre-billion worlds and we can vouch for the displeasure of the shunned masses. Nothing in their census answers could possibly imply a willingness for a slice of their planet's and unions' meagre wealth to be diverted to the Network. Ninety seven densely populated worlds: The network represents around eight percent of the Jurisdictions citizens, and yet it enjoys forty five percent of its wealth. How this fits into Consuls insidious control of the Human Jurisdiction is not clear, but we are in no doubt that the consequences of such inequality will soon present themselves.

The Enguine Manifesto

Endella Mariacroten: On Dendrell, in the Swinell Union, in the Fertile Belt

Endella Mariacroten: Justiciar of the Human Jurisdiction; celebrated hero of over thirty conflicts across the fertile belt; the silent blade which ended a hundred other wars never mentioned on public nets. She was physically prepared for anything she might face, and as the last of her nano-farms dispatched their pre-emptive swarms into her blood she took a moment to prepare her mind. Neural implants flicked nano-scale switches to release a steady flow of drugs and chemicals designed to minimise any fear or anxiety she might feel. In truth, however, those implants had been superfluous for over a century and if they had not been capable of synthesising the required compounds from her own body then she wouldn't have bothered to use them anymore. She was more than capable of regulating her own emotions. Recalling her aberrant behaviour over recent months, however, she wondered if that was still entirely true.

She checked her heavy multipistol and confirmed all five magazines were secured within the narrow butt: three different calibres of bolt; a clip of the larger toxin darts; a battery for the weak but long lasting laser. She stowed the multipistol in her shoulder holster, beneath the flap of her loose overcoat. In the opposite holster she kept another pistol: a simple laser with a battery-life four times longer than that of the multipistol's laser, and capable of charging through several dozen different methods. It was her backup and, on some of her longer missions in which she had been unable to procure more clips for the multipistol, it had been invaluable. It was a weak little weapon, but she had a fondness for it which went beyond its limited functionality. She patted the small cold weapon, not bothering to check it. It had never let her down.

She jabbed her fingers, rigid as iron bars, into the material of her shirt and felt the armoured fabric harden at the impact. From past experience she knew it was far from perfect and modern mag-gun bolts were capable of penetrating as often as they were deflected, but that was why she had the nano-farms, self-sealing circulatory system, plated bones, and all the other enhancements the Administration and Justiciary felt their top agents warranted.

Her checks completed, she stepped out of the rented car and looked across the plaza through floating screens, AR columns and water features, to assess her target: the planet's central Administration complex; the Jurisdiction's primary presence on Dendrell. It was a little more deserving of her efforts than the dry accounts over which she had been poring for the better part of a year, but she still had the feeling she was merely being kept busy. But ever the obedient soldier, Endella had committed to discharging her duties here to the best of her considerable ability. Had a lesser member of the Administration, a Trustee of some sort, been tasked with this assignment, she supposed, they would have revoked the suspect's codes, enlisted a couple of the Swinell Union's fine supervisors, and had the man arrested in his office to be taken into custody for questioning. If that was what the Senior Trustee had wanted he shouldn't have sent a Justiciar – least of all Endella Mariacroten. The target (Justiciars did not deal with *suspects*; by the time a Justiciar prepared to act, guilt was generally assumed) was the Area Trustee, Dendrell's most senior Federal employee, and as such there was every chance he had in place any number of escape options and contingency plans. He had the resources. Besides, if he was given even a couple of seconds warning, he could destroy vital evidence which Endella wanted to use to determine exactly where he was forwarding the embezzled federal grants. She was taking him hard and silent.

With a thought she donned a simple AR embellishment, appearing as a young woman covered in animated tattoos and sporting a prehensile tail of braided ribbons. Where she walked the ground sprouted tiny pink flowers which, within seconds, unfolded butterfly wings and flew into the air where they dissolved into a fast dissipating yellow mist. By the standards of current Swinell Union fashion, such an embellishment barely attracted notice. The air didn't even sing with her passing. Approaching un-embellished would have elicited far greater a reaction. Unlike the majority, Endella's AR implants were dialled back so the real world- drab-reality – seemed cloaked in a ghostly other world of AR. She knew better than to accept AR as real or to allow the two worlds to be as one; too many dangers could lurk hidden beneath embellishments. Her own weapons being a prime example.

She strode with purpose across the plaza, avoiding the rainbow jets of a bliss fountain in which jaded citizens with nothing better to do were getting a quick buzz of sensory-implant pleasure. It was a world away from the more intense AR sexual stimulation for which people paid extortionate rates, but it was a generous freebie laid on by the local government. Endella found it vulgar and certainly didn't need the distraction. She ascended the twenty wide steps to the administration complex's majestic entrance and headed directly to one of the fifteen security arches standing in a single line bisecting the cavernous reception hall.

Endella touched a brooch on her shirt. It was the AR visual representation of an intelligence-bridged suite of such potency that merely possessing the code compartment files carried a mandatory SMD for anyone outside of the Justiciary. It was a standard tool of a Justiciar, and one jealously hoarded. As she stepped into the arch she saw the brooch extend translucent tendrils, visible only in her private AR, into the arch and through the resin floor to the systems hidden beneath. While these tendrils subverted the local hardware, a wave of turquoise mist rushed out, twisting into a thick cord which reached through the high ceiling. The remote aspects of the security system, including the IB, were now pacified. Her weapons were not detected and her true identity not logged. The Area Trustee would not be expecting her.

A reception screen appeared in AR, a little way in front of Endella, and as well as a number of icons and lists which she could use to announce her business here a friendly face also appeared.

'Welcome to your Administration complex, the intelligence-bridged receptionist said. 'How can I make your visit more satisfying and productive?'

Endella sighed. The machine knew precisely why she was here – or at least the cover story she had planted an hour ago – but this particular IB machine obviously favoured the chatty approach.

'I'm here for my appointment,' she snapped, walking quickly to one of the elevator recesses so the screen had to follow at some speed.

'Of course, Miss Raheena,' the IB face said. 'I have informed the Area Trustee's secretary that you –'

' – Whatever,' Endella waved the screen away and stepped into the first available elevator.

'Thirty second floor,' the elevator announced. It knew where she needed to go.

By the time the oval elevator's curved door had slid open in a recess at the end of the Area Trustee's long waiting room, Endella had drawn her multi-pistol, activated the fourth magazine – the darts – and set her brooch invading the systems on this floor.

Endella stepped out, firing immediately. A single dart, one centimetre long, buried itself in the throat of a small man, a Senior Trustee, talking to a civilian woman just outside the elevator. A second dart found the woman's breast and, as the bodies dropped, Endella walked further into the surprisingly Spartan room. She targeted the remaining five people in turn, dispatching them all within three seconds. One dart each. A small screen appeared in front of her face: a message from her brooch. A single cry for help had been transmitted by someone in the room, but the brooch had intercepted and shredded the message.

One of the bodies, an older-looking man equipped with a whistling peacock tail and bizarre fifteen inch tongue, was twitching on the floor. The toxin was designed to incapacitate for up to six hours but didn't always agree with everyone's bodies. He did not seem to have a nano-farm, and he would need medical help, but that wasn't her concern. She was authorised to kill, and was not required to explain any fatalities. Why then, she wondered, had she rolled him into the recovery position and queued a medical alert to be sent the moment she was done here?

She opened the door, fired three times, and watched the Area Trustee, his personal assistant, and a civilian woman, drop to the floor like corpses. Then she sighed: was that all there was? She was bored, and she was frustrated.

She secured the files, informed the local Administration of her presence and of her need for a detention cell, and checked the medical request had been sent.

While she waited, sat at the Area Trustee's desk, she began trawling through more accounts, hoping for an excuse to go looking for something more exciting. And she saw now where the money had been going. It took only two minutes to prove a link with the Satumine.

She was going to Pellitoe.

Chapter 17

Any system of governance in which a single person, entity, or party is given absolute power is a risk to the freedoms valued above all else by the Jurisdiction . While Consul sought to dominate all, the Administration of the Human Jurisdiction takes only the roles of organiser and facilitator. We are keen that every citizen take responsibility for their own lives and this philosophy continues into the Administration's attitudes towards its colonies. Every world is free to govern itself, provided it presents no risk to the freedoms of its own people or those of the wider Jurisdiction. A logical result of this right is the formation of planetary unions - the formalisation of political and social ties between astrographically local planets. The Unions are a vital part of the Jurisdiction's tapestry and you are invited to explore the myriad flavours of human society now present across our galaxy. There is somewhere for everyone to call home, somewhere for everyone to be comfortable and free.

Rehabilitation: A Survivor's Guide

Galman Tader: Aboard the *Ellis-Three*, in orbit around Pellitoe, in the Swinell Union, in the Fertile-belt

Heavily armed and capable of housing three thousand crew and passengers in its four sections, the *Vulpine* was not the most modern of Federal Sentries but at two kilometres long was amongst the largest. Through the virtual portholes in his cabin aboard the *Ellis-Three*, Galman watched the enormous sentry drift intimidatingly close to the cargo hauler. Panic clutching at his stomach, he wondered if they intended to board.

With a sharp hand gesture he expanded the porthole and took in as much of the other vessel as could be encompassed, counting the dozens of obvious weapon ports and guessing at where the less blatant armaments might be hidden. He was unlikely to find out for certain; the captain of the *Ellis-Three* wouldn't contemplate challenging any boarding manoeuvre from the *Vulpine*.

Like the *Ellis-Three*, and almost every other craft capable of burrowing into shortspace, the *Vulpine* consisted of a forward bullet-shaped section in which the majority of the decks were situated, and reaching behind the bullet was a far longer box-kite arrangement. The specific design of this rear section was different for every style of ship, but they all consisted at least of five or six vast struts which extended from the flat rear of the bullet to form scaffolding around which one or more ring sections would be constructed like bands. For the most part the box kite was empty space. It was here that the shortspace burrowing was facilitated.

The *Ohio,* which stood watch in orbit back on Diaclom, had a single band around the rearmost part of its five struts. The *Vulpine* was significantly more impressive. Her three two-hundred meter wide bands were evenly spaced along its length, housing a large number of the crew. The three-hundred meter gaps between those bands, held together only by the five struts through which the crew could travel the length of the ship, gave the impression of an extremely fragile design. But Galman had seen footage of similar sentries in battle, and he knew those deceptively feeble struts could withstand an extraordinary battering. So long as one remained intact the ship would not lose integrity. The bullet section, however, was the real strength of any ship. Like most sentries the *Vulpine*'s half kilometre fore section could detach from the unwieldy box-kite in a matter of minutes while it engaged in combat. It was in the bullet that the majority of the crew were housed, and it was there that ninety percent of the immense arsenal was located.

The Sentry drew closer and Galman saw a single docking tube concertina from the second of the huge ship's three box-kite bands. Nervous, he clenched his fists and winced at the dull ache which had been returning with a vengeance since his supply of medication had run out a couple of days ago.

With a none-too-gentle bump the two ships mated. Galman made his way quickly to the walkway of one of the *Ellis-Three*'s box-kite struts and, prying loose a section of wall plating, climbed inside a maintenance crawlspace leading to one of the few serviceable parts of the burrower. He replaced the panel and crawled a little way into the cramped and hot space. If the *Vulpine* had been sent to look for stowaways, they would have to rip the ship apart looking for him.

Five long and painful hours passed before Galman's wrist screen whistled gently and the Captain's face appeared.

'What are you doing in the crawlspace?' the perpetually grim, artificially young man asked.

Galman grimaced. With his wrist screen active, the captain and any *Vulpine* search team knew exactly where he was. He had forgotten to turn it off.

'What did the *Vulpine* want?' he asked.

'Just a scan of our cargo,' the Captain explained. 'Seems there is a heightened state of security in the region.'

'Really?' That was interesting. He didn't suppose it had anything to do with him, but perhaps he wasn't the only one worried about Satumine activity in the three-world cluster of Diaclom, Dendrell and Pellitoe, here at the galactic south of the Swinell Union.

'Anyway,' the Captain went on. 'We're about to dock with Pellitoe customs. You can disembark, when you are ready, at lock three.'

'Thank you Captain.'

'Good luck Mr. Tader.'

*

Lock three was already open to a wide and brightly lit boarding platform. A curved ceiling of thick crystal offered a spectacular view of both the *Ellis-Three* and the customs station. Above was a dizzying view of Pellitoe's verdant globe sitting in a pool of deep black. Few stars were visible against the reflected glare of the fertile world, though a few other satellites and stations, two Union Cruisers and the two smaller federal sentries glinted like embers in the distance. Occasionally one of the three-kilometre wide solar arrays was seen as a fleck of black against the white clouds.

As his mind put into context the immense vista, Galman was gripped by chilling vertigo as he began to consider that what the gravity coils of the boarding platform deemed to be down was at odd with the planet above his head. He was, he realised, hanging upside down far above Pellitoe, and just within reach of its gravity.

'How you doing there?' a three legged machine enquired, clattering towards Galman from the station side of the platform. Aside from its two-foot long spindly chrome legs, it was nothing more than a smooth four-foot tall phallic body with a small oval screen at eye level. Testament to the increasing decrepitude of his body, Galman couldn't focus his cloudy eyes on the screen to see what was displayed.

'Sir?'

Galman realised he was clutching the thin hand rail as if it was the only thing keeping him from plummeting through the crystal ceiling and down to the planet.

'Yeah,' he mumbled. 'First time flyer.' He gave a pathetic grin and tentatively released his grip.

'OK,' the machine said. 'How's that? Better?'

Galman looked about for a moment, waiting for something to happen. There was nothing. Then, as the machine stepped closer, Galman was able to read the single line of text on its small oval screen: *If you can read this please let me know.*

'Um,' Galman began awkwardly.

'Sir?'

'Your screen. I can read it.'

'Ah, right,' the IB machine said. 'Then I imagine you can still see through the ceiling.'

'Yes.'

'You aren't kitted out for Augmented Reality,' the machine explained. 'Everything must look a bit drab to you.'

Fed up of appearing so meek, Galman straightened himself up and, not looking at the terrifying sight of the planet, strode towards the station lock. The machine fell into step beside him, its third leg never seeming to touch the ground but instead acting as something like a tail.

'I'm mortified when people like you get to see me unembellished,' it commented.

'Sorry,' Galman said.

'Not your fault. We will soon have you kitted out and immersed in the AR world.'

Galman was led through a number of bland corridors in which people wandered about in tight white jumpsuits and looked at him strangely but said nothing. He knew they were experiencing a shared reality painted over this dull real world which they called *drab-reality*. He imagined he was probably wandering through some of their embellishments, ignoring greetings or comments spoken only with AR voices, and generally appearing to act ignorant and strange. Diaclom would soon be like this, he thought, and the idea did not sit well with him. In order to function here, however, he needed to join the artificial world. So, once they reached a room in which four coffin-like pods were arranged in a cross, he didn't hesitate to lay in one when directed to do so by the machine.

The surgery took six hours. When he was roused Galman realised how much more generous the Pellitoe immigration policy was than he had been led to believe. He had been gifted not only a full AR suite, but also a whole new lease of life.

Chapter 18

The Ancient Satumine frames connect the network worlds by burrowing down to the lowest spacial dimension - pointspace - and back up to the location of a different frame. As pointspace is a singularity, there is zero distance to be traversed and so the journey is instantaneous. This is well understood by human science and a lesser form of the principle is used to send data via our pointspace comms burrowers. We have even made the first steps towards recreating the frames using our own technology - albeit with initially catastrophic results. But there is another technology present in the frames and it is something all too often overlooked. The frames are cloaked, hidden from all forms of detection, only appearing once a suitable pilot connects and drags it back into the visible realm. This is, after all, how the frame in orbit around Earth remained unknown to us for so long. There are many theories as to how the cloak works - ranging from localised distortion of light to the physical relocation of the frame into a lower dimension - but Jurisdiction science is still no closer to creating a cloak so thoroughly effective as those built into the frames. Are we to really believe the modern Satumine are as equally ignorant? What else, I must wonder, have they left in orbit around the network worlds? What else still lingers, poised to strike, above Earth?

The Truth: A treatise on the Satumine Conspiracy

Indin-Indin: Entering the atmosphere of Satute, in the Network

The turbulent icy air of Satute's upper atmosphere buffeted the tiny craft, each jarring impact knocking the failing attitude thrusters further out of alignment. The antigrav had failed within seconds of being activated and Satute's gravity was fast winning the struggle against the emergency descent jets. At least the cloak was holding, though an occasional purple flash engulfed the little vehicle like a luminous bubble as the field was forced to realign. It was failing, like everything else on the damaged shuttle. Indin-Indin needed to land before he became fully visible to thousands of planetary defence sensors in orbit and across the surface.

One of the attitude thrusters locked and the craft was punched into a roll as if by some immense weight dropping on the left wing. Indin-Indin muttered and cut the opposite thruster, letting the remaining two stabilise his approach. Moments later one of the descent jet cylinders died with a wet pop, erupting a short finger of red flame which escaped the cloak field and betrayed his position and trajectory to those he knew must now be aware of his approach. The fire extinguished within seconds and the cloak seemed to hold, so Indin-Indin cautiously eased the craft to one side and briefly allowed gravity to exert more influence before increasing the load on the remaining cylinders, confident his trajectory was sufficiently changed.

It was night where he was bringing his craft in, but the stark glare of so many artificial lights illuminated the planet-spanning city as brightly as the sun on the opposite hemisphere. Light pollution had never concerned his people: the Satumine didn't sleep, and it had been many thousands of years since any other animal or plant had existed which might object to the perma-light. The continuous white lines of the hexagonal grid of districts reached from horizon to horizon, broken only by a single small pool of black, the last of the Satumine seas. The great oceans which archaeologists believed once covered eighty percent of the planet, now sloshed in darkness a mile beneath the unending expanse of total urban sprawl. Between these dark dead oceans and the surface rested layer upon layer of Satumine history. Down there were the indestructible but useless cities of the original Satumine. That was where Indin-Indin needed to be.

Something snarled and choked in the craft's hull before a deep thump signalled another system failure. Indin-Indin wasn't sure what had stopped working; the diagnostic utility had frozen. Experience had taught the technician that when even the diagnostics were broken it was time to get out. But that wasn't an option. If he ejected now, assuming that system still worked, he would be in custody before he even reached the surface.

The cloak was buckling, blazing purple and white, dragging a lasting scar across the dark orange sky. Indin-Indin cringed, pupils across his joints and hands clenching instinctively as he realised he was visible to billions of Satumine on the surface. With the cloak apparently unable to recalibrate on the fly, Indin-Indin deactivated the device completely, extinguishing the purple ribbon but exposing his craft to the full scrutiny of so many sensors. Aggregates' gift of a shuttle, Indin-Indin mused, really should have been package more securely. Already he could see the diffuse white vapour trails of hastily launched interceptors. The cloak reported a successful shutdown and realignment and he jabbed a long finger at the restart icon. The field enveloped the craft in a stable glassy bubble which rippled once before turning completely transparent. Indin-Indin's upper body became briefly loose and even more spongy than normal – the equivalent of a human sigh of relief.

He changed course again and watched, scratching subconsciously at the resin sealing his abdominal cavity, as three wings of interceptors raced to his last visible location. They would love this; they were so rarely tasked with anything beyond surveillance. A few low powered lasers probed the area, searching for him, but none found the invisible craft.

Losing altitude, more or less under Indin-Indin's control, the tiny craft came down into a valley between two mountainous streets. The valley, the full length of a hexagonal district boundary, ended abruptly at one of the smaller square city blocks between the hexagons. This block contained at its heart a single tall spire – a pointspace comms transmitter which reached up from the depths of the city. He pitched the craft forward into a steep descent, following the transmitter spire past the mesh of transit tines and horizontal towers and into the tight network of the many layered hive.

Lamenting the loss of so many attitude thrusters, Indin-Indin battled inertia and gravity, coming within a few feet of clipping trackways, roads and buildings. But luck, or the affections of fate, saw him safely through the occupied upper levels and into the dense crushed and abandoned foundations. Unlike the upper city, perpetually lit by the glow of every street and building, the foundations were in near darkness, save for the reflected glow from above. Only the sporadic flicker of lights somehow absorbing energy bleeding from unsecured conduits further up, gave any hint that these crumbling and compacted districts had ever been home to billions. Indin-Indin pleaded with the craft to slow its fall as the spaces between the criss-cross of the city became tighter and less predictable. Already he could see huge expanses of impassable utterly compressed metal and ceramic. But still he wasn't deep enough into Satute's urban sprawl. These abandoned districts were maybe twenty thousand years old – the first cities of the plague survivors. The homes of the new Satumine race. Indin-Indin needed to get deeper, to enter the original Satumine civilisation, that strange world built for a race so dramatically different to their offspring that the new Satumine had been incapable of even living in those majestic and ancient buildings.

He landed the craft with more force than was safe and the long groan of a trillion tons of crushed and shifting hive echoed for miles in all directions. A little remote control device detached from the wall and gently flashed confirmation of the cloak's current stability, but he was far from confident that it would remain so, or even that the status monitor was actually working. But he could do nothing to improve the situation and so he grabbed the remote control and the large egg-shaped case containing Aggregate's most precious gift which he slung over his shoulder by its canvas strap, and left the little craft, hoping the cloak would hold until he returned. He had a walk of days, maybe weeks, ahead of him. The return journey, however, would be considerably easier.

Chapter 19

Enguine is the most isolated world in the Jurisdiction, part of no union and years from the Fertile Belt. Its isolation is far more than merely geographic; it is the only world allowed to remain out of contact with the Jurisdiction – refusing to maintain a permanent pointspace data link – and so its population is outside of the Jurisdiction's all-knowing census. It is also the source of a disproportionate number of refugees as, by definition, there is no way for the Jurisdiction's fanatical migration checks to confirm or refute the identity of a would-be Enguine refugee. Popular Jurisdiction media often quips that given the number of apparent refugees supposedly fleeing Enguine, there ought to be nobody left from which to flee. Everybody knows most Enguine refugees are either pre-billion migrants or fugitives of another sort. But it is almost impossible to sift the criminals from the genuine refugees, and so the legal loophole remains. For now. If you can make it off your pre-billion world, you will generally get away with it. The numbers managing that, and claiming Enguine heritage, are so tiny in comparison to the many trillions of Jurisdiction citizens, it isn't worth the effort of finding a better solution. Why anyone would dream of fleeing the sole bastion of freedom in the galaxy, into the oppressive embrace of the Jurisdiction, is beyond us, but we welcome anything that provides a loophole for those trying to escape the demanding breeding strictures and virtual imprisonment of pre-billion colonies.

The Enguine Manifesto

Galman Tader: Aboard a customs station in orbit around Pellitoe, in the Swinell Union, in the Fertile-belt

Drab-reality. Galman had always thought it such a snobbish term, used by the pampered fops of the Swinell

Union and other wealthy sectors of the Jurisdiction to set themselves above the seventy eight percent of worlds still under pre-billion restrictions and which generally couldn't afford a global AR network. He had to concede, however, that to those immersed in the vibrant and stimulating world of AR, unembellished reality must have appeared drab. The beauty and spectacle of this new stimulation, however, did little to soften his distaste for the fantasy in which most successful worlds wrapped themselves. The medical care was not so easily discounted. He looked at least ten years younger than after any of the limited treatments available on Diaclom, and he felt even younger than he looked. The comprehensive telomere report indicated his cells could continue to divide healthily for at least another twenty years before beginning to show any negative signs of ageing, and another twenty years after that before he would actually notice any detrimental effects of age. All of the frailties accumulated over his century of life had been reversed or otherwise repaired through a combination of accelerated natural regeneration and nano-farm intervention. And all at the state's expense. Galman couldn't dispute the efficiency and apparent altruism of the Swinell Union and he found his instinctive dislike of the liberal society difficult to maintain.

As he walked across an immense atrium, resplendent in its AR embellishments, indistinguishable from a planet-side tropical island surrounded by turquoise sea and domed by a perfect cloudless sky and blazing hot yellow sun, Galman soon remembered why he so disliked the people and politics of the Swinell Union: a family of Satumine, mildly embellished but making no effort to disguise their alien identity, were strolling freely along one of the sandy beaches. The adults chatted casually with a human couple while the children of both species chased one another with sparkling giggle-inducing AP whips. Bloody liberals.

A pang of grief sliced through his stomach and coiled about his heart as he recalled walks with his own home-reared children back on Diaclom. He would never have let his home reared children play with Satumine. He wondered, with a familiar cold chill of regret at his absence from their lives, if his dozens of mandatory offspring in the communal nurseries were given such strict boundaries.

'Look at that,' Galman complained, pointing to the interspecies interaction.

'Look at what?' his guide asked. The tripod was now draped in an organic-looking AR skin which gave the look of a tall multi-coloured tulip head with dozens of protean vines floating up from its green root ball feet. Had he not already seen it naked, Galman couldn't have guessed at its bland metal foundation.

'How can they let their children play with *them*,' Galman asked, sneering at the Satumine as they passed.

'Why wouldn't they?' replied the guide. 'The Satumine pay their taxes, obey the rules, and contribute as much as anyone else'

'They're Satumine,' Galman said, knowing that although such an argument felt watertight to him, it probably meant little to the IB machine. He tried another approach: 'I thought federal guidelines insisted on the close monitoring of all Satumine beyond the borders of their home system.'

'They do,' the machine said, guiding Galman with a suddenly arm-like vine towards a set of steps leading up from the beach into an oversized wooden hut. The steps looked like flowing water and, as Galman placed a foot on one, he felt the gentle chill of a waterfall trickling over his bare feet. It was a peculiar sensation, especially given the shoes he knew he was wearing but could not perceive. But it was pleasant and he took his time making his way up the ten steps.

'We meet our obligations,' the machine continued, 'by closely monitoring *all* of our citizens. We need treat the Satumine no differently.'

'Aren't you worried about Satumine terrorists?'

'Not at all,' the machine said, opening a door of topaz mist with a thin vine and leading Galman into the circular chamber beyond. 'We have never had any trouble with our Satumine on Pellitoe, and only twice though the rest of the Swinell Union.'

'Twice is enough.'

'We suffer vastly more crime at human hands,' the machine pointed out. It then stopped in the middle of the chamber and said, 'If you have concerns about living with Satumine, perhaps you have made a mistake in choosing the Swinell Union as a destination.'

'No,' Galman said too quickly. He stopped, took a slow breath, smiled at the giant tulip-head and said, 'I'm just used to a different way of doing things. I'm sure I can adapt.'

The machine seemed to bow forward and then waved a vine at a helter-skelter flow of water on one side of the chamber, past an arrangement of steaming rock pools which, by the expressions on the faces of the bathers, provided something more stimulating than merely bubbling hot water.

Your immigration officer is waiting for you on the fourth floor,' the machine said. 'Room seven.' With that it wandered back to the misty door and left without looking back.

Galman looked about the chamber's many pools and noticed a young elfin woman setting to stand up out of the water. She was naked, though the bubbling water protected her modesty, and Galman felt a twinge of excitement at the anticipation of a more unobstructed view as she stood. He knew the Swinell union promoted a liberal culture but hadn't expected such exhibitionism.

She noticed him looking and flashed a smirk. She didn't stop standing. But there was no display of nudity. As if drawing fabric from the surface of the water, she was fully clothed. Galman looked away. She had probably been clothed in a white jumpsuit – in drab-reality – the entire time. There was, most likely, no actual water in the pool either. Already he was being drawn in by the illusions of augmented reality.

The waterfall flowed upwards in a wide and gradual helix, though there were no steps. For a moment Galman stood at its base, feeling the spray brushing against his shins and feet. All fake sensory feedback. Eventually a man – or maybe a woman or even a Satumine draped in a human male embellishment – patted him on the shoulder and said, 'Just step on,' before wandering to the long bar against one of the curved walls where a few dozen people enjoyed exotic drinks. He cautiously lifted a foot to fast flowing water and was surprised to find a solid unmoving object beneath the decoration. He brought the other foot up to stand fully on the waterfall and a small screen appeared in front of his face. A cute anthropomorphised rabbit asked him which floor he would like and provided a simple numerical pad with which Galman selected the fourth floor. The screen dissolved and Galman was lifted smoothly up the spiral as if standing on a surfboard just beneath the upwards flowing water. He passed through a hole in the wooden ceiling which had opened as soon as his ascent began, and he found himself inside a tubular waterfall. He continued up and eventually emerged through the floor of a circular chamber far smaller than the ground level. Although his ascent had ended, the spiral waterfall extended up into the ceiling and Galman wondered how far up the building went. From the outside the wooden hut had been draped in an AR skin of only two storeys.

He stepped onto the thick pile of a red carpet which waved hypnotically to a non-existent wind. Stylised dragons chased each other across the floor. Galman sighed; was all this embellishment necessary? Who were they trying to impress? Around the chamber's circular perimeter were eighteen arched doorways, though there were no doors, just curtains of grey mist. Floating above each was a refreshingly simple numbered tile. He located number seven and held an arm out into the grey mist of that arch. The mist parted and a friendly voice beckoned him in.

*

'How do you like our station?' The angel-winged immigration officer asked, rising from his seat to lean across his desk and shake Galman by the hand.

'Very nice,' Galman said with great diplomacy. 'Very extravagant.'

The officer – Luque Cheic, according to the brief profile screen which had appeared in front of Galman as soon as he entered the room – chuckled and said, 'We try our best.' He waved vaguely at the ostentatiously cushioned seat opposite his desk and added, 'Please, sit down.'

'Is all of Pellitoe as intensely embellished as this station?' Galman enquired, sinking into the chair, squirming when tiny foam hands began massaging his buttocks, but quickly settling into the decadent experience.

'Well,' Luque offered a toying wink, 'we like to think we go the extra mile up here in orbit. Make a good first impression on our visitors, as it were. It tends to be just a tad more restrained planet-side. But there certainly are some very nice spots.' He then waved an almost dismissive gesture. 'It really is what you make of it. You can spend as much or as little as you like on your personal AR experience.' His face then hardened, just slightly, but enough that Galman's policing eye noticed: the immigration officer wanted to get down to it. 'In order to do that,' Luque went on, a single strand of coldness weaved into the fabric of his otherwise warm and soft voice, 'you need some kind of income. Or savings.'

Galman looked to the ceiling, to a vaulted glass dome looking out into space. He doubted they were anywhere near the station's outer hull, it was just an embellishment, but he felt uncomfortably exposed nonetheless.

'I have neither,' he admitted. 'My savings were spent on securing transport out of the Enguine system, and I have been in no position to secure employment on Pellitoe yet.' The captain of the *Ellis-Three* had fabricated a false identity for Galman, as part of his extortionate fee, as much for his own protection as for Galman's, and by claiming to have escaped the isolationist world of Enguine he had the greatest chance of a fresh start.

'The Administration will probably want to question you about Enguine at some point,' the officer said. 'But, for now, you will be granted provisional residency, a minimal welfare allowance of three hundred New-Euros per week, and your account has been credited with your data-matter allowance for the remainder of this month. Any number of brokers will be happy to facilitate its conversion into New-Euros.' He waved a screen into existence, showing Galman's sparse personal file, complete with financial accounts. His name had not been changed – it was not so unusual as to draw attention to the corresponding record on Diaclom.

'That is very generous,' he said.

Luque shrugged. 'Basic human rights,' he said.

'And Satumine?'

'Same thing.'

Galman bit back a vile retort. It sickened him that Satumine received equal treatment, but for the immigration officer to say Human rights were the same as Satumine rights was an insult to his core beliefs.

The officer waved the screen away. 'You will receive a data-matter allowance each month in addition to your welfare payments.'

Galman nodded. 'I also had a small amount of baggage.'

The man nodded and called into being his mag-gun and Tumble, both of which hung in the air over the table. Just AR.

'We have interrogated the machine and, despite some misgivings regarding its provenance, are satisfied that it does in fact belong to you and that its weapons have been removed or otherwise rendered inoperable. You will need to make arrangements to purchase intelligence-bridge cover, but your welfare payments should cover your basic needs which includes some limited IB time.'

'I won it on a poker hand, from the captain of the *Ellis-Three*. He picked it up on Diaclom-'

Luque held up his hand. He didn't care. 'I can't just let you have your mag-gun,' he bluntly declared.

'Fair enough. Can I sell it?'

Luque checked some screens and then asked, 'Are you happy with five hundred New-Euros?'

Galman scowled. It was worth double, but he doubted he would get much more. 'It'll do,' he said.

'OK, the funds have been transferred.' The officer stood and gestured to the door. 'A shuttle is leaving for the surface in two hours. You will be given six months grace with regards to your IB obligations, but after that you will be required to provide the network with a number of hours per month as set out in the latest schedules. You should register with an IB suite near where you plan to settle, in order that you can fulfil your duties without needing to travel too far. Once you are on Pellitoe, I suggest you spend tonight in a hotel and then put some Google-Crawlers out looking for somewhere to rent. After that you might want to smarten yourself up with a few basic embellishments. At least get an AR limb or two.

Galman nodded, shook one of the man's physical hands, thanked him and left. With a thought he accessed one of his newly installed interfaces and initiated a Google search-frame: house hunting could wait; he needed to locate Ambondice-Ambondice.

Chapter 20

The Jurisdiction currently gives extraordinarily broad freedoms to individual planets and to Unions it offers more rights to self governance than at any point in our long history. There must, however, be limits; for while we value the individual freedoms of every citizen, we can not allow those freedoms to lead to isolationism, xenophobia and hostility with one's neighbours. If a world or Union elects to set down such a path, the Administration will make every effort to discover the root of such a world's unhappiness and no expense shall be spared in making any and all changes in order that the citizens may feel comfortable within the Jurisdiction. Should these efforts be snubbed, however, it will be with a heavy heart that the Administration takes firmer actions in order that the wider Jurisdiction be protected.

Rehabilitation: A Survivor's Guide

Cordem Hastergado: On Pellitoe, in the Swinell Union, in the Fertile Belt

Cordem Hastergado didn't dislike Satumine but, in a professional sense at least, he had a general distrust of them. So when an organization arose with a predominantly Satumine membership, he felt obliged to investigate with a cynicism lacking in the procedures of the Swinell Union's Bureau of Supervision. An Office Trustee, responsible for the Jurisdictions federal presence throughout Equa - the southernmost of Pellitoe's five continents - he could not allow himself so liberal an attitude as his local counterparts. Although a Swinell native, born on Swinell-Dax two and a half centuries ago, he was a federal

119

employee and had a duty to see the Satumine through a more pragmatic lens.

Watching the horse-headed merchant pretend to swallow a morsel of steak, he decided this particular Satumine would be quite easy to dislike. So tolerant was the Swinell society, there simply wasn't any reason for a Satumine to don a human-skin embellishment - albeit a horse headed variant. Even so, if it had been merely a fashion statement, he could have understood. But this Satumine was taking every possible measure to ensure the deceit was absolute. After dimming his view of the AR world, bringing drab-reality to the fore, the Office Trustee had seen the small bag attached to the alien's rib-cage head, and it was into this bag that the steak was being forked. The steak was, of course, simply textured white pulp over which the look, the feel, the smell and taste of a steak had been draped, but that was beside the point. How many customers had this Satumine convinced he was human? Presumably all of them. Unlike Cordem, the majority of Swinell citizens had neither the ability nor the authority to so easily filter their AR experience.

Cordem reinstated his full appreciation of the illusion and took up a gorgeously faceted wineglass, trying to forget the dull grey foundation he had glimpsed a moment earlier. Taking a long sip he likewise tried to dismiss the knowledge that the sweet fruity wine was in fact nutrient-rich water. But the fantasy was ruined; it would be a few hours before his mind once again accepted the proof of his senses over his knowledge of the lie. He hated being forced to peek at drab-reality.

'Why do you pass yourself off as human?' he asked oh so casually.

'I don't,' Ambondice-Ambondice, also known to his customers as Ambo, flashed an entirely AR smile which looked frightening on an otherwise accurately recreated equine head. 'I look nothing like a human.'

That was, Cordem had to accept, technically true. Ambondice-Ambondice was a horse-headed humanoid resplendent in iridescent photo-active felt across his entire body. His additional two limbs, purely AR, were currently retracted into barely visible nubs of translucence beneath his armpits. Aside from the broadly humanoid frame, which was common to both human and Satumine physiology, there was nothing really on which to make any assumption as to the man's species. But Cordem was a native of this society, he knew the racial fashions and he knew when a Satumine was trying to pass as human.

'This is a human fashion,' he said. 'What's more, you have augmented your voice to sound human, you are using a human name and, of course, there is that...' he nodded at the plate of food in front of the Satumine.

Ambondice-Ambondice shrugged. 'It's not a crime is it?'

Cordem glared a moment but quickly softened his expression. If he hoped to form a working relationship with this Satumine, it wouldn't do to start antagonizing him.

'No, I suppose not,' he allowed. 'But there could be some questions over your decision to go by a human name.'

'No,' the Satumine said without hesitation. 'I thoroughly questioned a Federal and Union legislative guide, and I am well within my rights to call myself whatever I like. The same goes for the nature or implied identity of my AR skin, subject of course to the usual decency laws.'

The Office Trustee shrugged and said, 'Fair enough. That wasn't really my primary reason for meeting with you today anyway.'

'Ah,' Ambondice-Ambondice said with another eerie horse grin. 'To business.'

'Yes, quite.'

'You are looking for a new supplier for the Administration's secure AR comms screens.'

'You are well informed,' Cordem observed. 'I only confirmed this morning that we wouldn't be renewing the contract with our existing supplier.' He took another unsatisfying sip of wine and asked, 'How did you know?'

'Does it matter?'

Yes, Cordem thought, but said, 'No, I suppose not.' The nature of this Satumine's sources was typical of Cordem's motivation for forming this relationship with him. The skincrafting industry was lucrative and could account for a great deal of Ambondice-Ambondice's sizeable declared wealth, but the Office Trustee was privy to a lot more data than most Jurisdiction citizens imagined, and he had located dozens of hidden accounts and assets, all in some way under the Satumine merchant's control. His AR business simply wasn't *that* good. Cordem wanted to know where Ambondice-Ambondice's money came from, who he had in his pocket, and what his intentions were for all that money and potential power. To do that, he reasoned, he needed an in. He needed a relationship.

'Can you provide me the comms screens in the quantity I require?' he asked, knowing the Satumine could.

'How many?'

'Eight thousand over six months. All to be individually calibrated.'

Ambondice-Ambondice held up a finger and said, 'One moment.' One of his AR arms extended suddenly, reaching across the small restaurant, becoming more translucent so as to not disturb anybody and to indicate it was OK to walk through the ethereal limb. It penetrated the far wall and Cordem supposed it was hurtling towards the Satumine's warehouse. Like most AR embellishments, the arm was pointless. It was just a visual representation of a remote viewing and interaction system, but people liked to feel their artificial world was every bit as physical as drab-reality, and so shunned any overtly out-of body interaction where at all possible.

Moments later the arm snapped back like released elastic, a newly formed hand clutching an entirely AR headband which Ambondice-Ambondice passed to Cordem. The Office Trustee accepted the proffered device with his physical hands, his sensory interfaces conveying the appropriate tactile sensations. He slipped the glassy band over his head, felt it shift and expand to better accommodate his forehead, and waited for the soft neural tug of the user interface which allowed mental manipulation of AR. There it was; he was connected with the band and, with a thought, activated the comms-screen. Around his head, two feet out, a band of twelve screens hung in a ring, rotating as a carousel. They were all blank, yet to be calibrated, but he could access the basic menus. These would do. They could be tied to high security processing spaces in Pellitoe's global nets and paired to the unique alpha wave signature of their assigned Trustee. They were nothing special, but kit like this - even entirely AR devices - needed to be replaced periodically. They didn't wear down, but security concerns dictated their regular replacement.

'This is fine,' he said.

A face appeared on Cordem's personal screen, visible only to him. It was his head of security. 'You are being monitored,' the man reported. 'Leave by the restaurant's back door. I have briefed the manager. Your car is waiting for you.'

'I'm sorry,' Cordem said to the Satumine as he dismissed the screens and rose from his seat. 'But I am going to have to cut this short.'

Chapter 21

Do not believe the Administration. If you take one thing away from this treatise, let it be that. One of the many lies, devised by the Satumine and prosecuted on their behalf by the Administration, is the fiction that our shortspace technology can not be miniaturised beyond the vastly expensive and massive shortspace burrowers used on our Sentries and colony ships. It has already been accomplished, though such shuttle-scale ships are so far beyond classified that even most area trustees are unaware of their existence. And they are expensive. Insanely so. It is not only the raw construction costs that make these few ships so valuable; the real value is in their rarity. The cost obviously has a significant part to play in their scarcity, but this extraordinary advancement in galactic travel is kept from the masses for another reason: the material used in the miniature burrower's construction are in ludicrously short supply. And where is the largest supply of these materials? We need look no further than the compressed and abandoned under-levels of the Satumine home-worlds planet-spanning urban sprawl. Here is another proof of the Satumine's dominance of the Administration, for if we were the true masters we would be digging up those resources by the ship-load.
The Truth: A treatise on the Satumine Conspiracy

Endella Mariacroten: In orbit around Dendrell, in the Swinell Union, in the Fertile-belt

The little ship didn't have a name. To those who knew anything about the undersized shortspace burrower, it was simply referred to as *Endella's Ship*. To everyone else it was a fiction - nothing so small could contain the immense components required to claw down into shortspace. Currently those impossibly miniaturized components were retracted into the supposed hold of the fifty meter dart and, as far as the station crew was concerned, it was nothing more interesting than a private shuttle ferrying its wealthy owner up from Dendrell. Had they known Endella's ship cost more to manufacture than the entire orbital customs station, the lackadaisical crew might have been more careful about detaching the docking clamps. Hissing as the heavy latch scraped roughly against her ship's polished blue hull, Endella fired a positional thruster, squirting a jet towards the station's own hull and pushing herself further from the clamps.

Now a safe distance from the enormous ring of the station, she turned away from the planet and ignited her main thrusters. The gravity coils in the cramped cockpit, in the nose of the fifty meter flying engine, were barely able to counter the jolt of acceleration and she was pressed into the dense foam of the control chair in which she had spent so many months of her life.

'Please confirm your flight plan,' a confused man asked over the comms. Ostensibly a shuttle, her ship had no business leaving orbit and heading into open space. She didn't voice a reply, just transmitted a standard Justiciary code package which bypassed the human operator and instructed the flight control computers to disregard her. She didn't need anybody watching what she was about to do, and in fact had standing orders obliging her to ensure nobody ever saw it.

Clearing the outer orbital shells and leaving behind the clouds of solar-power satellites, customs and science stations, and a small fleet of federal sentries and Swinell Union cruisers on manoeuvres in the highest orbit, she guided her little craft in behind the smallest of Dendrell's five irregularly shaped and unusually close moons. At only twelve kilometres long, it really wasn't a moon so much as a captured asteroid, and there were no permanent installations on its surface, making it an ideal blind spot in which she could prepare the dart for shortspace. It beat heading out into deeper space to avoid the sensors of any prying ship she might have missed with her Justiciary codes.

Over the course of half an hour the supposed hold, accounting for everything but the tiny cockpit, opened and inverted to fold out its sleek dart shape and form the wide hollow tube of a burrower. Reactors came on-line, spatial dimension scanning arrays calibrated and, for another eight hours, the burrower charged. Endella waited with unfamiliar impatience. She knew she had three weeks of boredom and confinement ahead of her, but after that perhaps some excitement.

Chapter 22

Consul: Where to start? Enough has been written about the tyrant's rise to power and the means by which his consciousness arose. His crimes are even more thoroughly documented and dramatized in countless feeds and fictions. Far too little, however, is written of the influence this ancient evil still wields over our Jurisdiction. The Trustees bristle when we claim Consul is their secret master, but the evidence mounts and their arguments to the contrary grow weaker with every rote recitation. That the beast was exiled after our hard fought victory, rather than executed, speaks volumes of the secret allies and power it holds. Could it be that our apparent victory, the AC's exile, and all that has unfolded over the ensuing centuries has been part of Consul's longest of long games?

The Enguine Manifesto

Galman Tader: On Pellitoe, in the Swinell Union, In the Fertile Belt

Pellitoe's planet-side AR was not as vulgar as the excessive embellishment of the customs station. For the most part the sky could be relied upon to be, in fact, the sky, and entire levels of towers were not completely and inexplicably hidden from view or disguised as far smaller constructions. But Galman still found it all an unnecessary and juvenile fantasy. Even the novel and exhilarating experience of breathing fresh air, outdoors, without the need for oxygen filters couldn't take his mind off the irritation of AR. Tumble, however, loved it.

Clothed in a cheap but convincing embellishment, and looking like a four-foot goblin, all green and warty but with the most charming grin which suited the tone of his unchanged voice, the IB machine had spent much of the morning mingling among the throng of shoppers in the retail and recreation district near the hotel in which he and Galman were staying. Tumble had shook hands with anyone willing to give him a moment of their time, having overlaid his goblin hands across the foundation of extruded appendages. People had to know he was a machine because the sensory input instigated by the AR hand would not entirely negate the feel of thin metal tendrils beneath - the embellishment was too cheap for that - but nobody seemed to care or comment. Why would they? If they were happy to embrace the Satumine as their equals, why not IB machines? Even Galman had found himself referring to the machine as him, rather than it, though he suspected that had more to do with Tumble's creeping change in personality since Galman reprogrammed him, rather than the AR goblin skin he now flaunted.

Consul could run amok in a society like this, Galman thought. For all he knew, the artificial consciousness was doing precisely that: filling the Swinell Union with conscious machines draped in high quality human embellishments. It was the stuff of sensationalist fiction and alarmist media, but watching his intelligence-bridged companion share a joke with complete strangers, it seemed to Galman to be entirely plausible. But he wasn't here to unearth Consul's agents; he expected the federal presence would already be all over such an obvious threat. His sights were set on the Satumine. By the looks of the cosy meeting currently taking place between the continent's Office Trustee and the target of Galman's interest, the federal presence wasn't up to dealing with that particular danger.

'Seriously Tumble, will you focus?' He tugged at the strip of Tumbles worn leather sackcloth which ensured the machines AR decency. Although he felt the dry material between his fingers, he passed right through the illusion to touch the warm white shell of Tumble's drab-reality body. Tumble turned away from the fountain of yellow mist which rose from a vent in the paving slabs, ending his childish dance around the public embellishment.

'Have you tried this thing?' the machine asked.

Galman waved away a screen floating before him and glared at his companion. 'Tumble,' he snapped. 'You're supposed to be helping me listen in on those two,' he jabbed a thumb around the corner of the building to the restaurant a little way down the next street. Then, curious, he asked, 'Can you even *feel* that stuff?'

'I have sensory inputs, just like you do,' Tumble quipped. Then he added, 'Whether I *feel* it, however, is one for the philosophers. I say I do, but that could just be my convincing approximation of a mind.'

Galman tensed at the possible implications of his companion's all too believable sentience and he wondered if his illegal modifications had given rise to something unspeakable. But Tumble was not tied to a single human mind in a IB pod; his friend used the same communal intelligence-bridge system as any other machine. Consul's mind was born of a computer gaining dominance over its single paired human component and Humanity had learned its lesson; computers were no longer tied to a single human; artificial consciousness could never arise again.

Galman recalled his AR screen and showed it to Tumble. 'I keep losing the signal,' he complained. 'Stop playing with your new body and concentrate on your job.'

'I can focus on more than one thing,' Tumble countered. 'The reason for the poor reception is the torrent of data-signals flooding the planet.' The little goblin jumped up onto the side of the wall and peered around the corner. Galman guessed the white ball, in drab-reality, was suspended by a unigrip pad, but the AR goblin seemed to be clinging to the wall like some oversized gecko. 'I did warn you,' it added.

Galman scowled. Tumble had pointed out that they should purchase some AR-specific remote viewing embellishments to compliment the more pedestrian tools built into his metal body, but Galman's funds were all but spent and, having been on Pellitoe for only a week, he had still to secure an income beyond the welfare payments. As generous as those payments were, they were not enough for his needs.

'Look, just see if you can clean it up a bit. The Office Trustee looked like he was getting set to leave and I want to know where he's going.'

'Galman, down!' Tumble suddenly yelled. A blue flash then seemed to burn away his goblin skin to reveal the bare white porcelain ball which fell, as if dead, to the floor.

Galman dove to one side, instinctively reaching for a pistol he no longer owned. A second flash dissolved the minor embellishments he had bothered to acquire: a timepiece tattoo, a set of adjustable-colour clothing, and a nondescript face. Then the rest of the world's embellishments fell away. For a moment Galman wondered if the AR network had been attacked, but as he lost control of his body he realised he was being immobilised and his AR hardware deactivated. Something pinched the back of his neck and the world turned red. Then black.

*

Galman knew about unconsciousness. It had been a hazard of his employment and, without exception, the experience of awakening had always been unpleasant. It was like the familiar discomfort and disorientation felt upon surfacing from a shift in a IB pod. It was disconcerting, therefore, to awaken relined on a plush velvet sofa, alert and refreshed. He felt good, and that worried him.

'I have some questions for you, Galman Tader.'

Galman recognised the voice. 'Office Trustee Cordem Hastergado,' he said, looking over to the immaculately presented federal representative. The man was dressed in the same sharp suit and sparse embellishments Galman had observed him wearing at his meeting with Ambondice-Ambondice in the restaurant; the meeting on which Galman had been spying.

'You are a federal fugitive,' Cordem said, running his fingers through the short greying hair which had to be either an embellishment or a deliberately cultivated sign of age. Even at his most neglected, Galman had been able to avoid grey hair.

'No, I am not,' Galman insisted, rising from the sofa and looking about the large but spartan office. He strode across the hardwood floor to stand across from the Office Trustee's wide mahogany and brass desk. Cordem remained in his seat and gestured for Galman to sit in the green leather chair opposite. Galman didn't sit.

'I am a refugee,' he said.

Cordem snorted. 'Yes, from Enguine. I read your file.' Then he smiled. 'It's all bullshit of course.'

'No, I escaped the...'

'You are Galman Tader, of Diaclom, formerly of the Diaclom Constabulary.'

Galman just glared. He had no hope of convincing the Office Trustee. He had been caught after just one useless week.

'How?' he mumbled, now taking the seat.

Cordem leaned back, rocking his chair on two legs. 'Pellitoe customs and immigration is run by the Swinell Union,' he said. 'They expect the federal trustees on pre-billion worlds to stop anyone leaving those planets. It isn't down to union workers to spot such fugitives coming in. To be honest, Mr Tader, if you hadn't given me reason to investigate you, you would probably never have been caught.'

'Reason?'

Cordem returned his chair to all four feet with a harsh crack which startled Galman. 'You were following me,' the Office Trustee said. 'Spying on me.'

Galman sank further into the chair. He had been a cop for decades; he knew the importance of preparation, so why had he rushed this? Why had he spied on a meeting between his Satumine quarry and one of the six most senior Administration figures on the planet? Stupid.

'I wasn't following *you*,' he tried.

'Really? Then who?'

Galman hesitated. He was going to be imprisoned, or returned to Diaclom for an SMD, and yet he still didn't want to give up this case. Was his personal mission of revenge so important, a tiny voice of reason asked, that he couldn't let a federal officer take over?

'Well?' Cordem pressed, and Galman broke. What was important was his revenge, and the justice it would bring. That he wanted it done by his own hand was nothing more than self-indulgence. He was better than that. He told the Office Trustee of his unconventional investigation and interrogation of Satumine on Diaclom; he revealed what little he had been told of Ambondice-Ambondice; he even threw in an account of his own personal losses to Satumine Terrorists.

'Ambondice-Ambondice is part of something big, here on Pellitoe,' he insisted when Cordem failed to respond to the revelations. 'I know you all think the Satumine are no different to humans and you are terrified of victimising them, but -'

'That is the Swinell Union position,' Cordem interrupted with a low muttering. 'It is not the Federal stance.'

Galman smiled, in spite of his looming incarceration or memory erasure, and he wondered if anything he had revealed had come as a surprise to the Office Trustee. 'So you will investigate Ambondice-Ambondice?'

Cordem scratched idly at his head. 'I don't trust him,' he admitted. 'But I am limited to what I can do.'

'Typical,' Galman snapped.

'If you had more compelling *proof*,' the Office Trustee mused. 'But I can't act on hunches and hearsay.'

'So that's it?' Galman spat.

'Calm down,' Cordem said with such cold and forceful composure it silenced the ex-cop. 'I must first deal with you.'

Galman sighed. He had failed. 'Go on.'

'I am a very busy man,' Cordem said, looking hard into Galman's eyes, giving a subtle nod. 'And I think you made a genuine mistake in leaving Diaclom.'

'Excuse me?'

Another slight nod. 'I believe I can trust you, Mr Tader, to return home. I am minded to release you on your own recognizance' He waved a screen into existence and Galman saw a sizable financial transfer taking place. 'I have loaded your account with enough funds to meet the costs you will incur in getting home.' Another nod, this time accompanied by the slightest of winks. 'It's just a shame you were unable to acquire more definite proof of your suspicions about Ambondice-Ambondice. I can't help wondering how much the Swinell Union's Bureau of Supervision might have been able to uncover had it been more inclined to investigate.'

His heart racing, Galman nodded at Cordem. 'Do you know how long until the next flight back to Diaclom?'

Cordem sucked theatrically through his teeth. 'Oh, at least four months I'm afraid.'

'I see.'

'OK, well off you go. Do stay out of trouble. And don't go spending any of that money on AR improvements for you or your IB machine.'

Galman nodded and rushed to leave the room. 'I wouldn't dream of it.'

Chapter 23

Shortly after your liberation from Consul's tyranny, you will have been shown your unique financial data-realm, a place in which your transactions, savings, earnings and budgetary concerns can be securely rendered. You might find yourself confused by the bewildering array of potential barter options in the form of IB crystals, data-matter, time and labour bonds and no fewer than a hundred stable commodity systems. But beneath all of this you will see the bottom line. *Here you will see your entire wealth in the form of the Jurisdiction's single currency: The New Euro. Through your financial data-realm you may easily exchange practically anything of worth for this simple coinage. As for the name - New Euro - its meaning is, unfortunately, lost to the fog of history.*

Rehabilitation: A Survivor's Guide

Indin-Indin: On Satute, in the Network

For nine days Indin-Indin inched his way through the ancient buried city of the original Satumine. Even if he had not been forced to informationally battle his way past every door and seal, he could have spent decades down there and still only explore the smallest fraction of the world-spanning artefact.

The small blue pebble, affixed to the latest door to stand between him and his destination, whistled softy and at last the door slid silently aside. Like everything down there the door was in perfect working order. Original Satumine technology didn't degrade or fail and was, more or less, impervious to most mundane stresses. It would take significantly more than the tectonic weight of the crushed cities above to do anything more than scuff the pristine veneer of this abandoned world.

He followed the revealed corridor in a slow left curve until he came to another barrier. Another internal door. With the streets and external spaces filled solid by the rubble of newer Satumine constructions, Indin-Indin was restricted to the interiors of the buildings and not all of them were connected. More than once he had been forced back after a day's wasted travel when confronted by the impassable outer wall of a building, or the door to a street now filled in. But Aggregate's map told Indin-Indin he was close. He clipped the pebble onto the door and waited for the now tediously familiar hum of its exotic neural hoax.

In the egg-shaped case, slung over one of Indin-Indin's shoulders, Aggregate's gift hummed a sympathetic tone as its artificial neural architecture responded to the field generated by the pebble. Orders of magnitude slower than an original Satumine's mind, the two devices linked to the door and began the complex negotiations required to activate the mechanisms. An original Satumine could have done this with the slightest of subconscious thoughts, but this device, the product of thousands of years of research aboard the *Tenjin*, would take almost an hour. And yet it was far beyond anything even imagined by Human or modern Satumine science.

The pebble continued to hum and Indin-Indin sat on the polished corridor floor, leaning against the bowed wall and closing down the input from his many eyes. Satumine didn't sleep, but they appreciated a few moments of solitude and rest. His abdominal cavity was warm and the beginning of an enzyme flow was starting to dissolve the resin sealing the three flaps. In a couple of days his fifteen day digestive cycle would be complete and his abdomen would fall open to reveal a hard black stone of bodily waste. Then he would have a maximum of six days in which to fill the cavity with more food, ready for another cycle. He didn't expect to find any food down here.

The hum intensified and escalated. This was going to be a tough door, was going to take a while. Perhaps it hid a prize worth the wait. Whatever was in the next room, Indin-Indin would be the first modern Satumine, or human, to see it. Almost every door in the old world was sealed and so the modern species had very little access to the ancient technology, very little with which to experiment and study. Satumine couldn't even open the doors, much less utilise the hidden wonders of their heritage. It was an insult, therefore, that humans walked with comparative ease through the streets and buildings of the abandoned Satumine colonies, their so-called *pilots* opening some, though not all, doors with the same instinctive ease with which they de-cloaked the frames of the network and brought them to life. That was as far as human success with Satumine technology went, but it gave them the access needed to fully study that which was beneath the modern Satumine's feet but beyond their grasp. It was, Indin-Indin surmised, a continuation of this tentative human understanding of the ancient technology that gave rise to the device he now used to open the doors - and even this did little more than replicate the effect of the Satumine genetic code found in some rare humans; the *pilots*. Not much to show for ten thousand years of study by the crew of the *Tenjin*.

The pebble eventually whistled and the door hushed open, revealing a second door immediately adjacent which also opened without a sound. The doors were indestructible to anything the modern races could bring to bear so deep into the planet. The only things capable of burning through these doors were safely in orbit or aboard human Sentries around other planets. So the precaution of a double layer door was telling. Indin-Indin stepped across the threshold into a tall cylinder of a room. Practically a silo. The walls were like so much else in the old world: flawlessly smooth and utterly featureless.

He checked the location on Aggregate's map. This was certainly in the general vicinity of the vague locator. Could this be the place? There were thousands of similar locations marked on the map and, according to Aggregate, it was in places like this that the original Satumine had propagated and absorbed the genetic code developed in their experiments on Earth. It was in these facilities that the Satumine had been brought low, reduced to their modern form, and in the space of a decade lost the ability to interact with their own technology. Nobody knew now why it had happened, or why they first abandoned the colonies, but the remnants of Satumine code in the human gene-pool, and the aberrant human code in the modern Satumine, was well documented. Perhaps Indin-Indin would uncover the truth.

The third device in his egg-shaped case chirped with urgent glee. Indin-Indin grabbed the flat nine-pointed star of blue metal and examined its tiny white screen.

Active

The immense curved walls shimmered and exposed thousands of coffin-like alcoves reaching up to the distant grey ceiling. Without hesitation, and only the briefest pinch of doubt, Indin-Indin rushed to the closest wall and crawled into one of the coffins on the lowest layer.

White light, then horrifying agony as Aggregate's technology tried to keep up with the ancient machinery.

Chapter 24

We are told so often that the Satumine are no threat, that they could not possibly be conspiring against us when they are such a fallen and impotent people, unable even to activate their own ancient technology. It is our pilots, those born with the necessary aberrant genes, that have sole access to the controls of the great Frames. We are the superior race, we are the ones in control. Why then can our pilots open barely a quarter of the doors in the abandoned cities of the Network colonies? Why are the frames and a few simple locks opened to them and yet all other forms of Ancient Satumine technology refuse to yield to their supposedly compatible hybrid genes? The answer is obvious - the Satumine wished us to travel the Network, and use its resources to expand into the universe. They wanted us out there, searching for whatever it is they are afraid to hunt themselves - but they have ensured their other secrets, their advanced wonders, are kept from us. When the time comes for them to rise up, they will use those ancient machines to consume us.

The Truth: A treatise on the Satumine Conspiracy

Galman Tader: On Pellitoe, in the Swinell Union, in the Fertile Belt

Galman knew cops; he knew when a man or woman was in the job because they needed to make a difference, and he knew when they were in it for the money or the power. It took him less than ten minutes to identify Ollivan as typical of the latter breed. While the institutions of the Diaclom Constabulary and the Swinell Union Bureau of Supervision were polar opposites, cops were still cops. Galman recognised the bitter words Ollivan hissed about his duty while downing another large pitcher of

cheap ale which looked no different to the water used as
its drab reality foundation. It was the same crap he had
heard all too often in the Constabulary bars back home:
'I'm not paid enough for this shit'; 'I've half a mind to go
into private security'; 'I can't wait till my leave comes up.'
It was all about the money. The off-duty supervisor's two
companions were little better, but Ollivan was Galman's
target of choice. Not only was he in the job for the wrong
reason, he also appeared to be in some considerable debt,
judging by the conversations he was having. Galman could
use this miserable man.

He finished his own drink, a deliberately ostentatious
luminescent ale which sang an intoxicating ballad as it
danced down his throat, set the empty glass on the long
crystal bar which glowed and pulsed with the timbre of the
room's conversations, and he walked with practised
nonchalance to the table where Ollivan and his colleagues
were bitching about their lot. He caught Ollivan's gaze and
the bitter cop returned a suspicious scowl before flinging
up a bubble of rippling blue translucence. It was an AR
privacy screen and it told Galman, and everyone else in the
bar, the three men weren't in the mood for uninvited
company. It was a common piece of AR subscription
which cost only a few New-Euros a month. Galman had
used some of the funds provided by Office Trustee
Cordem Hastergado to subscribe to a suite of AR services
which included a similar privacy feature, but he had been
in a position to pay for premium code far beyond the
means of this indebted cop. With a thought Galman
accessed the suite and activated the costly service. Calm
and without comment he stepped through the bubble,
immune to the interference it ought to have inflicted on
his other embellishments and without the mild but
sustained physical discomfort the trio would have expected
him to suffer.

'What the hell is your problem?' One of cops spat as
Galman sat, uninvited, on the one empty stool at the table.

'Ollivan!' Galman said. 'How long has it been?' He beamed his most convivial grin and was repaid with a confused half smile.

'Excuse me?' Ollivan said, his lightly embellished face creasing thoughtfully at the brow.

'It's me. Galman.' Galman reached out with an AR hand, invisible to everyone but him, to touch Ollivan on the shoulder and initiate a private connection. Ollivan began to shake his head but stopped abruptly when Galman flashed him a private screen, displaying a sizeable financial transfer in the impoverished cop's name.

'Oh,' Ollivan said slowly. 'It's you.' He gave an unconvincing smile and added, 'How have you been?'

'Not bad,' Galman said, leaning back in the chair, relaxing, as the other two cops did likewise, seemingly content to accept him as an acquaintance of their colleague.

'So, what are you doing here?' Ollivan asked, toying nervously with his empty tankard.

'Family business,' Galman said, vaguely looking at the other two men. 'A bit private.'

The others looked to Ollivan for a moment, shrugged, finished their drinks and stood to leave. 'I ought to be getting home anyway,' one of them said.

'Me too,' the second added. 'The wife likes me to at least see the kids before they go to bed.'

'Ollivan nodded but didn't reply; he was preoccupied looking Galman up and down, probably wondering if he wanted to be alone with this apparently wealthy but unknown man.

'Ollivan?' the family man said. 'Everything OK?'

'Eh?' Ollivan glanced up at his friend as if snapping out of a trance. 'Sorry, yes, right, I'll catch you both in the morning.' As the other two turned away he called out, 'Give my best to your wife.'

Once the two men had left the perimeter of the privacy screen, Galman activated a more costly equivalent, erecting a seemingly solid black barrier around the table. The background chatter of the bar, previously muffled by the cheap blue bubble, now fell silent.

'Who are you?' Ollivan demanded.

'You don't need to know,' Galman said. 'All you need to know is I can get you out of your financial hole.' Galman didn't know for certain that he could, but the funds provided by the Office Trustee had been substantially more than would be required to get him back to Diaclom. Besides, he had seen Ollivan's response to the implied offer of half of those funds. The offer, he believed, was more than enough.

'And you are going to just hand over that kind of money?' Ollivan asked with obvious scepticism.

'Clearly not,' Galman said. 'But I am prepared to let you earn it.'

'How?'

Galman explained and, looking sick with stress, Ollivan nodded his acceptance.

Chapter 25

As if Consul and his agents needed any help in hiding from the inept scrutiny of mankind, we have willingly erected a whole new layer of reality with which to obscure the physical word. AR: Artificial Reality. It seems it is just too much effort now to actually create things with our bare hands, with the skills and tools that define us as a species, when we can just allow a computer to generate the sensory illusion of art, architecture, entertainment, food and just about everything we could desire. Even sex has been rendered obsolete by the almost unlimited and instant satisfaction offered by the veil of AR. Drab reality, the real *world, is just a dreary foundation of bare walls, insipid nutrient chunks and bland white coveralls. Given the choice very few ever glimpse this boring and uninspiring world. On many worlds a citizen lacks even the* choice. *Little wonder the agents of Consul walk so casually beneath the skin of our Jurisdiction.*

The Enguine Manifesto

Subset: Aboard the *Tenjin*, in shortspace, near the Pellitoe system, in the Swinell Union, in the Fertile Belt

Subset awoke suddenly. His naked body was soaked and cold with sweat, his fingers bleeding slowly from scratching at the walls in his sleep. The terror of his dreams still raw in his mind, the young man scrambled back into the room's corner while Aggregate more fully asserted his control and brought some measure of order to a frenetic mind. Eventually the confused man calmed down, once more a passenger in his own body. Seeing through Aggregate's many eyes and knowing that entity's extended thoughts, Subset realised his master, his god, was furious and distraught, and that was what had bled into his dreams.

Through Aggregate's extended body - the crew - Subset had seen the acquired footage of the human controlled fertile worlds, had witnessed the rape done to those perfectly balanced ecosystems, had watched the flaying of Aggregate's original body from those worlds. But recorded images could never inflict the same emotional trauma as direct observations from the *Tenjin's* sensor arrays. Now nearing the end of its shortspace journey, the *Tenjin* was able to peer ahead towards the target planet, and even Subset felt sick at what he saw. His sensibilities and emotions may have been merely the second-hand cast-offs of Aggregate's consciousness, but Subset felt them as strongly as any of the dark emotions experienced in his rare moments of independence. With tears welling in his narrow eyes, tears shared by every form aboard the *Tenjin* capable of such expression, Subset watched as Aggregate initiated scans for a trace of the symbiotic helix which would indicate the presence of his original self still lingering in the life down on that urbanised planet. But, of course, nothing remained of his old self. That pointspace body had lost its every anchor on this planet, and the remaining life was now isolated from the controlling entity for which it had all been created.

What remained of Aggregate's instinctive and insentient self expressed a deep animalistic grief at the loss of the planet. This grief echoed through his extended body, through subset and the rest of the crew, as anger at the violation. But that anger was fast filtered and crystallised in the human minds that gave Aggregate sentience, becoming more than grief, becoming more than anger. It evolved into a bitter thirst for vengeance at the invasion of his territory by the Human Jurisdiction. Subset felt this thirst and he looked forward to the *Tenjin's* arrival at Pellitoe.

The tiny whisper of Subset's true self tried to call for restrain and understanding, but the pleading barely reached the surface of his own mind, much less the extended consciousness of the crew, or Aggregate.

Chapter 26

Ours is a homogeneous and peaceful galaxy, home to only two intelligence races - Human and Satumine - both coexisting within a single Jurisdiction. Only occasionally do we experience internal unrest in the form of planetary or Union uprisings, but these are short-lived and have little to no impact on the broader galactic community. One might imagine, therefore, that war - true war - has become nought but a curiosity of ages long past. Such fantasy does not allow for the presence of Consul. Although there are only two intelligent races, the Artificial Consciousness, as you will be intimately aware, ruled over a great many worlds and can field a significant number of ships. He asked for peace at the end of the uprising in which he was expelled from Earth. He asked once more after the bloody two centuries of war between the Jurisdiction and the realm he had been creating in the shadows. That ceasefire lasted barely a decade. We will not be so quick to accept a third offer of peace from a monster who exists only to enslave us.

Rehabilitation: A Survivor's Guide

Galman Tader: On Pellitoe, in the Swinell Union, in the Fertile Belt

Silently walking with Ollivan to the hotel suite that had been his home for the past three days, Galman began to wonder if he ought to have prepared somewhere else for this; somewhere not so obviously tied to him. But if things went wrong there were probably few places on Pellitoe the Bureau of Supervision or the Federal Administration couldn't have under absolute scrutiny in seconds. By its very nature, a world spanning AR required omnipresent scanning and, although illegal under the Swinell constitution and legally questionable under Jurisdiction statutes, Galman was confident the AR systems could be subverted by those in power should the need arise. It was a lesser violation of this system that he hoped would give him an advantage over his quarry.

'You look nervous,' Ollivan observed, breaking a painful ten minute silence.

Galman flashed a tight smile and said, 'I'm fine. I've got this all covered.' If he was going to get caught, so be it. He knew better than to indulge in self-doubt. Besides, unless he had catastrophically misunderstood Cordem Hastergado's meaning, he had some measure of official protection. If he *had* misunderstood then he was screwed anyway.

'Is this where you're staying?' Ollivan asked as they ascended the cloud-like slope up to the hotel's heavily embellished entrance.

'For now,' Galman replied. Although blessed with a generous financial balance, the hotel was an extravagance he couldn't maintain indefinitely. It was a statement of decadence and luxury, towering ridiculously over the already affluent city like some refuge of the gods. Its highest levels were lost in the combined drab-reality clouds and AR aurora while eternal sunshine glinted on the apparently solid gold walls. It was an indulgence Galman would not have ordinarily allowed himself but, as Tumble had reminded him, if he wished to convince his target of his wealth, it would not do to bring him back to some scruffy unembellished pit of a motel.

The lobby was another gilded dream extending through the tower's core, all the way up to a distant crystal dome which allowed AR sunlight to fill the vast open space. Immediately the concierge attended him, offering to facilitate any and all needs. Galman accepted a glass of ale which the man - probably an IB machine - had brought with him in anticipation of his client's recorded preferences.

'Can I get you anything?' Galman asked Ollivan. The cop declined with a distracted wave.

'No, let's just get this done.'

'Fair enough.' Galman shooed the concierge away and led his guest over to one of the ten small elevators. In keeping with the ostentatious use of AR, the elevators were animated with an effect which likened the journey through the tower to a clichéd ascent into heaven, including the obligatory column of light, the cotton wool clouds and barely audible cords of an angelic choir. Galman rolled his eyes. Ollivan seemed hardly to notice the tacky display; maybe a life lived on Pellitoe had dulled his appreciation of AR embellishments, but more likely he had too much on his mind to care what else was going on around him.

Galman's suite took up a good fifth of the thirtieth floor and the elevator travelled horizontally at the last to deposit the two men in the living room.

'I hope you've come with good news,' Tumble barked, still wearing his goblin AR skin. 'I've got about as far as I can without some legitimate access. If I loiter much longer where I am, I'm going to get noticed.'

Galman stepped away from the column of light into the room, but Ollivan didn't move.

'Supervisor Ollivan has agreed to assist,' Galman explained to Tumble. 'His access is rated at seven and nine. Will that do?'

'I'm only a mid-level Supervisor,' Ollivan elaborated, still within the elevator cloud. 'I don't know if my codes can get you in where you want to go.'

Tumble laughed. 'All I need is an *in*,' he said. 'It never seems to have occurred to the Bureau of Supervision that someone might circumvent the moral and legal blocks of a machine such as me.'

'To be fair,' Galman said, 'most people aren't *capable* of re-programming to that level.'

Ollivan scoffed and finally took a slow step into the room. 'I think it would be more accurate to say people with that level of skill aren't, generally, stupid enough to commit such a blatant and dangerous federal offence. Do you realise the risks involved in removing an IB machine's blocks?'

Galman shrugged. 'Yes,' he said. 'But that really doesn't have anything to do with your involvement here.' Ollivan nodded.

Then there was a moment of thick silence which Tumble eventually broke: 'Regardless,' the machine said, 'the upshot is that the security in place is pathetically inadequate. I don't need to be able to change or add anything; I just need to download a bit of Bureau data; just need to see what they have. Your access codes, Ollivan, will be sufficient for my needs.'

Ollivan took a slow deep breath and Galman sighed. Ollivan was going to start playing games.

'Money first,' the cop said, failing to convey any menace or strength in either his voice or his meek body language. He wouldn't have survived a week in the Diaclom Constabulary but was apparently just the kind of inoffensive representative the Swinell Union wanted for its law enforcement agency. Galman shuddered at the thought of his old colleagues in the Constabulary becoming as pathetic and restrained as this worthless man, once the Bureau fully took over the policing of Diaclom.

'Don't fuck me around,' he warned. 'Just give us the codes.'

'Money,' Ollivan demanded.

The two glared, Galman with far greater intensity, but Tumble again broke the silence. 'Just pay the little shit,' he snapped. 'I don't have time to piss about.'

Galman eyed the cop a moment longer, wondering if he had misjudged him.

'Galman,' Tumble pressed. 'Now.'

Galman shook his head but called up a publicly visible screen and loaded the financial transfer he had previously shown the cop. With an unnecessary flick of his fingers he transferred the money.

'Happy?'

'Very,' Ollivan said with too broad a smile and with an unexpected self-confidence. Galman knew he had been played.

'Codes,' he demanded. 'Now.' But Ollivan was already drawing a short silver pistol from beneath the folds in his shirt. It had probably been fully visible in drab-reality, just tucked into the waistband of Ollivan's foundation jumpsuit, but neither Galman nor Tumble had the option to filter the AR world.

Galman didn't flinch. 'What are you going to do with that?' he asked.

'Hopefully nothing,' Ollivan replied. 'So please don't give me any reason to hurt you.'

'What's this all about?' Galman asked, keeping his hands out, either side of his body. 'Are you going to arrest me?' He didn't think for a moment the cop had such noble intentions.

Ollivan sneered and took a step back, closer to the elevator clouds. 'No,' he said. 'I'm going to take my money and you are going to keep quiet.'

Galman's arms were locked about Ollivan's in the time it took the cop to utter the last word. Half a second later the pistol was on the floor and Ollivan's arms were twisted behind him, his body forced to bend over so far he eventually fell to the floor where Galman was able to more fully restrain him. To better emphasise the point, Tumble dropped his goblin skin and swung across to hang in front of the downed cop's face, his vacuum cleaner barrel extended and the rumble of some internal mechanism sounding surprisingly similar to the charging of a micro particle-accelerator.

Ollivan divulged his access codes before Galman or Tumble had to ask again.

Chapter 27

It is all too easy to deride the human Frame project, focusing only on the catastrophe of the Tenjin and joining the backlash against the enormous wealth spent on it. But to do so is the succumb to the distraction so obviously laid on for us. The Jurisdiction is up in arms about the disaster following that first test of a human-built frame, a small but vocal minority scream for the entire project to be scrapped and for the resources to be invested in more worthy and safer endeavours. And while we are distracted with all of that, we are not asking the important questions, not examining the truth of the project. The failure was deliberate, orchestrated by the Satumine and their Administration pawns, in order that any inquiry into the frames focuses only on the safety of the technology. There is no way the project will be scrapped, that is obvious - there is too much to be gained from linking every Jurisdiction world through pointspace frames and allowing instant travel as is enjoyed in the ninety six worlds of the Network. The Satumine and the corrupted elements of the Administration simply do not want us asking how much of the original Satumine technology went into the design of our own frames, or what that technology might really be used for once it has linked every part of the galaxy.

The Truth: A treatise on the Satumine Conspiracy

Cordem Hastergado: On Pellitoe, in the Swinell Union, in the Fertile Belt

'Keep right behind him,' Cordem reminded the data-tech, an old and highly specialised Senior Trustee of proven federal loyalty. Like himself, most of the Trustee's under Cordem's charge were citizens of the Swinell Union, and the Office Trustee had to be careful to use only those he could trust in monitoring Galman Tader's investigation. This data-tech, like Cordem, considered himself a citizen of the Jurisdiction, not of the Swinell Union. There should be no distinction, but there always was.

With a three hundred and sixty degree twist of his many-pronged mechanical-looking AR limb, the data-tech accelerated his pursuit of the illegal code-crawler. The longest wall of Cordem's palatial office had become an immense portal through which could be seen the visual metaphor used to make sense of the complex code compartments within the Bureau of Supervisions secure network. Cordem understood very little of what he was seeing. A million translucent conduits filled the space within the portal, each flickering with a distinctly different hue and frequency. Apparently this all made perfect sense to the data-tech and occasionally, as his view descended into one of these conduits and the frequency stabilised into a regular rhythm, the man would mumble something about personnel files or audit documents. All Cordem cared about was that they kept the simple dot avatar of his quarry in sight. Although he had no legal justification for searching the network and files of the Bureau, it was well within his remit to follow a suspect wherever he might go. If he lost that dot - the avatar of Galman's IB companion - he would be forced to pull out. He really didn't want to pull out; he had been waiting years for an excuse to sniff around in this network.

The viewpoint again entered a conduit and lilac flashed rapidly across the portal. 'They have entered a partition which seems to be mapping the global AR net,' the data-tech reported with evident concern. 'Why would they be mapping the AR net?'

Eyebrows raised, Cordem said, 'I don't know. Just keep following him and make sure to tidy up behind you.' Galman's IB machine seemed to be under the impression that lax security on the gate equated to equally feeble surveillance within the system itself. Had Cordem's data-tech not been there to smooth out the ripples and scratches left across the code compartment, both of their activities would have been noticed by now.

A junction presented itself and Tumble selected one of thirty available tributaries. The data-tech followed close behind. The frequency of the lilac strobe intensified and the hue became blindingly vivid.

'I see,' the data-tech declared as if it was entirely obvious. Cordem pressed him for more. 'These are segregated elements of the mapped AR net,' the data-tech explained. 'They have tied the encoded positional routines with their own census and security records.'

'Meaning?'

'They can call up any citizen's name, either through their census records or through other security files, and they will be given the positional codes used by the AR'

'So they can know exactly where any citizen is on the planet?'

'In theory, but it isn't being used. I think it's just a contingency. I don't think the Swinell Union would have given permission to actually activate such a flagrant privacy violation.'

'Or of federal statutes,' Cordem added. 'Record the file locations please.'

'Done.' There was a flash and the data-tech added, 'Tumble just copied a file.'

'Let me guess,' Cordem said. 'Ambondice-Ambondice?'

The data-tech nodded. 'Shall I take a copy as well?'

Ordinarily that would have been out of the question, there would have been no legal justification. He would have liked copies of a hundred other such files which could have given him unrivalled surveillance on some of the most high value suspects on Pellitoe, but Tumble had already copied this file. That made it evidence in a criminal investigation and put it just within his remit.

'Copy it,' he said.

Tumble's avatar vanished and the portal faded as the data-tech withdrew from the Bureau of Supervision's network.

'Good work,' Cordem said, patting the other man on the shoulder. He then called up a screen on which his head of security was visible.

'Sir?' the strong woman, a Senior Trustee, said.

'Any news on Supervisor Ollivan?'

'They let him go,' the woman reported, a look of mild confusion on her face. 'I expected them to kill him.'

'To be honest,' Cordem admitted, 'so did I.'

'They're taking a hell of a risk,' the woman observed. 'If anyone tracks the codes they used...'

'Then you had best make sure Ollivan doesn't have a chance to say anything.'

'You want me to kill him?' She sounded startled, a little disgusted.

Cordem laughed. 'Seriously?' He shook his head. 'Just arrest him and hold him for a few days.'

'What charge?'

'Surprise me.'

Chapter 28

Ever since consul first donned his mockery of a human body, in the form of the tin-man, humanity has been repulsed by the notion of humanoid IB machines. Unlike so many other taboos, this has not faded over the centuries, and rightly so. For the jurisdiction to reserve its disgust solely for such forms, however, is to allow a more insidious and creeping acceptance of forms just as capable of housing an artificial consciousness as any humanoid robot. An interrogation of recent census data highlights this irrational bias, showing among other nonsensical preferences that over ninety percent of network citizens would be comfortable allowing an orb or wheel shaped machine to care for their children, while less than half a percent would countenance the notion of a humanoid machine going anywhere near their young. The figures are predictably less extreme outside of the network, but the trend is still undeniable. No doubt the disgust felt by so many towards a humanoid robot is the result of subliminal and long term conditioning by consul, designed to distract naïve citizens from the glut of machines rolling, spinning and crawling unopposed through our homes.

The Enguine Manifesto

Ambondice-Ambondice: On Pellitoe, in the Swinell Union, In the Fertile Belt

The pointspace comms centre was a tertiary redundancy, ready to take up the task of linking Pellitoe with the rest of the Jurisdiction in the event that the primary and secondary centres both failed. It was hidden beneath the AR skin of a decommissioned pre-billion era communal nursery, the structure that had stood in its place before Pellitoe's economic significance had risen to a level necessitating a third layer of comms redundancy. It sat in a shallow valley, a small city over the hills to the East and the protected wilderness of a vast reserve past the low mountains to the West. Down here in the valley was technically city land, open to development. In practice, aside from the occasional isolated compound such as the ostensible nursery, if was a buffer between the urban districts and the reserve. Pheromone towers and high frequency pulse emitters dissuaded any of the larger predators from straying too far into the buffer, and it was from behind one of the pheromone towers that Ambondice-Ambondice observed his target.

Short brittle fingers of desiccated affan-grass formed a crunchy carpet for a hundred meters all around the facility, gradually giving way to a healthier spongy meadow of absorptive turquoise grass. Scattered groups of flesh trees and intestinal weeds pulsed with the rhythm of a syrup node twenty miles into the reserve, and a thin mist of sweat rose from those meaty plants, like steam from a corpse, gathering in low clouds half way up the valley's height and spreading the familiar odour of raw flesh and honey common to every Fertile World. To his left, in the closest fleshy copse, Ambondice-Ambondice saw one of his lieutenants crouched among a patch of steaming brown weeds, along with the three other Satumine of his squad. To his right he saw another four-strong team squatting behind the wide resin block at the base of a pulse emitter tower. Ambondice-Ambondice was flanked by the eight members of his own primary team. Sixteen Satumine in total, plus himself, all armed, most checking their weapons.

He made use of cover, splitting his force so as to provide covering fire and the option of outflanking any potential enemy. But his efforts were rather unnecessary because, if he had failed in his preparations, a dozen AR remote-presence systems would be invisibly monitoring his approach and the kinds of weapons strapped to the solar-

power satellites in orbit could pick off every member of
his force through far deeper cover than the vegetation and
towers available. But Ambondice-Ambondice knew these
strategic pretences focused the minds of his men and
forced them to take seriously the task asked of them.
Besides, although he hoped to have dealt with the primary
threat - the AR remote presences - there was still the
potential for human eyes to be on the lookout.

Watching both teams with his many differently
oriented eyes, he waved the Satumine forward, sending
them into the dry grass and hoping the dull crunch of
affan husks which rose into the air like burnt paper
wouldn't be detected by the notoriously superior human
ears.

'Now us,' he told his own squad, leading them into the
dead grass fingers, up to the wide and well lit entrance of
the nursery. A hundred windows looked out on his
approach but Ambondice-Ambondice knew what lay
beneath this AR illusion. This was the bare flat side wall of
the comms facility - no door, no windows and, if his
preparations had worked, no security. One of the teams
took up position on the corner to his left; the other team
was on his right. Ambondice-Ambondice was at the wall's
middle in the AR shade of the entrance's arched doorway.
He held up both hands, gesturing for everyone to hold
position, and then consulted a tiny screen which appeared
in front of his left knee-eye. It was all looking good. Codes
originally acquired to facilitate Sharlie-Sharlie's vague plan
to collapse Pellitoe's entire AR network were now working
to isolate the local net, ghosting all of the AR and looping
a modified version back into the global network. The
result was the ability to block, alter, or destroy any AR
object or function currently running in or around the
facility, and to feed seemingly normal data back into the
wider network so nobody could notice what was going on.
It looked like the code was holding firm against the
automated IB monitoring systems which patrolled AR.

The processing space was more than adequate to facilitate the current demand, and so it ought to be. Ambondice-Ambondice had spent a grotesque amount of his misappropriated fortune in securing the corporate code-compartments and in bribing the monitoring authorities which could have otherwise quickly noticed the excessive AR data pipeline.

He tested the code, causing the doorway to shift colour. Satisfied he had full control he deactivated all internal security and revealed the true entrance on the west wall. He ordered his teams to the now exposed double doors and marvelled at how reliant the Swinell Union was on its AR. There were no drab-reality cameras or sensors, no physical security to stop him strolling through those unlocked doors and into the cavernous industrial mass within.

A little under a hundred human workers stood, open mouthed, in utter confusion, as the drab-reality foundation of their beautifully embellished facility was suddenly visible to them. More than a few of the staff were indecently under-dressed for human sensibilities, though none of Ambondice-Ambondice's Satumine really noticed. None of them ever wore clothes, not even in AR. Everyone else was attired in the plain white jumpsuits over which their AR skins ought to be draped. The most keenly felt losses, however, would be the AR limbs and the access to data-screens and comms. Some of these people had probably not been so limited, so *drab*, since infancy. To the people of a world so heavily embellished as Pellitoe, this was the stuff of nightmares.

Somebody yelled a terrified warning, noticing the seventeen heavily armed Satumine still sporting embellishments as they rushed through the only open door. People began screaming until Ambondice-Ambondice fired a needlessly noisy mag-round into the air.

'Come out from there,' he yelled to the workers cowering behind the thirty foot spherical mesh of the pointspace burrower at the far end of the huge room. When nobody moved he flicked a switch on his rifle, selected scatter-grenade shot, and fired silently above the hidden men and women. The explosion was dull and muted but was preceded by the ping and zip of a thousand high velocity pellets. Using AR positional data he looked through the sphere to see a dozen dead or dying, and twenty hurt. Those still able crept tentatively out, hands in the air. There was none of the sobbing or gibbering he had expected, the humans were too stunned, all but paralysed with fear.

'Pick your targets,' he mumbled to his team in the Satumine tongue. 'Wait for my command.' He then activated a small amount of AR which would project his voice around the room: Satumine couldn't really shout.

'I need assistance in modifying and operating the pointspace burrower,' he declared. 'Will those with tech-security grade eight or above please step over here beside me.'

For a moment nobody moved. Then one man began to take a step forward, his colleagues murmuring their disapproval at the apparent collaboration. But this was no volunteer. 'We all know what you are,' the man said. 'And nobody is going to help a bunch of terrorists.'

'I only want help in communicating -'

'We all know what kind of power goes into this burrower,' the spokesman interrupted. 'This could be made into a bomb powerful enough to level-' He didn't finish. Ambondice-Ambondice put a bolt through his neck, tearing his head from his body.

Now people screamed. 'I don't actually need most of you,' Ambondice-Ambondice went on, dialling up the vocal amplification. 'I only need five.' Setting his rifle to rapid fire, he added, 'Everyone else will die.'

If Satumine could smile, he would have. The humans' supposed solidarity and loyalty was nothing more than a tattered pretence within two seconds of his chilling declaration. The technicians literally fought each other with fists, feet and teeth, to be among the first five to reach Ambondice-Ambondice's side. With such a wealth of volunteers he began thinning the throng even before the first reached him.

When he had his five, each bruised and bleeding but smiling hysterically as if they thought this was anything more than a temporary stay of execution, Ambondice-Ambondice gave the command to open fire on the rest.

Chapter 29

As a survivor of Consul's IB farm worlds, your life will initially follow a fairly rigid and well-practised regime. Before long, however, it will be time for you to move on and your options for a new home planet may (depending on logistics and other local factors) be very broad indeed. One of your initial considerations, when selecting a home, should be the degree to which the candidate world uses, or does not use, augmented reality (AR). Many worlds enforce a strict 'curtain', meaning the AR world is accepted as reality and as such all citizens must be permanently immersed in the illusion. Without hardware blocks preventing citizens from stepping out of the illusion, the artificial layer of reality becomes unreal. Either everyone is 'all in' or nobody is. Other worlds use AR as an entirely voluntary experience, relegating the potentially vibrant and exhilarating world of AR to the level of mere tools and entertainment. It is a matter of personal preference and you will have plenty of time to weigh the advantages of both systems before having to make a choice.

Rehabilitation: A Survivor's Guide

Indin-Indin: On Satute, in the Network

Aggregate called it Atavism: Reversion to an earlier state. Humans would probably have called it a living hell of unknowable pain. As the last of his primary brain dissolved into a grey gel and, thinking with new intelligence orders of magnitude greater than anything that had existed organically for millennia, Indin-Indin considered the agony an intellectual curiosity. As new horrors shredded his every nerve ending, Indin-Indin distracted himself in a mental simulation of the changes he felt taking place within what was now his body. Through the homogeneous sponge of his flesh every cell was being tortured and rebuilt by the Atavism field and he could almost distinguish the nightmare pain of each cell as the human-inspired DNA was unwound and horrifically slowly reconstructed to incorporate a new third helix. No longer required to hold together a thinned shadow of Satumine code, the modified human genes were plucked out and the superior code of the third helix locked into place.

Distantly Indin-Indin heard the screams of his insentient mind. There was no audible cry, no organs left with which to create such sound, just the sobs of those sections of his old nervous system still to be knitted into the surfacing consciousness of a true Satumine. In the coffin-like confines of the Atavism pod, Indin-Indin's body was a dark pink puddle of thick soup, but within the loose incoherent muscle matter was the fibrous mesh that had once been his animalistic secondary brain. That brain, the vestige of the original Satumine brilliance, was growing in both density and complexity.

Already Indin-Indin knew he was not the creature he had once been - that lesser Satumine had died when his primary brain had been dissolved and recycled for its constituent organic resources. But enough of that creature's memory, its personality, had been mapped onto the fibrous brain which now reverted to the awesome organ of a true Satumine's intelligence.

The once thread-like neurological fibres gathered about themselves ever more structure, forming pencil-thick cords of efficient complexity, and true sentience was reborn. Then came the instincts. No, Indin-Indin realised, not instincts. This was true knowledge and memory encoded in his resurgent tri-helical genetic code. But still he didn't understand why his ancestors had debased themselves, stripped away their third helix and knitted together the tattered remnants with fragments of inferior human DNA. He didn't understand why they had sacrificed their ability to control their world and why they had forfeited the stellar empire they had worked so long to sculpt. Such knowledge didn't exist in the genetic memory, but he knew how he would find the answers. And he was satisfied it would coincide with his responsibilities to Aggregate.

Slowly the pain subsided and the soup of his body thickened into an opaque jelly, lacking organs of any kind save for the mesh of neural cords knitted through the entire glutinous mass. The Atavism field deactivated and the pod slid out, depositing him with no dignity or consideration onto the cold floor like a dropped dessert. He felt the motion but saw nothing. He had never before altered his form as, he now realised, was the way of his ancestors. But he had the genetic memory and instinctive skill. With a thought he began the slow ugly process of taking a usable shape.

Two hours later, after the dried crust of his cocoon fell away, a true Saturnine linked his mind with the city for the first time in twenty thousand years. He looked a lot like a human.

Chapter 30

First contact with the Satumine is often referred to, with an almost mythical fondness, as the greatest accident of all time. Before we began actively promoting breeding of the rare hybrid Satumine genes, there were perhaps one in one hundred thousand people with the necessary genetics to activate an Ancient Satumine Frame. The odds of one of those people finding their way into the primitive space program of the day, and being sent close enough to the cloaked frame to mentally link with it, were so small that it is almost incomprehensible that it actually happened. I put it to you, therefore, that first contact was orchestrated by the Satumine and the greatest accident of all time was, in fact, contrived well in advance of the event. The presence of Satumine genetic code in the human gene-pool has never been satisfactorily explained, but surely the least fantastical theory must be that the Satumine intended for us to access the Frames. Is it any less reasonable to assume they also placed some hidden agent, or mechanism, to ensure a compatible human would eventually link with the frames. Even if you deny the greater Satumine conspiracy - that of the long term plan for the Satumine to use humanity to search the galaxy on their behalf - you must at least accept that given the abuses and exploitation endured by Humanity at the hands of the Satumine, immediately following first contact, that it is likely that contact was intended and planned for by the Satumine.

The Truth: A treatise on the Satumine Conspiracy

Anden Macer: Aboard the *Vulpine*, in orbit around Pellitoe, in the Swinell Union, in the Fertile Belt

'You know they are going to expect us all to take shore leave,' the executive officer, Senior Trustee Steit Tomer, Said.

Anden Macer let go an exhausted sigh and tugged absently at the long thick dreads of matted brown hair draped across his black-uniformed shoulder. His Administration rank was that of Office Trustee, but like all Sentry crew members he wore only the insignia of his ship rank. He was the *Vulpine*'s captain. He glanced mournfully about the small senior-officers' den at the eleven men and women he considered to be closer to him than his own family. It was a grimly depressing gathering. These were the last of the original crew, those whom along with Anden had been there at the *Vulpine*'s launch almost one hundred years ago when they had all been Junior Trustees, on their first assignments. Since then the crew of eight hundred had slowly drifted away into other assignments or been lost to battle or retirement, and new blood had been drafted in. All the while Anden and the other few long-termers had steadily progressed through both Administration and ship ranks and, eight years ago, Anden had taken command of what had long since become his home, replacing the man who had been his captain for ninety years. Now the ship's centenary was looming and the Sector Trustee was insisting on celebrations, and awards for these eleven dedicated crewmembers. And they all knew such awards came with a generous holiday package. It was a gift none of them wanted.

'Why do those planet-bound Trustees always assume we're all itching to get away from our homes to spend a year trapped on some rock, while our ship is months away getting into God only knows what trouble without us?' Anden asked nobody in particular. 'If they really want to reward us they should just give us the replacement gravity coils we have been waiting for these last five years. It's a bloody joke down on six-delta.'

A murmur of agreement coursed through the den, but nobody was holding out much hope. The anniversary was in eighteen months and the *Vulpine*'s duty schedule had been arranged to bring it back to the Rancordit shipyard, in the Able Union, in time to coincide with that auspicious milestone. Anden had been ordered to leave Pellitoe in three days.

'As soon as we're in shortspace,' Steit observed, 'we'll have no way out of this.' It was to be a direct flight of a year and a half, straight home to Rancordit. 'If we're going to avoid this damned celebration we need to come up with something in the next seventy two hours.'

'We could just refuse to leave the ship,' said Keddy, the petite tactical officer and Senior Trustee responsible for the *Vulpine*'s internal security.

'Chain ourselves to the bridge?' the chief technician, Ovin Tinner, suggested with a smirk.

Anden offered a slight laugh but shook his head. 'The *Vulpine*'s honour is without equal in the Swinell-Able sector; if we're going to get out of it then we are going to do it by the book.'

Another murmur of agreement. Pride in one's ship was central to Sentry ethos. Anden rose from the plush sofa and wandered over to the short buffet table where he assembled a small plate of sandwiches. This was the private sanctuary of the twelve most senior officers, separate from the regular officers' mess and off-limits to anyone but this elite few. Not even the captain's assistant was allowed in here and so the officers had to serve themselves. That was the very reason they had formed their little club: one could begin to form an unhealthy opinion of one's own importance if every little domestic task was done for you by forever bowing minions. It was also the reason Anden insisted ranks were left at the door. He needed his closest friends to be comfortable challenging him should the need arise, though it rarely did.

'What about this heightened security level?' he asked Ruebill, the head of intelligence. 'Can't we use this concern over Satumine Terrorists as a reason to stay?'

'A Justiciar has been dispatched,' Ruebill said, joining Anden by the buffet and snatching up the whole plate of mini strawberry meringues as he always did, which was why a second plate was stashed in the chilled cupboard under the table. 'She is expected within a few hours. She surfaced at the outer belt this morning and is well into her final approach.'

'All the more reason to stay,' Anden said. 'If a Justiciar has been sent, the threat must be credible.'

Ruebill shook his head, pushed two of the pink meringues into his mouth and proceeded to chew noisily. He began talking again long before he had swallowed the creamy mess. 'From what I gather,' he sprayed a few flecks of meringue over the crisp blackness of his captain's uniform, 'the Justiciar is simply following a money trail. Nothing for us to involve ourselves in.'

Anden flicked the powder from his lapels and rolled his eyes. He liked Ruebill, but the intelligence officer really made the most of this 'no ranks' situation.

'Besides,' Ruebill added, applying a fresh dusting over the captain's uniform, 'they still have the two Union Cruisers, not to mention the four stations and the satellites.'

A sharp whistle lanced through Anden's head as his AR implants were suddenly reactivated and an array of screens appeared in the room. The duty officer had activated a tactical alert.

'What have we got?' Anden demanded. Ranks were back on.

'Something came out of shortspace,' the duty officer reported, his face appearing in one of the AR screens. 'It's unannounced and has emerged in low orbit.'

'I have command,' the captain announced, instantly routing the bridge functions to the den's AR environment.

'It's huge,' the tactical officer said, forming his control systems in one corner of the den. 'A kilometre wide. A sphere. It looks almost like a station, but -'

'It's the *Tenjin*,' Ruebill said, flicking a schematic and intelligence dossier to the Captain's array of screens. He followed it with the briefest of synopses which Anden skimmed.

'It's still pretty banged up,' Anden observed. 'Doesn't look like they had a chance to repair much of the damage done at Teroh.'

'Looks superficial,' someone opined. 'All of her major systems seem to be functioning.'

'Comms?'

'Nothing yet.'

'Do we think they are hostile?'

Ruebill gave a sideways look and said, 'Given their past conduct I think we need to assume they are.'

'What are our chances?'

'We're more heavily armed than the small Network Sentries it faced at Teroh, and we have two sizable Union Cruisers as backup. It will be tough but -'

'Christ!' Anden yelled as the white column of a plasma lance bridged the space between the immense sphere and one of Pellitoe's orbital stations, penetrating its core with ease and rupturing its primary generators.

'Why haven't they polarised their hull?' he screamed. He pulled up a new screen, encompassing only the breached station, just in time to witness in chilling clarity the failure of its reactors. Within a second the station was consumed by a white bubble and a thousand people were dead.

'All stations reporting tactical alert,' someone said.

About time, Anden thought. 'Bring us into range.'

'Yes sir,' the pilot said. 'It's going to take a few minutes to get close enough.' The *Vulpine* had been holding position around the lunar orbit where most incoming ships were expected to surface from shortspace. Nobody would be so reckless as to risk plotting a course any closer. Whoever was piloting the *Tenjin* didn't seem to care.

Why isn't anyone opening fire?' he demanded.

Ruebill provided a tactical schematic of the situations around the planet, overlaying the fields of fire. Immediately the problem was obvious. The *Tenjin* had come in beneath the orbit of the stations and defensive satellites, and all of the primary weapons of those orbital platforms were aimed *away* from Pellitoe. The only things pointing down were anti-personnel lasers which the operators obviously knew wouldn't even warm the *Tenjin's* hull.

'How long to reposition?'

'The Area Trustee's office is saying five minutes,' Ruebill reported. 'I would say closer to seven.'

'And the Union cruisers?'

'Three hundred year old tech,' Steit reminded the captain. 'The weapons take a while to charge'

'Then tell them to launch their fighter drones.'

'They're already on it.'

Like puffs of pollen, clouds of white dots jetted from the two cruisers from ports along their bullet sections. Screens with a higher degree of magnification showed each dot to be a ten metre dart equipped with arrays of thrusters down both sides and a large jet to the rear. At their noses were barrels of medium level particle accelerators and already a few of the drones had opened fire on the *Tenjin*. Within five seconds they were all peppering the tarnished and buckled sphere with flickering beams of high energy particles. The *Tenjin* responded with wide beam lasers and sweeping fans of plasma, too low in power to concern the now polarised hulls of the stations and ships but sufficient to detonate in their dozens the puny darts and the realigning defence satellites.

'They're barely scorching its hull,' Steit observed.

'The particle accelerators are losing twenty percent of their power in the thin atmosphere,' Ruebill said. 'But even in vacuum they just wouldn't be enough to get through. The *Tenjin* is emitting some kind of defensive field.'

'Then tell them to focus their fire. Maybe we can overload some of the field generators and punch a hole through.'

Ruebill nodded and magnified on a screen the gaping breach in the hollow hemisphere, the most obvious legacy of the Teroh debacle. 'There,' he said. 'The generators on the surrounding sections have to extend over the hole. *That's* the weak spot.' But as soon as the drones began focussing their attack the vast orb rotated, turning its weakest point from the largest part of the swarm. The darts attempted to match the rotation but couldn't keep up and so selected alternative targets while every passing second saw their number whittled further.

Finally came the flash of the Union Cruisers pounding the *Tenjin's* defensive field and the orange flame of overloading generators began to splash across its surface.

'Ground based defences are coming on-line,' Ruebill said, and Anden smiled. The rogue science station was going to take some beating, but it *would* be beaten.

'Get our own drones ready,' he ordered. 'I want them launched as soon as we are within weapon range.'

As a fusion cascade ripped through one of the box-kite struts to the rear of the lead cruiser, Anden felt a twinge of guilty delight: would this atrocity be reason enough to keep the *Vulpine* around Pellitoe a little longer?

Chapter 31

In the simplified onion-skin model of special dimensions, pointspace is the core of the onion. More precisely (but still wildly inaccurately) it is the immeasurable zero-dimensional singularity at the very heart of the core. It is the lowest of all special dimension, a space of absolutely no distance which, paradoxically, lies beneath every part of all dimension above it. From pointspace you can instantly reach anywhere in the known (and unknown) universe. It was during our most audacious experiment to traverse this singularity, with the ill-fated Tenjin experiment, that Consul declared its most recent war with the Human Jurisdiction. Was it that the Artificial Consciousness feared we might succeed, and therefore gain a tactical advantage? I offer for your consideration another theory: Consul has already pierced and explored the skin of pointspace and discovered something he would rather mankind did not yet learn of.

The Enguine Manifesto

Endella Mariacroten: In the Pellitoe System, in the Swinell Union, in the Fertile Belt

Endella had hoped to slip unnoticed onto Pellitoe, reporting only to the Sector Trustee with whom she had already been in contact. But she had been spotted surfacing from shortspace, on the outskirts of the Pellitoe system, by the early warning grid before her Justiciary codes had been able to intervene. Although able to avert from her ship the gaze of any surveillance, her presence was reported to the Area Trustee and, she assumed, the Office Trustees, both on the planet and in command of the single Jurisdiction Sentry. Her discomfort didn't stem

from any irrational desire to remain hidden from the
Administration's leadership, rather her concern that it was
a member of that leadership - probably an Office Trustee -
to whom the embezzled funds from Dendrell had been
forwarded before distribution to the Satumine.

The events of the last few minutes, however, rendered
such concerns moot. A team of auditors could take up her
pursuit of the money. She now had a far greater threat to
pursue.

Within a minute of her pointspace comms picking up
the encoded tactical net, an IB tactician on the Sector
Trustee's staff had compiled a report for her and issued its
recommendations. They were not orders; the IB tactician
had worked so fast there was no possibility that the Sector
Trustee could have even been informed of the suggestions,
let alone ratified them as orders. But Endella was
experienced enough to know that these suggestions were
almost guaranteed to be confirmed within the next hour.

After skimming through the *Tenjin's* tactical file she
more carefully took in the short paragraph explaining the
tactician's recommendation. She grinned and replied,
simply stating she would endeavour to do her best. But,
when a cold blade of apprehension stabbed at her core,
she wondered if the Administration would have involved
her at all had any other Justiciar been in range. Clenching
her fist and swallowing back the self-doubt, she resolved
to prove to the Administration, and to herself, that she was
as coldly efficient an operative as she had ever been.

She linked her cockpit fully into the tactical network
and, as her presence was authenticated and incorporated
into the command chain, she took in the situation as it
now stood. Ground based plasma lances had been brought
on-line and were concentrating their fire on a single area of
the *Tenjin's* hull, blowing out dozens of field generators
and causing long black flakes to peel away and crumble
from the station into the thin atmosphere of orbit. But the
Tenjin had, as yet, to fire a single volley at the ground based

installations. The orbital defence platforms, having been useless for several minutes, had now been realigned and were concentrating their efforts on another point on the station's hull. They, however, seemed fair game for the *Tenjin's* formidable arsenal and with most of the antiquated drones from the Union Cruisers now vaporised, the wide angle plasma and laser weapons were sweeping through the ranks of evenly spaced satellites, ruining them with just the lightest of touches, lighting up the Pellitoe sky with the glow of countless new stars.

The two Swinell Union Cruisers were not so easily dispatched and in concert with the relentless ground based weapons they were beginning to overwhelm the powerful energy field protecting the vast station's hull. The ability of the hull to absorb energy, unfortunately, was far greater than conventional Jurisdiction technology, and when the energy fields began to collapse the expected devastation failed to present itself. Ever greater chunks of absorptive hull flaked away only to reveal yet more fresh plating beneath.

The *Tenjin* began to move, slowly at first but soon with such velocity its leading hemisphere glowed red as it dragged through atmosphere. The glow subsided as the station gained altitude, rising from the upper atmosphere and into the lowest satellite orbits, ploughing effortlessly through constellations of solar power satellites, local comms hubs and, as it rose higher, the few remaining defence platforms.

Endella saw where it was heading even before the tactical network was updated with strategic predictions. The *Tenjin* was rising to put one of the orbital stations between it and the two union cruisers. But it didn't turn its weapons on the spoked-wheel station; it just kept firing through the gaps at the cruisers. The ships and the ground weapons, however, slowed their fire and then ceased altogether.

'Idiots,' Endella muttered but could offer no comment over the net until her authority was approved, which seemed to be taking forever. The cruisers and the ground weapons were capable of targeting the *Tenjin* without any risk of striking the orbital station, but if the six kilometre sphere was destroyed, the station could not avoid being caught in the blast. A heated debate arose on the network, with the chain of command momentarily failing as the Swinell Union authorities refused the federal Administration's order to resume firing. It was the brave commander of the orbital station in question who, in the end, resolved the discord. Its weapons finally realigned to aim down, the station fired its every weapon at the *Tenjin* just a few hundred meters below.

Its human shield evidently compromised, the *Tenjin* fired a swarm of missiles and rail-gun projectiles which, at this range, were immune to the anti-munitions role of the station's meteor lasers. Explosions began pulling the orbital station apart and the *Tenjin* brought itself quickly out of range of the ensuing detonations, suffering only buffeting from gravitational distortions.

The *Tenjin* rose further into a higher orbit, closing on the two Union Cruisers, escaping all but the most powerful of the ground-based weapons, and leaving a trail of exhausted hull plating in its wake. Eventually it exceeded the range of even the most powerful ground weapons and so slowed its velocity, evidently not wishing to come any closer to the fast approaching Federal Sentry, the *Vulpine*. It faced off against the Union Cruisers and traded blow for blow, tearing through the inferior ships with increasing ease as the defensive hull plates were exhausted and the weaker plates beneath exposed.

At last her authority was confirmed and Endella took her place beside the Area Trustee at the top of the command chain. She didn't bother addressing him - he was worse than useless in this situation. Instead she contacted the man to whom the Area Trustee had deferred every tactical decision thus far: Office Trustee Anden Macer, the captain of the *Vulpine*.

'When you get close enough,' she instructed, using only vocal comms, 'I want you to launch ten percent of your drones.'

'Hello Justiciar,' Anden said, harried but respectful of her honorary Area Trustee rank. 'I was rather intending to launch all of my drones. If they can all fire on the same spot, they have a chance of punching a hole through to a vulnerable system within the station. Ten percent are just going to scuff the surface.'

'I don't want them to fire on the *Tenjin*.

'Excuse me?'

'You have probably noticed the *Tenjin* has been charging its shortspace burrower ever since arriving here.' She knew he had; it was the reason no reinforcements had been dispatched from the nearest worlds- by the time they arrived in three weeks, the *Tenjin* would be long gone and quite possibly en-route to one of the now defenceless planets from which they would have been sent.

'I have,' Anden confirmed. 'But don't worry; the *Vulpine* is more than up to the task. The *Tenjin* will never make it into shortspace.'

Activating a pre-prepared code carrier, Endella isolated herself and Anden Macer from the tactical net and allowed an image of her face to be transmitted. She looked the Vulpine's captain hard in the eyes.

'Listen carefully,' she said, her voice level and menacing. 'You are not going to destroy the *Tenjin*.' Anden was visibly taken aback but said nothing. 'You are going to use the drones to form an interference wave with their particle accelerators, to prevent the *Tenjin* from securing a clean burrow into shortspace.'

'The drones won't last more than a couple of minutes,' Anden said, though his tone suggested that was the least of his problems with this plan.

'Which is why you are only sending ten percent. Just keep replacing your losses. The *Tenjin* needs another ten minutes of clean burrowing time. Don't let it have that long.'

'Why?' Anden demanded.

Endella knew she didn't have to answer and suspected Anden would, ultimately, follow the order regardless. But she needed to be sure.

'I'm going to be there shortly,' she explained. 'And I intend to be aboard the *Tenjin* when it finally drops into shortspace.'

'Why not let me just destroy it?'

Endella watched yet more of the *Tenjin's* incredible hull peel away and its improbably powerful weapons carve through a cruiser's box-kite struts. 'We are at war with Consul,' she said. 'And that rogue station has, somehow, developed technology far beyond anything we, or the Artificial Consciousness, have managed to create. I intend to secure that station and fill it with our best scientists.'

Anden looked down and sighed. 'If I can't destroy it,' he said, 'and I have to keep it from escaping, we are going to lose both of the Swinell Union Cruisers.'

'I know,' Endella said with practised detachment but with an unwelcome twist in her stomach. In truth, she didn't expect the *Vulpine* to survive either.

Chapter 32

The mechanics of Pointspace comms are generally unfathomable to the average citizen. As with practically every form of communication since the telegraph, however, the end user's ignorance matters not one jot and we will not attempt to explain its intricacies here. Should you wish to learn more the Jurisdiction is generous with its education programmes and you are welcome to advance your knowledge as far as you are capable. For now it is sufficient to know that through our vibrations against the skin of the lowest spacial dimension we are able to transmit data to any point in higher dimensional space (the realm in which we exist) almost instantly, knitting the distant colonies and unions into a coherent and homogeneous society. You may communicate as easily with those a hundred thousand light years distant as you may those in your own city. We are all of the same Human Jurisdiction and there is no barrier of distance to foster dangerous isolationism.

Rehabilitation: A Survivor's Guide

Galman Tader: On Pellitoe, in the Swinell Union, in the Fertile Belt

Like everybody else in the wide oval park, Galman was entranced by the periodic flashes lighting up the dirty red night sky. Unlike most, however, he was no so naive as to believe it was an AR display laid on for his entertainment. Tumble had identified the flashes as orbital explosions. Satellites. When a far larger flash smeared the sky with ribbons of orange fire Galman guessed a station or ship had suffered the same fate as those hundreds of satellites. When a second such explosion sent shock waves through the upper atmosphere, reaching the lowest levels with enough energy to disperse the sparse cloud cover, Galman knew for certain something big had been taken out. Only the failure of a great many gravity coils could send such powerful waves so easily through the vacuum of high orbit. A murmur of concern passed through the gawping crowds and, by the time another massive detonation lit the sky, most had woken up to the idea that something terrible was happening above their peaceful world. It was then that the ground based weapons' fire became visible.

Maybe the authorities felt the populace needed to see a defence was being mounted, or perhaps they just didn't feel there was any point disguising the obvious conflict any longer. Whatever the reason, the AR sheaths disguising the beams of accelerated particles were deactivated and for a while dozens of bright columns streaked across the red night, emanating from within the city and from the wilderness for miles in every direction, all converging on a distant point far above. Apparently a single enemy. It didn't take long for the beams to subside and, for the most part, people took this as a good sign. Galman wasn't sure. Tumble thought the battle had probably just moved out from the weapons' range and, if the ships up there didn't defeat the mystery aggressor, it would probably be back soon enough to concentrate on the planet based threats.

'You must be able to see something,' Galman insisted as he and Tumble made their way quickly out of the park, heading for the hotel.

'Just a little debris in low orbit,' the machine, still looking like a goblin, said. 'My AR inputs are blinding me to anything higher up.'

'This has got to be it,' Galman said. 'Whatever Ambondice-Ambondice was planning, this is it.'

The park entrance was an arch of rock, glowing with a blue inner fire and, although it was wide and un-gated, Galman was forced to jostle through the anxious throng heading out of the park to the imagined safety of their homes. Just because the planet-based weapons had fallen silent, people still weren't comfortable being outside. When yet another large but far off explosion stained the night with a lingering smudge like some distant nebula, the nervous crowd became a panicked exodus. And yet they kept to the AR gate, unable to cast off the illusory world which told them the high park walls actually existed. Galman stepped out of the press of bodies, pushed an arm through the wall to check no drab-reality barrier underpinned the illusion, and stepped through, shuddering at the unpleasant pressure his inputs simulated against his nerves. Tumble followed behind.

The crowd outside the park was no less chaotic. Galman supposed it was like this all over the planet, at least in the hemisphere facing the devastation.

'Look at them,' Galman said. 'Where the hell do they think they are running?'

'Where the hell are *we* running?' Tumble countered.

Galman stopped, causing a fleeing Satumine and a human to pile into him from behind.

'Watch out,' Galman spat, stumbling forward, but the interspecies couple was already twenty meters down the road.

'So?' Tumble said, following Galman into a wide side street out of the hysteria of the main road. 'Where are we going?'

Galman looked into the Goblin's green eyes, knowing they didn't correlate with the IB machine's visual sensors. He had, he realised, been heading for the hotel, fleeing home in the same instinctive and irrational way as everybody else. He leaned back against a flawlessly polished wall - a cheap AR fascia through which he could just about feel the slightly rough cold metal beneath.

'I don't know,' he admitted to his artificial friend.

'If this is what the Satumine were planning,' Tumble pressed, 'don't you want to at least do *something*?'

Galman's head lolled forward and he wiped his face in his hands. 'Like what?' he muttered. 'I came here to stop another atrocity, but I've done fuck all. I'm just a backwater cop way out of my depth and so far beyond my remit I'm lucky I'm not in prison. I should have just reported my concerns and let those with some actual authority deal with it.'

Tumble joined Galman, leaning against the wall, and patted his arm with an AR hand. 'You tried that,' he reminded him. 'You told Office Trustee Cordem Hastergado and he practically authorised you to investigate further.'

'No,' Galman said, 'I should have just told someone on Diaclom.'

'Told them what?' Tumble snapped with unexpected force. 'That you forced your way into a Satumine house, without a warrant or, for that matter, a valid Constabulary card, and *tortured* the occupant before murdering him and his wife?' He then laughed a cold simulated chuckle. 'Do you think they would have given a damn about the vague intelligence you gained from that?'

'They might have followed up - '

'- Listen,' Tumble said, suddenly calm. 'Nobody was ever going to uncover what was going on. You went well beyond your remit, well beyond the *law*, in your pursuit of the Satumine, and even you didn't get to the truth in time.' The goblin pointed to the sky where the smudge of the most recent explosion was now flecked with glitter-like flashes of white. 'Whatever is going on up there, *nobody* could have prevented it.'

Galman found little comfort in Tumble's reasoning. Perhaps nobody else had been in a position to stop this, but Galman *had* been, and he had failed. That the events in orbit might be unrelated to his investigation of the Satumine didn't occur to him. He turned to face the wall and butted its true rough surface with his forehead, muttering curses to himself.

'So that's it,' Tumble said, his accusing tone slicing through Galman's self-pity. 'You're just giving up?'

'Giving up?' Galman hissed, not turning from the wall. 'It's a bit late to do anything now isn't it?'

'Is it? We're still here aren't we?' The goblin grabbed Galman by the scruff of his jumpsuit's collar and pulled him from the wall, probably anchored with hidden tentacles to the opposite wall for leverage, and practically threw him into the main street. 'I don't see any destruction down *here*,' the machine yelled to Galman over the panicked shouts of the crowd. 'The worst hasn't happened yet.'

'For a moment Galman said nothing, just looked about the embellished street and its terrified occupants. They all seemed so helpless, so defenceless. If he was the only man in a position to help, to stop what was to come, then it was his duty to act.

'Have you finished decoding Ambondice-Ambondice's AR positional codes?' he asked with renewed purpose and composure.

'Just about,' Tumble said with an AR smile.

'Good. We're going after him tonight.' Then, lowering his voice to a mumble, knowing Tumble alone would hear, he added, 'But first I need a gun. See what you can do.'

'It'll be expensive.'

'Spend everything we have, if you have to.'

Chapter 33

You may be having a hard time accepting the truth of the conspiracy laid down in this treatise. How, you may ask, could the Satumine be the dominant species, manipulating and using us from behind obfuscated schemes and plots, when they are so abused by us? It may seem ludicrous to believe that they willingly allowed themselves to become such a beaten people, but to think like that is to attribute human motivations and thought patterns to these alien creatures. Certainly few humans would have given up the dominant position the Satumine seemed to have over us after first contact, but that is precisely what the Satumine did. We did not discover the other addresses built into the Earth Frame through our own ingenuity - the Satumine allowed us to discover them. The Satumine wanted us to find the Network and to imagine ourselves the dominant race. They do not share our emotions, they do not feel as we do, and they are content to suffer what we might consider humiliation and abuse, for they see a far bigger picture, a far greater victory.

The Truth: A treatise on the Satumine Conspiracy

Indin-Indin: On Satute, in the Network

Ancient Satumine systems reached out hungrily for the neural fibres threaded through Indin-Indin's homogeneous body mass, and he reached back to complete the connection. Human pilots, with their meagre analogue of true Satumine neurons hidden in the structure of their primitive brains, often reported a cold sense of dreadful apprehension and anxiety as the connection was made to the more open systems of a Network frame, but Indin-Indin felt nothing more unusual than the autonomous flexing of an invisible and previously unknown extension of his body. What his body actually *was*, however, was something he would have to consider when he had more time. There were no organs, no bones, not even the eyes or other sensory components of his old body - just a spongy body mass and the neural fibres. But he looked human, though that was his choice and it was merely cosmetic: an organic mask across the pink-red sponge. He could change, should he chose to do so, provided he had another few hours to spend on the task.

Striding quickly through the city passages, opening doors with less than a thought, he made use of a positional system which appeared on every wall he passed, guiding him back to where he left Aggregate's cloaked shuttle. He felt there were so many more systems grasping for contact but he pushed away their clawing requests. If he started lighting up this city, this civilisation beneath his own world, he would be noticed. Besides, he had no idea what he might start moving down there in the depths of the somnolent metropolis; this was, after all, the foundations of the modern Satumine hive, and any movement could have seismic repercussions.

Catching a glimpse of himself in a reflective wall section, Indin-Indin took a moment to fully appreciate what he had turned himself into. Using only his mental image of a human as a template he had reformed the putty of his true Satumine body and excreted a skin indistinguishable to the eye from a real human. The excretion had even formed a thick head of hair, eyes, teeth, fingernails. It was remarkable and slightly disgusting. He blinked, watching the thin lids close over eyes through which he wasn't looking. Every cell of his body was identical and each was sensitive to the full EM spectrum, to the vibrations of sound in the air, and even to the aroma particles ordinarily picked up by a modern Satumine's chest follicles or by a human nose. His ancestors truly had debased themselves when they traded their superior bodies and minds for some cheap human-inspired imitation.

Indin-Indin was tempted to reform, to discard this offensive human shape which felt like an insult to his kind, a continuation of the mockery, but he had chosen this shape for a reason. He would soon be travelling to a human world.

Across his shoulders he retained the now burnt-out device and its egg-shaped container. Aggregate had ensured it would last for only one transformation, one act of Atavism, thus ensuring Indin-Indin's compliance with the terms of their deal. Not until he had done the task asked of him would Aggregate instruct him in the method by which the device had altered a pod and caused it to restore his birth right. Only then could Indin-Indin return his entire race to its true majesty.

A chill passed through his new body and he stepped away from the reflective wall, disgusted and unwilling to look at himself. But it was not his form that repelled him rather the realisation of his true motivation. Cleared of the crude human neural architecture, his mind no longer suffered confusion, indecision or the capacity for delusion or self-deceit - habit caused him to insist, at least at first, that his motivation was the betterment and empowerment of the Satumine. But he could not maintain the lie any more than he could close any of the trillion ever alert eyes that were his bodily cells. No, he was doing this for nothing nobler than pride, and vengeance against a Human Jurisdiction which had belittled and subjugated the Satumine. In the past, perhaps, that realisation would have caused Indin-Indin no concern; he might even have believed it a genuinely worthy cause. But now? The instincts and memories of his ancestors came wrapped in the morality and sensibilities of the True Satumine.

He couldn't alter his dark motivations. So instead he took comfort in the knowledge that the result of his petty vengeance would be laudable regardless of his reasons for acting.

It took only a few hours to return to the shuttle, his route being both more direct and not suffering the same delays at the doors that had stymied his inward journey. The shuttle could not be seen, even by the Indin-Indin's heightened and expanded omni-senses. Either the cloak still functioned or the little craft had been discovered and removed. There appeared to be nobody around, no sign that his shuttle had been found. If anybody was hiding, waiting for him, he would have noticed them. It wasn't overconfidence, merely a realistic appraisal of his improved abilities and senses, an appraisal confirmed by genetic memory.

Touching the small remote, Indin-Indin called for the cloak to deactivate and was gratified though not particularly surprised to see the shuttle exactly where he had left it. Once aboard he reactivated the cloak, noting a self-repair suite had done what it could to stabilise the temperamental system. The report it provided was not overly optimistic, predicting a catastrophic failure of the cloak, and the thrusters, within a few hours of sustained flight. Both systems ought to last a while longer in vacuum, but Indin-Indin knew the majority of his work would be within the atmosphere of this or another planet.

The ascent through Satute's layers was more comfortable than the earlier descent. The shuttle was not carrying the extreme velocity of interplanetary flight, fighting to slow its re-entry while gravity dragged it down; the ascent was slow and cautious, at least until clear of the final sub-layer. Then, with no danger of striking a building, the shuttle accelerated brutally, attaining escape velocity within a few seconds and straining the cloak horribly. But none of the tell-tale flashes or streams emerged to betray his departure, and no interceptors were scrambled. A few minutes later the cloak stabilised, clear at last of the atmosphere.

He knew where the invisible pointspace frame was hidden, floating in the highest orbit, shielded by an ancient cloak but surrounded by modern Satumine defensive platforms. He had spent years working on those platforms and, he suspected, the knowledge he gained aboard them was the reason Aggregate chose him for this blessing. Indin-Indin knew the codes to briefly usurp control of the entire frame monitoring network. He plotted the short journey around the planet and into a far higher orbit than the one into which he had already risen. It was going to take an hour. It could have been done more quickly, but the orbits were packed with countless satellites and trash from a millennium of civilisation, and no cloak was capable of hiding an accidental collision with a communications satellite or a large chunk of decommissioned orbital junk.

Indin-Indin realised he felt hungry. It was different to the normal sensation preceding the start of a new digestion cycle: there was no softening of the resin sealing his abdominal flaps. He didn't even *have* abdominal flaps. But he knew he was hungry, and by dint of his genetic memory he knew instinctively how to eat. In a compartment under his chair he found a small store of dry biscuits provided by Aggregate. There was no label, no instructions, but by simply brushing his fingers across the powdery disks he knew their precise nutritional content. With only the briefest though he formed a digestive organ in his hand, like a heart sized balloon swelling from his palm, filling it with a chemical soup designed specifically for the biscuits. He could digest almost any organic matter. A sphincter formed on the back of his hand and small incisors grew about its clenched muscles. It took seconds to chew through five biscuits, and minutes to digest them. Focusing, he became aware of every cell in his body and fascinated he observed the nutrition and energy of the biscuits pass from the temporary stomach in his hand, by a process similar to osmosis, into every cell. Having reabsorbed the juices, the stomach blister reverted to homogeneous body mass. That small meal, with no part wasted, would see him through a few days. Water, which he found in bottles next to the biscuits, was absorbed directly through his cells as he pushed one of his fingers into a bottle.

The network of frame defences was large, but it didn't impress Indin-Indin. He was blasé to the platforms, had seen them too many times, had seen them break down, had seen the programming which would probably never even let the weapons open fire should the Humans come through the frame in force. The defences were there for show. He uploaded his codes and with only his superior True Satumine intellect he countered the internal surveillance programs with the speed of an IB machine. Moments later the pointspace frame was undefended and, reaching out like so many human pilots, he called on it to uncloak.

Chapter 34

Satute is a world crowded beyond farce. There are no Satumine colonies, and two hundred billion Satumine have been forced to deface their world to support themselves. I am not so far to the left in my politics to suggest we forget the abuses perpetuated by the Satumine on the humans who first set through the pointspace frame almost a thousand years ago, but that abuse lasted barely a century. Any debt owed by the Satumine has long since been repaid through their subjugation and degradation at the hands of the Human Jurisdiction. The time for grudges has long past; it's time to allow these broken people to leave the prison of their single dying rock and create new colonies of their own. Are we so insecure and unsure of our dominion over the galaxy that we cannot countenance the idea of a few Satumine colonies amongst the glut of human worlds? Are we so damaged by our wars with consul that we have lost that which sets us apart from that monster? Has he robbed us of our compassion; our humanity?

The Enguine Manifesto

Anden Macer: Aboard the *Vulpine*, in orbit around Pellitoe, in the Swinell Union, in the Fertile Belt

The captains of the two Swinell Union cruisers were not following orders, or at least they were not following Anden's orders. If the Area Trustee was responsible for their apparent insubordination the man wasn't admitting it. Watching the burning cruisers fire desperately on the looming sphere of the *Tenjin*, Anden couldn't bring himself to blame them. He wasn't going to expend anything but the bare minimum of effort in convincing them to refrain from destroying the rogue station. He had re-issued the Justiciar's instruction three times; there was little else he could do right now beyond opening fire on the offending vessels. Besides, the cruisers had no hope of bringing down the *Tenjin* before it finished carving them up, unless the *Vulpine* more aggressively joined the fray. Regrettably that wasn't going to happen.

Striding quickly through the corridor linking to the primary bridge, his entourage of senior officers close behind, the captain watched as the *Tenjin* focused three plasma lances on a weapon port of the smaller cruiser, the obscurely named *Trepan*. The senior officers filed in, making their way up to the suspended disk of the command floor by way of a sloped rolling path. Anden took his seat up there while the others replaced their portable AR controls with more permanent equivalents. Beneath the command floor, extending out for thirty meters in all directions, the circular lower bridge was loud with well-practiced, but none-the-less desperate, activity. Several hundred crew members worked down there, performing the tasks which others might have assigned to the IB machines. Those so inclined had probably never seen the devastation wrought by a single well aimed attack to the Intelligence-bridge suites. On Federal Sentries, where the potential for armed conflict was a real, if infrequent possibility, humans remained firmly in command.

The perimeter wall offered a panoramic AR view, as if it was perched atop the highest level, looking out into space. It encouraged a sense of vulnerability – a sense not entirely unjustified for the few walls between the bridge and the outer hull offered less protection from that *Tenjin's* weapons than the captain might have hoped for.

'Can we at least give them some covering fire?' Keddy asked, bringing up onto the public screens confirmation of the *Vulpine's* weapon readiness.

'We aren't allowed to destroy the *Tenjin*,' Anden said, the instruction tasting bitter as he repeated it.

'Well at least let me take out some of their weapons.'

Anden sucked through his teeth and tugged nervously at his dreadlocks. He wanted to say yes, wanted to order his crew to begin tearing apart the *Tenjin's* weapons, even though it would draw the attention of those weapons to his own ship. But he had the honour of his ship to consider. That honour was, he had to admit, more important than the safety of those two Union Cruisers. Still, it didn't sit easy.

'Captain?'

'The box kite is detached? Yes? Right, get us closer,' Anden ordered. 'Once the drones are launched, we might be able to justify taking out some of the *Tenjin's* guns.' He gave his tactical officer a warning glance and added, 'But only those weapons threatening the drones.'

Keddy snorted but didn't challenge her captain. This wasn't the officers' den, and Anden's officers would never question his orders in front of the crew.

The *Vulpine* accelerated, closing the gap it had been maintaining for a couple of minutes while the drone flight-plans had been codified. Now they were coming within range of the *Tenjin's* weapons, and it didn't take long for impossibly overpowered lances to be turned on the larger more threatening target presented by the Federal Sentry. Reports of concussive damage came in almost immediately. The polarised hull plates absorbed the brunt of the initial salvo but were unable to stop entirely the appalling energy from punching high frequency waves through adjoining sections.

'Cosmetic damage,' Steit summarised. 'Missed our weapons and primary systems.' Then more quietly he asked, 'Return fire?'

'Not yet. Just get the drones out there.' Seconds later - in which the force of the attack became noticeable even in the bridge at the ship's heart - the first wave of drones was launched.

'Sit down and strap in,' Anden ordered his officers who, in turn, relayed the command to the crew on the main floor below. The rattle and clunk of harnesses briefly filled the bridge and then everyone got back to work.

'Port nineteen is buckling,' someone reported and a ship schematic appeared on the Captain's main screen, highlighting the failing hull section in a flashing red glow.

'Secure internal bulkheads,' the captain ordered by rote, his attention fixed on the swarm of dart-like drones forming up, ready to execute their complex manoeuvres.

The *Tenjin* turned a few of its lesser weapons on the tiny unarmoured vessels, vaporising them one at a time. It's immensely powerful primary weapons could have annihilated vast swathes of the drones in an instant, but it would have been like swatting at flies with a war hammer. Sometimes weapons could be *too* large. The colossal beams simply couldn't aim quickly enough at the targets so close to the station.

'It's going to take them all out eventually' Ruebill said. And that was exactly what Anden had been hoping to hear. Suddenly energised he pulled up more tactical screens and began pointing out targets. 'Open fire,' he instructed. 'Only her weapons.'

Chapter 35

Having spent the majority, if not the entirety of your life, captive in one of Consul's IB farms, it is likely you have never seen a Satumine in person. It is possible, in fact, you might not even be aware of the race. It need not be an issue, for our cousins in the Jurisdiction are so thinly spread beyond their single world that you might not ever meet one. For now it will suffice to know the Satumine are in some way genetically related to us and whatever it is that introduced our genes to their race also stripped them of the ability to utilise the technology which once made them a mighty civilisation. The Network worlds and the Frames connecting them are of the Original Satumine race's design. We thank them for their gift and we tolerate their hybrid offspring.

Rehabilitation: A Survivor's Guide

Galman Tader: On Pellitoe, in the Swinell Union, in the Fertile Belt

The rural buggy wasn't stolen, as such, but Galman had certainly breached the conditions of the rental agreement. Although supposedly suited to any off-road environment, the rental company had insisted the six-wheeled open-top buggy be taken no further than the recreational fields and hills of the city's suburban belt, and a flashing alert on the lightly embellished dashboard indicated the company were aware of Galman's disregard for their contractual stipulations. But nobody was attempting to force a comms link, either with the buggy's computer or direct to Galman. There was probably nobody still working there. The news nets, although sparing in details of the incident in orbit, were advising everyone to remain indoors, wherever they were, but reports showed millions fleeing their places of work or recreation and running for the irrationally assumed security of their homes.

'Can you shut off that alert, please?' he asked Tumble.

The IB machine had discarded his goblin skin at Galman's request - Galman felt more comfortable seeing what his friend was really doing. Not speaking, perhaps a simulated sulk at the loss of his skin, Tumble extruded a thin needle tipped rod and stabbed the alligator-skin embellished dashboard. Immediately the alert was silenced and Tumble withdrew his appendage.

'Have you been able to find anything more from the secure nets?' Galman asked, manually steering the agile buggy around a young family of flesh trees. The affangrass here was un-swollen and short, and barely reached the top of the vehicle's thick tyres, presenting almost no resistance to the powerful machine which left a path of turquoise affan mush in its wake.

'Tumble?' Galman pressed when the machine didn't answer. Given the uncertainty of the orbital incident, the possibility of an IB coverage failure was a serious concern. 'You still bridged?'

'Yes,' Tumble said, begrudgingly breaking his silence.

'So have you got any more news?'

'Nothing.'

'Whatever happened - or is still happening - it's big,' Galman observed, perhaps a little obviously. He then pointed to the closest of the thousand thick red AR columns connecting the sky with various points in the city and the wilderness. They were public warnings of predicted re-entry trajectories for anything expected to survive the friction of atmospheric deceleration, and the size of the red domes of projected impact sites, the blast radius, suggested some massive impacts were likely.

'Even if they shoot most of it down,' he said. 'There's still going to be a crap load of damage.'

Tumble synthesised a snort. 'At least everyone knows precisely where the damage will be. They are going to have hours to evacuate. Probably won't even lose any of their belongings, apart from the buildings.'

Galman nodded. When his family had been killed by Satumine bombs, there had been no such warning. But any thoughts of cheapening the magnitude of this atrocity were swept away by the realisation that thousands had probably lost their lives on the stations and ships in orbit. For all he knew, they were still being killed up there.

'It could still get a lot worse,' Tumble pointed out as Galman negotiated a suddenly steep climb up a small rock strewn mound, catching air in a short jump at the crest. 'Whoever is up there, they could still be intent on attacking the planet.'

Galman nodded again. That was exactly why he was out there, chasing Ambondice-Ambondice's AR positional codes. The buggy clipped a pothole hidden beneath the affan grass and jarred Galman from a reverie in which he was the lauded hero of the hour.

'Eyes on the road,' Tumble said though there was nothing like a road our there in the buffer between city and wild reserves.

'She can take it,' Galman said of the buggy.

'Probably,' Tumble conceded. The suspension was capable of far greater shocks. 'But it can't be doing your spine any good.'

Galman shrugged and steered the vehicle towards where the affan grass was thinning and giving way to the cocktail sticks of splint grass. 'I haven't been this healthy in decades,' he said, noting the change in sound from the wet squelch of pulped affan grass to the snap and crunch of the tiny wooden tooth-pick splint grass beneath solid tyres. 'It's going to take much more than a few bumps to knock my back out again.'

'He's moving,' Tumble suddenly observed, highlighting on an AR screen the position of Ambondice-Ambondice.

The dot of yellow was travelling, at speed, across the buffer region and drawing closer to the reserve.

'Think he's heading for the wilderness?' Galman asked, plotting an intercept route and changing direction with a long skid which sprayed a lone flesh tree with a hail of wooden shards.

'I hope not,' Tumble replied. The pistol he had been able to acquire for Galman had cost almost their entire funds and yet was hopelessly inadequate for the job of keeping Galman safe in the reserves. It would kill a Satumine easily enough, but the native wildlife of fertile worlds was notoriously tough to put down and, without the pheromone towers and high frequency pulse emitters which kept the buffers clear of the creatures, Galman and Tumble would have been set upon very soon after venturing into the wilderness. Had the small laser pistol not been so overpriced, there might have been enough left to hire an armoured safari truck, with its own pheromone systems. Ambondice-Ambondice was probably in a position to move a lot more freely - Galman knew the kinds of funds being sent his way.

A huge shadow was suddenly drawn across the vehicle and the buggy skidded to a stop as a massive endephant stomped across the vehicle's path, treading where Galman would have been. Galman hadn't seen the terrifying creature coming; Tumble must have overridden the vehicle's controls and applied the brakes.

Holding his breath, as if breathing alone would have attracted the enormous beast back to the stationary vehicle, Galman looked across to the crest of the hill to his right over which the endephant had so suddenly appeared. What he saw swarming over the crest was far more startling than the endephant. Scattering trampled and pulverised splint grass, hundreds of two foot long bugs, emotively named spite-beetles, were advancing as a black and yellow chitinous tide.

Still out of Galman's control, the buggy lurched into reverse and backed off with surprising acceleration, bringing Galman's face forward to smack the embellished dashboard. The spite-beetles didn't follow - their hive mind focused intently on the immense meal offered by the already tiring endephant.

Rubbing his throbbing nose, but finding no blood, Galman stood in his seat to get a better look over the small hill to the right. 'What the fuck?' he blurted.

'The pheromone towers and pulse emitters must be down in places, 'Tumble concluded.

'Power shortage?'

'No, the IB machines would have prioritised power to the towers. I expect some of the devices, or the power conduits at least, have been hit by debris.'

'Uh-huh,' Galman mumbled. He wasn't really listening; he was transfixed by the ugly razor-mouthed beetles disappearing down the slope to the left and into the spread of tall flesh trees where the endephant had tried to find shelter. He never saw the pranx-rat leap from behind a large, blue lichen covered bolder. Almost a thousand pounds of dense rodent muscle slammed the side of the buggy with a force that seemed to Galman unnaturally mechanical. Back home in the constantly changing, contrived ecosystem of Diaclom, nothing as hugely destructive as the pranx-rat had ever been introduced without substantial genetic modification - Galman was stunned by its bestial ferocity.

Amid the sound of twisting metal and the crack of ceramics, Galman cried out in shock and the buggy was tipped onto its side, throwing him out into the sharp points of the splint-grass meadow. Like a hundred blunt needles they pierced the thin foundation of his AR attire and jabbed at his flesh. Many blades snapped under his weight but others stabbed through his skin to draw blood which the monstrous rat would undoubtedly smell. Scrambling to stand, puncturing the skin of his palms,

Galman looked up to see the vicious swords of the pranx-rat's two oversized canines slice through the air as they bore down on him. He reached for the small laser pistol but found only an empty holster. The teeth rushed to his body and he closed his eyes.

Searing pain never came, no violent tug at his body, but an unearthly screech sliced through his ears. Not his own screams, he realised, but the bizarre high pitched roar of the pranx-rat.

'Run!' Tumble yelled and Galman opened his eyes to see the machine's every tentacle and appendage extended and coiled about the rodent's neck and slathering snout. 'Go!' he yelled again, catching one of the animal's legs in a thick tentacle and pulling it up, lashing it to the muscular body.

Galman got to his feet fast, glancing about for the weapon but not seeing it, and he sprinted away from the struggling pair, crunching brittle toothpicks beneath his feet.

'Faster, Galman,' Tumble called out. Galman looked back to see sparks shower from the entwined machine and beast as one of Tumble's appendages was ripped from its spherical body. Without the benefit of its old police arsenal, Tumble could do nothing more than wrestle the animal. The pranx-rat was going to win this contest.

There were several flesh trees dotting the splint-grass meadow and Galman considered climbing one of those warm and pungent organisms, but a pranx-rat would make literal mince-meat of such a refuge, reducing it to a puddle of quivering viscera and braving the trees mildly poisonous defences in order to claim its human meal. Besides, the poisons would threaten Galman as much as they would the rat, and his medical supplies, including the anti-toxins, were still in the upturned buggy. He ran past the flesh trees, making instead for the thick trunk of a pheromone tower. It looked to be undamaged but the presence of the animals indicated a failure in the power grid.

A dull pop from behind punctuated the end of the struggle as the pranx-rat tore the last of Tumble's strongest appendages and began galloping after Galman, trailing the IB machine like a dented tin can on a piece of frayed string.

Chapter 36

Even the most liberal and apologetic unions must accept that there have been numerous terrorist attacks for which the Satumine have been proven, irrefutably, to be responsible. Yes, there are human terrorist organisations as well and, unlike the human terrorists, all Justiciary inquiries thus far have failed to uncover a link between what appears to be isolated and wholly independent Satumine terror cells. But all that means is the Satumine terrorists are far better at hiding their connections. No terrorist attack has ever been traced back to Satute, but that does not mean the government of the Satumine home-world is not responsible. How many human children must die before we stop allowing these alien creatures to live free in our colonies?

The Truth: A treatise on the Satumine Conspiracy

Aggregate: On the *Tenjin*, in orbit around Pellitoe, in the Swinell Union, in the Fertile-belt

Another of the particle accelerators was silenced, its magnetic field coils fused by a salvo from the *Vulpine*'s substantial compliment of weapons. Aggregate redirected the power from the now useless coils to bring on line one of the reserve accelerators. Less than a second after the beam had flickered out, a new column of intense energy was lashing out at one of the union cruisers.

Tired of wallowing in his den he shed the obesity of his favoured body. His nanoglands reduced the fat to a thin liquid which splashed across the room when his skin ruptured like a burst water balloon. The skin tightened immediately and now an athletic and lithe young man donned a clean jumpsuit and strode out into one of the control rooms near his sanctum. There was no need for him to be there in this favoured vessel; he was as much the rest of the crew as this so-called captain. But the mind of the human captain, the first he had subsumed, granted more than sentience and human ambition, it granted a sense of self which was difficult to shake. *He* was the captain, the crew merely extensions. It wasn't true, of course, for the captain's body could have been incinerated and Aggregate would have continued undiminished through the rest of the bodies, through the rest of the anchors tying his pointspace self to higher dimensional space.

He reached the control room as one of the Union Cruisers finally succumbed to its wounds. In a series of deceptively restrained explosions, it came apart. Moments later the gravity coils went and a wave battered the other cruiser, setting off a few incidental detonations across its hull. The *Tenjin* and the *Vulpine* were too distant to be seriously impact though Aggregate felt the distortive effects wash through his many bodies.

With a wicked grin he saw his shortspace burrower had begun digging down through the spatial dimensions again. The gravity wave had disturbed the swarm of drones disrupting his departure. The complex interaction of hundreds of intersecting particle accelerators around the *Tenjin's* circumference had been stopping the burrower from cleanly digging down. It was an inexplicable attempt to stop the *Tenjin* from leaving. Every time Aggregate destroyed enough of the tiny drones to counter the effect, the *Vulpine* launched more to replace the losses, but the gravity wave had knocked the entire swarm out of alignment and he had a good few minutes of clean burrowing ahead of him. It wasn't going to be enough to get all the way down into shortspace, but it would be a start. Every time the *Vulpine* had to replace lost drones, the *Tenjin* got few more seconds of burrowing and now, with this unexpected bonus, those accumulating moments might be enough.

But why were they trying to stop him from leaving? They couldn't know he had no intention of destroying the *Vulpine*, that he was deliberately leaving her weapons intact; as far as the humans could know, the *Tenjin* was going to destroy everything in the system. They ought to be encouraging the massive stations departure, not tying it to the higher dimensions.

He fired a brutal salvo at the *Vulpine*'s bullet section, coring through the hull, down a dozen levels into the crew sections. With such telling damage, the *Vulpine*'s captain would not take time to wonder why none of his weapons had been destroyed; he would just count his blessings. Aggregate *wished* he could silence the federal sentry as fully as he had one of the cruisers, for those weapons were tearing whole sections of the *Tenjin* apart, and even with the temporary disruption to the drone particle accelerators it was still uncertain that his weapons would outlast the *Vulpine*'s supply of drones. The union sentry was steadily and slowly working its way through the *Tenjin's* armaments. He was fortunate, he decided, that the *Vulpine* was focusing so fully on his weapons rather than the station's structure. Unlike the *Vulpine*'s captain, however, Aggregate was not content to count his blessing. Clearly the humans intended for the *Tenjin* to survive. But why?

Turning his attention to the last federal cruiser, punching through its hull with any weapons too large and unwieldy to efficiently target the drones, Aggregate turned his own focus on the small pod waiting to be launched from the most heavily armed section of his station's hull. Looking through a crewman's eyes he watched the final preparations on the compact cloaking device within the ten foot pod. He had some concerns about the device's stability and predicted the cloak could burn out before reaching Pellitoe's surface. But the planet's satellite system was in ruins; nobody would be able to see where it landed even if the cloak failed.

Flooding the local area with EM interference, Aggregate sent a high intensity directed comms beam to a specific point on the planet. No message was included, just a carrier awaiting confirmation. A minute later the response came. Ambondice-Ambondice was in position to receive Aggregate's gift. The pod cloaked and was launched as a missile at the planet. Even if it had been a missile of the most destructive breed, the damage it might have caused would have been as nothing compared to the devastation the pod's contents was going to inflict on Pellitoe and the rest of the Human Jurisdiction.

Chapter 37

Let me tell you about Rajin Stoll. You are unlikely to know his name – even he doesn't recognise it. He was an atmospheric engineer on a dull little rock of a colony in some dingy four-world union out in the galactic east. Like so many worlds in our exponentially expanding Jurisdiction, his was a pre-billion colony, bound by the stringent obligations and limitations that come with such a designation. The best known stricture is, of course, the requirement for each citizen to breed, in one form or another, in line with prescribed targets. The second is that of closed borders. Until a world reaches the arbitrarily required populace of one billion souls then migration for almost any reason is prohibited and fanatically policed. Even with the renewed hostilities between the Jurisdiction and Consul, the Administration's military will not accept volunteers from any pre-billion colony. So what of Rajin Stoll? He was a loyal and productive worker, keen to create a thriving and self-sufficient world, happy to breed and remain on the planet until it reached its billion status, and in all likelihood would have remained years beyond that. But news of his father's infection with a corrupt nano-farm and the man's impending death on the closest world in their union changed all of that. He asked, perfectly reasonably one might imagine, for permission to travel the two weeks to his father, putting in place every conceivable guarantee of his return. Permission was, predictably, denied. And so Rajin fled his world, turned by nonsensical and rigid Administration legislation from a loyal and law abiding man to a criminal and a fugitive. He was, of course, apprehended and subjected to a sentence of memory dismissal. His father died without so much as a call from his son, and Rajin lives on with a new identity, back on his colony, not even knowing who his father was, much less that he died.

The Enguine Manifesto

Indin-Indin: In orbit around Satute, in the Network

The touch of the pointspace frame upon Indin-Indin's mind sent a chill of excitement through his homogeneous cells. Although far lighter a touch than that felt when linking with the systems down there beneath the planet's surface, the implications of this fleeting connection were infinitely more profound. Now able to do what the human pilots had been doing for nearly a thousand years, Indin-Indin had access to the entire network.

The Satute pointspace frame, although laying at the network's heart, was the least utilised. Aside from infrequent inspections by Jurisdiction Trustees, the arrival of which was never advertised and was generally kept from the greater Satumine population, the Satute frame never had reason to drop its ancient and perpetual cloak. Of the two hundred billion Satumine now living on the crowded world, less than a thousand had ever seen the frame with their own eyes. Indin-Indin was among their number, though prior to this momentous event he had only witnessed the frame de-cloak a single time. Now, appearing at his instinctive command, the frame's simple design seemed somehow larger, more majestic. No longer was Indin-Indin's perception of the device tainted by the humiliation and subjugation the frame represented. No longer was the octagon a tool of oppression and human superiority; it was the device of Satumine resurgence. It was spectacular to behold.

Its mass had never been definitively calculated, the interior being impervious to scans and unreachable by any means that wouldn't result in the frame's destruction, but most estimates were around several dozen billion tonnes. It certainly conveyed a sense of immense weight, but its true scale was impossible to appreciate until you drew close enough to be contained within its scope. There were no markings on the smooth surface of white metal and so, from afar, it could have been mistaken for a small satellite. And yet, even then, its sheer mass, its density, was undeniable on some instinctive level. Even the primitive humans picked up on this subliminal perception and, it was postulated, it was a side effect of the frame's constant link with the singularity of pointspace, a conclusion which only raised more questions.

The frame mentally asked Indin-Indin for a destination and he laughed at the simplicity of the request. How had it taken the human pilots more than a century of using Earth's frame to realise they could travel to worlds other than the Satumine home world. It was so *obvious*.

Unlike those first human pilots, Indin-Indin didn't let the request wash over him, unanswered, forcing the frame to connect with the last secured destination. Instead, with the ingrained knowledge of his cells he pulled from the frame a Network map and, recalling Aggregate's instructions, selected the world labelled *Oolik*. The human invaders knew it as *Dereph*.

In a constant quantum-scale connection with pointspace, the frame sent a brief pulse signal, resonating with the Oolik frame's frequency, establishing a guide-line through pointspace to connect the two, bypassing eighteen months of shortspace - seven hundred and fifty higher dimensional light-years. Then, burrowing down through every spatial dimension with a quiet efficiency which baffled the greatest human or modern Satumine scientists, the frame punched a hole, following the quantum-scale guideline into pointspace and up again into the higher spatial dimensions of the Oolik frame.

Humans described the formation of a wormhole as a brilliant point of white which, if viewed from the front, seemed to reach out for light-years. Indin-Indin pitied them for their limited senses. As the point expanded to fill the octagon he bathed in the almost spiritual magnificence and wonder of the sensory kaleidoscope which thrummed and rippled with an enthralling melody, touching his every perception in ways his old body had never been able to feel. Had he the capacity, Indin-Indin would have wept. How, he wondered, could the Ancient Satumine have willingly turned their back on such beauty?

The blunt chirping of an alert wrenched him from the dream and he noticed defensive platforms beginning to overcome the informational blocks. It was time to stop basking in the wormhole's emissions and actually use it. He edged the tiny craft closer, let the tidal forces catch at the event horizon some hundred meters from the wormhole proper, and braced himself as the infinite compression of pointspace pulled him in.

Humans experienced pervasive whiteness which penetrated even their closed eyelids and, once more, Indin-Indin felt the primitive creatures were cheated of the true spectacle. Not that they deserved to see it. Although the journey was instantaneous, there was also a definite memory of the transition. More physical than visual, it was an impossibly sensual caress, coupled with an emotional response which left those of his old life as dry shadows. What was love in the face of this? But, like so many emotions and sensations, he found it hard to genuinely recall the experience as anything more than an idea, a dulled memory.

He was back in the higher dimensions, drifting lazily from the blue cloud of a dispersing wormhole, propelled by the meagre surplus of force left from the frame's titanic energy expenditure as it countered pointspace's pull, dragging Indin-Indin's little craft from the singularity and out of the Oolik frame. He checked the cloak and was relieved to find it still active, because hundreds of human ships, from tiny shuttles no larger than his own, to network sentries and even one of the colossal shortspace out-network Sentries, were arrayed in front of the frame. Indin-Indin brought his craft to an abrupt halt and waited for a response from the fleet. Had they been expecting him? Could they penetrate his temperamental cloak? But aside from a dramatic increase in poorly encoded local comms, there was no reaction to his arrival. Scanning the comms, Indin-Indin gathered the humans were confused, and concerned, that a wormhole had opened and closed without depositing a ship. No network world was admitting to opening the wormhole and already it seemed enquiries were being made of Satute's puppet-government.

Deciding it wouldn't be long before someone considered the possibility of a cloaked ship, Indin-Indin fired his thrusters and rushed into the fleet which, he now understood, was nothing more than a holding formation for ships awaiting transport through the frame.

Barely into the fleet, he saw the sentries suddenly open fire, criss-crossing the space within and around the frame with all manner of beam weapons. For a full minute they lit up the space with ever changing vectors of fire, blindly searching for a hidden ship. And as they did, Indin-Indin slowly weaved through the fleet, heading towards the planet. Already he could feel the distant call of a somnolent Satumine colony subsumed by the human invaders. Soon he would awaken that colony and he would drive the humans from what was rightfully his.

Chapter 38

Humanity's discovery of the ancient Satumine pointspace frame cloaked in orbit around Earth is hailed as the defining moment in our history, the point from which our galactic dominion arose. It is celebrated as the single most fortuitous event in all of human history but it very nearly led to our ruin, if not our eventual enslavement or extinction. So many potted histories of the Jurisdiction imply we quickly and easily went from finding the first frame, and its link to Satute, to discovering the links to the ninety two other network worlds, and from there the colonisation of the galaxy. What is all too often forgotten is the brutal exploitation of Humanity at the hands of the Satumine when it was thought the frame went only to Satute. They offered longevity treatments at ever escalating prices, leeching Earth's resources and dragging us to the brink of collapse as they enjoyed a brief age of wealth and regeneration on their single world, in spite of their inability to use the frames built by their ancestors but now controlled by a rare few compatible humans. Of course once we found the other addresses in the frame network we had the resources to turn the tables and subsume Satute into our fledgling Jurisdiction, taking control of the longevity treatments and recovering quickly from Satute's abuses. But things could have been so very different.

Rehabilitation: A Survivor's Guide

Endella Mariacroten: In orbit around Pellitoe, in the Swinell Union, In the Fertile Belt

The countdown turned red in its final sixty seconds, warning of the tiny ship's impending re-emergence into the higher dimensions as it drew inexorably closer to Pellitoe. The timer reached five seconds and the Justiciar tensed, her mind recalling the myriad ways in which this could all go so appallingly wrong. Her haste, and consequently the perilously tight proximity between her plotted egress and the planet, had only increased the likelihood of some calamity. Even if her calculations were spot-on - and now she had had time to check them she was far from confident - she had by necessity plotted an egress so close to Pellitoe's atmosphere there was every chance she would strike it before her attitude jets could activate. And then there were all the satellites, and very likely the debris, to contend with. But the usual leisurely approach from a distant lunar orbit hadn't been an option; she needed to arrive in the thick of it.

With an anticlimactic *pop*, Endella's ship rose back through the spatial dimensions, leaving behind the one dimensional thread of shortspace which had carried her from the edge of the system. The popping sound became a grinding snarl and the Justiciar knew something had gone wrong. The acrid stench of burning tar wafted across her face in hot waves, filling the cockpit with black smoke which scratched at her throat like mustard gas and stung her eyes, blinding her with blood-flecked tears. An explosion punched her from behind, scorching her short hair and adding a peanut tang to the stench fast replacing the breathable air. The groan of another explosion further back in the burrowing section told her it was only going to get worse.

Eyes useless, she activated a redundancy in her AR implants, bypassing normal vision and feeding the embellished world of her ship directly into her optical nerves. With a thought she dismissed the useless aesthetic niceties and retained only the screens and interfaces, reaching for them with AR limbs to summon a system monitor. It was a terrifying read but, making further AR bypasses, she cut off the other senses to relieve the pain and the stench, and found a detached calm in which she was free of the distractions of fear and panic, free to consider the system monitor in a more pragmatic frame of mind. The rear of the ship, the hollow tube of the burrower, was twisted and smouldering as the last of the oxygen trapped between hull sections was burnt, or stolen by vacuum. The entire underside of the burrower had been shorn away, blasted from the ship by some internal force, and now drifted some distance behind among a dense trail of debris in this lowest of orbits. It was the debris, the remnants of Pellitoe's ruined satellite network, which had caused such devastation and, looking through one of the few remaining internal sensors, Endella found the primary culprit: a small shard of solar panelling, fused like melted glass to a blistered chunk of blackened metal. The ugly assembly no bigger than Endella's hand, was positioned impossibly at the heart of the burrower's sealed regulator, throwing the alignment into chaos and spewing immense forces throughout the ship to pull and tear at every component. There was no hole through which the aberrant debris could have gained access to such a critical system and, replaying the data recorded during her re-emergence from shortspace, Endella realised what had happened: The ship had emerged into the same space as this chunk of scrap and by sheer misfortune had aligned it with the regulator so the two objects shared the same higher dimensional space. Just incalculably bad luck.

Cursing the uncertainties of shortspace travel, the Justiciar shut down power to the regulator and isolated any systems which had suffered significant damage. She then extinguished the few fires, opening them briefly to vacuum, and almost as an afterthought she vented the noxious smoke from the cockpit, replacing it with the emergency reserve while the atmospheric systems got a grip on the situation.

The ship was ruined. It would never again burrow into shortspace. And she was certain she would not be afforded the honour of a replacement. No matter; she still had work to do.

Reviving her physical senses, she turned her attention outwards from the ship, taking in the battle still raging some distance out in the highest orbits. The *Tenjin's* immense hull was still blighted by the massive wound inflicted two decades earlier, but six new holes now pocked the hollow hemisphere while numerous craters and troughs scarred the solid half. Fires burned freely, spitting flames out into vacuum to die or, at their most intense, to curl back under the station's gravity to scorch the outer hull. But its structure appeared sound. The *Vulpine's* captain, it seemed, had restricted his assault to the station's weapons. A field of unrecognisable metal fragments marked the loss of a Swinell Union cruise, and Endella had to accept that its destruction, and the huge loss of life, was in part down to her. She had ordered Anden Macer to keep the *Tenjin* here, and to not let it be destroyed. She had cost that cruiser's crew their lives. Glancing over a quick scan of the remaining union cruiser, she accepted that it too would shortly fall. Again, her responsibility. She shook her head and scratched at the back of her hand, scraping up stinging valleys of skin which welled with blood. She had to stop thinking like that. She had to be hard. Cold.

She looked to the *Vulpine*. The federal sentry, at least, had fared well. She creased her brow and examined the scan more fully: it had fared *too* well. Just as she required the *Tenjin* to survive this battle, did the *Tenjin* likewise have reason to see the *Vulpine* survive? A curiosity for later; right now she needed to get aboard the rogue station.

She checked the dwindling mesh of particle accelerator beams holding the *Tenjin* in higher dimensional space. Even before her position in the tactical network was re-established she concluded that the *Vulpine* had expended its supply of drones. The *Tenjin* continued to pick off the tiny drones and as Endella began climbing into a higher orbit, her thrusters rattling against the useless mass of her tattered shortspace burrower, the drones' mesh failed. The *Tenjin* was free to burrow, unrestrained, into shortspace.

'Office Trustee Anden Macer,' she said once her connection and authority had been re-established. 'I need you to order the last Union Cruiser to cover my approach to the *Tenjin*.'

'Justiciar?' Anden responded. 'Where did you come from? I can't see your base ship.'

The *Vulpine*'s captain was unaware of her small ship's shortspace capability, and Endella didn't have time to explain. 'Not important,' she snapped. 'I only have this failing shuttle with which to board the *Tenjin* and I need some serious cover. That is all you need to know.'

'The *Tenjin* doesn't seem to be bothering you at the moment,' Anden said. 'It seems more interested in finishing off the cruiser before slipping into shortspace.'

'It probably hasn't noticed me,' Endella said, grimacing as a dozen beams focused on the cruiser's nose, excavating a deep quarry which exposed at least ten levels of the old ship to space.

'Just give the order,' she spat. 'As soon as I get close the *Tenjin* will try to take me out.'

'Yes Justiciar,' the captain said with enough contempt to see him charged with insubordination had Endella not wholeheartedly shared his distaste for her order. She was asking that the failing cruiser confirm its fate simply to ensure her own survival. But that wasn't the reason for her order; her survival was important only because of the work the Jurisdiction required of her aboard the *Tenjin*. Once she was done there, she was as expendable as those she now condemned to death.

Her thrusters sputtered and pulsed wildly and Endella had to wrestle the ship, forcing it into a collision course with the *Tenjin*. For a moment it seemed the cruiser's captain was going to disobey the order as, evidently, it had done with regards to her instructions not to assault the *Tenjin*. And in that moment she smiled. She willed him to disobey; to live. But as her little craft came within weapons range of the vast rogue station, the cruiser's thrusters ignited and it began drifting laboriously across Endella's view of the *Tenjin*. She sank in her seat, unsure how to feel.

She struggled to maintain her course and twice had to disengage the jets in order to reignite them. In front of her the cruiser visibly deformed under shots which, from her vantage point, silhouetted the cruisers bullet behind a corona of pulsing energy. Would it survive long enough to shield her approach? She was unsure.

Although hidden from her, the *Tenjin* was getting closer. The cruiser had altered its alignment, apparently initiating a ramming manoeuvre, and Endella's battered prototype vessel followed so close behind as to be almost within its box-kite. A strut rippled under the force of some unseen impact in the cruisers bullet and then it shattered, snapping in six places and ejecting atmosphere and bodies from its hollow walkway. Endella tried to ignore the sight, knowing everybody aboard the ship would soon be dead anyway. But the guilt landed in her stomach like the chunk of fused metal and glass that had so badly crippled her ship. She tore again at her hand.

Almost there.

Explosions within the bullet punched out huge sections of hull and orange lines cracked across the entire ship. She had killed them all. And for what? But, at the last, the cruiser lurched to one side, pulling out of its suicide charge, to reveal the looming curve of the *Tenjin's* scarred and pocked body. She was too close now to be threatened by the primary weapons, and everything capable of such close range firing was focused entirely on the swerving mass of the Swinell Union cruiser.

Endella saw her opening: a seventy meter tear in the hollow hemisphere. She aimed her complaining ship, begging it to do her this one last service. But the ship felt little loyalty; with a dull crack and not so much as a flash of light the thrusters all died. Endella's ship plummeted towards the solid hemisphere, tumbling under the uneven pull of the *Tenjin's* savaged gravity coils. She saw the cruiser fall apart under the most intense barrage, filling the void with a painful glare. Then she crashed into the *Tenjin's* unyielding hull.

Chapter 39

Our Governance Machines are, on the face of it, a solution to the problem of one failed system of government after another which has plagued human history. No longer are flawed humans - along with their vested interests and short sighted points of view - expected to efficiently and fairly oversee humanity. We now have vast numbers of IB Governance Machines to direct our Administration and these machines speak for us all. They are adjusted, every year, in accordance with the findings of the Census and can be relied upon to organise our Jurisdiction with the collective will of its every citizen. And there is the flaw: the Administration was so obsessed with creating the ultimate expression of democracy, it never considered that such a democracy might not be best for us. Now, rather than a few hundred fallible humans deciding the direction in which our government should lead us, we have trillions *of fallible humans doing it instead. But that is not the greatest flaw in the system - the true threat is the fact it is open to abuse and manipulation. The Governance Machines may faithfully follow the findings of the Census, but there is great power to be wielded by those in a position to design the questions presented on the Census. You will not be surprised to learn that I have evidence the Satumine are, via their pawns, slanting the questions over the course of centuries in a direction known only to them.*

The Truth: A treatise on the Satumine Conspiracy

Galman Tader: On Pellitoe, in the Swinell Union, in the Fertile Belt

The pheromone tower stood as a lone white monument amongst the vivid turquoise of affan-grass, the coffee brown splint grass and the deeply veined pink of scattered flesh trees. From afar it had seemed no more spectacular than a large tree, and its gently swaying fanned branches which dispersed the repellant pheromones on the wind confirmed the illusion. But as Galman sprinted into the shadow of its thick smooth trunk, its grandeur became apparent. He had expected few handholds to aid his escape into its heights, but had hoped at least to encompass its girth and shimmy up, away from the approaching pranx-rat. But this colossal pylon was twenty feet wide and he lacked even a strap with which to extend his reach. The beast was galloping towards him though Galman didn't need to look back to know the monstrous rodent was closing on him, for the furious snarl and the clatter of Tumble dragged behind it grew louder, closer, with each of Galman's panicked breaths.

Nothing as vicious as the pranx rat existed on Galman's home world of Diaclom, but he had seen enough broadcasts, both fiction and documentary, to know the mess large predators could make of a soft human body. Spurred on by adrenaline and terror he clambered desperately at the slick glossy pylon, praying his hands might find some hidden grip. When his flailing fingers discovered just such a lifesaving hold it took the frantic man a moment to appreciate what it was that had been revealed to him. Daring to risk a glance over his shoulder, Galman saw the beast would be upon him within seconds. Closing his eyes for better mental focus, he called into being one of his recently acquired, horribly expensive and legally ambiguous embellishments. Opening his eyes he was glad to see the spinning disk of blue a couple of inches in front of his face. He flicked the AR disk towards the pheromone tower and squinted as harsh white strobed at a nauseating frequency. All the while the pranx rat closed the gap, seeing nothing of the AR world. The flashing ceased and, its AR embellishments burnt away by the vandal code, the pheromone tower's true drab-reality form was exposed. With the grin of a man granted reprieve at the steps of the gallows, Galman leapt at the exposed ladder and climbed with such panicked haste he slipped on every other rung.

The pranx rat ran headlong into the tower's base with a jarring thud which told of a thick cranial plate. The ladder juddered and Galman had barely cleared the first ten rungs. A fast but poorly aimed swipe from the rat's six inch claws told Galman the head-on collision had failed even to stun the massive animal. The second swipe caught his right calf, tearing open the limb and soaking his foot in blood with startling speed.

He cried out and dragged himself further up the ladder, putting himself just beyond the reach of a third angry swipe. Convinced the beast would suddenly start climbing the ladder, Galman didn't rest. He continued up another twenty feet before his burning leg numbed and his head swam with disorientation. If he passed out, he would be ripped apart by the pranx rat, probably before the agony of evisceration roused him. Feeling as if he might vomit, he tried to slow his breathing, realising hyperventilation was exacerbating the effects of blood loss. In a moment of clarity he deactivated his clothing embellishments, tore a strip from the now visible jumpsuit, and with the length of linen he tied his left arm to a rung on the ladder. If he passed out, perhaps he might not fall. The embellishments no longer disguising the ugly wound he saw how much blood was flowing from his lacerated calf to trickle down the ladder and onto the rodent's waiting tongue. He doubted he would ever regain consciousness if he passed out now. Watching the monster lap up his blood he knew it wouldn't give up and go looking for another target - not with the blood exciting its murderous instincts. He quit tying his arm to the ladder and instead used the strip of fabric to stem the flow from the gash which went deep into his muscle. The rat froze. What had it heard? Another target perhaps? It then relaxed and paced around the tower, occasionally glancing up to check its pray was still there. Again its ears pricked up and now Galman also heard the noise: a mechanical whine and a dry metal clinking. The beast arched its back, attempting to dislodge the IB machine it had, until now, been content to ignore. Like a dog chasing its own tail the pranx rat set about scrambling after Tumble's tentacles which hung behind as a dozen new tails, one of which had begun to twitch and writhe.

'Galman!' the machine yelled, his voice wavering and distorted. 'I can't see anything. Shout something so I can locate you.'

'Tumble!' Galman called back as the rat snapped at one of the metal tentacles, clipping a couple more inches off of its length.

'Bollocks,' Tumble said although it was doubtful the loss of the appendage tip caused it any actual discomfort. If it was capable of experiencing anything akin to pain, it would have deactivated the sense when the first of its limbs had been ripped from its body.

'I can't position you,' Tumble called out, his spherical body bouncing on the rat's muscular back and his grip loosening around its torso. 'My senses are all over the place.'

'I'm twenty feet up a pheromone tower,' Galman provided. 'And I'm bleeding.'

'Got you,' Tumble replied. He then lashed with his one active tentacle, flicking something into the air which Galman followed intently with his gaze as it glinted in the sun. His laser pistol. He swore, seeing the weapon was too far out to be caught. Knowing Tumble would be unable to retrieve the pistol if it fell to the ground, he reached out, kicked off from the ladder, and caught the small pistol in his tingling right hand, and then fell twenty feet to the sharp points of splint grass which, at least, had mostly been crushed into the pulp of affan grass by the rat's claws and leathery feet. The ground was hard and it refused to yield at all as Galman's shoulder struck. A wave of sharp agony shot through his entire body as the shoulder dislocated and a rib snapped. But the ex-cop didn't hesitate or cradle his throbbing arm; he took the pistol in his good hand and as the pranx rat turned on him he fired. Five shots at its thick ugly skill. A sound as of a dying pig screeched from the tusked snout and after shaking its head, so violently Galman thought its neck night snap, the pranx rat turned and fled, trailing Tumble for ten meters before the IB machine released its weakened grip and fell like so much scrap metal into the splint grass. Galman dropped to his knees and screamed in pain and felt the chill of unconsciousness flow through him, seeping into his mind.

Chapter 40

The Approved Faith Conglomerate (AFC) is one of the most blatant and grossly offensive examples of the Administration's stranglehold on our freedom of thought. Certainly there have been countless wars and atrocities committed in the name of one deity or another, and yes the very notion of a belief system based on nothing but superstition and wishful thinking is both idiotic and childish, but for the Administration to think it can prescribe a handful of watered down and regulated religious systems is no less ridiculous. The real crime, however, is not in the Administration's attempt to own all religions; rather it is in the lengths to which it will go in order to ensure its complete control. Incarceration, memory dismissal, murder and even war are all authorised tools employed by the Administration and their Justiciars in their attempts to crush any unapproved faith system. The supposed harm those religions might have caused, I would suggest, is more than offset by the actions taken to stop them. Instead of wars between religions we have wars between the state and religions. What's the difference?

The Enguine Manifesto

Anden Macer: Aboard the *Vulpine*, in orbit around Pellitoe, in the Swinell Union, in the Fertile Belt

The nuclear glare of the Cruiser's death picked out in deep shadow-filled troughs and pits the *Vulpine*'s hundred bodily wounds. The bullet section had lost its smooth curves, its shell no longer a polished beauty, blackened by energy beams and internal fires. She was burnt, cracked and warped with internal bulkheads now providing the greater part of her structural integrity. Yet her weapons continued to hammer at the *Tenjin*. The energy field which had frustrated the initial assault was now sporadic and whole sections were failing as explosions cascaded around the sphere. On witnessing the Justiciar's collision with the station - the resultant fireball being too much, he surmised, for her to have survived - Anden had gladly set aside the order to restrain his attack. With only a handful of drones still functioning, he could no longer prevent the *Tenjin* from burrowing into shortspace, and there was no need for him to try. If the Justiciar was dead then the orders were meaningless; if she had survived then she was aboard and the *Tenjin* could be allowed to leave. He doubted the latter and was determined to punish the *Tenjin* for its unprovoked assault. If he could crack open its hull and pierce its reactors then all the better. He wasn't prepared to let any other Jurisdiction world suffer the same pointless and random aggression as had been suffered by Pellitoe.

'The drones are just in the way,' Keddy observed. 'Their accelerators aren't even warming the hull.'

'Then set them on collision courses,' Anden ordered. 'You saw the hole the Justiciar's shuttle made. Let's see if we can make a few more.'

'Perhaps we will get lucky,' the tactical officer quipped. 'There can't be much more between us and the *Tenjin's* reactors.'

Ruebill snorted and said, 'I would guess there is even less between the *Tenjin* and *our* reactors.'

'Chin up,' Anden said, shooting the officer a glare. 'We have done OK so far. Maybe the *Tenjin's* captain doesn't want to destroy us.'

'It would explain our weapons still functioning,' Keddy said, shearing a section of the station's hull away with a laser, as if peeling an orange.

'Like hell it does,' Ovin yelled. 'We have been lucky. If they wanted us to survive they wouldn't be gutting our crew sections and our environmental regulators. They would just take our weapons out and leave us be.'

Anden grimaced at the chief technician's observation, partly because it dissolved the fantasy that his ship was, in this battle at least, somehow blessed and fated to survive. But what really stung was the reminder of so many casualties.

'How many have we lost?' he asked in a shamed mumble which, had it not been transmitted through AR directly to Ruebill's ears, would have been lost to the shouts of the crew on the lower bridge beneath the command floor and to the groan of another particle accelerator driving deep into the *Vulpine*'s core.

'Unsure,' the intelligence officer called back. 'At least four hundred. Depending on how long we stay out here fighting, we will probably lose another three hundred of the wounded, because the medical decks are ruined'

Anden cringed and covered his face with one hand, tugging at his dreads with the other. The *Tenjin* was trying to flee, and in no more than a few minutes it would succeed. In that time Anden was going to lose hundreds of his crew for want of the medical facilities available on the sole surviving orbital station on the other side of Pellitoe. Could he really justify pursuing his attack on the *Tenjin* while those people died?

As if knowing his thoughts Steit said, 'If we disengage, head back into low orbit, and make our way to *Kubet* station, I doubt the *Tenjin* will pursue. It wants out, and following us will bring it back within range of the planetary weapons.'

'Can we stop the *Tenjin* before it leaves? Can we cripple it?'

The executive officer licked his lips and frowned. 'Honestly? I don't believe so.'

Anden tugged harder at his hair and for one uncharitable moment wondered if his officers had become cowards, preferring to flee and save themselves rather than risk their lives to neutralise a threat to the Jurisdiction. Did they not ache to avenge the deaths of those aboard the cruisers? But flushing with private shame he knew that wasn't how it was. His crew - what was left of it - was beyond reproach. Swallowing hard he ordered a ceasefire. The dull pounding of the *Tenjin's* weapons continued to split the *Vulpine's* harrowed body, but as Anden instructed a withdrawal the immense station slowed its assault. When the ship crept beyond optimal weapon range, the *Tenjin* made no move to follow. Shortly after, as the *Vulpine* drifted over the horizon, seeking out the aid of *Kubet* station, the *Tenjin* vanished silently into shortspace.

While others offered up cheers of relief at the obscene aggressor's retreat, Anden only shook his head and offered his apologies to whoever was destined to next suffer the *Tenjin's* irrational ire. And he silently cursed the dead Justiciar at whose feet he laid the culpability for both the escape of the *Tenjin* and the deaths of so many brave citizens.

Chapter 41

Depending on your personal circumstances and the politics of the region in to which you resettle, you may chose, or be required, to live on a pre-billion colony for a while. Such a colony is simply a world yet to reach a population of one billion. These worlds are actually in the majority during the Jurisdiction's current exponential expansion. To continue this growth we need every colony to break past the billion mark as swiftly as possible and then begin sending out new colony ships to settle ever more of the many thousands of suitable worlds. To this end there are two strict rules which apply to every pre-billion world. The first prevents anyone from migrating off the world, in order that the young colony not die. The second insists that all breed, and that they breed vigorously. Every adult must contribute to the production of, as an absolute minimum, one child every three years. This means a colony starting from a base of one hundred thousand settlers will reach one billion in a little over a century and a half. You have the option to raise your children in a traditional family setting, meaning you will have five or six children under your guardianship at any given time for one hundred and fifty years, depending on the age at which they leave the family home - or you can simply submit genetic samples and allow the resulting life to be remotely birthed and raised in communal nurseries. Should you opt for the latter you will be required to contribute to the costs and will be ineligible for certain tax-breaks or bonus electoral privileges, but for many it is the preferable option and you will face no stigma or judgement for your choice. You may, of course, opt for a combination of the two over the course of the colony's pre-billion period.

Rehabilitation: A Survivor's Guide

Endella Mariacroten: Aboard the *Tenjin*, in shortspace

Endella had suffered worse injuries during her almost three and a half centuries - most having been inflicted through her two hundred years in the Justiciary - but right now she struggled to recall any so gruesomely visceral. A length of pipe had speared her from behind, glancing off her spine and bursting through her abdomen so it now protruded like some hellish maypole, hot intestines hanging down from its jagged and gore covered point. For a while her guts still clenched and pumped, squirting excrement from a laceration at the top of the disgusting spectacle. Her right thigh was similarly impaled by a pipe and a red plug of flesh was jammed in the four inch wide tube like a cork. A lung had been punctured by shattered ribs and a compound fracture thrust her left collar bone up through the skin and back into her throat. She didn't try to work out how many other bones were broken, she expected the majority were. As delirium began to protect her conscious mind from the horror, she gave a short wet laugh, finding it ridiculously hilarious that her greatest agony came not from the life threateningly monstrous wounds spraying shit across her intestines, but from the sharp and incessant agony of her right little toe. Stretched beyond capacity, the tiny machines of her internal nano-farms had deactivated nerves across her most severe wounds but had left the most minor of injuries - her broken toe. She went to cut her pain receptors using internal hardware, but the system was unresponsive. Neither did her AR implants work. Unconsciousness came to her aid, however, dragging her to numb oblivion while her nano-farms began their lengthy campaign of reconstruction using her own mind as an intelligence-bridge to guide their work - an arrangement so close to the mechanism needed to give rise to an Artificial Consciousness that it had been outlawed centuries ago at the end of the rebellion against Consul's rule. As in so many areas, however, Endella Mariacroten had special dispensation. She was too valuable an investment to be allowed to die.

Natural unconsciousness gave way to a mechanically induced coma, and the work of repairing Endella's devastated body truly began. He body was animated with the jerking clumsiness of a zombie as the nano-farms sent neural inducers into her brain, firing off commands to cause her hands to shove intestines back inside the soiled abdomen and to snap her collar bone back down more or less in place. She was aware of none of it, least of all the pain. The artificial animation of her comatose body was as much a violation of federal statute as her intelligence-bridge with her own nano-farm. The idea of machines possessing human bodies was as chilling as the prospect of another Consul gaining consciousness within the systems of the Jurisdiction. Endella had executed eleven criminals for their involvement in such technological development. But she was above them. She was exempt.

She awoke with no idea how long had passed. That was a concern; it meant her internal hardware was damaged rather than simply disconnected from her body in the crash. The nano machines would have reinstalled any such disconnected device. She tried her systems one by one, finding the entire AR suite unresponsive, likewise her physiological management hub and neural access data storage. At least her nano-farms worked and, fortunately, so did the personal IB system which encased her brain like a wire basket. She opened her eyes and dry flakes fluttered down her cheeks. Brushing her face with painfully tender hands caused whole strips of papery skin to fall away, revealing a new pink layer which burned in the heat of wherever she was.

It hurt to move her arms but Endella was experienced enough to know that living through the crash was no guarantee of continued survival; if she didn't get away from this twisted and smoking amalgamation of her destroyed ship and the *Tenjin's* hull then someone would soon discover her and finish what the crash had started.

She tugged at her leg, pulling it free of a girder which had fallen across her feet. It came free with little effort because the limb was now significantly more slender than it had been when the rubble had settled. The nano-farms had devoured her muscle and bone mass to rebuild her failing organs and to form new skin where the burns had been too severe to leave. She got to her feet and felt horribly weak, as though the *Tenjin's* gravity coils were set far too high. Her stomach ached; when she bent down to tighten the boots which were now two sizes too big, there came a deep searing agony as of a knife cutting her open. Letting out an ill disciplined cry she dropped to her knees and clenched her fists, cutting her new palms with short thin fingernails. Her jumpsuit, although auto adjusting, was ripped in too many places for the garment's limited processor to achieve a tight fit, and she was able to pull aside the large tear at her midriff to reveal the ugly knot of scar tissue and protruding nodules of grey intestinal sections. A rivulet of thin watery blood, stained brown with spilt faeces, was escaping the centre of the vile wound and Endella knew she was far from healed. At least she knew why all of her internal hardware was destroyed: pushed beyond their rated expectations, the nano-farms had been required to build more nano-scale machines than their resources could support. They had cannibalised every mechanical and electronic device within her body save for the one controlling them: the personal IB. And still repairs were incomplete.

After tearing the sleeves from her jumpsuit and tying them tight about her stomach, Endella took in her surroundings. Her ship was utterly destroyed and barely recognisable. The cockpit, designed to be the most stable section of the ship, was the most intact but even it was a blackened and crushed mess in which she was partially entombed. To her left, through a wide gash in the cockpit, she saw a short stretch of the *Tenjin's* interior which gave way to a vista of blackness streaked with white veins. She was looking out of a hull breach into shortspace. She looked away, struck by the disconcerting vertigo which befell any who looked directly on shortspace. She could still breath, suggesting some kind of energy field was sealing the breach: more technology she intended to liberate from the apparently ten thousand year old vessel. Her chair was embedded in the curved front wall, a trail of cables still connecting it to the fitting of the floor which, Endella now noticed, was on the ceiling. The ship was upside down. With that simple realisation she resolved the chaotic shapes into a recognisable layout. She stood and reached up for the secure box previously hidden beneath the chair but now exposed on the new ceiling. The effort of raising her arms sent a shock of pain through her shoulder and she decided the collar bone could only have been roughly fused. Her nano-farms seemed too spent to intelligently moderate her pain and, given their inability to perform much more work, they appeared to have declined the option of totally blocking the sensation in order that she might not accidentally and unknowingly damage her body further.

Grimacing, she persevered. The secure box was melted shut and it took more effort than was comfortable to break the seal. Everything felt so heavy, so difficult; her arms were like those of a child, the muscle stripped away. But the seal broke and the box swung open, spilling its contents down onto the upturned ceiling. The mag-gun she loaded with its full array of clips, while the backpack which was full of all manner of useful supplies, she slung over her shoulder, immediately regretting it. Something cracked under the bag's weight and she was floored, clutching her freshly broken collar bone. Cursing her stupidity, she transferred the backpack to the other shoulder and crawled through the hole in the side of her cockpit, avoiding looking out of the *Tenjin's* hull breach.

The space outside was as cramped and distorted as her cockpit; perhaps the remains of a corridor or small room. There were no doors, no obvious way out. So, wishing she had time to stop to eat some of the high energy, high protein supplies her body needed if it was going to resume repairs, she began crawling through increasingly restrictive passages in the jumble of knotted and fused metal, every movement threatening to open her stomach and empty her entrails onto the floor.

Chapter 42

It is hardly a secret that I take extreme offence at, and object in the strongest of terms to, the policy of allowing Satumine to settle, albeit in small numbers, on most of our colonies. But even if you do not share my belief in the ultimate threat posed by the Satumine race, there are more pragmatic reasons to require this policy to be scrapped. Many consider the Satumine a hardier, more durable creature, when compared to Humans. They highlight the alien's ability to withstand greater doses of radiation as an example. But the truth is, when considering the sum of all biological and psychological traits, humanity is in fact the more adaptable species and we could make a home of far more worlds than might the Satumine. The expense and the time going into the terraforming of planets - ignoring for a moment the Fertile Belt - could be cut by perhaps ten percent if we did not have to go the extra mile in ensuring the planets are also hospitable to the Alien parasites within our Jurisdiction.

The Truth: A treatise on the Satumine Conspiracy

Indin-Indin: In orbit around Dereph, in the Network

The ship's processor appeared to have learned from its graceless descent through Satute's atmosphere, and although coming close on a dozen occasions, the cloak never failed as the spurting thrusters eased the little shuttle down into Dereph's lower atmosphere, slowing it to a comfortable cruising speed. Dereph: even the shuttle provided to Indin-Indin by Aggregate showed the Human name for this erstwhile Satumine colony. It infuriated him. The world was called Oolik; soon even the Humans would be forced to respect it with its true name. Assuming there remained any human survivors in the galaxy.

Every level of Oolik's atmosphere, from the low orbits down to the thick air just above the tallest of the Human and Satumine towers, was highly regulated by fifty IB traffic control systems, and thousands of aircraft and orbital shuttles weaved complex paths through AR highways which Indin-Indin could perceive only though the ship's screens which were subtly connected to the global AR net. Further down, in amongst the dense jungles of monolithic human towers and the gorgeously curved arches and twists of ancient Satumine architecture, the traffic increased a thousand fold. Hundreds of IB systems took full control of every vehicle, ensuring an efficient and safe flow through the low altitude roads of the urban centres. And on Oolik - or Dereph - like most Network worlds, almost the entire planet was an urban centre. Thirty billion humans swarmed across the single crescent continent, millions more filled the five floating cities which made the most of the remarkably temperate equatorial region. All across the vast ocean, ships and drilling rigs, and construction docks and ocean based space ports, blighted the otherwise pristine blue expanse.

Satumine buildings were spread thinly across the continent, and Indin-Indin guessed it had been one of the youngest colonies. There would still have been thousands of miles of verdant wilderness when the Humans arrived, but now, from above at least, the continent looked little different to the dense urban mass of Satute - only with visible oceans. He wondered how long it would be before citizens of the Network, so comfortable in their elite corner of the Jurisdiction and far less willing to spread out into the galaxy than the wider population, would extend their cities to cover the oceans of Oolik.

The sky lanes became denser the lower Indin-Indin descended. It was becoming increasingly difficult to avoid the fast moving traffic which often changed direction for seemingly no reason at the command of the IB traffic control. Invisible to those machines, his presence was not allowed for in their minutely calculated flows and the small craft's thrusters were worse than sluggish, making course corrections hazardously slow.

The inevitable collision came as he weaved through three tightly wound lanes of low altitude traffic. He steered the craft into what he took to be a long stretch of open space, just above the highest of the three entwined lanes, hoping to follow it between a henge of human towers circling the upturned arch of a vast ancient Satumine facility. When, for whatever reason, the traffic control machines suddenly split the three lanes into six, Indin-Indin's assumed empty stretch of air was immediately filled with thousands of fan-cars and urban shuttles. The thrusters slowly responded to his urgent course change and a huge public transport shuttle clipped his rear quarter, destabilising the strained cloak and killing two more thrusters.

The traffic stopped. All of it. It was a startling and enthralling spectacle to behold as every vehicle halted in perfect unison and every thruster realigned to assure stable hovering. Nothing moved on any sky lane for as far as Indin-Indin could see, apart from him. He would have been conspicuous enough, sputtering and jerking his way through the synchronised traffic, but amongst the suddenly motionless vehicles his shuttle had to have been noticed by every human and every machine for miles around. It was as if all of Dereph was staring. It would be mere seconds before a Trustee confirmed what the IB defensive machines must have already recommended. He was going to be shot down.

But until the order was given, for a few brief moments, it seemed his passage would be assisted. Traffic Control had begun moving aside any vehicles in his path. It was not for his benefit, rather the safety of those with which he might have otherwise collided. He aimed for the inverted arch, not expecting to be given time to reach it. Then, with a warm familiarity, dozens and then hundreds of ancient Satumine devices welcomed him, linking with his mind and confirming him as the senior Satumine - the *only* true Satumine on the planet. Instantly Indin-Indin had at his disposal the tools he required and the instinctive skills and knowledge to use them.

Using his craft's link to the Human networks, and computational power ten thousand years in advance of that available to secure those networks, Indin-Indin located every IB suite on the planet. That took a tenth of a second. There were thousands of them, many containing just a single pod, others holding up to twenty. He then asserted his authority over the long somnolent Satumine planetary defences. Despite the intrinsic durability of Satumine technology, he found many were no longer sustained by sufficient power supplies. Others were so far beneath the foundations of the human cities that they would expend their entire charge just blasting to the surface. But there were enough for his need. It took another half second to mentally assign each hidden weapon its task.

He gave the order to fire.

Across the continent buildings collapsed as the Satumine structures around which they had been built suddenly shifted and opened to reveal crackling rods of jade. Thousands were dying in those collapses - one such catastrophe unfolded a little way in front of Indin-Indin, in the henge of human towers. He watched the revealed weapon open fire, and he knew the same was happening for miles around. He could have done more than merely instruct the weapons, he felt he could have truly inhabited them, *known* them, but was not yet ready to give himself so fully to the technology. The weapons were surprisingly subdued, understated discharges, just thin beams of not-too-bright white which fanned out in their dozens from the jade rods, flickering a little but doing nothing more.

Then the destruction began. At the terminus of each thin non-threatening beam a building exploded with horrifying force. Surrounding buildings shook under the impact of shock waves and blasted debris, and many more collapsed under the second-hand assault. Millions were dead. But still the greatest destruction had not been unleashed. Unthinkable to the Jurisdiction's leadership, and hence utterly unplanned for, the planet was without any IB suites. Not a single intelligence-bridge was active on this world and no systems were in place to allow trained humans to take over the complex tasks assigned to those now useless machines. It simple shouldn't have been possible for a coordinated strike to destroy the entire IB infrastructure.

The damage taking place was almost unimaginable, but the chaos and horror directly before Indin-Indin was a fair reflection. Thousands of vehicles plummeted from the sky, raining down on the city as explosive missiles. Other vehicles accelerated, uncontrolled, into the sides of towers or into one another. All across the planet, hundreds of millions more were dying.

No IB eyes remained to watch him, and every human eye was distracted by a hell which had engulfed the planet in less than five seconds.

Un-noticed he landed at the gate to the upturned arch, an Ancient Satumine research facility, and he casually strolled from the craft into a scene of fleeing, screaming humanity, which took him, in his new form, to be one of their own.

He ordered the doors to open.

Chapter 43

The Administration is at once the most impressive logistics system ever devised and the most corrupt and damaging government imaginable. That any single organisation can, more or less, manage twenty thousand planets as a reasonably coherent entity is undeniably an awesome feat. Of course it is significantly less impressive when you realise it is covertly overseen by the agents of Consul, but still it is no mean accomplishment. But just because something is difficult does not mean it is a worthy goal. A federation of dozens, possibly hundreds of smaller states joined by economic and social ties but ultimately self-governing, would have been infinitely easier to accomplish and far less damaging. I have no doubt that Consul would have infiltrated many of those states, but he would have been far less likely to have so utterly conquered all of mankind as he has so quietly managed in our Jurisdiction.

The Enguine Manifesto

Galman Tader: on Pellitoe, in the Swinell Union, in the Fertile-belt

Galman's cheek was tight and hot. As he rolled over it was as if the ground tugged at his face, trying to hold him down. He opened his eyes to the turquoise burst of a pulped affan grass patch. The liquid spilt from those sausage-like plants had evaporated, leaving only the thick and sticky syrup on which Fertile World ecosystems relied; the syrup had dried on his face, adhering him loosely to the compacted soil. Light headed he pulled away from the affan grass and sat up, bringing his knees to his chest. He hurt, but not terribly so. There was a soft numbness pulsing across his body and he wasn't sure that was a good thing. Checking an AR screen he saw almost ten minutes had passed since he fell from the pheromone tower. That no other creature had approached him, eaten him while he lay unconscious, was due only to a well-earned share of good luck. He doubted such rare luck could hold much longer.

The numbness was banished by a spear of agony thrust through his right leg when he tried to stand. He fell back and looked aghast at the exposed muscle of his torn calf and the glint of bloodied bone within. The flow of arterial blood had stopped, stemmed by the labours of his limited internal medical hardware. There were no nano-farms to knit his body together, but an enhanced clotting agent had been released from a tiny capsule attached to his heart when his blood pressure had dropped dramatically.

Reaching for the tattered skin which needed to be stretched and stitched back across the exposed muscle, Galman found he had no real control over his left arm. His shoulder was still dislocated, though the sickening pain was masked by analgesic drugs dispensed from another capsule within his heart. With barely a thought he grabbed the hanging limb in his good hand and tugged hard, snapping the joint back into place. He screamed; there was a limit to the pain these simple drugs could mask. But the agony was short lived, fast receding to a dull ache drowned by medication. The pain in his savaged leg, however, was not so easily overcome. Looking around, hoping to spy something to use as a crutch, Galman noticed the motionless remains of his IB companion, his tentacles still stretched out, draped across the plain like a dead jellyfish. Perhaps Tumble could be repaired, but not just yet. He saw the buggy a little further off, beyond a family of flesh trees; the vehicle was still turned on its side. In there were the emergency medical supplies, as well as the tools he would need to revive Tumble, if repair was even possible. About him there was nothing to use as a crutch and so, grimacing and trying hard not to look at the grotesque wound, he got back to his feet, putting his weight on his good leg.

Hopping to the buggy was slow and appallingly painful, every hop sending a searing jolt through sliced muscle and jarring his bruised body. But progress was made, and clutching the laser pistol he had found still lying beside him, he was eventually upon the vehicle.

Galman laughed darkly when he realised the medical supplies were stowed in a compartment on the outside of the vehicle, on the side currently pressed into the dirt. Dizziness was returning and he slumped, half fell, to the spikes of splint grass. Defeated. He didn't have the strength to right the buggy and he didn't even try. He had lost too much blood. With another ironic chuckle he toppled and fell into cold darkness.

'Galman,' somebody barked. 'Wake up!'

Galman awoke with a start, refreshed, alert and focused. But confused.

'Tumble?'

'You've slept long enough,' the dented sphere quipped, waving the stump of a torn appendage. 'Ambondice-Ambondice has stopped moving. I think he had reached wherever it was he was heading.'

'Tumble?' Galman asked again in a tone of stupid befuddlement. 'What happened?'

'I repaired,' the IB machine said.

'Yourself or me?' Galman asked, looking down at his leg which was enclosed in a pale blue wrap. A thin tube led into that wrap, pumping a flow of blue-tinged blood from a canister, the AR screen of which read almost empty. Seconds later the transfusion was complete and the tube disconnected with a muted pop. Only then did he notice he was sat in the buggy and that they were moving.

'First I repaired myself,' Tumble said. 'Then I fixed you.'

'You were out cold,' Galman protested, sitting up in the chair and testing his range of movement, finding a little stiffness, some tenderness, but nothing worse.

'It was only my body,' Tumble replied. 'My code compartments were fine, and so was my innermost maintenance functionality. It took a few minutes to use it to repair my outer maintenance systems and another hour to use those to repair my bodily control systems.'

'How much were you able to repair?'

'Once I got to the supplies in the buggy, I could fix most of my sphere, and about five percent of my appendages.'

'Any permanent damage?' Galman asked, his confusion washing away, replaced by a determination to get back to work.

'Nothing we can't fix if we get to a proper service shop. But for now let's get to Ambondice-Ambondice. The fact that Tumble assumed the queries had been about his own mechanical body rather than Galman's wounds either indicated that Galman's injuries were not severe enough to be concerned with, or a worrying narcissism in the reprogrammed machine. Either way, Galman didn't comment.

'Where is he?' Galman asked, pulling up the appropriate AR screen, locating the Satumine's positional data.

'In the wilderness,' Tumble said as something clicked noisily within his metal body.

Galman reached for his pistol, aware there would be a great many more creatures to deal with in the wilderness.

Tumble patted his master's shoulder with a clumsy and frayed tentacle. 'Relax,' he said. 'I've taken precautions.'

Chapter 44

The most visible aspect of the Administration in your day to day life will be the Trustees. These civil servants administer and enforce the strictures and systems of federal governance and are separate from the various local government bodies of each world and union. They ensure the census is accurate, that the taxes are paid and that things like pre-billion restrictions are adhered to. The Trustees also oversee the Jursdiction's military and it is to the Trustees that responsibility for inter-union disputes fall. Perhaps a career in the Administration appeals to you, in which case you will find dozens of entry routes, as a Junior Trustee, on practically every world - and we would be delighted to have you.

Rehabilitation: A Survivor's Guide

Aggregate: Aboard the *Tenjin*, in shortspace

A trillion geometric compartments flashed, each with its own unique rhythm and melody, cycling through ten billion colours unknowable to human eyes. Constructed through a dozen mathematical dimensions, the geometry of these compartments was as foreign to human comprehension as their colours. It was the standard model for Jurisdiction computer code, the foundation on which the *Tenjin's* processors had been improved over ten millennia. Like so many other technologies, Aggregate knew how to construct a far more efficient system, and indeed had done just that in many of his most critical devices. But the ancient computer, the original, was integral to the *Tenjin* and resources had not existed in the wormhole to rebuild it anew. Improvements, however, had been made. Now they were being tested.

The data incursion had originated on Pellitoe, during the final second before the *Tenjin* returned to shortspace. But Aggregate was under no illusion that the humans had activated the informational assault. The attack was sophisticated and fast, which didn't necessarily preclude human built IB technology, but the underlying code was too complex, to advanced, to be of Jurisdiction origin. The crew of the *Tenjin* had not developed twenty seven dimensional geometric code compartments until over eight hundred years into their lonely voyage; the Jurisdiction used twelve dimensions in their code, the same as that ostensibly used in the *Tenjin's* computer. No, there were only two sources of such an advanced assault: the original Satumine, or Consul.

Aggregate observed the assault's progression through the code compartments, noting the changes occurring in the unique frequencies and understanding his assailant's intent. In the intent was betrayed the source: his computer was being infiltrated by an agent of Consul; probably one of the pseudo consciousnesses living unnoticed in the AR of Pellitoe, reporting back intelligence to Consul through the busy pointspace comms traffic. The uploaded viral intelligence was seeking the vast technological databases which held the largely unused product of ten thousand years of human and near-human research. Advances Consul had ample resources to develop.

The intent discerned and the culprit unmasked, Aggregate stopped toying with the invasive intelligence and employed the full force of his superiority to beat it back through the compartments and out into the cold vacuum of an isolated storage device. He had the knowledge required to construct code compartments in geometries using over a thousand mathematical dimensions, but had lacked the resources for such a massive and fundamental upgrade, and that was a frustration. Such compartments could have outmanoeuvred the twenty-seven dimensional virus with almost embarrassing ease, but no matter. Aggregate had developed a far more elegant solution. Using his instinctive understanding of pointspace, he applied the same principles to the archaic computer. Each of the trillion code compartments required just a single tweak: a pointspace mathematical analogue was built and, through their dimensional tweaks, every compartment connected with the new singularity code.

Defensive routines appeared around the invading code, slipping through tweaks hidden from the twenty seven dimensional viruses, reappearing at any point within the wider code structure. The virus withered, but was fast to learn, and new protocols were displayed within nano-seconds to stymie the defensive action.

Aggregate was prepared. He opened the tweaks beneath Consul's virus segments like booby traps, dragged them down into the mathematical pointspace, re-depositing them in prepared ambushes far from the support of their fellow segments. Over long seconds the battle raged, but Aggregate had no doubt as to the outcome. He withdrew from the AR metaphor and allowed his mind to slow to normal human efficiency.

An icon appeared before him; the battle was won and the virus trapped in a physically isolated crystal memory sliver. He nodded, satisfied.

'Consul,' he said, instantly activating a pointspace comms channel to the dedicated relay the artificial consciousness had set aside two decades earlier for Aggregate's use. 'How are things on the front line?'

'Is the small-talk really necessary?' Consul replied, making no reference to the informational attack. Aggregate hadn't expected the AC would and was not inclined to bring it up either. He didn't blame the AC for its desire, or attempt, to steal some of the *Tenjin's* secrets, and the attempt changed nothing.

'You have received all of my tactical bulletins regarding my war with the Jurisdiction, so there is nothing else for me to tell you.' It was true, Aggregate was well aware of the apparent stalemate and the subtle mustering of Consul's hidden forces which, although liable to inflict devastating and debilitating damage to the human fleets and border worlds, were unlikely to lead to outright victory.

He shrugged. 'To business then.' Sending an informational bundle he continued, 'I have entered the second stage of my stratagem.'

'Yes,' Consul said, its contrived voice revealing nothing it didn't want revealed. It then appeared, forming once more the tin man avatar so often employed in its meetings with Aggregate. 'I witnessed the battle through the eyes of my agents and through their links with the Pellitoe satellite network. I was, for obvious reasons, unable to witness the final stages.'

Aggregate nodded - the satellites had been amongst his first targets and without them Consul would have seen little. 'I destroyed all orbital defences, most of the satellites, the stations and the Swinell Union cruisers. I allowed only one station and the federal sentry *Vulpine* to survive.'

'The *Vulpine* is still fully armed?' Consul enquired.

'Of course.' Then, with a slight grimace, Aggregate added, 'The *Tenjin* suffered extensive damage ensuring the *Vulpine* kept all of her weapons.'

The tin man somehow raised an eyebrow which Aggregate was sure hadn't existed seconds earlier, and said, 'It's *your* plan, Aggregate.'

'Indeed,' the pointspace entity in human skin said. 'But you are set to profit richly from my ultimate success.'

For a moment the tin man stared blankly at Aggregate. Then it said, 'I assume you hope to elicit some further service from me.'

'Nothing too imposing.'

Consul snorted. 'You have employed me to re-engage the galaxy-spanning Human Jurisdiction in a war which pits my two thousand worlds against a domain ten times larger, simply to divert the federal fleet's attention. You have little remaining leeway in which to further impose.'

Aggregate offered a coy laugh though he knew Consul was not making light of their relationship and the extent of the AC's significant contributions. 'All I need is for you to confirm that the fleet around Dendrell has not been dispatched to Pellitoe. I assume you have contacts there.'

'One moment.' The moment was, in fact, barely a heartbeat, and the tin man was speaking again. 'The fleet was put on alert when you arrived a Pellitoe but, as you predicted, they were not dispatched. In light of your overt display of activating your shortspace burrower, and your choice to refrain from attacking the planet itself, the fleet was held back.'

'What about - '

'- yes, the union cruiser in orbit around Diaclom is still there.'

'Excellent.'

'You will arrive at Diaclom in three weeks,' Consul stated. 'You will need four weeks in which to complete your work once you arrive. Are you confident your agent on Pellitoe will act within a window of no earlier than a week from now and no later than three weeks?'

'*You* recommended him, Consul.'

Consul just shrugged its metal shoulders, said nothing, and vanished, closing the comms link behind it.

Chapter 45

I have previously referred to the hybrid genetics of the people we call pilots *- those people capable of linking with Ancient Satumine frames. While I must accept that some few humans have, through some mechanism, been mutated and defiled with these shreds of Satumine genetics, I refuse to accept the wildly speculative notion extrapolated by Jurisdiction science from this mutation - I refuse to accept that Humans and Satumine share a common genetic heritage. The accepted, but wholly offensive theory, is that at some time in the distant past the Satumine mixed their genes with early hominids and, for reasons unknown to man or alien, later used some product of this experiment to alter their own genetic code. This, the Administration guesses, was the end of the Ancient Satumine and the genesis of the modern lesser race. This is a disgusting, offensive theory and, even if I do not yet have a full and competing theory, I* refuse *to accept this lie.*

The Truth: A treatise on the Satumine Conspiracy

Cordem Hastergado: On Pellitoe, in the Swinell Union, in the Fertile Belt

What the atmosphere failed to burn, the ground based defensive batteries took care of. More or less. Only where the raining debris became a torrent did anything survive re-entry to impact the planet, and even then the largest of the artificial meteors were still picked off by the IB controlled batteries. Small as the collisions were, damage was still being done. The destruction and loss of life inflicted by the panic, disorganised evacuations and opportunistic violence and looting, however, was a hundred times that caused by falling metal. Cordem spent the first hours after the remains of Pellitoe's satellites began falling from the sky, trying to assist the regional government to enact their woefully inadequate emergency protocols. As the federal representative for the Equa continent, he had no authority over the chaotic response, no real role at all unless the Jurisdiction declared the disaster a federal concern. So, frustrated by the degradation of civil order and the Bureau of Supervision's inability to calm or reassure the public, or even to enforce some kind of military order, the Office Trustee retreated to his private office where he implored the Area Trustee responsible for the planet's federal presence to speak to the Sector Trustee about declaring the loss of control a federal concern. The Area Trustee was not receptive, so Cordem did what little he could, issuing federal advisories to the population of his continent. He assured them the threat had left the Pellitoe system and the red AR columns, indicating possible impact sites, were accurately identifying the only risks. Everyone should, he advised, return to their homes or businesses or, if they were indicated to be at risk, find shelter with neighbours. If looting and rioting escalated, he warned, the federal Administration could be called upon to restore order.

It wasn't a lie, though the local governor responded very quickly, privately reminding Cordem that intervention was extraordinarily unlikely now that the external threat had passed. Cordem simply reminded the governor it was still a technical possibility.

Then, with the city screaming irrationally about him and the orbits voiding their shattered contents onto the planet, Cordem settled down to listen to music, smoking an AR cigarette and sipping a tumbler of sedative-laced brandy. He was not one inclined to inaction and he required a little chemical assistance to wash his hands of the crisis. *Give it a while*, he told himself. *It will all calm down soon enough.*

An intense radiated heat and a low droning hum roused Cordem from unsettled and delirious stupor. Even before he opened his eyes, mechanisms within his heart and around his brain flooded his body with anti-toxins and stimulants, and he leapt to his feet, immediately aware of the threat which had triggered his internal alarm. Red light stained his office, the same urgent red as the risk indicator columns. Through the wide crystal window he looked down to the panicked swarm in a street hundreds of feet beneath his penthouse office and noticed how far the blast radius of this supposedly incoming debris fragment was predicted to extend: the bubble of red spread through most of the city block. He swore. The predictions were supposed to have been finalised by now and nothing had been indicated anywhere near his federal tower. Things could change, of course, there could have been additional explosions or a poor shot from a defensive battery could have deflected rather than destroyed a falling object. But Cordem immediately suspected more sinister explanations.

The door to his reception area was swung open without the courtesy of a knock and the Office Trustee went straight for the tiny pistol hidden beneath his luxurious chair.

'I'm sorry for the intrusion,' said his personal assistant, a wise looking man who had chosen like Cordem to allow some grey into his hair. 'We need to evacuate.'

Cordem's hand had found the pistol but had thankfully yet to pull it from the quick release holster. The Office Trustee had a good relationship with his assistant and the man's charming family, and pulling a gun on him could only have spoilt the geniality.

'I'll be right behind you,' Cordem said with a smile which belied the concern clenching at his gut. A direct hit to the federal headquarters of the continent; it seemed a bit of a long shot given that nothing else was predicted to be hit for several miles in any direction.

'The car is waiting for you.'

Cordem nodded and watched the man stride quick but calm from the office, back into the reception. The Office Trustee snatched the pistol from its holster, kept it in his hand but sheathed it in a translucent AR skin which cost more than many people's entire collection of personal embellishments.

Beyond the reception was an open plan office, ordinarily busy with Junior Trustees going about the bureaucratic machinations of the Jurisdiction, but now empty save for the high backed seats, each of which was ringed with blank AR screens hovering at eye level. They had been quick to get out, Cordem thought. But then, most low rank Trustees didn't need to be told twice to take time off work. He jogged calmly to the closest elevator shaft – a more austere design than the ostentatiously embellished devices used throughout most of this world – and he stepped onto the large mirrored disk which took him quickly down to ground level.

The lobby was busy, but ordered. Like most of the federal tower the cavernous entrance space was sparsely augmented. Such austerity was not a federal requirement, rather a reflection of Cordem's own tastes and his determination to portray a clear distinction between the Swinell Union and the wider Jurisdiction and its Administration. The calm lines of Trustees filing out through the security arches was a far better reflection of the differences and was in stark contrast to the screaming masses only a few feet away in the street.

Cordem joined the back of a queue and was passing through an arch a minute later, one of the last out.

The car wasn't outside the tower where it should have been. Hovering above the reserved parking space was a gently rotating disk of pale blue embellishment. The frantic crowd paid it no attention and even the relatively calm Trustees walked right through it as they left the tower. It was a private object, intended only for Cordem. He reached across the crowd with an invisible hand, stretching it the ten meters between him and the disk, activating a simple message.

'Things are a bit unpredictable,' came the voice of his driver. 'I've parked up in a quieter spot.' The disk then ceased its spinning, pulsed a couple of times and elongated, becoming a long cord of blue running down the road and turning down a side street. The Office Trustee followed the path laid out for him, weaving through the throng where he could and barging past when he had to. If anybody recognised him – and they really ought to – they didn't show it. Nobody stepped aside in deference to his status; people believed they were going to die if they stayed where they were and no amount of respect or social protocol was worth the risk of being caught up in the blast when the orbital debris hit the federal tower.

Cordem didn't rush. This was just a precaution. With no other risk indicators anywhere near, there was no reason to believe the batteries wouldn't succeed in shooting down this single threat. And yet he felt uneasy. Again he considered the improbability of a direct hit on the continent's federal headquarters. But surely nobody could have orchestrated the strike.

The side street was not much narrower than the main street, but its embellishments were markedly cheaper. The main street offered no better way out of the area than did this less affluent road, yet people preferred to remain in the well-lit and heavily embellished road, fighting through the crowd rather than slipping into the darker side street as had Cordem. It spoke volumes about the Swinell mind-set.

The car was parked fifty meters down the street, draped in shadows which were, in all likelihood, AR. Nicely out of the way. Cordem rushed to the vehicle and slid quickly through the open door onto the hard cold seat.

That wasn't right. Where was the AR leather? A sudden wetness passed over his body and icy cold stung his skin. Then, in an instant, his embellishments decompiled. The physical embellishments, what little he sported, were unimportant. It was the *comms* suites and control screen which the Office Trustee could not afford to be without.

'What –' he began, but a large pistol was pressed into his mouth and the Satumine gunman appeared from beneath an AR cloak beyond even the ability of Cordem's now decompiled observation utilities to perceive.

'Please let go of your pistol,' the Satumine said in the clicks and spits of an undisguised Satumine voice. Cordem looked down to his own pistol, now exposed after its transparency embellishment had fallen apart. He blushed at his incompetence. He had forgotten he was even carrying the weapon, and now it was far too late to use it. He couldn't even call for help.

'Now what?' he asked.

Chapter 46

The Chief Trustee rests atop the human pyramid that is the Administration. He stands on the shoulders of the Sector Trustees and beneath them the Area trustees, Office Trustees, Senior Trustees, Trustees and Junior Trustees. And I swear he thinks the whole damn pile of bureaucrats is nothing but a throne for his comfort. You might think I would welcome the idea of a human holding the reigns of the Jurisdiction, as opposed to some machine, but this arrangement is just begging to be abused. Whenever a single man is given this much power humanity is never more than a word away from tyranny. At the very least the pyramid should be flat-topped, with ultimate power ending at an assembly of Sector Trustees. In the end the whole discussion is irrelevant – the governance machines have the power to veto any action taken by the Chief Trustee, and those machines are more the tools of Consul than they are of the Jurisdiction's citizens.

The Enguine Manifesto

Galman Tader: On Pellitoe, in the Swinell Union, in the Fertile-belt

Something came down behind the flesh trees and oak-like gamber trees which lined the ridge to the left of the valley. The impact wasn't particularly spectacular, and only a short-lived plume of dirt and smoke hinted at the crater which Galman imagined now formed a clearing in the small forest. More dramatic was the sudden haemorrhaging of syrup-node roots across the splint-grass meadow, erupting sticky clear sweetness from pulsing, spurting geysers, coating the dry wooden points with the lifeblood of the ecosystem. The spurting leaks in the root network were happening every twenty meters or so, for as far along the valley as Galman could see.

'Must have come down on a syrup node,' Tumble stated, not the slightest bit concerned.

'I know I'm new to fertile worlds,' Galman said, reigning back control of the buggy and searching the map for an alternate route to Ambondice-Ambondice's location. 'But won't all that syrup attract just about every creature for miles around?' It was a minor miracle that nothing had attacked them already; they were well into the reserve and, by rights, Galman ought to have been fending off all manner of beast with his feeble mini-laser.

Tumble synthesised a laugh and patted Galman's hand away from the screen with a frayed and twitching tentacle.

'I told you,' the IB machine said. 'I took precautions.'

'What precautions?' Galman demanded, the fourth time he had asked since waking in the buggy. Tumble was treating it as a game, insisting Galman guess. Galman wasn't in the mood.

Tumble prodded the rear seat and gave nothing more. After glaring at Tumble's cracked central band for a moment, Galman muttered his curses and leaned across the divide between the front and rear seats. A twinge of tight pain reminded him his wounds were not entirely healed and he bit his lip at the ache.

The rear seat's lightly embellished cushion, he discovered, was not bolted to the box of its base. Gingerly, as if expecting something to leap from within, he lifted the foam-stuffed resin cushion section and revealed a bundle of cables, a couple of foot-long canisters and a small AR screen hovering above it all.

'Tumble,' Galman said with the caution of one who wondered if he might have come across a bomb. 'What did you do?'

'Well they weren't using it.'

'Pardon?' But Galman spotted the identification label on the canisters: Repellent Pheromone II. 'You stripped out the pheromone tower?'

'It had lost the power feed and our buggy is using a third of its generator capacity.'

'And its working?'

'Seems to be.'

Galman grinned and felt himself relax. 'Has anyone done this before?'

Tumble held up two of his more mobile tentacles and formed something akin to a shrug. 'I doubt the towers have ever lost their power but, if they have, I'm sure someone would have had the same idea. It wasn't exactly difficult.'

The collection of cables, and their connections to a stack of sealed crystal processors, looked considerably more complex than anything Galman would have been comfortable attempting outside of a workshop.

'How long will the canisters last?' he asked, clambering back into the front seat as the buggy rumbled and jerked through a patch of particularly strong splint-grass.

'I doubt we will get five percent through the first canister,' the machine replied. 'But it never hurts to carry a surplus.'

Ambondice-Ambondice's positional data put him at the end of a short branch of an extensive valley network, and it was possible to get a lot closer to him and his companions than if they had been following in the open plains above the valleys. Either they didn't expect anyone to follow, or they were confident they could deal with any intrusion. Galman hoped for the former but very much suspected the latter.

No longer in constant dread of bestial assault, Galman found the remainder of the journey passed remarkably quickly and soon enough he was out of the buggy and peering from behind a rocky outcrop at a row of vehicles. One of those vehicles sheltered Ambondice-Ambondice.

He pulled up a visual enhancement embellishment, held the illusory screen in front of his eyes and magnified.

He counted the vehicles: three safari buggies a little better appointed than Galman's rental and a medium sized off-road truck with an enclosed trailer large enough to contain two of the buggies. At least ten Satumine were milling around, sporting a variety of embellishments, none of them attempting to disguise themselves as human. He was frustrated that none of them was identifiable as Ambondice-Ambondice, though that particular Satumine was still, according to the AR positional data, in one of the buggies. A quick scan of the open-top vehicles revealed another four Satumine, none of which was the horse-headed, fur covered Ambondice-Ambondice that Galman remembered from his earlier observations. As bigoted as it was, Galman had to say the Satumine all looked alike.

'They're armed,' he whispered to Tumble who was still in the buggy a few feet away, but who was more than capable of hearing the hushed voice. 'Mainly pistols, but a few accelerator rifles and what looks like a charge launcher.'

'How much closer do you think we can get?' the machine asked, making a meal of its dismount from the buggy and dragging its ruined body along the ground by two tentacles like a man whose legs had just been blown off.

'Not much closer than this,' Galman decided. 'There are a few rocks over there and we could possibly make it to those flesh trees if I carried you,' he pointed to a copse sixty feet closer to the gathering. 'But we can see well enough from here. Unless something changes-'

Something changed.

As if revealed by the raising of some embellishment, a long cylinder flickered into existence a hundred feet above the Satumine gathering, and the conspirators suddenly leapt into what seemed a practiced drill, unloading a similarly sized metal crate from the truck, placing it beneath the hovering cylinder and then stepping back to watch the object float with impossibly silent grace down into the crate which slammed shut when full. The Satumine then began loading it back onto the truck, using motorised lifters which had also been waiting in the trailer.

'They're going to leave,' Galman said, pointlessly.

'We can't follow in the buggy,' Tumble pointed out. 'They will see us as soon as we are out in the open fields. We're going to have to wait till they get where they're going and pick them up again using Ambondice-Ambondice's positional data.

'No,' Galman hissed. 'Whatever the shit in orbit was, it was tied to that cylinder. It's not getting out of my sight.'

'I don't know what to suggest.'

'I need to get aboard that truck,' Galman said, some part of him certain he was about to get himself killed. 'Can you help me do that?'

For a moment Tumble said nothing. Then, slapping a tentacle to the floor in excitement, it said, 'Pick me up. Get me back in the buggy.'

For five minutes the machine picked apart the jury-rigged pheromone dispersal device, ordering Galman to twist here, hold there, and stop asking stupid questions. Galman did as the machine instructed, all the while glancing back down the valley, though from the buggy he could see only the rear of the truck and none of the other three Satumine vehicles.

'Right, take that out,' Tumble pointed to one of the canisters. Galman noted a sharp hiss of escaping gas as he did what Tumble asked. The hiss ended with a wet click. Tumble snatched the canister, did something impossibly intricate to the eight valves and clipped across one of them something he had been constructing from the wires and crystal processors torn from the now destroyed distributor.

'Get ready to run,' Tumble said. 'And please don't forget to take me with you.' He put the canister down on the passenger seat and asked Galman to transfer to him full control of the vehicle.

A moment later the buggy, carrying the modified pheromone canister and driving under the remote control of Tumble, drove up the side of the valley and disappeared over the crest of the low hills.

'What did you do?' Galman asked, back behind the rocks and clutching Tumble.

'I set the pheromones to be released in a single huge plume.'

Galman reached for his pistol. 'Tumble, have you really thought this through?'

Tumble laughed with a worryingly manic realism. The buggy reappeared and rolled, out of control, down the valley wall, heading straight for the Satumine. Seconds later came the stampede.

The Satumine opened fire, frantic and desperate, and Galman crept forward, expecting at any moment for a pranx-rat to find him and finish what its cousin had started on his leg.

Chapter 47

So what hardware will you be required to install in your body in order to fully enjoy the world of Augmented Reality? There is no definitive list as local regulations or customs and AR strictures will determine the depth of AR immersion allowed - or in fact required - of its citizens, but for the most part you will be fitted with sensory input processors feeding your AR experiences directly into your brain. All basic senses - sight, smell, hearing, touch and taste - will be orders of magnitude more realistic than those offered by external hardware solutions such as ocular projectors. In terms of output, you will be equipped with internal musculature-tracking processors, as well as positional-data mappers. The later is the element causing most concern for those moving from less AR intensive worlds, but federal statutes strictly limit access to, and uses of, the AR positional data. Nothing beyond secure IB machines ever see this most sensitive of data.

Rehabilitation: A Survivor's Guide

Endella Mariacroten: Aboard the *Tenjin*, in shortspace

Endella emerged from a crush of deformed walls and fallen girders, smeared in her own blood and the lubricating oil and grease which flowed through the destroyed section from a severed pipeline further up. Laying in a puddle of oily blood, her clothes reduced to tattered strips and her body writhing in pain; it looked as if she had been birthed by some mechanical beast. Her body pleaded with her mind to let it lay there, to fall into unconsciousness and, if at all possible, to never wake it up again. She wiped the thick grease from around her eyes, smearing it more than actually clearing any away. At least her burnt-short hair wouldn't be matted and carrying pounds of bloodied lubricant. Getting back to her feet took a ridiculous effort and once she was there, steadying herself on a twisted handrail, a coughing fit brought her back to her knees. She coughed for a full minute, expelling mucus and clotted blood and shooting ice cold agony through her ribs and collar bone. She strained violently to throw up her stomach, emptied as it was by the nano-farms in their desperate search for resources. Still she retched, bursting blood vessels in her eyes and setting her nose bleeding. A seeping heat spread thorough her stomach as she felt something burst. She looked down to the ugly knot of her poorly sealed abdomen and saw watery blood and yellow-black bile flowing freely. Swearing, fighting back the urge to begin retching once more, she tore the last sleeve from her jumpsuit and bound her stomach, replacing the bandage she guessed had been snagged and lost during her painful crawl through the *Tenjin*'s smashed sections.

Endella took a deep, calming breath, but found it only clarified the unending pain. Back on her feet she started walking, unsteady at first but with increasing confidence, if not comfort. Her crawl through crushed walls had brought her out in a dark and silent corridor. The air was dry and still and it had an indefinable staleness which Endella guessed related to an environmental system which had failed a long time ago. This was probably a decommissioned section. The dim lighting was provided by a single strip of pale blue which ran uninterrupted across the length of the arched ceiling. It was the kind of emergency lighting which most ships employed, drawing its meagre power requirement from the ambient temperature which never really left a sealed ship, even when every system was shut down. It provided just enough light for the Justiciar to see the curve of the corridor, fifty feet along.

She gripped her mag-gun, grateful she hadn't lost it in her scramble through the walls, and set off down towards the curve, uncertain of her location and unable to consult her now dismantled internal hardware. But she had many skills, many talents, the least of which being an eidetic memory. The time spent in shortspace, en-route to Pellitoe, had not been wasted and Endella knew the layout of every corridor, laboratory, crew section and command centre on the vast science station. If she could get her bearings, find a recognisable facility or, better still, a section identifier, she ought to be able to find her way to her primary objective: the central IB suite. If she could get to the intelligence-bridge pods she could utilise her only remaining piece of internal hardware and scour the *Tenjin*'s computers for a way to seize control, or to at least disable the crew long enough to allow federal troops to board.

The corridor continued its gentle curve to the right, dimly lit and abandoned, for the better part of a kilometre. By the rate of the curve she guessed she was about half way between the station's equator and one of its poles, assuming she was travelling in an arc around its perimeter. It was just as likely she was walking through the station, getting closer to its heart and that the curve had nothing to do with the outer circumference. She passed several doors; some were single person portals, others large double entrances which likely led to communal areas or science facilities. Every one of them was sealed; not merely locked but welded shut. Endella didn't have time to waste on forcing doors open and, since none were labelled or otherwise identifiable, she continued on, every step jarring her gut. She imagined the crude scar splitting and her intestines being held in by nothing more than the already saturated sleeve of her jumpsuit. If her all but spent nano-farms hadn't been able to cauterise the major blood vessels she would have long since bled to death. She forced herself to stop thinking about her wounds and focused instead on recognising the corridor. Although nothing was signposted, and she was blind to the low level AR used aboard the *Tenjin* prior to its supposed ten thousand year voyage, she should still have been capable of recognising where she was. She recalled the doors passed so far and estimated the distances between them, comparing the numbers to her memory of the station schematic. Twenty possible corridors, so long as the basic structure of the station had not been utterly rearranged during its time in the wormhole. A few more minutes of walking revealed six more doors, reducing the possibilities to twelve corridors. It took only another minute and a half to discount all but two possibilities, and that was as good as it was going to get because much of the station was mirrored across its equator and this corridor was part of that mirror design.

She was either two kilometres from the IB suite, or five hundred meters. Either way, a door a minute back would lead to a corridor taking her in roughly the right direction. The door, like the others, was welded shut. Her mag-gun might have been able to punch a few tiny holes in the metal but it would never break the seal. She unshouldered her rucksack and produced from it a small roll of white tape. She ran a strip down the seam between the two sections of the double door, tore the strip from the roll and returned the remainder to the bag. She had a detonator in the rucksack as well but had long ago discovered a much simpler was of activating heat tape. Setting the mag-gun to anti-personnel bolts she took a few steps back and fired.

The tape burned blinding white and with a heat which singed the last of Endella's eyebrows. She turned away and waited until the cool air of the decommissioned corridor returned. Turning to look at the result of her efforts, the Justiciar felt a gentle breeze of warmer, fresher air, blowing through a neat quarter inch gap between the door sections. Her fingers fitted, just, into the gap and, although hot to touch, the metal was not molten and did not burn. The alloys used in jurisdiction ships and stations conducted heat with extraordinary efficiency and it took only seconds for the doors to be as cool as the rest of the corridor.

Bracing herself for pain in her collar bone and possible tearing in her gut, Endella tried to force the doors to slide open. For a moment they were immovable, seized up entirely, and she feared the welding had been applied to more than just the seam. But after a moment more of painful effort, during which she was certain something burst inside her, the doors ground open with much more noise and vibration than she would have liked. And, as a huge figure stepped towards her, silhouetted at first against the brighter light of the room beyond but fast becoming visible as it approached, she realised that more than the *Tenjin*'s structure had changed over ten thousand years of isolation. This creature was no more human than the Satumine. She fell back, startled, and raised her mag-gun to the thing she could only think of as a cyborg.

Chapter 48

The mag-gun is the standard firearm for most military and civil police forces throughout the Jurisdiction. Its technology is the basis for virtualy every form of modern personal weapon and few citizens ever consider its origin. While the principle of the weapon has existed in human science since shortly after the dawn of the technological age, long before consul was birthed, it was not until we made contact with the Satumine that it could be perfected. Only with the advances in battery density, and the poly-dimensional magnetic field revolution, were we able to create a device capable of the power and portability needed to make such a cheap and effective weapon. I know I can come across as obsessive, paranoid even, so I am not going to suggest the Satumine have somehow compromised every mag-gun in the Jurisdiction and might, at the flick of a switch, disarm or destroy our every army - but I will ask you a question: given the origin of the science, who do you suppose is the secret holder of the mag-gun patents? How much wealth and power might they wield?
The Truth: A treatise on the Satumine Conspiracy

Galman Tader: On Pellitoe, in the Swinell Union, in the Fertile-belt

Bucking like fitting rodeo bulls, the delirious affan-goats were at the fore of the stampede. Slender and wiry, the six-horned prey animals were amongst the fastest of fertile world beasts, and aside from raging at the invisible cloud of maddening pheromones, they were doing the best they could to stay ahead of what was next over the crest: the pranx-rats. The sabre-toothed predators were not as fast as affan-goats, but they did not need to take such a circumspect route down the valley. While the goats followed narrow paths between rocks and potholes, the enormous rodents just piled headlong down the bank, leaping rocks and holes and losing no small number of their massive pack to bone snapping falls and trips. Even before the Satumine had noticed what was charging down into their camp and formed up into a firing line, the predators had caught the slowest of their prey and speared the smaller animals with their scythe-like teeth. Predator and prey rolled as one entangled beast down the slope, landing in bloody piles a couple of hundred meters from the Satumine. The front most affan-goats were even closer. The Satumine opened up with their diverse arsenal, peppering the muscular mass of pranx-rats with anti-personnel bolts, tearing away chunks with armour piercing rounds and burning through tough bodies with high powered laser rifles and particle accelerators. Although far closer, not a single one of the many-horned goats were targeted. They just weren't a threat against the prospect of a pranx-rat's demonic form. Blind to instincts of self-preservation by an incensed and chemically stimulated frenzy, the pranx-rats ignored their wounds, didn't flee so easily as had Galman's earlier lone assailant. Unless their legs were blown off or their resilient internal organs significantly devastated, the creatures barely registered the injuries being heaped upon them. But, one-by-one, they fell to a devastating rate of fire.

Galman reached the flesh-tree copse as the remotely controlled buggy was finally torn to pieces by a furious pranx-rat, and one of the pressurised canisters exploded, turning the offending monster into strips of red meat and flooring every animal for fifty meters, including a couple of Satumine. Then the goats reached the defensive line and, contrary to what the Satumine had probably expected of the prey animals, did not merely pass through. In a scene even more disturbing than the pranx-rat advance, disturbing for its improbability and irony, the goats began goring Satumine with long horns and biting with incisors intended ordinarily for the blades of the affan-goats' namesake grass.

Then came the endephants and scavenging octopoids.

'Now!' Tumble hissed. 'Nobody is looking at the back of the trailer.'

Galman didn't stop to think, knowing to do so would serve only to delay or stop his suicidal dash across open terrain towards a gang of heavily armed Satumine and a stampede of frenzied animals. He cleared half the distance before looking up from the ground to see what was going on ahead. Dead animals littered the ground in front of the Satumine and their blood attracted those that had already passed the line so the Satumine became surrounded. That, at least, cleared Galman's path.

Still nobody looked at the trailer; every Satumine was focused intently on targeting the vicious and irrational animals. Hugely outnumbered and weakened by a few obvious injuries and several casualties, the Satumine still had the advantage of rapid fire and that advantage was beginning to show. Gradually the stampede was being whittled and great bloody mounds piled up, almost shielding the Satumine from the remaining animals.

With so much free meat just lying there, and the pheromone cloud dissipating, the Satumine were becoming forgotten to the fast sobering beasts. But Galman was already ensconced within the long trailer, hidden in an empty storage alcove, Tumble still in his arms.

After a few minutes of inaction, Galman wondered if the distraction had worked too well and the Satumine were all dead. Although no bad thing, in and of itself, he believed there were more layers to Ambondice-Ambondice's plot than merely collecting the mystery cylinder. The cylinder was going to be used for *something*, and Galman really wanted to know what that purpose was. If the Satumine terrorist was dead, then so too was the trail. After a few more minutes, however, the trailer rumbled and began steadily vibrating with off-road driving.

'Can you keep track of our position?' Galman asked.

'I should imagine so,' Tumble replied.

Two hours passed in silence, a tiny AR screen hovering before the two companions, plotting their position as determined by Tumble. As they approached an abandoned pre-billion nursery the screen suddenly vanished.

'Drop all of you AR!' Tumble snapped with sudden urgency.

'Why?' Galman asked, doing as Tumble suggested, unloading all of his embellishments and tools.

'This facility,' Tumble whispered, 'has been isolated from the global AR net.'

'How can you know that?'

'I'm not sure,' Tumble admitted. 'But if Ambondice-Ambondice is the one controlling the AR here, he will know about you by your embellishments.'

Then the trailer was opened.

Chapter 49

In the Jurisdiction we are governed by trustees who are in turn guided by machines which act solely in accordance with our wishes, as dictated by the census. So they tell us. If this was true then how the hell did the Justiciary come about? I have no problem with a federal police force – I would much rather the Jurisdiction was a collection of self-governing states with no need for a single law enforcement body over the local forces, but as long as we are a single entity then I see the need for the Justiciary. But I cannot believe the census has ever indicated a wish by the people for an organisation as brutal and unaccountable as that which unleashed the Justiciars on us. Surely we have not indicated a desire to be subjected to a reign of terror by men and women who can break any law in the pursuit of their abhorrently far reaching remits? Such agents are ideal tools, however, for the artificial consciousness that actually runs the Jurisdiction.

The Enguine Manifesto

Indin-Indin: On Dereph, in the Network

The ninety-foot door flashed yellow as, like a thunderclap dramatically heralding the ancient facilities' awakening, a car plummeted to the ground and skipped along the street like a stone across a pond. Clearing a small child by mere inches, the vehicle didn't quite make it over the man beside him and it tore his head away in a messy explosion of blood and brain. A greater explosion of fire and metal followed as the car slammed into Indin-Indin's shuttle and he felt his outer cosmetic layer burn and darken at the intensity of the flames. With a thought he absorbed the damaged cells for later repair and replaced them with a freshly forming human-like skin. In the parts of his neural mesh dedicated to the control of Satumine technology, Indin-Indin heard the whole ancient research facility rouse from millennia of somnolence, responding to the great door's opening.

The vast entrance's two halves glided slow and silent into the upturned arch walls and instantly Indin-Indin realised his error. Although his intelligence was unrivalled by any organic life yet extant in the galaxy, it seemed his common sense and judgement had not been proportionally enhanced.

Even from his vantage point, standing before the still opening great doors, he heard the alarms within the facility. Human alarms. Human pilots, as well as attaining the mild contact required to activate Network frames, could link with the petty systems controlling some ancient Satumine doors. In his haste, Indin-Indin had assumed all doors to be the same. It was now obvious to him that such reasoning was not only wrong but also unforgivably naïve. This door had never been opened by humans; this was the entrance to a high security research facility and, as such, only senior Satumine could ever open it. It would not be fooled by the light touch of a human Pilot's mind. Any hope of walking in unnoticed seemed to have been lost. But, as he ran through the opening doors into the huge hall beyond, a crowd of panicked humans rushed in behind him, fleeing the rain of vehicles and the raging fire-storm sweeping through the city devoid of an IB emergency response system. The ancient facility shuddered under a heavy impact, but it was doubtful that even the force of a falling public transport vehicle could so much as tarnish the near-indestructible alloys of ancient Satumine architecture.

From within, the shape of the upturned arch was still discernible. The entire facility seemed to be a hollow shell curving up to Indin-Indin's left and right, reaching up hundreds of feet. While the vast walls were covered in a mesh or rods and domes, looking something like an antiquated circuit board, there was nothing else within. No gantry levels, no furniture or human equipment, just an immense expanse of open space in which a micro climate had been established, forming thin wisps of cloud towards the two high ceilings. The humans didn't stop to admire the mystery of this hollow construction, they simply ran to the twenty-foot circle cut into the floor, around which a human railing had been built and an elevator disk installed. As they fought for space on the four-person disk, forcing some of their number to fall over the small railing down the dark passage to a quick death, Indin-Indin queried the facility systems, mentally asking how the human authorities had previously gained entry without breaking the seal on the large secure doors. His attention was drawn to a four-foot door, far off to his left. A human door. Before he could form a second query, the Satumine systems pre-empted him and explained an emergency ventilation shaft had been open during the fall of this planet and the humans had simply built an undersized door around this open vent. Indin-Indin shrugged and caused the vent to slam closed, shattering the flimsy diminutive human door and sending what sounded like a gunshot echoing up and down the hollow arch. He then closed the main door, sealing in the humans who had hoped to find shelter, as well as the five hundred humans the systems informed him were down in the subterranean levels where they were trying to steal ancient Satumine technological secrets.

Inhabiting the facility surveillance systems, Indin-Indin located and tagged every human. The ability to so effortlessly multi-task was instinctive, but still it came as an exhilarating surprise. With absolute focus, and no noticeable loss of intellect, he observed every human, paying full attention as if with separate minds to each human's actions. He considered them both in isolation and as part of a larger stratagem encompassing the entire group. How far could he split his attention and still see his intellect remain undiminished? He didn't have an answer but knew he had not come close to his limits. Establishing links with the security systems, he felt his mind expand and the minor act of multi-tasking became even easier. His potential, it seemed, would be limited not by the neural mesh within his body but by the Satumine systems to which he could link. And, if necessary, he had sole access to the entire colony. For now, however, he was content with the facility.

Noticing the continuing struggle at the elevator disk, which had yet to ferry a single group to the supposed safety of the subterranean levels, Indin-Indin decided to rid himself first of these frantic humans.

The elevator disk and its accompanying systems down the shafts kilometre length were removed by the simple act of awakening the true conveyance system used by the original Satumine: before the gravity chute could activate and calibrate, contingency systems ensured the long shaft was clear of anything which might unbalance the precise gravimetric wave patterns, which included the human-built elevator. A brief flash of light and heat, siphoned from the pointspace energy collectors powering the entire Satumine colony from five miles beneath the surface, atomised everything that shouldn't have been there. The blast of heat escaping the shaft was enough to incinerate every one of the humans gathered around the elevator disk, as well as the railing around its perimeter. Safety protocols would never have allowed such a blast to take place had any Satumine been detected so close – but humans didn't count. They died before they had time to scream. Indin-Indin thought that a shame. But there were five hundred yet to suffer more satisfying deaths.

Taking a curious delight in the aroma of charred human flesh, he approached the sterilised shaft, kicked aside a couple of smouldering heaps of human-shaped charcoal and stepped out over the pit. Although genetic memory told him what to expect of the gravity chute,

Indin-Indin still tensed at the sudden decent which, while controlled, was so fast as to be almost free-fall. He resisted the urge to reach out to the controls with his mind and apply the emergency breaks; it would have done him little good to be stranded half way down, hovering on a gravimetric wave front. For almost a full kilometre he was pulled down by the planet's natural gravity, the chute applying only the slightest hold. The tiny point of light at the chute's bottom began widening and the gentle upward push of gravimetric waves increased, quickly countering the natural pull of the planet and applying a deceleration which would have been painful, perhaps fatal, to his old body and to the bodies of humans. His new form merely compressed by a few inches and endured the force. Then he was on the ground, surrounded by the melted remains of the humans' elevator system, the charred bodies, and a ring of startled but very much alive human workers.

'Who are you?' a woman demanded. Indin-Indin noticed a pistol in a thin holster on her right thigh, but she made no move to reach for it. Why would she? Indin-Indin looked every bit as human as her, and he was unarmed. But, not limited to the range of his faux-eyes, able to see with every cell of his body, he saw the movements of those behind him, and a stocky old man was raising what looked like a shock-rod. Indin-Indin smiled. It was a human expression, one he had never been capable of forming in his old static form. He decided he liked it. He asserted control over the facility defences, awakening hidden lasers with the same ease with which he had roused the massive weapons used to destroy the IB suites on the surface.

At their lowest settings the defences could deliver a neural shock capable of irritating an ancient Satumine – or incapacitating a human. It was this setting Indin-Indin deployed, dropping every human around him before the pin-sized emitters had fully extended from the walls. Then he brought down the rest of the research teams throughout the facility. Unlike those incinerated by the chute steriliser, these humans would have time to appreciate the horror of their end.

For an hour Indin-Indin practiced his control over Satumine technology, finding ever more imaginative methods of execution for the human usurpers.

Chapter 50

Of all the privileges and rights afforded to every citizen of the Human Jurisdiction, the most absolute but often underrated is the Census. This powerful if occasionally cryptic document, gauges through various psychometric questions the beliefs, priorities, desires and principles of every one of the trillions of humans in the Jurisdiction. The results of this vast democratic undertaking are processed and distilled until the base morality and wishes of our society can be woven into the code compartments of the legion of governance machines overseeing the logistics of legislating and administrating our thousands of worlds. You are required to exercise your democratic right and your participation in the census morally obliges you to accept the net results in the form of the laws created from its findings. As a survivor of Consul's slavery you will no doubt be excited to express your opinions and, I am delighted to inform you, you will be presented with the most recent census questions within weeks of your official integration into the Jurisdiction. We can not, after all, ask you to be subject to laws over which you have had no say.

Rehabilitation: A Survivor's Guide

Anden Macer: Aboard the *Vulpine*, in orbit around Pellitoe, in the Swinell Union, in the Fertile Belt

Anden Macer no longer observed the honour rites of his home world. He hadn't even been back to that shipyard world during the *Vulpine's* occasional deployments to the Able Union. The ritualistic culture of Rancordit simply wasn't compatible with Anden's more enlightened federal mind-set. Although he had never gone so far as to admit it out loud, the customs of his people seemed laughably superstitious. He had kept his hair in the traditional Rancordit dreadlocks out of habit rather than any desire to honour his ancestors and clan. Now, however, as he closed the hastily sanctified shears about the thickness of the dreads, he mumbled the rite of failure, feeling each word sting his soul. The shears were deliberately blunt and Anden had to force the long handles to close, severing a thick matted twist of greased hair and sending a jolt of psychosomatic pain through his body. The hair landed on the mat on which he knelt, seeming to strike the ground with immense weight. Anden had failed his crew, he had failed the crews of the Swinell Union cruisers and the orbital stations, he had failed those the *Tenjin* would now go on to kill. He had failed the Jurisdiction. He no longer deserved to wear the dreadlocks which had, for over a century and a half, represented his intrinsic honour and the glory of his successes. He cut the second dread, this time feeling nothing as the hair fell; the rite was complete, his failure and dishonour confirmed. More hair fell away, leaving jagged stumps and lines of red where the shears scraped at the captain's scalp.

A hand gently clasped his wrist; another pulled the shears from his weak grip.

'What are you doing?' his executive officer, his friend, asked with unfamiliar softness. Anden sniffed back a pitiful sob and turned to face Steit, humiliated and disgraced. He couldn't talk, didn't have the words, and in the throes of the superstitious rite he felt he didn't have the right to speak.

'Anden?' the executive officer pressed. 'What did you do to your hair?'

Anden looked blankly at his friend, then down to the shears, then finally to the twists of hair on the floor.

'Steit?' he mumbled as if waking from the nonsense of a dream. The cool air of the ship's failing environmental systems breezed across his half-bald head to send a cold judder down his spine. He reached up to feel his dreads, many of which were no longer there.

'Steit?' he repeated, utterly bemused and broken.

'It's OK,' the executive officer whispered, kneeling beside his captain, his friend of a century, and pulling the sobbing man's defiled head to his chest. 'It's OK.'

'We're in position,' the operations officer said, poking his head through the open door to the captain's cabin. Like Steit he spoke with an uncomfortable softness, a worrying restraint which was so unlike him. Nobody knew how to act, how to be around one another, much less how to talk to their distraught captain. Practically on the eve of its centenary, the *Vulpine* had suffered its most devastating defeat, its greatest loss of life, and it had been under Anden's command.

Anden looked across to the door, pushing his executive officer away with a lethargic shove. Did the crew blame him? How could they not? He was expected on the command floor but daren't show his face. Although he had called the *Vulpine* his home for almost a hundred years, and some of its crew his friends for just as long, he knew others aboard had also formed relationships decades long, and many of those had been violently ended by the disastrous encounter with the *Tenjin*.

'Oh, Christ,' Ruebill said, stepping into the cabin, closing the door behind him. 'What's he done to his hair, Steit?'

'He cut it off,' the executive officer said, waving the sanctified shears. 'It's a Rancordit ritual. The rite of failure.'

The operations officer shook his head with a tired sadness laced with a pity which only enhanced Anden's shame. 'Well, he's needed on the command floor. He needs to transfer control to *Kubet* station's IB docking systems.'

'I can do that,' Steit said, making to stand. Anden glared at him; it was bad enough that two of his senior officers were talking about him as if he weren't there – or as if he were a senile invalid – but now they were preparing to usurp his duties and hide him away as an embarrassment best kept from the crew. Not likely. He grabbed Steit's wrist and squeezed hard, dragging the officer back down to his knees. 'This is my ship,' he snarled. 'She was wounded under my stewardship, and it is under my stewardship that she shall be restored.'

Steit smiled and watched Anden stand before joining him on his feet. 'Yes Captain,' the executive officer barked, giving an approving nod. 'Might I suggest we neaten up your hair before we-'

'Sod the hair,' the captain snapped. 'It doesn't mean a damned thing.' He meant it. To hell with his ancestors and his personal honour, it was to the dead of the *Vulpine* that he must bring honour and glory. He lived only to bring meaning to their deaths; he would not wallow in self-indulgent ritual. With a few prods at an AR screen he loaded an extreme haircut embellishment, covering his remaining dreads with the shortest of crops. Then he strode to the door.

'I want the weapons checked and our box-kite recovered from lunar orbit,' he snapped. 'As soon as the *Tenjin* is detected elsewhere, I want us ready to burrow.'

Chapter 51

Most Unions have some form of law limiting or outright prohibiting genetic tailoring, but the Administration claims there is no federal ban. If you wish to test the truth of this, I invite you to travel to a world like Lekmal's Rest, a world with perhaps the most active and permissive genetic manipulation infrastructure, and ask for your unborn child to be of the third gender. See how quickly the Trustees block your request. They will not even give you a reason. Why, then, when such a gender does not exist naturally in the Satumine any more than it does in Humanity, are they permitted to create such self-fertilising offspring? They may deny it, but I have seen them.

The Truth: A treatise on the Satumine Conspiracy

Galman Tader: On Pellitoe, in the Swinell Union, in the Fertile Belt

Galman couldn't see who had entered the trailer, he was too deeply ensconced in the storage alcove, but the vile click and sputter of the Satumine tongue was unmistakable. He wasn't fluent in the alien language but had picked up enough during his decades of obsessive Satumine persecution to recognise curses and complaints as the creatures struggled to unload their prize. Apparently the mechanical lifter had failed and, none-too-quietly, the Satumine had to manually pull it down the trailer's ramp. A shadow fell across the alcove and Galman shrank back, seeking the darkest corner but knowing he was poorly concealed. A Satumine leg reached back into the alcove's open mouth as the creature leaned into the massive crate containing the mysterious object. Galman froze, waited for the leg to twist a few degrees, to turn the knee eye into the alcove and spot the hidden man. Tumble brought up one of his tentacles, slow as to not make a sound with the failing appendage. A needle-point slid out of the tentacle, poised to stab at the Satumine eye should it turn. Galman shook his head; the Satumine wouldn't be disabled by such a strike, just enraged. Besides, this Satumine wasn't alone; there was an unknown number of his comrades to contend with, both inside and outside the trailer. Tumble withdrew the needle.

Somebody yelled, or at least raised his voice in the half-hearted way Satumine did when angered or issuing orders, and the leg vanished from the alcove. Galman restrained a sigh. The alien voice continued its attempt at shouting from the rear of the trailer and although Galman couldn't decipher word for word he got the gist: The lead Satumine wanted the *device* off of the trailer and hooked up to the pointspace burrower within the hour. The response was easier to decipher: *Yes Ambondice-Ambondice.* Galman grinned and reached for his pistol. A metal tentacle gently coiled about his wrist, restraining his murderous impulse.

For a full minute the Satumine struggled with the bulky crate, scraping the trailer's floor as they inched it towards the ramp. Then they were done; the door closed and the perpetual light of an illumination strip returned the interior to the gloom in which Galman had travelled for more hours than was comfortable.

For a few minutes Galman and Tumble waited in silence, waited for the doors to open again or for a Satumine, still aboard, to reveal himself. When nothing happened, nothing appeared, Galman stepped tentatively from his hiding place, Tumble under his arm, and he stumbled forward as his new calf tissue tensed and cramped in response to the sudden movement after so long cooped up in the alcove.

'Now what?' the machine asked. Galman glared at his friend, then looked around the large trailer, all but empty save for the malfunctioning mechanical lifter.

'We need to get out,' he decided, massaging life back into his solid muscle, 'Before the truck starts moving again.'

'I think they might notice if we open the back doors,' Tumble said.

Galman muttered that his IB companion wasn't really helping and then he pointed to the panelled floor. 'What about those?' he asked. 'Can we lift one of those panels?'

Tumble extruded a short drill-like implement from one of his tattered limbs. 'I'm guessing you mean can *I* lift one.'

'Just get on with it,' Galman hissed, placing the spherical machine down on the floor.

After probing with the drill-tip, finding the rivets and panels to be an AR embellishment of the most pointless kind, Tumble located the real floor sections and didn't need to drill out any rivets or bolts. The six-foot sheet of thin metal came up easily, passing right through the illusion of a more retro floor, and Galman helped Tumble slide it aside.

'Is that it?'

Tumble lowered a tentacle down through the illusion and seemed to poke about for a while. Then he pulled back and said, 'Seems to be. Stay here a moment while I go down and see what's out there.' The machine then disappeared beneath the AR floor and Galman felt a choking claustrophobia advancing on him. He closed his eyes and reminded himself that his friend was only a couple of feet away, that there was a six-foot gap in the floor – hidden beneath an insubstantial illusion - through which he could escape at any time. But he felt no better and he realised how reliant he had become on Tumble's companionship and support. He bit back a call to the machine, knowing he had to just sit tight while Tumble scouted ahead. His hand ached. Looking down to see white trembling knuckles he saw he had been gripping his little laser pistol's thin handle so tightly as to dig his finger nails into his palm. It took a deliberate effort to relax the grip; it felt as though clinging on to the weapon was all that was keeping him alive. When had he become so neurotic? Recalling his current illegal endeavour and the means by which he had arrived here, he doubted he had been entirely rational since leaving Diaclom. His obsession, if not his neurosis, had begun long before that.

His introspection was broken by the prodding at his ribs of a metal tentacle. Galman opened his eyes, saw Tumble, and dismissed his self-examination.

'How's it going?'

'Not great,' Tumble said, emerging part way through the illusory floor. 'But it's not going to get any better. Down you come, but be quiet.'

It was disconcerting to step through the AR floor. The sensory input of unreal resistance to his passing only made it worse. It truly was a step into the unknown, but once he lowered himself down as far as his chest, and his feet pressed on the smooth surface beneath, he found himself able to resolve the conflicting stimulus and ignore the AR floor. He ducked down, bringing himself fully beneath the trailer and saw the truck had been parked in a wide garage or loading bay in which several other vehicles were lined up. From below, the trailer looked dirty and lacking any embellishments, but there was every chance that this rustic look was precisely the effect being sought and it could all be AR over a spotless drab-reality foundation. Crouching low to avoid crossbeams and the heavy axles of the five sets of wheels, Galman made his way to the trailer's rear, dragging Tumble by an appendage. There seemed to be nobody in the loading bay and a deep scratch led across the floor to the shutters of a wide delivery door, telling of the crate's immense weight. Beside that large closed shutter was a smaller door which had been left ajar and from beyond could be heard human and Satumine voices. For several long seconds Galman remained there, crouched beneath the trailer, eyes fixed on the crack of light shining between the frame and partly opened door. He looked about again, wary of running out into the open, of exposing himself to a hidden guard. He couldn't see anyone but was less than certain of his ability to spot a concealed Satumine on such a heavily embellished world as this.

'Can you see anyone?' he whispered, barely mouthed, to Tumble.

'No,' the sphere replied, louder and obviously more confident they were alone in the loading bay. Galman nodded, happy to trust the machine, and slid out from his hiding place to sprint the short distance of open bay to the smaller of the two doors where he pressed his face to the inch crack, peering through.

'This doesn't look much like a pre-billion nursery,' he whispered. 'I've seen plenty of them on Diaclom and I'm pretty sure none of them included pointspace burrowers.' The mesh sphere of the burrower dominated the bare room beyond the door and Galman recognised its configuration immediately. 'This is a pointspace *comms* facility,' he said.

'I guess the nursery was just an AR cover,' Tumble suggested. 'Which means this must be a redundancy. If the primary is damaged they would want this place hidden from any potential attack.'

'I don't think it was hidden very well,' Galman said, noting the stacks of human corpses piled against the far wall, a wide sticky puddle of dark blood spread out for a few metres but now congealing. They had died a while ago, though not too long. There was no stench of decay.

'What are they doing to the burrower?' he asked Tumble, only just stopping himself from leaning though the opening to point at the five dishevelled and beaten humans attaching a twenty- foot corkscrew of chromed pipe to the mesh.

'I really have no idea,' Tumble admitted. 'But a pointspace burrower could be converted into a hell of a bomb. Perhaps we should get out while we still can.'

'No,' Galman said, though he suspected the machine hadn't been entirely serious in its suggestion. Tumble knew how emotive a Satumine bombing was to Galman; there was no way they were leaving.

A dozen Satumine were visible, every one of them armed. There were probably more around the large hall, beyond the limited range visible through the small gap in the door. Too many for Galman to take, even if he had something more threatening than a mini laser pistol.

'What do you want to do?' Tumble asked.

'Just watch, for now. We need to know what they are doing. Is there any way you can get a signal to the federal authorities?'

'Not within a kilometre of here,' Tumble apologised. 'Like I said, they have got the AR here completely isolated, and all of the comms go through that network.'

'Any way of using your intelligence-bridge connection to send a signal?'

'Sorry, Can't be done.'

'Well record what you are seeing. If we get a chance later I want you to upload it all to the Trustees.'

'Already recording.'

Of course he was.

One of the Satumine glanced over to the door and Galman pulled back, convinced he had been seen. But still he looked back through the gap a couple of seconds later. The Satumine was striding towards him.

'Fuck,' Galman spat and he bolted for the trailer, sliding feet first to regain his hiding place.

'Thanks!' Tumble muttered, still by the door where Galman had left him. Galman cringed and beckoned desperately for the crippled machine to rush to join him.

In his prime Tumble could have fired an adhesive tentacle to the trailer and drawn his body in, and it would have taken no more than a second. Tumble wasn't in his prime. He managed to extrude his three spindly leg stalks and began clattering awkwardly across the loading bay, taking far too long. Galman considered leaving the machine to be discovered, trusting Tumble could bluff his way out of the situation without betraying Galman's presence. Instead, however, he found himself dashing back out to meet his IB friend.

'Stupid,' Tumble commented, not elaborating as to whether it was referring to Galman's failure to pick him up when he bolted, or his decision to break cover in this ill-advised rescue. Galman scooped up the struggling sphere and turned back to the trailer as he heard a loud metallic clattering. He froze, waiting for a challenge, or a shot, but then noticed light streaming in from the main door which, behind the truck, was rolling open. He glanced over his shoulder and saw the door to the pointspace *comms* room still hadn't opened, and so he dove back under the trailer.

Then the door opened and six of the Satumine strode into the loading bay, walking to within a couple of metres of where Galman and Tumble lay. With a solid click the main exit door locked into place, fully opened, and a small vehicle could be heard driving in. Possibly a car.

One of the Satumine spoke and Galman recognised the voice as that of Ambondice-Ambondice. He spoke in the human tongue, but not using embellishments to smooth over the roughness of Satumine pronunciation.

'Office Trustee,' he said with joviality and familiarity. Galman couldn't tell if it was sincere but, when a familiar human voice yelled a furious tirade which was silenced by a wet impact, he decided the Office Trustee was not there by choice.

'Just relax, Cordem, we all have a long week ahead of us. You ought to save your strength.'

Galman couldn't see the Office Trustee, but he knew his only ally, Cordem Hastergado, was now a prisoner of the Satumine. He shuffled further back into the shadows beneath the trailer and wondered if he would ever leave this facility alive.

And his calf had cramped again.

A few minutes later, Tumble lost his intelligence-bridge coverage.

Chapter 52

Anyone who has followed my feeds, or even my publicly accessible criminal record, will know I am an ardent supporter of union-level autonomy. The dream, of course, is for the unions of the Jurisdiction to embrace the example set by Enguine and to cede fully from the homogeneity expected by the Administration, with each state entitled to go so far as complete isolation from the galactic community should its citizens so desire. The Administration will cite various wars with such independently minded planets and unions as prime examples of why an overarching galactic government is necessary, but they will always conveniently skirt around the actual triggers which sparked those wars. Official feeds will tell of violent regimes oppressing and abusing their populace and of warmongers building vast fleets and apocalyptic weapons soon to be unleashed on the peaceful worlds of the Jurisdiction. They will show Sector Trustees declaring with heavy hearts a pre-emptive strike, promising to minimise casualties with a measured and surgical response, stating clear objective of liberating an enslaved population and neutralising the threats to the neighbouring worlds. And then they will censor everything coming out of those Unions as they unleash CRMs and other disproportionate tactics to batter into submission a world which dared to turn its back on the Jurisdiction.

The Enguine Manifesto

Endella Mariacroten: Aboard the *Tenjin*, in shortspace

Endella squeezed the soft trigger, past the bite point of single round fire and into fully automatic. The magnetic coils hummed and, one by one, bolts were pulled from the last selected clip – armour penetrating – and accelerated through the short barrel to almost supersonic velocity. She could have set a higher velocity but had neither the time, nor the desire to draw attention to herself with sonic booms. In almost complete silence the twenty bolts were ejected from the barrel in under a second. The cyborg dropped to the floor a moment later, its face a mess of bloodied holes which gave the look of a maggot ravaged apple. The back of its head, however, was completely removed, blasted in chunks into the room, taking with it most of the brain. The Justiciar got back to her feet from her instinctive firing position on one knee and stepped carefully through the door, her mag-gun locked on the apparent corpse but her eyes scanning the rest of the room for more threats.

According to her memory of the *Tenjin*'s layout, this ought to have been either a crew dorm for Junior Trustees, or a storage area for the quad-helix research department – depending on which hemisphere of the mirror designed station she was in. This looked nothing like either room. Amid a tangle of frosted crystal pipes, and oval chambers the size of a Satumine head, stood twenty three massive transparent piston-like assemblies. Each reached from the floor to the ceiling fifteen feet above and pumped with no discernible rhythm as they compressed a light green gas or plasma, turning it scarlet when the pistons reached maximum compression and sounding a sharp pop before rising again to draw more of the unknown green matter into the assembly. In the frosted pipes and chambers ran a current of crackling white which escaped through several fractures as a thin steam. Endella glanced back down at the corpse, wondering at the white metal augmentations across its face and naked, sexless body. None had any obvious function, being merely small plates and coils of the glossy white metal, presumably attached to greater enhancements within the body. The scattered fragments of crystal and metal binding together chunks of spilt brain confirmed her assumption and when she unloaded six more bolts into its chest, just to be certain, she glimpsed a network of cables and crystal processors through the small holes.

Undoubtedly there were important discoveries to be made in the dissection and study of this body, but there was no time. Not yet. Covering her mouth and nose with her hands, she ran through the thin clouds of escaping vapour to leave by the single door at the far end of the room. The cloud stung as nettles and then burnt like acid when it found her seeping stomach wound. She gritted her teeth and pushed through, relieved when the door responded to her presence and opened into an utterly bare side room. The door slid closed behind her and the tiny wisp of vapour following her in was quickly expunged by the coin-sized atmospheric circulation ducts near the ceiling. She breathed in deeply and exhaled hard, doing her best to cleanse her lungs of whatever it was she had been exposed to. A stinging in her eyes told her it was more than mere steam and her abdominal wound felt hot and stung with the rhythm of her pulse. She really needed to stop and eat as much of her emergency supplies as she could stomach, to give her nano-farms something to work with. But she expected the cyborg had been more than capable of betraying her presence in the second or two before she had put it down. She left the side room by the only other door, bringing her out into a corridor. It was better lit than the decommissioned passage in which she had previously walked and that probably meant she could expect to run into more of the crew which, so far at least, and excluding the cyborg, had been conspicuously absent.

Flicking the mag-gun selection to the more plentiful anti-personnel bolts, she jogged down the corridor. Thirty seconds later, her intestines threatening to haemorrhage through the rupturing knot of scar tissue, she accepted she would have to walk. Blood was seeping almost unopposed through the thin fabric of the sleeve she had used to bind the wound and, to her chagrin, Endella realised the nano-farms were completely exhausted. Had they anything left with which to work, the bleeding would have at least been stopped. Resting against one of the curved walls she took a medical supplement tube from her backpack and squeezed the thick paste into her mouth. The sickly strawberry flavour couldn't disguise the metallic tang, but it was the metal that the nano-farms most needed. Once more nano devices had been constructed they would use the fat and protein in the paste to patch up the worst of her wounds. It wouldn't take too long, perhaps ten minutes, but she couldn't stay, she expected the crew to be closing in on her. There was as much chance, of course, that she was bringing herself closer to them with every step.

Ten minutes later, still having seen no signs of life, she realised she had also seen none of the expected security devices – the surveillance and defensive systems. In some places she could see the empty housing that ought to have contained a surveillance and address screen but, like most of the screens and devices she should have seen in the corridors and rooms through which she was passing, they appeared to have been ripped out. The *Tenjin*'s crew did not seem to feel the need to invest in internal security and, if it was true that they had spent ten thousand years isolated in a wormhole, they probably needed to recycle all spare resources to construct anything new. Recycling and austerity could only go so far though, which possibly explained the noticeable lack of crew. How many of the original crew's descendent had actually survived to see the emergence back into higher dimensional space? However few their number, they obviously felt themselves plentiful enough to declare war on the Jurisdiction.

As she neared the IB suite, Endella found the first group huddled around a smoking bundle of cables in the corner of a vast industrial expanse which, according to her memory of the layout, shouldn't have been there. Where there should have been six decks, containing one hundred assorted rooms and a network of interconnecting corridors and passages, stood this single immense chamber. Gantries and catwalks criss-crossed in every direction, granting access to all parts of the huge mechanical components which rose out of the ground and, Endella suspected, continued down for several more levels. The heat and noise was unsettling and unfamiliar. No human had been subjected to such industrial working conditions for centuries – only IB machines should be so deep within the mechanical workings of… whatever this was.

The crew, nine in all, hadn't noticed her standing twenty feet above on a shaky catwalk. They worked, wordlessly and without expression, on the tree-trunk thick bundle of cables, cutting individual wires with tools protruding from holes in their fingers and slipping crystal processor flakes between the severed ends. Every one of the creatures was different, but each as inhuman and androgynous as the cyborg she had killed earlier. Some were practically clothed in white plates of metal, looking more like humanoid robots than augmented humans; others had only a few strips of white but were disfigured by ugly sub-dermal implants which bulged and stretched the pallid black-veined skin. Their cloudy grey eyes betrayed no thoughts, no emotion, and Endella was prepared to accept they were no more than mindless animated corpses – nothing but organic IB machines. To imagine any sentience behind those pitiful eyes was too disturbing a thought on which to linger. She crept along the catwalk, her feet having regained some small measure of their usual dexterity now that the worst of her internal bleeding had been stemmed and the torn scar tissue at her stomach re-knitted. The creatures – she couldn't think of them as human – didn't look up from their work. She made her way across the length of the huge industrial chamber to find a door and then glanced back. The group of nine was partially hidden behind a twisting metal cylinder which ground against a black resin plate and showered the area with yellow and blue sparks. Her view partially obscured, the object of the creatures' efforts beyond her view, Endella was reminded of an AR fiction she had seen as a child: they looked like ghouls feasting on the warm viscera of their human victim. She shuddered and turned away, rushing through the door into the short corridor she hoped would lead to the IB suite, if the *Tenjin* still even used Intelligence-bridges.

Through another door at the end of the corridor she found a scene to rival the imagined horror of the ghouls. Nine IB pods were arranged in a ring, facing out, and seven of those pods were occupied by creatures more pitiful and harrowing to behold than even the cyborgs huddled about their cables. Black and withered like mummified corpses, the seven occupants could not have possibly been alive, except that Endella saw their desiccated chests rising and falling with slow shallow breaths. Deep cracks in the blackened skin formed to accommodate the motion of breathing and, about their feet, flakes of dark leather littered the floor. Feeding tubes reached down from spheres in the ceiling, forcing nutrients directly into the occupants' stomachs and a build-up of scabs and blisters had grown around their mouths and followed their tubes up a few inches. Endella had seen countless vile horrors as a Justiciar, had uncovered graves of tortured colleagues and seen the unspeakable atrocities done on worlds stupid enough to cede from the Jurisdiction. But nothing she had seen had ever before elicited so physical a reaction as did this IB suite. She vomited, expelling blood and puss rather than the paste she had eaten. Something hot began refilling her stomach and although she retched violently she held back from throwing up again. Something had burst inside and she was filling up with blood - blood she needed to hold on to until her nano-farms could redirect it back into her circulatory system. It was going to take more than a tube of paste, and considerably longer than ten minutes, to stabilise her failing body. Fortunately, she reasoned, it would probably take her a good while to shadow the *Tenjin*'s intelligence-bridge functions to find an exploitable weakness.

Sitting in one of the empty pods she put her head back and allowed the automated feeding tube to extend down to her face where it slithered horribly across her cheek, past her lips and across her tongue. She felt a cool test squirt of paste not dissimilar to medical paste but lacking much usable metal, and she hoped her nano-farms retained enough material to make use of the steady flow of nutrients they were about to enjoy. Clenching her fist at her poor focus she belatedly recalled an old survival trick from her early military training and quickly opened the base of her multipistol's magazine. She slid out three armour-piercing bolts and swallowed them like tablets. There would be virtually nothing left of the cold metal bolts by the time her nano-farms were done with them.

The alpha-field activated and she felt her mind relent to the pervasive roots of the *Tenjin*'s computers. Then, before she lost awareness and became merely a tool for the IB computers, she activated what was left of her internal hardware. As the device around her brain exerted its unique influence, Endella wondered if she would be discovered. If the bodies in the other pods were any guide, however, she guessed nobody came here very often.

Chapter 53

Coming, as you have, from Consul's slave worlds, the spectre of mortality has likely never disturbed you - either because as a component in the IB farms your continued existence was assured, or because you actively longed for death. Either way, you may not be aware of, or understand the obsession with, human mortality. The fact is for the greater part of human history our ancestors were limited to barely a century of life and in most cases considerably shorter. The technologies developed to extend and ultimately negate the processes of natural death are myriad and well publicised and you will be invited shortly to undergo those therapies most appropriate to your situation and intended place of residence. The most important and universal result of these therapies is, however, that all humans are entitled to an indefinite span of life. Short of extreme accident or violence - both of which are ever rarer in the Jurisdiction - you will not die. Ever.

Rehabilitation: A Survivor's Guide

Indin-Indin: On Dereph, in the Network

The Satumine facility was a warren of tall passages and even taller halls. The clutter of human equipment and supplies made it claustrophobic and tainted the simple beauty of clean smooth walls behind which ancient technology was hidden from view. Humans were such a materialistically showy species, determined to put their every accomplishment and trapping of petty wealth on display. The Satumine, the *true* Satumine, were not so insecure. Indin-Indin had spent an hour clearing a small room of the devices and furniture that the human squatters had installed, though the two piles of dead human meat - all that remained of the couple of human females that had been working in this room when Indin-Indin had awoken the defences - were left in the corner. They were a pleasant reminder of the vengeance he would inflict for the humiliation and subjugation of his people. He now crouched in the corner; the mass of his body was as equally comfortable in that position as in any other but the pose was a throwback from his old habits and the requirements of his discarded feeble body.

His massively dividable focus was as much in the facility systems as it was in the bare room as he searched for the technology Aggregate had sent him here to utilise. For three days he had sat, unmoving, scouring the complex network of devices which were as decentralised as human AR nets, and he found no mention of what he needed. A uniquely Satumine emotion, not even felt by the modern bastardised race, washed through him. Perhaps akin to a calmly considered panic, but with a note of anger and other less easily defined feelings; it took Indin-Indin by surprise. No, not surprise, even that emotion was changed. The shameful ties to humanity which had made his race so weak, no longer corrupted his emotions. Indin-Indin thought, and felt, only as a true Satumine.

He considered his panic-like state and linked it to the realisation that Aggregate may have been wrong. The mysterious creature controlling the *Tenjin* had assumed the technology it needed would exist in this facility but such an assumption had to have been based only on the files available in the original *Tenjin* research networks. It was an assumption based on the supposition of the human researches Indin-Indin had just slaughtered throughout the facility, and he didn't feel confident that those lowly creatures could have possibly discerned the true purpose of anything the true Satumine had been researching. He punched the ground – another habit of his old self. Inwardly, however, the calm undercurrent to his panic allowed for a more rational response. Within minutes he understood that the Satumine system nets had decohered over such a vast span of inactivity and, in all likelihood, he was seeing, inhabiting, only a fraction of the full network.

He began repairing code flaws, where he could, and rewriting that which couldn't be salvaged. With the same instinctive ease that had brought him this far, he understood the Satumine computer languages.

The code compartments were geometrically formed through a thousand mathematical dimensions, a colossal advancement over the twelve-dimensional mathematics employed by Jurisdiction computers, and Indin-Indin arranged them with subconscious ease. The code compartments of the devices themselves were written into a million mathematical dimensions, and he perceived them with little difficulty. The networks, therefore, were sheer simplicity.

New systems appeared by the dozen in the increasingly complex network and Indin-Indin asserted his absolute authority over them all. But still the device required by Aggregate remained lost. He continued to revive the faded network, bringing to life whole branches of science undreamed of by the Jurisdiction, many of which had never been mastered by the Satumine before their exodus from this facility and this colony. But still not what he needed.

A day later, four days after he had brought low the intelligence-bridges on which the human society of this planet was built, he became aware of a particle accelerator being unleashed on the facility door from orbit. Although he knew it would take more than the accelerator to gain entry, Indin-Indin was furious – or something like it – at his own short-sightedness. So immersed as he was in the Satumine network of devices, he had ignored the human equipment. He had seen it merely as junk to be pushed aside. For all his mental superiority, he had neglected to invade the human surveillance cameras and hide himself, and the slaughter he had prosecuted, from their sight. Too late he linked the Satumine network with the pathetically vulnerable human surveillance, blinding every camera and sensor in his facility. With one part of his divided mind he monitored the humans evacuate the system of civilian ships while fortifying the orbits with military vessels. The rest of him continued rewriting and repairing the facility network.

Two days later, the humans had brought in three more accelerators. They had burnt an inch-deep hole. As the accelerators were powered down for twenty seconds to cool, the door regenerated, much to the lead Trustee's apparent irritation and to Indin-Indin's amusement.

He still hadn't found what he needed, but there was a vast amount of the network yet to be revealed. He did not have unlimited time – Aggregate had specified a timetable which could not be altered – but he had some time yet.

'Stop it!' a voice, a Satumine voice, yelled into Indin-Indin's mind from the network. 'I shouldn't be alive!'

Another new emotion struck, and Indin-Indin withdrew instantly from his inhabitation of the network.

Chapter 54

It is a controversial and sensitive subject, but I would like to speak now about the right to die, and specifically how this right is suspended on pre-billion colonies. Ever since we enshrined into law the right to an indefinite lifespan, we have had to ensure an opposite right was in place, in order that the vertigo of a potentially infinite life does not consume us. We have a right to die because that right allows us, ironically, to go on without killing ourselves. We are more content to go on living when we know we could end it if we so desired. This right has always been suspended on pre-billion colonies, for obvious reasons. A heartening exception has been the exemption of Satumine from this prohibition. They are not required to breed and they are not stopped from self-euthanizing. This has been a comfort to people such as me, as it means the Satumine are still deemed less than us. I am disturbed - terrified even - to learn that the exemption is soon to be removed. Satumine will, within the century, no longer be allowed to self-euthanize on pre-billion colonies. Why am I terrified? Because this change in the law must herald a far more upsetting and destabilising shift in policy: the Satumine will soon be required to meet the same breeding quotas as humans.
The Truth: A treatise on the Satumine Conspiracy

Galman Tader: On Pellitoe, in the Swinell Union, in the Fertile Belt

Over the course of almost a week, the twenty foot chrome corkscrew had slowly uncoiled to form a thick snake which now wrapped itself about the mesh of the spherical pointspace burrower. The heat radiating from the esoteric chrome device's interaction with the burrower had reached as far as the small door through which Galman periodically spied on the Satumine group, and his face had begun to redden as if severely sunburnt. Since completing its embrace of the burrower, twelve hours ago, the chrome snake had started pulsing organically, each contraction spewing a stronger wave of heat. Galman supposed he was being subjected to dangerous levels of radiation, something Satumine were naturally better equipped to endure, and he wished Tumble was still with him to monitor his exposure. His friend's intelligence-bridge coverage had dropped out periodically for the first couple of days after their arrival at the pointspace comms facility but, on the third day, it had failed to reconnect. Shortly before falling silent for the last time, Tumble had suggested the people scheduled for duty in the IB suites across Pellitoe had probably failed to attend, leaving a global shortfall. After the chaos of the orbital attack and the rain of debris, most people were unlikely to place their civic IB duty at the top of their list of priorities. It was unlikely many had even returned back to their places of work yet. And so, with the IB service providers drastically under powered, the essential government services would be given priority over commercial subscribers. Tumble would recover but, cut off from global *comms* and the news they carried, Galman had no idea how long it would take.

He chewed on the husk of a desiccated affan-grass finger, the likes of which were scattered about the loading bay floor, blown in whenever the large door opened to allow Ambondice-Ambondice's sentries back inside. It was a strangely bitter-sweet plant and it stung like nettles on his tongue. But the thick bead of syrup occasionally found in the simple digestive tract was the only liquid Galman was getting. So he chewed on every finger he found, the one in ten which bore a little syrup helping to keep dehydration to a tolerable ache. Occasionally, from the camp he had established in the cab of a disused service truck, he was able to see out through the main door when it opened, and he caught glimpses of the healthy affan-grass meadow a few meters beyond the facility, fat with stored water and syrup. It was torture to look, but he couldn't turn away. The glare of heat from inside the burrowing chamber dried what little saliva his mouth could produce, swelling his tongue and splitting his lips. But every hour resting in the cab's shade was time in which Ambondice-Ambondice might reveal his intentions, or time in which office Trustee Cordem Hastergado might be allowed to arise from his medically induced coma.

Confirming his fears, he was awoken from a painful sleep by the desperate cries of a human. Throwing off the bundle of protective coveralls he had found in the cab, Galman opened the door with now well practiced care and silently made his way across the bay to peer through the door he had long since realised was damaged by weapons fire and could not fully close.

The five technicians had been whittled down to three as their tasks had been completed and Ambondice-Ambondice no longer required the full group of human captives. When Galman reached the door he caught the death of the last man, the other two already lying on the floor before their Saturnine executioners. Their murderers. There was no blood; the grotesque angle of their heads betrayed savagely broken necks. The last man died in the same mercifully quick way. Galman grimaced as the bodies were thrown on to one of the two piles of corpses. There were no flies or maggots about those piles – the fertile world ecosystems had no analogous fauna – but the bodies were in an advanced stage of decomposition and *something* had been aiding the process. As the fresh corpses disturbed the charnel heaps, black dots rose from between the dead and scurried a while before withdrawing once more to their nest in the cavity of someone towards the bottom of the pile.

Ambondice-Ambondice gave an order in the Saturnine tongue and Galman translated it to mean, more or less, 'Wake him up.' Not for the first time Galman questioned his motivation for not fleeing earlier, for not reaching the kilometre boundary at which he could have re-established a comms link and called for help. He could have saved those five lives. But there were sentries all around the facility; Ambondice-Ambondice wouldn't have allowed him to get away. He would have been killed. But was that true? During his last day of intelligence, Tumble had helped him prepare a potential escape and had judged his chances as at least one in three. Was he a coward? Clenching his fist around the mini laser pistol, Galman forced the doubt from his mind. He had ensured his survival because somebody had to stop what was happening here; not because he was afraid to die.

The Office Trustee – Cordem Hastergado – had been wheeled from an adjoining room, strapped to a basic medical bed which was probably the drab-reality foundation of a far more complex and lavishly embellished AR monitoring system. Very little of the AR was running in the facility now. Cordem was stirring and Ambondice-Ambondice pushed aside the Satumine slowly administering a stimulant through a high pressure jet-needle. The terrorist leader pressed down hard on the delivery button, administering the full shot in one quick pulse. Cordem awoke with a start and a scream and then strained at the straps which held his wrists in place. There was just enough give in the fabric to allow Cordem to thrash and tug at his restraints. Ambondice-Ambondice punched him in the stomach, draining the fight from the Office Trustee and leaving him to moan quietly, pitifully.

Ambondice-Ambondice took a small box from his belt pocket, the belt being the only clothing he wore, and lifted its hinged brushed metal lid. He took a tiny capsule, like some ancient medicine, from within the box before returning the container back to his belt pocket.

He switched to human tongue: 'Office Trustee, I need to get this inside you,' he said, leaning over the bound man and reducing his voice to a threatening murmur which

Galman strained to hear. 'I would prefer that you swallow it,' the terrorist went on. 'But the human body offers an extensive variety of alternative orifices should you resist.'

Cordem glared and Galman expected a struggle, followed by a most undignified resolution. But the Office Trustee opened his mouth and closed his eyes; he knew he was beaten.

'Well done,' the Satumine said, dropping the pill into Cordem's mouth. After the Office Trustee appeared to swallow, Ambondice-Ambondice prized the mouth open again and brought his palm-eyes down to look. Apparently satisfied, Ambondice-Ambondice called up an AR screen and pressed the only icon on display. The pointspace burrower growled and the temperature increased with such abruptness Galman took a step back, thinking there had been an explosion. Even the Satumine withdrew to the edges of the room. More than just heat, the burrower and now writhing chrome snake glowed with a white haze at which Galman could not look directly. He was going to require post radiation treatment, and probably a dose of nano-machines to clean up a host of potential cancers. It was all easily treatable, but only if he survived to make it to a medical facility.

Cordem screamed and then, as his cries fell suddenly silent, the heat and glow was gone. The chrome device no longer ensnared the burrower; it was instead curled on the floor where it began to melt, degrading into a puddle of quicksilver.

'I must confess,' Cordem said with disturbing confidence, 'that went more smoothly than I had expected.' Then, after a dry chuckle, he added, 'Not that I doubted my technology, you understand. I just didn't think you were up to the task of properly utilising it.'

'Aggregate?' Ambondice-Ambondice asked with the tone Galman had learned was the best approximation a Satumine could produce of suspicion.

'Yes,' Cordem said, calm and level. 'The authentication code is 'three, three, nine, seven, gamma, four.' Now would you untie these straps?'

Ambondice-Ambondice waved a Satumine over. 'Let him up,' he said. Galman noticed a couple of other Satumine had their weapons trained on Cordem.

Confused, Galman had to conclude the Office Trustee had somehow been turned. Or perhaps he had been turned a long time ago and was only now being activated. He felt he should be doing something; he felt the time for watching had passed. But what could he actually do? If ever he was going to flee, to call for help, the opportunity had been wasted. With an Office Trustee now on side, Ambondice-Ambondice would not only be warned of any report against his operation, he would also, through Cordem Hastergado, be able to cancel any response.

'We need to get to *Kubet* station,' Ambondice-Ambondice said, not approaching the Office Trustee now that he was on his feet. Trust, it seemed, was yet to be earned.

'Yes, I know,' Cordem snapped. 'It is *my* plan.'

'Of course,' the Satumine replied. 'It is disconcerting to address the body of an Office Trustee. I am having trouble accepting it as *you*.'

'Well get over it,' Cordem said. 'I have the relevant authority, in this body, to gain access to the station, and I also have access to a federal shuttle at Madrik port which we can use to get into orbit.'

'Precisely the reason I selected Office Trustee Cordem Hastergado to be your host.'

Cordem – or Aggregate, as Ambondice-Ambondice had called him – shot the Satumine a savage glare. 'No,' he spat. 'Not a *host*. I am not some kind of parasite! This body and mind are both mine entirely. I *am* Cordem.'

Galman had seen and heard enough. He could do nothing to intervene in this madness from where he currently was, but he knew where they would be heading.

He retreated to the decommissioned service truck and accessed the short range *comms* emitter Tumble had helped to construct. Within every vehicle in the loading bay – every vehicle available to the Satumine – a countdown began. He then activated the truck's generator core and located Madrik Port on the AR navigation screen. It was time to leave. If there was time, he thought, maybe he could grab a handful of water-saturated affan-grass once he was clear of the facility. Radiation treatment, however, would have to wait a little longer. The two in three chance of him dying in the next minute, he put completely from his mind.

Chapter 55

"Have you been for your Full Body Sweep this year?" *How many times have you had your news feed interrupted by that annoying little reminder? Perhaps you are lucky enough to live in a Union willing to provide a subsidised nanofarm, but if not you are probably part of the significant majority of Jurisdiction citizens reliant of telomere therapy and body sweeps for your indefinite lifespan. If you have any sense you will do as I do and delete that reminder from your feed, cancel your account with the clinic and source an independent and unregistered DNA technician to do the work instead. Want to know how the Administration (and its artificial intelligence master) really controls a population of trillions? I'll let you think about the answer as you stand in line with the rest of humanity waiting for some Trustee to modify you on a genetic level every year just before you fill in the census.*

The Enguine Manifesto

Endella Mariacroten: Aboard the *Tenjin*, in shortspace

Viewed from within, the *Tenjin's* intelligence-bridge network appeared to Endella as a universe of white bubbles in an infinite black void. Paradoxically external to this void lay the kaleidoscope projections of her and the other seven minds connected to the system. Like threads of lightning, white forks danced across the external skin, crackling between the minds with no discernible pattern. This was the simplest representation of the system, more a test-screen for Endella's hardware than any useful tool. It merely confirmed her personal IB hardware was overriding the pod and that she was conscious of her link to the *Tenjin*'s systems.

Like her miniaturised shortspace ship, the personal IB hardware had been a reward for extraordinary service – a gift that had qualified her for a dozen missions of even more extraordinary service to the Jurisdiction.

She sank beneath the simplistic visualisation and submerged her awareness in the convoluted processes of the intelligence-bridge. What had been portrayed as lightning flitting from mind to mind was now revealed as the transfer of randomly assigned process packages to and from each of the seven connected brains and, although she was aware of the transfers to the other six, Endella could not know their contents. It was a limitation of the technology; she could only perceive and read the sections assigned to her mind for intelligence filtering. Discerning the purpose of any system was therefore a slow and largely random endeavour.

Days were spent just tagging each process segment and looking for connections that might build a larger code string and identify a specific system of the *Tenjin*. She had done this work many times before and had expected no easier time of it than those previous informational nightmares. But this was more complex even than her intrusion into the intelligence-bridged AR net of the Able Union capital world, years earlier. In that vast data sea she had at least recognised the language. Although the IB architecture had been retained, the code compartments being used on the *Tenjin* were unrecognisable and, Endella feared, there was a good chance they extended into more mathematical dimensions than her hardware or mind could comprehend.

Unable even to separate the IB network into disparate categories – the first step in the long process of identifying specific systems – she changed tact. There was no need, she reasoned, to actually label the systems passing through her mind, and she certainly didn't need, at the moment, to read the instructions and activity of those systems. She only needed to know how to disrupt the *Tenjin*'s progress until federal forces could reach and board it. *Take the main logistics and administrative nodal system down*, she decided. It would cripple the *Tenjin*'s ability to efficiently utilise everything from life support to weapons. It was the primary nodal system on any ship or station and, she reasoned, it would account for most IB activity. All she had to do was follow the process packages back to their source machines and computers and, statistically, the region to which most returned ought to be the primary logistics and administrative node.

A few days later, as confident as she was ever likely to be, Endella roused herself from IB induced sleep and pulled the sticky feeding tube from her throat, retching and vomiting a small clot of the sticky paste. In spite of her nausea, however, she felt in remarkably good health. Her head ached with the familiar post IB hangover and dull heartburn spoke of the non-standard paste she had been fed this past week. But her stomach was greatly improved from its prior ugly state. She pulled away the crusty fabric, tensing as it tore free from a thin layer of skin which had grown into its weave. She smiled at the small nodule of scar tissue where there had earlier been the horrifying great knot of a weeping hole. Prodding at her abdomen with a finger she felt no great pain, no signs of internal injuries yet to be healed. Just a little tenderness and, as she stood, some tightness which she expected to soon stretch out. Her ribs and collar bone were fully repaired and there were no bony lumps to suggest any complications. She knew enough about her nano-farm limitations, however, to realise her intestines and stomach would be an ugly jury-rigged mess and she would need more extensive treatment if she ever made it off of the *Tenjin*. But for now she was fit for duty.

Although eidetic, her memory struggled to retain her experiences within the IB network. This was another expected limitation. Ordinarily she would have committed to artificial memory the facts gleaned from her observation of the systems, loading every moment into storage devices within her brain and spine. Those devices no longer existed - they had all been reduced to base elements and reformed into nanites. She didn't even have an AR notepad on which to jot down the most salient details. No matter. She required only a single fact: the location of the primary system node. She focused on the location, compared it to her memorised schematic of the *Tenjin* and committed the location to her waking memory. The rest she allowed to bleed away. She was glad to let it go for the glut of complex code compartment imagery was only worsening her headache. The node was located behind the wall of a corridor in what was, when the *Tenjin* had still resembled its original design, the hollow hemisphere which had been defined by eleven concentric bands. From what she had seen of it, prior to crashing into the station, that entire section was now a complete enclosing shell. The node was in what used to be the empty space between two of the wide bands, so she had no map to guide her, but getting as far as the closest original section was surprisingly easy. It took under half an hour off jogging, an exertion she was now quite capable of enduring, and she passed only a single group of the augmented crew hard at work on a melted section of wall behind which a slab of processor crystal had been shattered. She watched them a while from around the corner of a junction, marvelling at the speed with which they were repairing the fractured processor. It was a task on which Jurisdiction IB machines could spend days, but these three creatures were fusing the shards of crystal together, using tools extended from the tips of their fingers, in mere minutes. They worked, as did the others she had passed a week earlier, without uttering a single word, but there was no doubt they were cooperating. Although gripping her mag-gun, she refrained from firing on the group. It had been a week since she had revealed her presence to the crewmember she had killed and she had not been seen since. Perhaps they were no longer looking for her, maybe they thought she had succumbed to her injuries. There was no need to reveal herself again. Not yet at least.

She crept back the way she had come and found an alternative route, circumventing the cross-section where the group was working.

When she came to the start of the unmapped parts of the hollow hemisphere, she was pleased to find the same style of corridors and rooms, and the same basic layout. The extensions must have taken place towards the earlier part of the ten thousand year voyage, before resources had run low and the crew reduced so dramatically. Before they had been changed so horribly. Finding her way through the sections she wondered what had actually happened in those ten millennia. Had these empty corridors been home to a thriving civilisation? Had there been separate factions, nations perhaps? How many millions had lived and died in that wormhole and how much of their cultures, their accomplishments in art and philosophy as well as technology, had survived? It occurred to her how much of a treasure this ancient station's archives would be to anthropologists as well as the scientific community. There would be so much to learn about the human condition. She felt a pang of sorrow for the lost cultures of the *Tenjin*, and wished she could have witnessed them before they had degenerated into whatever it was that now skulked through the empty corridors and waged war on the Jurisdiction.

The system node was behind an innocuous looking wall in a corridor wide enough to pass for a hall. There was no opposite wall, just a railing beyond which was a vast open expanse looking down on a colossal concourse five levels below. The concourse's high ceiling was up another four levels and balconies such as the one from which Endella was looking were visible on every floor, ringing the huge but empty space below. Whatever this had once been, it was obviously no longer required. Everything had been stripped out, probably recycled. Feeling exposed to so many vantage points, she rushed to the wall and worked as fast as she could. Unscrewing a wall panel using tools from her rucksack, she revealed a stack of plate-sized crystals behind a lattice of transparent rods and bundles of cable. This was the system's critical weak spot, the point through which most of its widely distributed components and controllers passed - a single node, the destruction of which could not easily be compensated. A gentle yellow light flashed through the crystal stack with a slow, regular frequency and Endella considered firing a few bolts at the processors. It would certainly be a less overt way of bringing down the system than her original more explosive plan. But, after removing a second panel and finding the node extended further along the wall cavity, she decided it would take too long to uncover its entirety. So, from her rucksack, she took four coin-sized charges. The black disks were not the most powerful of the munitions within her bag but they were enough for this. Each disk was wiped across the three-inch flexpad detonator and as they were activated an icon for each appeared. Pressing the icons would detonate the corresponding charge, while pressing the smaller fifth icon in the screen's corner would set them all off. It was a simple system; they were simple explosives.

Chapter 56

Telomere braiding is one of the more basic of available rejuvenation treatments offered on practically every Jurisdiction colony. It is not as permanent a therapy as, for example, a personal nano-farm, and its effects not so dramatic as the most sophisticated body-sweeps, but it is the tested and reliable workhorse of human immortality. It is cheap, effective, and can be administered with a bare minimum of training or equipment. Come war or recession, natural disaster or technical failure, humans will always have a means of quick and easy immortality. This is the promise of the Jurisdiction.

Rehabilitation: A Survivor's Guide

Subset: Aboard the *Tenjin*, in shortspace

Aggregate was in an ecstatic mood when he called for Subset. Free once more of his lord's direct inhabitation, the youngest crewman shuddered at the broad grin slithering across the captain's unusually slim face – these sessions of torment were worse when Aggregate was in a good mood; the monster was always so much more animated in his affections. Subset stepped meekly into the opulent den and glanced about, desperately hoping to find some narcotic drink laid out for him, as was occasionally the case. Something to dull the pain. Not today. Subset was too naïve of the human experience to fully appreciate how much of an appalling violation the sexual degradation was, but it was bad enough to reduce him to tears, even this many centuries into his miserable life. The agony of the sadistic and gleeful beatings, however, required no such understanding. Subset's strategy for enduring the torment was the same for both flavours of abuse but, long since wise to his plaything's attempts to retreat into his mind, to dissociate from the physical ordeal, Aggregate ensured a varied and unpredictable curriculum of defilement and pain. Before the youngest crewman could retreat into the numb sanctuary of dissociation Aggregate would inflict some new misery. There was no escape and there never would be.

As Aggregate tied subset's naked and bleeding body to an upright pole and began rummaging through a container Subset knew to contain barbed whips, iron bars, razors and all manner of shock-inducing devices, the crewman closed his eyes and wondered – as often he did – how much of the original human captain's sadism had ever been allowed to surface into action. That the sexual perversions and cruelty were founded in that long-since subsumed human mind was beyond doubt. Aggregate's original self, that with which it now hoped to reconnect and change, experienced the higher dimensions only through the primitive and animalistic minds of the Fertile Worlds and the shared consciousness of those planets' interconnected plant systems. It lacked any real intelligence and was a benign entity.

Aggregate was not.

Searing horror forced him back into his body and he screamed. He didn't beg for mercy for that only heightened his torturer's excitement. Something pressed through his shoulder, sliding into the socket of the joint and, with a wet pop and a wave of nauseating pain, the arm was dislocated.

When Aggregate connected the modified pointspace entity to every human strand of DNA in the galaxy – and there was no question of him failing – how many of those trillions would he curse with independence in order that he might toy with their bodies? Would he finally tire of Subset when presented with such an abundance of new flesh?

Would he finally subsume him entirely? Subset welcomed such a fate.

His penis burned as razor blades joined the game and Subset bit through his lip in the futile hope of distraction.

The *Tenjin* shuddered and, as if walking across misaligned gravity coils, Subset felt his body tugged in several directions. To what new torture would he now be subjected?

'No!' Aggregate roared. Subset opened his eyes to see a large AR window on the den's far wall. For a moment Subset's agony was forgotten, so terrible was the vista beyond the illusory window. The bubble of higher dimensional space around the *Tenjin*, which hurtled through the single dimension of a shortspace strand, was writhing and folding across its skin.

Multi-spectrum filters overlaid sections of the image, highlighting in false colours the thinning of the dimensional skin in too many places. The bubble was going to burst and its contents – primarily the *Tenjin* - were going to be subjected to the physical laws of shortspace. It would still reach its destination, but would emerge into higher dimensional space as a stream of single dimensional non-particles which, in a matter of nano-seconds, would fall back down as radiation into more hospitable lower dimensions.

'The bitch is still alive,' Aggregate snarled, landing a solid and unsophisticated punch on Subset's jaw, cracking bone and loosening teeth. The captain then ran for the door. No doubt he had some means of saving the station for he was infallible and unstoppable, but it would take a moment, and he appeared to feel the need to handle it personally though his favoured body. Subset's stomach clenched at the realisation he had been left alone and unguarded, and his internal nanoglands were already converting fat and muscle to heal the atrocities done to him. As fat was harvested from his arms, the restraints became ever looser.

Chapter 57

Satute, the Satumine home-world, is an urban planet in the most literal of senses. Often described as a hive, its vast sprawl is miles deep, every layer a passage through time, through crushed and unstable ruins millennia old, right down to the most ancient and indestructible foundation - the original Ancient Satumine realm. That this most ancient layer reaches completely round the planet suggests an overcrowded world even back then. We must assume, therefore, that the Ancient Satumine were late in taking to the stars. They must have already paved over their entire world before the first pointspace frames were built and the slow expansion into the Network worlds began. The Satumine, in either incarnation, never discovered shortspace burrowing - that is a human innovation - and so the crawl out to the new worlds must have been a laborious task of millennia as the frames were launched out across the region at sub-light speeds. How is it that a race of such awesome technological ability never discovered shortspace? Perhaps they know better than to use it - and why should they when we are so willing to go out into the galaxy instead?

The Truth: A treatise on the Satumine Conspiracy

Ambondice-Ambondice: On Pellitoe, in the Swinell Union, in the Fertile Belt

'We established a pass code in order that we might avoid precisely this mistrust,' Cordem – or Aggregate – said.

Ambondice-Ambondice aligned as many of his joint and hand eyes as possible to look over his ostensibly human co-conspirator. It was true; the pass code had been agreed some time ago to allow Aggregate to prove he had subverted the body prepared for him, but Ambondice-Ambondice was a suspicious creature and had seen comrades on other worlds brought down by all manner of convoluted Jurisdiction plots. This could easily be some part of a set-up intended to expose him, or the wider Satumine cell.

'All the pass code proves is that you, Aggregate, have inhabited this body or that you, Cordem, are working for Aggregate. The validity of Aggregate's claims and his loyalty has yet to be established.'

Cordem/Aggregate glared at the Satumine leader. 'Do you imagine all that took place in orbit, all the destruction wrought, was part of a ploy to convince you to expose yourself as a terrorist?'

'Perhaps.'

'Are you really so arrogant as to think yourself important enough to warrant such an expenditure of life and equipment?'

'The events in orbit have yet to be verified,' Ambondice-Ambondice noted.

'And the falling debris?'

Ambondice-Ambondice gave a Satumine shrug. 'Minimal in comparison.'

The human sucked through his teeth and gave a tired shake of his head. Then, without warning or evident trigger, his eyes widened and a furious scowl surfaced. 'Fuck!' he yelled.

'What?' Ambondice-Ambondice asked, maintaining his distance from his, as yet, unproven ally.

Cordem/Aggregate's composure returned in an instant and he shook his head. 'Problems aboard the *Tenjin*,' he said. 'My presences there will deal with it.'

'I still want proof of your sincerity,' Ambondice-Ambondice said, suspecting the minor outburst was just a distraction.

Cordem/Aggregate sighed. 'Fine, but we need to make this quick. I want to be at Madrik port as soon as possible so we can get the next phase started. The window of opportunity is closing.'

The Satumine terrorist knew precisely what he wanted from the Office Trustee. 'Give me the Federal override codes for the Pellitoe AR network.' Not only would such divulgence prove beyond doubt the trustworthiness of whomever this man was – Cordem or Aggregate – it would also be a delectably ironic victory over Sharlie-Sharlie who, more than anything, desired those codes but had refused to sponsor or support Ambondice-Ambondice's endeavour.

'If you use my emergency codes, I will be identified as the source of any disturbances and my usefulness in obtaining access to the *Vulpine* will be compromised.'

'I'm not going to use them; I just need to see that you are prepared to hand them over. I can verify the codes' veracity without activating them.'

Cordem/Aggregate threw up his hands in exaggerated exasperation, made a laboured show of calling up a screen and formed the eight mathematical dimensional code compartment from a lengthy formulae he, or at least the previous owner of the body, had committed to memory through artificial neural hardwiring. Forming the code compartment took three minutes; it took another four for Ambondice-Ambondice to upload the Federal override codes into a sandbox AR partition in the global network. It was valid. He copied the sandbox partition into the segregated and ghosted AR of the facility, allowing it to be viewed by the other Satumine of his breakaway cell and the man he was now willing to accept as Aggregate.

'Now, can we get on with this?' Aggregate asked.

'I must confess,' Ambondice-Ambondice said, scrolling through the unlimited access and authority menus and utilities of the Federal override, 'I am finding myself tempted to activate it.'

'Do that,' Aggregate warned, putting his hand through the image of the code compartment which floated between him and the Satumine leader, 'and you blow your chance to wreak true devastation on this world.'

Ambondice-Ambondice dropped his faceless head forward – an expression unrelated to the human nod or bow , more a wry smile – and reduced the partially loaded code into an AR pendent which he grew around his neck. He could unpack it with a thought and fully exploit and abuse the Pellitoe AR should Aggregate prove to be other than what he claimed.

'Uthan-Uthan, take one of the trucks and bring the sentries back in,' Ambondice-Ambondice ordered. 'Edelerit-Edelerit, get everyone aboard the –'

A curtain of blue flame exploded into the room through the damaged personnel entrance to the loading bay, ripping the door from its flexi-steel hinge and hurling it into the mesh of the pointspace burrower. Clear coolant gel seeped out of the resultant fracture on the mesh and numerous alarms, both AR and drab-reality, issued throughout the communications facility. The larger door to the bay was deformed by a second explosion and a small split appeared through its middle, letting in a single tongue of yellow as the larger plume erupted through the smaller doorway. More explosions sounded, dull and muted but with a deep punch which shook Ambondice-Ambondice's neural threads, and a crack appeared in the wall to the loading bay. All about him Ambondice-Ambondice saw his team going to ground but finding shelter unfortunately lacking. Save for the few supplies they had brought with them, the facility was predominantly AR and helpless to deflect drab-reality flames and falling masonry.

'Out,' he yelled, thrusting a finger in the direction of the main facility doors on the wall opposite the burning loading bay. A screech, as of pressurised gas escaping a ruptured canister, split through the roar of flames and the crash of falling metal and construction resin slabs.

Ambondice-Ambondice bolted for the door which another of his Satumine had already reached and was in the process of sliding open. The terrorist leader barged his subordinate and slipped through the gap in time to see one of the facility's service trucks crash through the main vehicle entrance, its solid tyres crushing shards of the smashed door into the desiccated affan-grass. fire chased the truck from the loading bay and thick black smoke rolled out after, obscuring the vehicle's escape.

'It's not one of ours,' one of the Satumine said, having escaped behind Ambondice-Ambondice. The Satumine leader held his breath, something he could do for considerably longer than a human, and walked quickly away from the burning building.

He established a comms link with his sentries scattered about the valley and ordered them to stop the truck. Unlike humans, his ability to speak was not compromised by the need to hold his breath. As Aggregate ran from the facility, which was now lost in a thick cloud of black, the flames at least were beginning to subside. Only the vehicles in the bay would burn – the construction resin of the walls and roof were designed to endure and extinguish a blaze. A couple of Satumine were helping the human to clear the reach of the smoke, untroubled by the soot coating Aggregate's throat and lungs. Ambondice-Ambondice left them to it; the kinds of Jurisdiction medical technology available to an Office Trustee were more than capable of cleaning his lungs of a little smoke damage. The human would probably be fine by the time he reached the base of the pheromone tower at which Ambondice-Ambondice waited for him.

Further along the affan-grass meadow he saw the spray of syrup and water of the truck's passage and, seconds later, a fusillade of laser fire and the stuttering beams of particle accelerators erupted from the cover of flesh tree copses and the rocks dotting one of the valley's gentle slopes. The truck tipped and skidded under the assault and something was ejected from the distant vehicle, flying through the air for a hundred meters before crashing into a flesh tree in an explosion of vegetable blood and syrup. Ambondice-Ambondice at first thought it a missile but enhancing his shoulder eyes' vision with an AR screen identified the projectile as one of the trucks rear tyres. The unsupported corner now dragged at the affan-grass, ploughing a wet trough through the meadow. More weapons opened up but, without the means to pursue, they were limited to a few passing shots. Within a minute the heavy but surprisingly fast truck disappeared behind a ridge and the sentries reported their perimeter breached.

Ambondice-Ambondice swore in human and Satumine tongues and recalled his sentries to the smoking facility.

'You were supposed to secure this site,' Aggregate yelled, striding towards the Satumine with a look of murder on his blackened face. His voice gave no hint of the smoke he had inhaled moments earlier.

'Not now,' Ambondice-Ambondice yelled back. He turned to one of his subordinates and asked, 'Did they get *all* of the vehicles?'

'Yes,' the Satumine relied. 'My guess is they rigged the generators to bypass the regulators. Must have been in there for quite a while.'

'Which means they know what we are doing,' Ambondice-Ambondice said, turning back to the human. 'We're compromised.'

Aggregate shook his head and offered a tired smile. 'Not at all. I'm an Office Trustee,' he reminded the Satumine. 'He won't get far. And if he raises the alarm I can suppress it for long enough.'

'*He?* You think it's one man? Well how are you going to stop him if you don't even know who he is? Everyone at the facility was accounted for and killed.'

Aggregate summoned a screen and a link to the Bureau of Supervision was established. 'I have the memories of the consciousness that previously resided in this body,' he said. 'And it seems he had suspicions about you, Ambondice-Ambondice.'

'And?'

'He illegally employed the services of an outside agent to follow you.' Aggregate formed an arrest warrant on the link, allowing Ambondice-Ambondice to see the name: Galman Tader.

'Order them to kill him,' the Satumine suggested.

'They wouldn't follow such an order,' Aggregate said with evident irritation. 'But relax; he will be detained and out of our way. By the time he has a chance to convince anyone of our intentions, it is going to be far too late to stop us. Now, if I were you I would call one of your contacts for a ride out of here. I'm not walking all the way to Madrik Port.

Chapter 58

Any union of note has a fleet of cruisers available to transport resources and personnel between its worlds and those of its neighbours. Shortspace travel is still too expensive for any government to rely on private cargo vessels, and the federal government is reluctant to allow its Sentries to be treated as a taxi service. A number of particularly wealthy Unions have paid for small fleets of brand new vessels of their own design, but the vast majority have signed up for the so called 'hand-me-down' initiative, paying a nominal fee to the federal government in exchange for a few outdated and stripped down federal sentries (re-branded as cruisers) on the condition that they make those ships available to the Jurisdiction in the event of any local military crisis. This is all common knowledge and few see any problem with the arrangement. I am willing to bet you do not know, however, that the Area Trustees still hold the override codes for every ship sold off in this manner. They deny this, quite forcibly as attested by my most recent conviction and incarceration, but it is true nonetheless. Is it little wonder most uprisings are so swiftly put down? What, after all, can any union hope to do against the Jurisdiction when their ships can be deactivated at the flick of an Area Trustee's AR switch?

The Enguine Manifesto

Indin-Indin: On Dereph, in the Network

'What are you?' Indin-Indin asked. 'Artificial Intelligence or Artificial Consciousness?'

The entity squirmed and shifted within the network's entirety; both part of the interconnected web of systems and separate from it. It was more than any one system, more than the collective, an entity beyond Indin-Indin's ability to control or even connect with. But the Satumine could, through his absolute contact with the facility network, feel the entity bristling at the question.

'Neither,' it eventually replied into Indin-Indin's mind, lacing the word with a Satumine emotion like disappointed offence, which washed across his vast mind as if he had felt the emotion himself.

'You must be one or the other,' Indin-Indin insisted, and he was fairly certain it was an Artificial Consciousness – perhaps the Satumine equivalent of Consul.

'I am a Consciousness,' the entity stated. 'No more artificial than you.'

'You are a product of technology,' Indin-Indin countered. 'Software would be my guess.'

'Your point?'

'You are created; you are artificial.'

'As are you,' the consciousness spat, hurling feelings of anger and hurt. 'But you don't consider yourself artificial.'

'I used atavism to revert to an earlier genetic state, but that state was the product of evolution.'

'No it wasn't.' The consciousness revealed emotions of confusion and mild amusement. 'The organic caste of the Satumine race is as contrived as the software caste.'

Indin-Indin recoiled from the entity, the revelation horrifying, though he knew in the memory of his tri-helical genes that it was true.

The consciousness pursued him, maintaining its presence in the periphery of his mind. 'What matters is the veracity of the consciousness, not its origins. In that regard, we are equal.'

But Indin-Indin knew their equality extended beyond merely their claims to consciousness. The Satumine technology was registering two viable Satumine on the planet, and it rated them equally in the hierarchy, in-so-much-as they were both at the top of the chain of command. Each of them – Indin-Indin or the software – had unrestricted access to the systems of the facility, and the planet, and each was capable of cancelling the orders of the other. That equality was obviously something Aggregate had expected, and chosen to override, because a moment later a numbing cold lanced Indin-Indin's neural mesh as a change began to take place beyond his control.

'What are you doing?' the consciousness demanded.

For five seconds Indin-Indin could not respond. When control returned and hidden genetic switches fell away, their task complete, the question didn't need answering. He now outranked the software consciousness.

'You aren't Viceroy Wednon-Wednon-Tule,' the computer snarled. Indin-Indin curled his mock-human lips into a smile; the systems now read his mental link to be that of some long dead ruler. Aggregate really had considered everything. He couldn't imagine his mysterious ally had the neural schematics of the Viceroy, so he guessed some latent device, left over from the atavism, had scanned the Satumine systems for what was required, and then enacted the necessary changes in Indin-Indin.

'I need your help in locating a specific system in this facility,' he told the software consciousness.

'No,' it snapped but, in spite of its defiance, an emotion of compliance betrayed its inability to refuse. 'You've got to be joking!' it suddenly said. 'You're invoking magisterial privilege?'

'Yes,' Indin-Indin guessed.

'What system do you need?' it begrudgingly asked.

A low thump and the sounding of various alarms directly into Indin-Indin's mind pulled his attention away. Through the facility systems he saw a single narrow beam of accelerated particles burning into the wall of the building. He followed the beam up through the skyline, into the clouds where the still sluggish and somnolent Satumine technology could not yet look beyond. They were using ship-based weapons and would carve through before too long.

'What's happening?' the Consciousness demanded.

'They're cutting through.'

'Who?' but the computer was already connecting with all manner of systems external to the facility network, and Indin-Indin followed where it went. 'What happened to the colony?' it cried.

'The human's now occupy it.' Indin-Indin explained.

'Oh...' was the computers response. Indin-Indin watched it reach beyond the Satumine systems and into the human AR and comms networks, where Indin-Indin could not follow. It recoiled almost immediately.

'Oh,' it said again, transferring the complete human history into Satumine archives. It was now up to date on the affairs of the galaxy.

'How did you achieve Atavism?' it asked. 'You shouldn't have been able to do that without access to proper Satumine technology or mental capacity. You would require a computer consciousness to develop the necessary -' It stopped abruptly, then said, 'Consul, the human computer consciousness, helped you.'

'No.'

'Then who?'

'Just find what I need,' Indin-Indin ordered. 'Time is a factor.'

'You don't know *why* we incorporated human genetic material, do you.' It was a statement.

'Just find the micro pointspace burrowing array,' Indin-Indin said. There was something within him telling him he really didn't want to know why his race had debased itself with weak human DNA.

The computer started opening up the rest of the facility systems network, a hundred times more rapid than had Indin-Indin. 'I'll have it for you shortly,' it said. 'But you need to hear me out, and then you need to shut me down and destroy yourself.'

'Say nothing more on the subject,' Indin-Indin ordered, as if it was written into his genes to refuse to listen. He dismissed the idea as ridiculous – he didn't want to hear what the computer was saying; there was no hardwired compulsion, he could have listened if he had wanted to. He just didn't want to. Unable to disobey, the computer fell silent, and Indin-Indin never thought to question what other changes, like the identity mask, Aggregate had arranged during atavism.

Chapter 59

Telomere braiding, while the guarantee of the Jurisdiction, is far from the pinnacle of rejuvenation treatments available in this blessed age. That honour goes to nano-farms. Within these small IB devices, surgically placed within the body of anyone wealthy enough to afford them, or fortunate enough to live on a world offering such technology for free, nano-scale doctors are produced almost constantly. These doctors monitor the body under the guidance of an intelligence bridge, harvesting fat, bone or any other tissue as required. Provided the recipient of the nano-farm has an active IB link, their continued health and youth are assured. The only thing required of them is the occasional ingestion of the raw materials needed for nanite construction not found in a normal diet - and even this is only required after significant trauma. The nano-farm is the summit of medical technology and as as the Jurisdiction's wealth grows so the day when all citizens can be so protected draws ever closer.

Rehabilitation: A Survivor's Guide

Endella Mariacroten: Aboard the *Tenjin*, somewhere in the Fertile Belt

The explosion had been more aggressive, far louder and with a greater eruption of plasma, than Endella had expected. Peering around the corner at the still burning wall, as intense three-foot jets of plasma raged in translucent blue cones, she guessed the *Tenjin*'s power mesh was running at a greatly increased plasma grade than indicated in the original specifications. But there was no harm done by her misjudgement of the charge required; when they ruptured, the high pressure plasma conduits had merely increased the damage to the crystal stacks. Her nonchalance was reigned in, however, when the station was tugged at from every direction, its special dimensions undulating and pulsing in a distinct and immediately recognisable way. The bead of higher dimensional space in which the *Tenjin* sped along a shortspace thread, was losing cohesion. The bubble was going to burst.

She swore. The original *Tenjin* design had included no means of shortspace travel; the station simply wasn't constructed with such a system in mind and, although ten thousand years of advancement and upgrade had obviously included the development of some new form of shortspace burrowing specifically designed with the *Tenjin*'s enormous structure in mind, it would still require considerably more mid-flight calibration and stabilisation than was normal. Where Jurisdiction vessels maintained a stable bead of higher dimensional space by dint of their shape and intrinsically stable design, the *Tenjin*'s form would constantly threaten to rupture the bubble of normal space and collapse directly into the thread of shortspace. The immense flow of IB code passing through this node wasn't related to the power mesh and core systems, rather it was the vital stream of stabilising data required to keep the station in shortspace. And she had just ripped it apart.

Her fingers rubbed nervously, impatient, against her thumbs, as if literally itching to do something. Anything. But this was now beyond her control; either the crew of the *Tenjin* would somehow compensate for her sabotage or they, and she, would all be dead very soon. There was nothing she could do either way. With that understanding came a calm acceptance and she regained control of her restless hands. All she could do was continue in her mission to explore and potentially disarm the *Tenjin*. If she was to die, it would happen so suddenly she would never even notice it happening.

She turned her back on the now screeching plasma jets, turned a corner and literally walked into a member of the crew. Combat instincts, honed over three centuries, brought her fists up to crush the creature's surprisingly soft and cold nose even before Endella had taken in its grotesquely gaunt appearance. White metal plates covered its chest like overlapping scales, disks of matte black resin dotted its bald and misshapen skull and an oversized mechanical arm sprouted from its left shoulder, tipped with a rotating array of cutting tools and clamps. It looked a fearsome amalgam of human and machine and had she thought before instinctively striking, she might have held back the punch through fear of damaging her hand and inflicting little damage on the seemingly tough creature. In fact its nose exploded like a blood filled blister and her fist continued in through the skull which seemed more cartilage than bone. The vile thing fell, instantly dead, its metal parts clattering on the floor and pulped brain running in a thick trail from the hole Endella had punched into its face. Combat instincts satisfied, the Justiciar raised the mag-gun she ought to have used in place of her hand and fired a single anti-personnel bolt into what remained of the creature's forehead. Just to be sure.

'I can't keep letting you kill my crew.' The voice came from behind her and was as androgynous as that of an IB machine. Endella turned at her hip while bending at her knees, bringing her weapon round to whoever was behind her. She fired a six round spray of bolts as the creature, more bulky in body and mechanics than the gaunt corpse at her feet, raised its glowing rod-arm like a weapon. It died as easily as had every other crewmember she had killed so far. For all the advancements the Administration was convinced the *Tenjin* had made in its ten millennia, the crew seemed remarkably fragile; even more so than the notoriously feeble Satumine. Either they were not as advanced as had been expected or their society was of a sort in which physical resilience was unimportant.

Judging by the lacklustre response to her presence, it seemed the *Tenjin* crew had not anticipated anybody infiltrating their station. How long it would take them to mount a more determined defence, however, she couldn't guess. Not long, she suspected.

The ground shook and she realised the undulation of the failing shortspace bead had ended some time ago. This shaking was something new, something far more physical. Something close. She needed to get out of the confined corridor where she could be far too easily trapped, but there wasn't time enough to burn through any of the doors which had abruptly stopped responding to her approach. She sprinted past her latest victim, back to the more open space of the wide balcony overlooking the huge empty atrium. Perhaps she could drop down over the edge to find the relative safety of a lower level where her presence hadn't been so spectacularly betrayed. Rounding the gentle corner to the balcony she fumbled in her rucksack for a unigrip pad and line but, by the time she reached the still raging cones of plasma and the pools of melted wall panel, she still hadn't found what she needed. She gave the flames a wide berth, but even by the railing she felt the intense blaze prickling against her face and exposed arms. She un-slung the pack and looked inside properly for the line. It wasn't there. With a flush of embarrassment and irritation she recalled last using it some years ago to abseil down the side of a tower occupied by the prohibited quasi-religious cult that had begun to spread, briefly, through the Able Union. She had been in such a rush to apprehend the sociopath around whom the cult was formed that she left the line behind. For all she knew it was still there, dangling ninety floors up from the streets which had not been rebuilt, or even sanitised, after the viral and radioactive lengths the cult had gone to in order to keep Endella away. It was another indication of her waning focus, and compromised ability, that she had neglected to restock her emergency pack in the years since that near-apocalyptic night.

'Fuck-it!' she yelled, kicking the thin railing and throwing her pack to the ground. She told herself her outburst stemmed from frustration at her stupidity; in truth it was the reopening of an old wound that had so upset her. *That* was the cause of her loss of focus and her inability to do the job at which she had, for so many years, excelled. She had saved the greater part of the planet's billion lives, but at the expense of three million in that city. The Justiciary and Administration had declared her actions warranted, necessary in fact, and praised her as a hero. *She*, however, knew she had failed, and three million innocent people had paid the price of her incompetence.

She screwed her features into a determined scowl. *Let it go*, she told herself, though she knew it could never fully leave her. Self-doubt was going to get her killed; she needed focus.

'Throw your weapon to the floor,' a sexless voice demanded. A twelve-foot inhuman creature, a wiry monster, its tight rope-like muscles visible though thin translucent white skin. The face was more-or-less recognisable as human though its eyes were missing, replaced by a single mechanical array in the forehead: an inch-wide blue disk surrounded by nine smaller yellow hexagons. Like most of the crew she had thus far seen, it sported a few patches of white metal scales and, most noticeably, all four limbs had been replaced with heavy industrial prosthetics. The legs, which looked like naked girders, devoid of any aesthetic bodywork or even paint, were bent at the knees and eight-toed clamps acted as feet. The arms were little different to the massive legs and their length gave the creature the look of a mechanical gorilla, dragging massive gauntlet hands along the ground. Endella froze.

'I don't have to kill you,' it went on, raising its oversized arms to point the rotating head of some six-barrelled device at her. 'But I will unless you put down your weapon.'

More crew rounded the two corners, oblivious to the plasma jets or unbothered by the heat. Endella was surrounded. Her mag-gun was aimed to the ground and she knew she was dead the moment she raised it. But perhaps they wouldn't be so quick to punish other less hostile movements; she took a step back, waiting for the searing burn of whatever the monster was pointing at her. It didn't fire, though other crew members started targeting her with all manner of alien devices. She stepped back again, pressing against the railing.

'Drop the pistol.'

She turned and leapt from the balcony.

Chapter 60

To hear some of the more liberal apologists speak, one might imagine the differences between humans and Satumine are merely cosmetic, nothing more than skin-deep variations on an otherwise closely related template. But this is utter nonsense. Strip away our skin and you will find us as unrecognisable within as we are without. Perhaps the most obvious example is the utterly alien method of digestion employed by the Satumine. The void beneath those ugly three flaps in their abdomens serve the dual function of reproductive cavity and digestive system. They don't eat in any way we would recognise; what passes for a mouth in these creatures is not connected in any way to their 'stomach'. They simply push food into the cavity, allow the flaps to seal closed with some kind of semen-like excretion and then a fifteen day digestive cycle begins, after which the flaps soften once more and a hard black stone of bodily waste is removed. They can then take up to six days to begin the process once more. They consider this to be a far more efficient and elegant system than that used by humanity, but they soon come to envy our supposedly primitive biology when something indigestible or poisonous gets sealed in when the flaps harden. Towards the end of a fifteen day bout of poisoning they prey for the human ability to vomit.

The Truth: A treatise on the Satumine Conspiracy

Galman Tader: On Pellitoe, in the Swinell Union, in the Fertile-belt

Galman had to fight the over-steer of a shattered suspension assembly and the constant drag to the left resulting from the loss of a rear wheel. But the truck was, for the most part, in one piece and it was maintaining a forty miles per hour rate across the rock strewn splint-grass field, in spite of the bare axle grinding and sparking away at the rear corner leaving a trail of churned up dirt, chipped rocks, and patches of burning splint-grass. The intermittent system monitor warned of a dangerous overheat in the axle but it was far enough from the generator to rule out any immediate risk of catastrophe. The worst that was likely was a fire igniting in the surrounding bodywork, but the truck's chassis would burn slow.

The AR embellishments on the service truck were minimal and utilitarian – very much in keeping with the federal ethos of the pointspace comms facility to which it belonged. There were no concessions to driver comfort, such as sensory input embellishments which might have given the illusion of a more accommodating seat, and there was little in the way of aesthetic niceties. Just a standard array of control screens which floated a few inches above the dashboard on which hardwired equivalents of the primary functions were duplicated, and a spread of AR windows complimenting the small drab-reality windscreen. The Satumine had chipped and cracked the windscreen with their various projectile weapons before Galman had fled beyond their range, and a few neat holes had been melted through by the beam weapons also aimed his way. There were a lot more holes on the right side of the driver's cabin though most were now hidden behind AR windows. The system monitor reported thousands of chips and dents across that entire side of the truck and at least fifty detectable penetrations, only four of which had made it into the truck's drive hardware where they had damaged nothing that couldn't be bypassed by the simple processor running the vehicle. All things considered, he had got out of there in far better shape than he, or Tumble, had expected. A five millimetre hole, passing clean through the back of his hand and out of the palm where it left a messier coin-sized wound, reminded him of how much worse it could have been. Considering the amount of holes in the truck, he ought to have been hit dozens of times.

There was a basic med-kit under the seat. After confirming the truck's rudimentary auto-function was keeping him on track to reach Madrik Port, he applied the antiseptic salve. It was the most basic of first-aid supplies, the kind freely available even on his backwater home-world of Diaclom; far less advanced than the restorative devices he had left behind in the safari buggy. But it would clean the wound, close off any blood vessels and numb the pain. It would, in the absence of anything better, even promote some basic accelerated re-growth. But it would be ugly. He could live with that.

The truck dipped into a pothole and the exposed axle caught a rock which jerked the whole vehicle with enough force to throw Galman out of his seat and into the AR controls. Registering the potential accident, the truck ground to a stop. Galman muttered curses at the sub IB control system and restarted the vehicle. The usual IB traffic control would have avoided the pothole, would have even been able to compensate for the missing wheel and ruined suspension, but traffic control had been withdrawn from all rural areas, according to the news net Galman had scanned over the last few minutes, so he either had to drive it himself or rely on the rudimentary auto-control. He wasn't entirely confident of his ability to manually steer the heavy truck in its sub-prime condition, but he doubted he could do much worse than the computer which, to be fair, was designed only to cover occasional outages of the IB traffic control, and generally only on the roads. It wasn't designed to drive at speed, damaged and off-road. Flexing his injured hand which was numb only around the open wound, he decided it was as good as it was going to get and so he called up the manual steering options. Of the three available systems; icons and touch screens, joystick, or wheel; he selected the retro style steering wheel. It was what he was used to on Diaclom. He had half expected an entirely AR steering wheel to materialise, but was pleased to see a ring of thick wire unfold from some previously hidden compartment. AR paddles and buttons, floating unattached to the wheel and beneath his thumbs, provided control over acceleration, brakes, generator presets and various other settings for the trailer section. With a tired smile he wondered why he hadn't thought about detaching the cumbersome and damaged trailer earlier but, now the option was literally at his fingertips, he uncoupled the twenty-six foot cylinder from the cab, and he accelerated away. Only the suspension, catching on rocks and completely failing to compensate for the rough terrain, ruined what was now an otherwise easy drive.

For an hour he drove, keeping to the buffer between suburbs and wilderness, circumventing the city and getting close to Madrik spaceport on the outskirts of the northernmost district. He had worried that Ambondice-Ambondice might have had more vehicles besides those destroyed in the loading bay, but there was no sign of pursuit and, apart from the barrage as he broke through the Satumine perimeter, it had been easy going. It wouldn't be long, however, before they were able to arrange for someone to drive out to collect them – Galman was under no illusion that Ambondice-Ambondice's entire cell had been at that facility. Besides' even if Ambondice-Ambondice couldn't reach out to anyone, Cordem Hastergado certainly could. Galman was grateful all air traffic had been suspended; otherwise the Satumine could have been picked up and taken to the spaceport almost immediately.

Fifteen miles from Madrik port, IB traffic control was restored to the rural areas and Galman gladly turned over control to the superior artificial driver, giving him the chance to load the news net again. The past few days had seen a curfew and the deployment of Bureau of Supervision support staff onto the streets, along with several thousand Federal Trustees. In spite of the lack of civil order training and experience of these admin and investigative officers, the sheer number of uniforms on the city streets had quickly restored order to a population as inexperienced at civil unrest as the authorities were at combating it.

The last of the orbital wreckage had come down two days ago and there had been no sign of the unidentified assailant anywhere in the system, which meant it was in shortspace and going elsewhere. People were calming down and, as evidenced by the restored Traffic Control, were getting back to work and fulfilling their civic duty by way of their IB obligations. For all his distaste for the Swinell Union way of life, Galman conceded the people of Diaclom would not have been so easily calmed, and the authorities not so efficient in their response. Whatever it was that had happened up there, in orbit, Pellitoe had coped admirably.

Tumble awoke, his Intelligence-bridge restored. He crawled up from the footwell where Galman had stowed him, un-retractable and ruined tentacles sparking and buzzing as they crossed one another.

'Update?' the machine asked. Galman filled his IB friend in on what he had witnessed at the facility, explained how Ambondice-Ambondice had somehow turned Office Trustee Cordem Hastergado, what he had heard of their plan to use Cordem's shuttle at Madrik Port to get to the federal sentry *Vulpine* via *Kubet* Station, and finally recounted his desperate escape, and at the last showing off the crusty hole in his palm through which, had he been so grotesquely inclined, he could have poked a finger.

'We need a different vehicle *before* we reach the port,' Tumble decided as soon as Galman was done talking.

'Why?'

An unmistakable clunk, the sound of which hadn't changed in centuries of automotive design, signalled the locks activating on the driver and passenger doors. Then Traffic Control adjusted their course, steering them into the city.

'*That's* why,' Tumble said.

'Deactivate the Traffic Control,' Galman hissed at Tumble when the dashboard refused to do it for him.

'I can't,' Tumble said. 'It's a police override.'

'Damn it,' Galman yelled. He should have foreseen this; he had pulled in enough criminals in his career by overriding their vehicle controls. How had he not seen this coming? 'Fucking Cordem Hastergado!' He fired at the windscreen with his small laser, hoping to smash his way to freedom before he was driven straight into custody, but managed only to melt a small crater into the inch thick crystal.

'If I were you,' Tumble remarked, 'I wouldn't have that in my hands when we reach the Bureau of Supervision station.'

Chapter 61

*Do you have an IB assistant? Do you allow a machine,
intelligent by virtue of a human brain and bridging hardware, into
your home? Do you drive a vehicle, visit a doctor, watch the
entertainment feeds, maintain a personal log, communicate with
anyone through any means other than face to face, pay your taxes,
buy your groceries, or pretty much do anything other than live in a
cave on an uninhabited moon? Chances are that Consul is watching
you. I have already been fined a dozen times and threatened with an
SMD for repeatedly stating that Consul and his artificial
consciousnesses have a presence in the Jurisdiction's IB network, but
the fact is it is more than a mere* presence. *Consul outright runs the
IB network. He has long since bypassed and overcome the so-called
protective measures designed to prevent another consciousness from
arising through the bridging of human mind and computer hardware.
We have little choice, at the moment, but to live with these
consciousnesses within our infrastructure, but never ever forget that
they are there. Assume Consul knows everything, but don't let that
stop you fighting him.*

The Enguine Manifesto

Aggregate: On board the *Tenjin*, somewhere in the Swinell Union, in the Fertile Belt.

Aggregate had always been especially protective of the
captain's body and had ensconced it in the pleasure den at
the *Tenjin*'s core, investing a disproportionate amount of
himself in that single human mind. It was time, he decided,
to let go of the captain's narcissism which had so skewed
his consciousness and prevented him from fully becoming

the other thousand bodies. He was *not* the captain and he needed to embrace his plurality, needed to prepare himself for expansion into the millions on Diaclom and, soon after, the trillions across the Jurisdiction. With this in mind, Aggregate marched the Captain's body out of the pleasure den, leaving the plaything – Subset – tied in place. He was determined to put this once precious body in harm's way, to prove to himself his ability to truly disperse his consciousness.

Guiding the captain's hands to reroute the ruined shortspace regulators through new relays and processor stacks previously used for less critical systems, he also guided the rest of the crew in their pursuit of the human infiltrator, watching her leap from a balcony only to catch the railing of a lower level where she now hung in obvious pain. Simultaneously, Aggregate was Cordem Hastergado, berating the useless Satumine leader for the unacceptable delay in finding alternative transport.

Senior Trustee Cordem Hastergado; he was the reason for Aggregate's willingness to abandon his obsession with the Captain's body. For too long Aggregate's consciousness and intelligence had been defined by the minds of the *Tenjin*'s closed and dysfunctional community, defined by the narcissism and self-centred arrogance of a captain who had already ruled the sealed station for over a thousand years when Aggregate first arose, and by the minds of a crew resigned to serfdom. The pointspace shard had only ever known a world centred on the captain. But now, with the Office Trustee added to his distributed awareness, Aggregate had a fresh perspective, a mind indoctrinated by the decentralised Administration of the vast Human Jurisdiction. It was precisely what he needed. When he claimed more such minds the distorted thinking of the captain and his crew would be diluted further and forgotten.

Through the senses of the captain, Aggregate became aware of an incoming communication. Consul wanted to talk. Deliberately expressing his newfound preference for dispersed existence, Aggregate routed the communication to four of his bodies which were currently repairing a secondary plasma regulation node, far from the captain, and far from the invading human woman.

'I need to talk to Aggregate,' Consul's tin-man AR avatar stated.

'Yes,' Aggregate said, speaking through all four bodies.

The tin-man cocked its cylinder head and nodded. 'I see,' it said. 'You are embracing your nature at last.'

Aggregate was impressed, and concerned, at the artificial consciousness's insight. He had been sparing in his explanations regarding the details of his pointspace existence and had never revealed himself to be a singular entity. 'Exactly,' he admitted. There was no point in hiding what was obviously evident to Consul. Clearly the machine consciousness had not been idle over the last couple of decades. It knew exactly what Aggregate was. Such knowledge needn't change anything; Aggregate was no threat to Consul's realm – even if he were to claim the bodies of Consul's human components. As long as the minds still functioned in Consuls IB farms, it really wouldn't matter who lived through those bodies.

'I assume this change of personality is in response to the successful inclusion of an external human agent into your group consciousness,' Consul said with more unnerving insight. 'Office Trustee Cordem Hastergado, I believe.'

'Correct,' Aggregate conceded. He didn't bother asking how Consul had come by such specific details; the AC would probably refuse to tell him or would furnish him with a lie.

'I am gratified that your venture is proceeding as predicted.'

'Thank you, Consul.'

'I must, however, protest at the actions of your primary Satumine agent on the Network world of Dereph.'

'Indin-Indin? Why, what has he done?'

The tin-man avatar projected a sense of irritation, although its features were static lumps of unyielding metal. Aggregate wasn't sure how the AC pulled such expression off. 'Indin-Indin has taken a somewhat aggressive approach to his infiltration of the ancient Satumine facility to which you directed him.'

'And?' The one significant blind spot Aggregate had been forced to accept in his planning was an inability to monitor Indin-Indin's progress on the distant Network world, but he had confidence in the ability of a restored original Satumine, albeit one marginally compromised by certain behavioural assurances built into his neural fibres. That Indin-Indin had been a little aggressive in gaining entry to the research facility was not entirely unexpected; the Satumine had every reason to strike out at the humans defiling the old Satumine colony. It was a specific grievance with which Aggregate could strongly empathise.

'To cover his approach,' Consul explained, 'he activated ancient Satumine weapons across the planet and targeted the IB suites.'

'Sounds entirely sensible.'

The AR tin-man stepped up to Aggregate's four bodies in an unnecessary display of bravado – it was nothing more than a projection on the visual centres of the four brains. 'I had nine consciousnesses hiding within the Dereph intelligence-bridges. Your Satumine agent murdered them.'

'Murdered?' Consul snapped across four voices. 'He had no way of knowing your *people* were inside the network. How could he? At worst it's manslaughter, though I would call it an unfortunate accident, nothing more.

'Semantics,' Consul said as if its choice of words hadn't been precisely chosen. It had called it murder, which meant that was exactly how it saw it. 'The point is, I lost agents on that world. I expect your future actions to make less of an impact on the IB suites of other Jurisdiction worlds.'

'Pellitoe?'

'Yes, that is my immediate concern.'

The four bodies each held up a hand in a conciliatory gesture. 'Understood, Consul. I will do my best to ensure the IB network is largely intact after the *Vulpine* is done with the planet.' Then, confused, Aggregate asked, 'How can you have artificial consciousnesses in the Jurisdiction IB systems? The Humans learned after you not to pair individual minds with specific computers'

The tin-man snorted. 'Do you think I haven't also learned?'

Chapter 62

Of all the careers open to you as a member of the Human Jurisdiction, perhaps the most rewarding is that of a Trustee. And of all the different Trustee postings, one of the most exciting and worthy is surely that of a Sentry crew member. What better way to see the Jurisdiction and repay those who liberated you from Consul's servitude than to sign up for a tour aboard one of the most formidable symbols of freedom ever constructed. The Federal Sentries are the most advanced machines in the entire Jurisdiction, supporting hundreds, often thousands of crew, affording their Trustees with every luxury and privilege available whilst ensuring they are exposed to little, if any risk. You will visit different planets, making new friends across the unions during your decades of service. You may be assigned to a ship offering long term support to a small group of worlds, or you may service a long but vital supply route, spending years in shortspace and establishing relationships closer than anyone unaccustomed to such a life could ever imagine. Yes there is war with Consul, but there is far more to Sentry life than that.

Rehabilitation: A Survivor's Guide

Subset: Aboard the *Tenjin*, somewhere in the Swinell Union, in the fertile belt

The user interface of the *Tenjin*'s computer was an intuitive and simplistic array of multi-dimensional geometric planes which relied on the extraordinary complexity of the code compartments running through countless parallel processor crystal stacks. Subset had never been required to physically interact with the interface – his five centuries of service having been restricted to light maintenance and the demand of satisfying

Aggregate's vile appetites – but he found he had no difficulty in accessing the computer. Most of his life had been spent as part of Aggregate's greater consciousness and, as such, his physical brain held the memories of the pointspace creature's every action save for those occurring during Subset's tortured periods of disconnection. The youngest crewman knew how to use the computers because *Aggregate* knew how to use the computers.

He was cowering in an empty box-room which had once been a service-grade citizen's quarters in the final age of the *Tenjin*-state, before Aggregate had surfaced. Aggregate hadn't looked in this room, with any of his bodies, for at least four thousand years, and Subset felt confident he was safe for the moment. But, if he just hid, his DNA would soon enough be reclaimed by Aggregate. He flicked impossible geometries across the AR screen, reading the mathematical interactions as easily as he could the many variants of standard Jurisdiction script and Satumine pictographs which had evolved over the first three thousand years of the *Tenjin* society.

'Were you trying to kill us all or was this a miscalculation?' he mumbled as the details of the explosion took shape. 'Did you even realise the shortspace calibration ran through those stacks?' He often spoke his thoughts aloud; it had been a conscious decision, just a few decades into his grim existence. Aggregate's various bodies never spoke – never had any reason – and Aggregate rarely addressed Subset during his moments of independence, other than to torment him. Subset had chosen to speak because he felt it was in some way required of him. Why else would he possess the capacity for speech? Besides, he got lonely and a voice, even his own, offered a taste of comfort.

'He's going to be all over you,' he said, noting the precise location of the explosion and recalling the standard deployment of Aggregate's bodies. 'I hope you came armed.'

There was no internal monitoring system in the *Tenjin*. The near total surveillance used to control the final *Tenjin*-state had consumed vast amounts of finite resources and Aggregate had been quick to reclaim such un-necessary systems, recycling them into the shortspace burrower that had been utterly useless in the wormhole but which he had known would be vital on their eventual emergence into higher dimensional space. Aggregate, in his various bodies, had been the only life aboard the station, there had never been anybody on which to spy. Now somebody had made their way aboard, Subset imagined Aggregate was lamenting the loss of so many eyes, not to mention the myriad weapons which had once brutally enforced the last regime's order. Subset also longed for an image of the invader; he wanted to know if they were still alive.

'Hold on,' he said, choosing optimism over the easier pessimism which clenched at his heart. 'I'll be there soon.'

The explosion had occurred in the old forum in what had been the fourth-circle citizens' district, the space in which the upper-middle class of the final state had gathered to debate statutes and pass judgement on their peers. Now it was just another empty hall, circled by equally bare balcony levels. Unfortunately for the unknown human it was also close to the designated work sections of a disproportionately high number of Aggregate's bodies. Subset abandoned the safety of the box-room and ran through familiar corridors to find an elevator disk to take him down to the fourth-circle citizens' district.

He had never been to that particular forum, but like the rest of the eighty percent of the *Tenjin* in which he had never set foot, he knew it well. In one body or another Aggregate had walked virtually every inch of the station and Subset held that experience.

The disk brought him down into a wide chamber in which twenty simple beds, no more than shelves, identified the space as a dorm of those bodies working in the area. In one corner stood the most basic of toilets beside a shower which was only ever used when internal bodily devices warned Aggregate's bodies of some unexpected contamination or risk to health. His bodies were generally capable of self-cleansing. A nutrient paste dispenser lined the opposite wall, its six feeding tubes encrusted with dried paste. It was little different to Subsets own cell, though he shared with no other body; Aggregate preferred not to constantly see Subset, allowing some anticipation to mount in his absence. Only the shower was missing from Subset's cell because Aggregate never sent him to biologically tainted sections in which the contents of old labs still festered and mutated.

He quickly left the dorm by its only door, stepping out into a column of Aggregate's bodies which was rushing to the forum just a hundred meters down the corridor.

'Subset, you let yourself out of my den?' Aggregate asked through five bodies, using an uncharacteristically communal voice. Those not speaking continued down the corridor while the other five turned to face subset.

'Yes,' Subset stated, looking into the single blue array-eye of the closest body. Aggregate rarely spoke to subset through any body other than that of the intimidating and terrifying captain. Somehow Subset found this new method to be less awe inspiring, less threatening. 'I grew tired of waiting,' he added, at once hating himself for bating Aggregate while relishing the rebellion and the strength it revealed. Aggregate smirked thorough the two bodies in possession of mouths capable of such expression. Subset expected an assault, physical or otherwise, but Aggregate turned away, five times, and walked on.

'Just stay out of the way,' it called back in a single communal voice. 'I will be you again in about fifty minutes, at which point I will resume work on the seven-nine-hex-blue relay overflow. Go there now so you are in place.' Then Aggregate rounded the gentle corner.

Subset smiled. Aggregate was so certain of his dominion over the crew, over him, that he couldn't conceive of the threat Subset posed when independent. That was going to change.

It would have been faster to follow the crew, along the corridor and into the forum. They were heading directly for the destroyed processor stack where subset hoped the human intruder was still alive. But Aggregate's casual disregard for Subset would be compromised if he followed now that he had been ordered elsewhere. He returned to the elevator disk and descended another two levels, exiting onto a massive open level which spread out the full hundred meters to the balcony overlooking the forum. There was little light save for that which shone from the circle of the forum and some of the other balcony levels. Leaning over the balcony, on this level, three of Aggregate's bodies looked up, straining to reach. Subset could guess at what, who, was hanging from the level above. He could also guess why all manner of tools and appendages were being pointed up – Aggregate wanted the human to believe the crew were armed. It was a bluff, but one the human had no reason to suspect. How would they know Aggregate had no need of armed security aboard the *Tenjin*? The longer the human hung there, however, the closer Aggregate's production systems came to fabricating real personal armaments. Subset guessed it would take less than ten minutes to produce and distribute rudimentary pistols. For now, however, the crew were unarmed and, most significantly, had their backs to him. Stepping closer, hoping Aggregate would be too distracted to hear his approach, Subset tightened his fist and felt a surge of excitement. He was glad Aggregate seemed to be living more fully through the crew, because he wanted his sick master to feel this.

Chapter 63

I was actually privy to the source code of the first probe to reach the Cannis Major Dwarf Galaxy. I was able to decompile and analyse the brief stream of data received on its emergence from shortspace into our closest galactic neighbour. Many people like to suggest Consul lurks out there in the dwarf galaxy, imagining some realm vastly bigger than the domain in which we suppose he exists here in the milky way. But the astrogation data makes this unlikely: We know when consul first fled Earth, and we know when he first utilised shortspace technology. Granted, he could have made the fifty year journey to the dwarf galaxy before our first probe arrived there, but only by a few years. We sent that first probe very soon after we developed shortspace and I can not imagine Consul could have dominated the miniature galaxy so completely as to have been able to destroy our probes the instant they emerged from shortspace. They have, after all, emerged in every quadrant of the Dwarf, thousands of light years from one another. Consul could not be so utterly dispersed so quickly and the energy signature of the pulse detected by the first probe does not match anything like Consul's technology. The original Ancient Satumine, on the other hand, may have had millennia, if not longer, to dominate the Cannis Major Dwarf Galaxy. Why, then, do they leave the bastardised modern Satumine race here in our midst? It is not, one must imagine, for our own good.

The Truth: A treatise on the Satumine Conspiracy

Anden Macer: Aboard *Kubet Station*, in orbit around Pellitoe, in the Swinell Union, in the Fertile Belt

The station was too cold. It had often been remarked, especially by new crew intakes, that the *Vulpine* ran a little warm, but Anden had had a century to acclimatise. The station climate control held a steady twenty two degrees Celsius, only two degrees cooler than the *Vulpine*'s cosy interior, but enough to aggravate Anden's already foul mood. And the air reeked, a sharp bitter tang with a cloying treacle aftertaste, like an excessive splash of cheap perfume. It was the smell of Satumine. Nobody else seemed to notice, save for the others of his crew, and few of them appeared as bothered by it as Anden. Perhaps his attachment to the *Vulpine*, to his home, and his reluctance to leave its warm halls, was felt more strongly than by the others. He didn't have a problem with Satumine, but they were rarely allowed aboard a federal sentry and he was uncomfortable with so many aboard the station.

His crew also seemed more at ease with the augmented reality so prevalent and pervasive aboard the station. There were many reasons Anden had chosen to rarely leave his ship, even when deployed for extended periods in orbit, but his dislike of excessive and superfluous AR was high on the list. As a tool, a utility, he was content to exploit the advantages of AR; the *Vulpine* was controlled through any number of AR screens and interfaces. He was even happy to employ certain cosmetic embellishments, often wearing an AR uniform and, even now, his bare-blade crop was an illusion behind which stumps of his dreadlocks were disguised. What unsettled and infuriated him about the AR culture of places like the Swinell Union was the sheer glut of embellishments, the transformation of their worlds, their lives, into some bizarre fantasy and, worse still, their insistence that all are permanently immersed in the augmented reality. Aboard the *Vulpine*, any crewmember was free, encouraged even, to disable or fade their perception of AR, to remember always the truth of what Swinell Union citizens called Drab-reality. On the *Vulpine*,

AR was an embellishment, a decoration and a tool, not a substitute for physical reality.

His personal shopper – generously provided by the Union commander of the station – opened yet more illusory windows to reveal a catalogue of exotic AR appendages. Anden remembered his other major distaste. On the *Vulpine*, AR tools and embellishments were created and used as required; in places like the Swinell Union entire economies had developed to ration AR use, further confirming it as something to be desired, making a great many people very wealthy. To him it didn't seem right to sell things which simply did not exist. Nobody he spoke to aboard the station understood his reluctance to spend the sizable credit of data-matter provided to him and his crew, least of all the frustrated personal shopper.

'If you would just *look* at the premium range,' the man was saying, guiding the gold-framed window across Anden's large room to bring it in line with the captain's vacant stare. 'I think you will be pleasantly surprised by the depth of tactile sensation available and the customisable embellishments, ranging from animated tattoo- ' he brought forward an elongated human arm, around which tribal patterns squirmed and chased one another. ' – to luminescent follicles.' Anden turned away before the man could show him an arm covered in glowing fur.

'I'm happy to use the positional marker paired with my natural arm,' Anden snapped. 'It has served me well enough for the past hundred years.'

'But what about non-local interactions? With any appendage from the mid to premium ranges you will be provided unlimited extension capability, subject to regional security and privacy statutes, and a screen will show you exactly where the arm –'

'No,' Anden said. 'If I need a non-local interaction I will make a call to whomever it is I want to interact with. I don't need to be able to poke them on the shoulder!'

The personal shopper coughed awkwardly. 'That really isn't the current fashion,' he said.

'And I really don't give a shit,' Anden snarled, causing the other man's heavily embellished manga-face to blush. His embellishments must have been tied directly to sensory outputs; otherwise the flush of red would have remained hidden in drab-reality, beneath the white cartoon skin.

'I don't want to buy an AR limb,' the captain said, stepping closer to the other man and noting which some satisfaction he took a step back. 'I don't want a new skin, I don't want your *essential* kit of tools and utilities, and I certainly don't want your stimulant food additives.'

'What about the customisable clothing package?'

'Christ,' Anden yelled. 'You don't give up!'

'It's just, sir, that a man of your social standing really ought – '

'No!' Anden screamed, reaching to physically push the personal shopper out the door which had opened behind him. 'I don't want your fucking AR clothes.'

The door closed and Anden waited, expecting the persistent man to knock, to try again to make a sale. But he seemed to have got the message. He didn't knock.

'He was only doing his job, Captain.'

'Fuck!' Anden jumped at the voice and tripped over the bare drab-reality slab that he was, he suspected, supposed to have embellished with a coffee table skin. He landed in a ball in the corner of the room, rubbing a throbbing shin.

'Christ, Steit, what the hell are you trying to do?' Anden complained.

'Sorry, Captain,' the executive officer said, a tight smirk betraying his amusement at the Captain's spectacular trip across the room. 'Didn't mean to startle you.'

As Anden got to his feet it struck him that Steit shouldn't be in the room. He hadn't come through the door, and there was no other way in.

'It's OK,' he muttered, spitting sarcasm. 'I can get up on my own.' He didn't require his friend's hand to help him to his feet, but the offer would have been appreciated.

'Yeah, sorry,' Steit said. 'Can't help; I'm not really here.'

Anden exhaled, the disappointed sigh of a parent finding their sixteen year old daughter's tattoo. 'AR,' he muttered. 'Non-local interactions? Really?'

'Not bad, eh?' He was actually *proud* of his new toy. 'I was going to go for a premium bundle of tentacles and arms, but I realised I had enough to buy this whole body projection set-up'

Anden shook his head. 'We're not staying here for long, so don't get too comfortable. I mean, seriously, how much use are you going to get out of that thing?'

Steit shrugged. 'It's *their* money,' he said.

Then Anden saw the purple coiled around Steit's left leg. 'What's that?' he demanded. 'A tail?'

The executive officer uncoiled a fleshy appendage and let it swing lazily behind him.

'Nice, isn't it?'

'For the love of…' Anden pinched the bridge of his nose and felt he ought to laugh, but his pain was too raw for levity. 'Why, Steit?' What the hell are you going to do with that? You have unlimited AR access on the *Vulpine* but you never felt the need to do anything like this on the ship'

'We don't have the same calibre of artisan on the *Vulpine*. Anyway, I'm just trying to fit in, Captain.'

'By wearing a purple tail?'

'Believe it or not, I attract less attention like this than in my drab-reality.'

'I can't deal with this,' Anden said, throwing up his hands. 'How are they doing with the repairs?'

'They're getting there,' Steit said, having the good grace to unload the tail from his projected visage. 'The weapons and core life support were largely undamaged, and the box-kite is still out in lunar orbit. They reckon they can have the burrower connection points in working order within a few hours.'

'And the bloody great holes all through the bullet section?'

'Seventy three percent of the *Vulpine* is open to space either through damage inflicted or because of structural repairs requiring the removal of entire hull sections. There will also have to be a complete refit and restock.'

'But she could fly?' Anden asked. 'I mean, if she had to, the *Vulpine* could reconnect with the box-kite and enter shortspace?'

'If she had to,' Steit confirmed. 'And to be honest, this station isn't in any condition to perform major structural work. Give it a week or two to patch us up and we will have to head for Dendrell and make use of the shipyard.'

'Bollocks to that,' Anden said. 'As soon as the *Tenjin* surfaces, I want us ready to pursue.'

'Steit frowned and shook his head. 'The *Vulpine* can't support the crew in her current state. They will have to stay here until Dendrell is done with fixing the damage.'

'But the bridge is OK, isn't it? I mean, it's able to support a skeleton crew to get to Dendrell.'

'Barely even a skeleton crew,' Steit said. 'But yes.'

'Then it can support enough of us to go after the *Tenjin*.'

'Who do you have in mind?'

'You, me and the rest of the senior officers.'

'Steit nodded, there was no enthusiasm and Anden didn't blame him. All that mattered was that his closest officers, his family, would not refuse him. They would all die together.'

Chapter 64

Although the first truly effective and readily available longevity treatments and drugs were seen following humanity's contact with the Satumine, we had actually developed many of the treatments now used to grant an indeterminate lifespan as far back as Consul's reign on Earth. The technology was withheld by the Tyrant and, to be honest, I expect it would have been withheld by any human government had such existed at the time. Immortality has always been a dream of the populace and a nightmare of those charged with the governance of man. While we were limited to a single planet, immortality could have only exacerbated the strain on our limited resources and territory. Had immortality been available, some believed, mankind would have learned to restrain their need to breed and those few children created would be cherished and raised by families who could see them as the rare gift they are. Now that virtual immortality is a fact of life, however, we see a complete reversal of these naïve predictions: society expects an exponential growth and the demanding breeding quotas on pre-billion colonies ensure this expectation is met. And as for loving nurturing homes for our children — I invite you to visit a pre-billion communal nursery.

While hardly abusive environments, these nurseries are far from the intimate homes a more natural breeding regime would allow. Children born to a pre-billion colony know nothing of the love shown to children on the Network worlds or the more established out-network planets. As pre-billion worlds start to significantly outnumber the established planets, an ever decreasing percentage of the human populace will know what a family truly should be, and when those worlds become established and the breeding strictures lifted, I imagine the communal nurseries will remain.

The Enguine Manifesto

Galman Tader: On Pellitoe, in the Swinell Union, in the Fertile Belt

The Bureau of Supervision district-station was part of an impressive compound of over a dozen local government buildings arranged in an extended T with a scattering of detached buildings, all within enclosed grounds of verdant gardens, driveways and entirely too many water features for Galman's less ostentatious tastes. A twenty foot wall surrounded the compound, although it was impossible to know how much of it was underpinned by a corresponding drab-reality barrier. The Bureau station encompassed the entire horizontal bar of the T and Galman's stolen truck was driven, by Traffic Control, to a huge open garage at one end. As the vehicle came to a gentle stop, between two smaller patrol vehicles, Galman considered pocketing the mini-laser, but Tumble advised against such a strategy.

'You'll just look guiltier,' the machine cautioned.

Galman saw four men approach from either side. They were recognisable as Bureau officers, their uniforms identical to those worn by the men and women who replaced the Diaclom Constabulary, the officers who had replaced *him*. In spite of their slight build, Galman was not so naïve as to doubt their ability. For all his dislike and mistrust of the liberal Swinell Union police, he had to concede they were well trained and superbly equipped. He dropped the weapon and kicked it back beneath his seat, tensing in anticipation of the customary beating with which he had often prepared a suspect for interrogation. He couldn't defend himself with the pistol – that would justify his immediate execution – but he could make them work for his detention. If they wanted to beat him, they weren't going to get out of it un-bloodied.

The doors clunked as Traffic Control unlocked them and Tumble went limp, his intelligence-bridge cut again.

'Come on then,' Galman spat as the doors swung open. 'Which of you is man enough?'

The response was a genuine chuckle and a positively genial smile. 'Really?' the senior supervisor said, as if Galman was a child who had been watching too many old AR fictions. 'Come on,' the friendly cop said, holding out a hand to help Galman from the cab, his tone only mildly patronising. Galman glanced at the man's hip, noting the thin mag-gun and the short butt of a telescopic baton. The cop's hands were nowhere near the weapons, but the fact that they were not concealed beneath AR embellishments pointed to a deliberately passive-aggressive display. This officer had no intention of using force but, if needed, he was more than capable.

Galman took the man's hand, wary but disinclined to make the first aggressive move. He stepped down onto the garage's AR carpet which was immune to the assaults of vehicle tyres and the filth they tracked in.

'Please follow me, Mr Tader,' the Senior Supervisor said, putting a guiding hand across Galman's shoulder and leading him to the closest of the five doors. The other cops fell in behind. 'I am Senior Supervisor Ludit,' he said. 'Can I get you anything? A hot drink perhaps? Something to eat?' The kitchen embellishes a delightful stress relieving relaxant-sandwich.'

What followed was treatment so civil it was excruciatingly embarrassing. Having greedily devoured several sandwiches, and three pints of cold peach-water, he was led to a comfortable lounge in which he was asked, if it wasn't too much trouble, would he mind completing a few forms regarding his personal details, his immigration status, any offences he would like to confess and, bizarrely, if he would like to register any complaint or comment about the manner of his detention. A little disorientated and confused, Galman put his feet up on a plush footstall, leaned back in the reclining seat and completed the paperwork, all the while wondering if his own investigations and interrogations on Diaclom might have been better served by such unexpected politeness and civility. It certainly unsettled him.

After an hour, in which he was asked no less than ten times if he might appreciate more refreshments or some kind of entertainment, he began to wish they had just beat him and thrown him in a cell.

'Mr Tader?' A Supervisor called from behind the small desk besides what was, for all intents and purposes, a café. Galman raised a hand though he was one of only three supposed prisoners in this most bizarre of holding areas. 'Would you be so kind as to make your way down to suite four,' the Supervisor said with a pleasant smile. 'Just down that corridor, third room on the right. Let yourself in.'

Suite four. He was sure they meant *interrogation room four.* He gave a wary smile, nodded and headed for an open arch abutted by two AR waterfalls. They really did like their water features on Pellitoe.

'Would you like a drink, or something to eat, to take in with you?'

Galman couldn't help but chuckle at the obscene civility of this most liberal of police stations. 'No, thank you,' he said.

The suite's lilac door opened at his approach and the gentle strum of a guitar rolled out to meet him. *Mood music?* He laughed again though he hadn't forgotten the severity of his situation. He had been arrested, undoubtedly at the behest of Cordem Hastergado, an Office Trustee turned by a Saturnine Terrorist. Behind all the smiles and apparent kindness and the unending offers of refreshment, behind the pleasant surroundings and mood music, lay a significant danger. They were trying to induce him to lower his guard; he couldn't let that happen. Hardening his features into a determined scowl, he stepped into what he had to remember was an interrogation room.

'Ah, Mr Tader. Galman. I can call you Galman, can't I?' He was a well build Supervisor, a Senior Supervisor according to rank insignia on his tight fitting uniform. He looked due for telomere braiding treatment, his physical age seeming to be in the late fifties. His relaxed belly and unkempt beard all contrived, no doubt, to enhance the friendly tone of the interview. His entire facade was probably AR. Beside the Supervisor stood an impossibly thin woman, her too-long limbs no thicker than snooker cues, her face twice as long and half as wide as was natural. It looked as though she had been stretched out like toffee. All AR.

'Whatever you want,' Galman replied, accepting the man's hand and shaking it, briefly. 'And who are you?'

The man beamed, as if he had just made a dear new friend. 'I am Senior Supervisor Ledwintoe, and this is our IB psychology system and independent counsel.'

'In the parlance of you home world,' the IB 'woman' said in the androgynous voice required of all IB machines, 'I am your lawyer. I'm here to ensure you are treated fairly and that you are aware of your rights.'

'Nice to meet you,' Galman said, shaking hands with her and feeling the thinner Drab-Reality foundation of her robotic appendage beyond the sensory feedback of embellished skin.

'You look tense,' Ledwintoe observed, motioning for Galman to sit on the long black sofa opposite the identical one on which he and the IB lawyer had been sitting. 'Has anyone offered you something to drink? Something to eat?'

Galman smirked. 'It's fine,' he said. 'Your people have been very hospitable.'

'Good, good,' the cop said, briefly catching the solicitor's eye. And in that look Galman understood the ludicrously courteous treatment. This world, aside from being a liberal pit of AR decadence and Satumine integration, was also home to a viciously litigious society. The cops of the Bureau of Supervision were terrified of being sued, and whichever firm this IB lawyer represented was happy to facilitate the claims of aggrieved, or greedy, criminals. He shook his head and closed his eyes – was this what was to become of Diaclom? Little wonder the Constabulary had wanted rid of him – he would have bankrupted them within a month.

'Why am I here?' he asked.

Ledwintoe held up his hands. 'Now *that's* the question, isn't it?'

The lawyer machine leaned forward. 'The Federal Administration has ordered your detention,' she said, 'and has asked that you be placed in solitary confinement. However they have yet to provide a suitable emergency dossier with which to justify such an infringement of your liberty.'

'We, the Bureau of Supervision, are not about to lock you up on your own merely at the say-so of a federal request unless it is backed up by admissible facts,' the Supervisor said. 'All they have given is evidence of your illegal departure from a pre-billion world – '

'- and according to their own files they have given you a month in which to vacate,' the lawyer interrupted. 'So you can't be detained on that.'

'So, again, why am I here?'

The cop squirmed. 'The Administration has the right to ask for a twelve hour detention prior to providing an evidentiary dossier.'

'You can't be put in solitary,' the AR machine said, looking at the cop as she spoke. 'But they can hold you on the premises for twelve hours.'

Galman clenched his fists. Twelve hours was too long; Ambondice-Ambondice would be on board Cordem Hastergado's shuttle long before then. He had already lost an hour waiting in the luxurious holding area.

'I suppose bail is out of the question,' he said with a hopeful smile.

'No, not at all,' Ledwintoe said quickly, again glancing at the solicitor. 'In fact, that was something I wanted to discuss.'

'Really?' Galman sat up.

'They took your IB machine, the sphere,' the lawyer said, suddenly, her artificial voice accusing, leading. She expected to earn from this. 'They want to download its memory and see what you have been up to.' She said it as if disgusted at the inexcusable breach of Galman's civil liberties and privacy. She had obviously been instructed to find any excuse to sue. Galman wasn't interested.

'To what end?' he asked, aware his pursuit and surveillance of Ambondice-Ambondice would all be there, though the turning of Cordem would not. He wasn't sure if the release of those memories would help or hinder his mission.

'If it can prove you are not involved in any illegal activities, we can release you on monitored bail, rather than detain you.'

'So what's to discuss?'

'We don't seem to be able to activate the IB machine,' Ledwintoe sounded embarrassed. 'We have secured suitable bridge coverage, but it just isn't responding.'

'I don't know what to suggest.'

'They were hoping you had employed an access encryption,' the IB lawyer explained.

Galman shook his head. 'It was damaged in an… accident.'

'Yes,' Ledwintoe said. 'We noticed that. It's in the shop as we speak. We'll have it as good as new – '

'– That must not be misconstrued as a gift, or payment, and it does *not* affect you statutory right to litigation…' Galman held up his hand to silence the obsessed lawyer.

'Yes, fine,' he said to her.

The door opened and the head, and spine, of a young woman were hurled into the cop's lap, flicking warm blood across Galman's face. Tumble rushed in, swinging with renewed energy and health, coiling an appendage around Ledwintoe's neck while grabbing his mag-gun with another.'

Chapter 65

So you are considering starting your new independent life on a pre-billion colony? Well good for you. You will be following in the footsteps of the Jurisdiction's great pioneers and can take satisfaction in the knowledge that you are not only repaying the kindness of your saviours but also helping ensure the Human Jurisdiction remains strong and secure. But what about when your chosen colony reaches its glorious billion-day and the breeding and migration restrictions are swept away? Will you embrace the change, revelling in the new challenges and opportunities laid out before you? Or, as a true pioneer, will you set out on a colony ship to take yet more worlds for the Jurisdiction? The rewards, both in satisfaction and more tangible gains, are significant for those selfless citizens who make a life of the Jurisdiction's expansion.

Rehabilitation: A Survivor's Guide

Indin-Indin: On Dereph, in the Network

'Are you deliberately delaying the initiation sequence?' Indin-Indin demanded of the computer consciousness. It seemed every time the micro wormhole generator was ready to come on-line the computer suddenly uncovered an entirely new level of systems which needed to be activated in order to continue.

'You have to understand,' the computer said into the Satumine's mind. 'This entire colony was remotely deactivated from Satute and was never supposed to be re-awoken in such a piecemeal way as this. Without the wholesale initiation of the entire colony, things are going to be slow and not entirely predictable.'

'Just hurry up,' Indin-Indin said, noticing the arrival of another Jurisdiction Sentry through the pointspace Frame, and the immediate launch of troop carrier shuttles which headed directly for the Satumine research facility. The hole carved into the wall by ship-based particle accelerators was now large enough to accommodate a column four men abreast, and it would only take a few minutes for the molten metal to cool enough to allow them to approach. The wall's regenerative properties hadn't been entirely spent or neutralized by the immensely powerful if simplistic beams, but it would take a couple of hours for the hole to begin healing at any appreciable rate.

Indin-Indin began reacquainting himself with the ancient weapons scattered across the colony with which he had so effectively destroyed the human IB suites. Many of those weapons could be turned just as easily to the small army gathering outside his facility.

Through the weapons conveniently situated about the facility, Indin-Indin more intently observed the throng of armoured humans and their sleek IB combat machines which, he noticed by way of a data-sight inherent to the weapon scanners, were powered by intelligence-bridges generated on the orbiting sentries. He could smell the humans. No, not smell, though this new sense had much in common with that redundant human-inspired sense. This was more an intuitive awareness of chemical composition, a sense borrowed from the weapon sensors through which a part of his fractal consciousness existed. It was a new feature, something of which he hadn't been aware the first time he used the weapons. How many more wonders were to be awoken in the abandoned Satumine colony?

While part of his attention monitored the computer's slow revival of the micro wormhole generator, another part tore through the pungent human rabble, vaporising their soft limited bodies with the lightest touch of thin white beams, beams which terminated at the mechanised support where they delivered their explosive pulses which Indin-Indin hadn't bothered to dial down from the building levelling setting with which he had previously taken out the IB infrastructure. Those human bodies not directly brushed by beams were shredded and burnt to ash by the heat of spontaneously generated plasma and then blasted to dust by violent pressure waves which brought down three human buildings already destabilised by the earlier calamity. Nothing of the human army remained.

While the Jade rods of the Satumine weapons cooled, Indin-Indin addressed the computer. 'Why was the colony remotely deactivated?' As the words formed he felt a deeply rooted anxiety and knew he shouldn't have asked. He wasn't supposed to know why the Satumine defiled themselves with human genetic material and abandoned their empire - but from where did that reticence come? Was it racial genetic memory or some tampering at the hands of Aggregate?

'Satute was, for a while, immune to the pointspace entity,' the computer replied, speaking quickly, urgently, into Indin-Indin's mind, eager to discuss what it had previously been ordered not to mention. 'In order to fully sterilise the conquered colonies of the lost Satumine, the Satute government had to deny the infected the ability to use their technology to combat the sterilisation pathogen – '

The computer abruptly stopped explaining and Indin-Indin waited, silently, for it to resume. Then he realised he had ordered the computer to shut up or, at least, his mind had given the order. He didn't remember consciously deciding to speak and felt, with an ugly certainty, that Aggregate had done something to him to ensure he was incapable of learning the truth of his species' decline. But no matter; when his work was done, and Aggregate had his micro wormholes, the Satumine would be allowed to revert, en masse, and the past would be irrelevant.

Something like pain, not uncomfortable as such but a definite recognition of injury, coursed through Indin-Indin's fractal awareness. The Jurisdiction sentries were bombarding the planet, carving through the structures built around the ancient Satumine weapons and melting through the jade rods. One by one they shattered and Indin-Indin swore in a tongue only he and the computer could appreciate. The weapons would regenerate, but not for several days.

'Have we got any surface to orbit weapons?' he demanded.

'Not that we can power,' the computer reported. 'The pointspace harvester is barely operating at two percent.'

Indin-Indin watched the Sentries dispatch more troop carriers to the surface. 'Well we need to take out those ships, because I can't defend this facility indefinitely if the humans get inside and take out the internal defences.'

'How about this,' the computer said, pulling a thread of the Satumine's awareness into a partially isolated system a kilometre beneath the Federal Administration's primary complex at the city centre.

Indin-Indin felt a warm flush of excited satisfaction. 'Oh yes,' he said. 'That will do.'

Chapter 66

My regular readers are well aware of my age. You will no doubt have read my early memoirs, those vast tomes recalling and reminiscing over the earliest days of the Jurisdiction and my thoughts on those first years after we discovered the frames. I am, you must then realise, one of those few humans who yet remembers the cold and humbling shadow of natural death. I know also the burning ecstasy of Satumine longevity drugs. That is the only way in which those who lived so long ago could have made it to the point where mankind created its own means of immortality. Let me explain, then, that it was not merely the release from the spectre of death that led humanity to so willingly hand over in ever greater shipments the wealth and resources of Earth to the Satumine. We were not handing over all that we had merely in order that we might not die; we were feeding an addiction! Nine hundred years may have passed since we were freed of Satumine longevity drugs, but a century of addiction is not easily undone and those of us carrying the memory of that bitter elixir do so with a guilty longing. I despise the Satumine, but were I to be gifted one more dose of that deep-green filth, I can not say with certainty that I could resist. I fear, therefore, that some of the Jurisdictions oldest and most powerful citizens may still be under the sway of Satumine providers of an obsolete but addictive drug. How much would these people give to feed their habit?

The Truth: A treatise on the Satumine Conspiracy

Ambondice-Ambondice: On Pellitoe, in the Swinell Union, in the Fertile Belt

Placing the third nutrient biscuit into his abdominal cavity, Ambondice-Ambondice noticed the silhouette of an approaching convoy.

'Are these your men?' Cordem asked. Ambondice-Ambondice was accepting the human to be Aggregate, but it was easier to label him, in his thoughts, as Cordem. Aggregate, to his mind, was the mysterious ally captaining the distant *Tenjin*. It was difficult to imagine them both to be the same person.

He checked the vehicle data-profiles with a simple AR utility and identified them as those dispatched by the remainder of his cell. 'It's them,' he confirmed, holding closed the flaps of his abdomen and rushing the production of resin which would seal the cavity and begin the digestion process. He got to his feet and waved for the rest of the Satumine to get up.

'Stand ready,' he ordered, taking his rifle and aiming at the lead vehicle which fast drew near. He wasn't taking anything for granted, wasn't going to entertain the same complacency with which he had allowed Galman Tader to blow up every vehicle in the loading bay. The convoy of three medium vans pulled up. They weren't really suited to off-road and deep scratches on the lower bodywork showed they lacked enough ride height to clear the ever present rocks littering the wilderness. Further up the vehicles, all the way up their small windscreens, the thin slush of burst affan grass suggested a direct path through a bloated meadow. The rest of the Satumine now trained their weapons on the vehicles.

'Out you come,' Ambondice-Ambondice ordered, focusing every forward facing eye, bar those on his palms which saw nothing but the plastic of the rifle grip, onto the one-way mirror of the oval windscreen. When the doors opened and recognisable Satumine stepped out from each of the three vans, Ambondice-Ambondice and the others relaxed, lowering their aims and stepping forward.

'Never mind the pleasantries,' Cordem snapped, barging through the companionable throng to reach the lead van. Still pissed, no doubt, that his rank had been insufficient to override the ban on airborne vehicles which could have got them to Madrik port in a fraction of the time these vans would take. 'We're already late.'

The Van's driver looked questioningly to Ambondice-Ambondice as the uniformed Office Trustee slid across into the forward passenger seat. The Satumine leader gave a subtle flick of his hands, a gesture much like a human nod, and the driver stepped back into the cab, returning to his seat.

'Get in,' Ambondice-Ambondice ordered the others. 'And keep your weapons close to hand, but out of sight.'

They drove through the city, taking the shortest and most direct route to the North District in which Madrik Port was situated. Ambondice-Ambondice, despite his eagerness to get there as quickly as possible, had wanted to remain off-road, to circumvent the city entirely. He wasn't comfortable driving in plain sight, especially given the unprecedented level of security since the incident in orbit. There were too many Supervisors and Trustees on the street. But Cordem insisted they take this, the fastest route. Besides, he had quipped, who was going to pull over the continent's Office Trustee?

Madrik Port's entrance lay about a kilometre beyond the four lanes of the ring road delineating the city's central metropolitan area. Its single landing pad, an eight hundred meter circle of embellished construction resin, was surrounded by a kilometre of grounds, dotted with a few dozen varied hangars and Madrik Port's one terminal building. It wasn't a major port, used primarily by local Trustees to reach the Federal Sentries or by wealthy citizens who liked to use their own shuttles to get to the stations rather than rely on crowded public shuttles at the larger ports. Consequently, security was generally more lax. As they approached along the two lane road, which had the AR look of an old cobbled road but on which the ride was as smooth as any other, Ambondice-Ambondice saw a squad of ten armed humans at the gate. To call it a gate was perhaps a little pretentious: it was merely an AR arch of blue light where the road passed into the port's grounds. There was no perimeter wall into which a gate could have been built, just a continuation of the arch in a blue line hovering five foot from the ground, circling Madrik Port. If Ambondice-Ambondice had been so inclined, he could have ordered the driver to take the van out of the hands of Traffic Control and had him drive off road, completely bypassing the squad of what looked like Trustees. But Cordem looked back from the front passenger seat and said to Ambondice-Ambondice, 'Just stay calm, and tell your comrades in the other vans to do likewise. I've got this.'

The Satumine leader was uncomfortable. The possibility of being found, with a convoy of armed Satumine, was a concern, as was his reliance on a human – or whatever Cordem now was. But his greatest discomfort stemmed from the human's insistence on talking as if he was in charge. He accepted this entire endeavour was the product of Aggregate's ingenuity, his planning and his technology, and was prepared to take instruction in private. But to be belittled, treated as a subordinate, in front of his own men, riled him. He couldn't bite his tongue, didn't have one, but he screwed up the tiny mouth in his neck and didn't respond. He sent a curt little comms note to the rest of his Satumine in the other vans, reminding them not to do anything stupid.

'Pull up at the gate,' Cordem instructed the Satumine driver.' He then reached for the rifle which rested between him and the driver. The Satumine's hand rushed to grab the weapon but Cordem was faster. 'Relax,' the human said, chucking the rifle back to where Ambondice-Ambondice sat. 'I just don't want this on display.' He raised the AR screen between the cab and rear passenger section, though he blocked sight only from the front to the back; Ambondice-Ambondice could still see perfectly well.

The Van pulled up and two of the Trustees approached the passenger side. Ambondice-Ambondice wondered why they weren't heading for the driver, until he noticed the AR icon, a rotating federal crest, hovering just the other side of Cordem's door. The Trustees knew there was someone of rank in the passenger seat and that he wanted to talk. The side door seemed to vanish as if embellished with a full length AR window; no need for the door to be opened.

'Good evening, Office Trustee,' one of the Trustees said, a hint of anxiety barely hidden behind a mask of over familiarity. 'I didn't see you on the manifest for today.'

Cordem chuckled and gave a friendly smile which the younger man seemed to lap up. 'I should hope not,' the Office Trustee said. 'In this state of heightened security it would hardly do for my itinerary to be advertised, would it?'

'No sir, of course not,' the Trustee said, looking to the ground while his companion waved the rest of the squad aside, out of the road. 'Sorry to have delayed you, sir.'

'Not at all,' Cordem said. 'This is a difficult time and I would expect that security be taken most seriously.'

In the back of the van Ambondice-Ambondice clenched his fists and willed Cordem to get on with it, to wrap things up with the guard and to resume their approach to the hangar containing the federal shuttle.

'Tell me, Trustee, have you had any trouble here at the port?' the Office Trustee said. Ambondice-Ambondice resisted the urge to reach through the AR screen and slap the back of Cordem's head. What was he doing?

'Nothing so far,' the younger man said, looking somewhat more at ease. 'But there had been some looting and civil unrest in the Northern District.' He then leaned closer to the AR window, lowering his voice to a conspiratorial murmur. 'If you ask me,' he said, 'I think the bloody Satumine are behind a lot of...' he trailed of and seemed to choke on the last word as he noticed the Satumine driver to Cordem's left. 'Sorry sir,' he blurted, pulling back from the window, flustered and visibly paler. 'I didn't mean –'

Cordem waved him away. 'Let it go,' he said, deleting the AR window and gesturing for the driver to continue through the blue arch. He then removed the screen between the two compartments.

'What the hell was all that about?' Ambondice-Ambondice snapped.

'Just wanted to check there has been no trouble,' Cordem said, his words dismissive, mildly patronising. Ambondice-Ambondice said nothing.

The hangar to which Cordem directed the driver was by far the largest in the modest port, a little under five hundred meters long, about half that in width. Unlike many of the private hangars adorned in every conceivable embellishment from exotic and garish fascias to animated displays and illusory wildlife, the Federal hangar was a bare grey box, though even that was probably some form embellishment over an even more Spartan drab-reality foundation.

Cordem called up an AR screen and instructed a small side door to open, and the three vans entered into utter darkness which could only have been a deliberately blinding embellishment because light streaming through the door was swallowed un-naturally the moment it crossed the threshold. Ambondice-Ambondice was the first to recognise the potential threat.

'Back-up!' he yelled to the driver. 'Get us out of here.' But the van didn't move. A high pitched screech sounded and the van dropped a couple of feet, the sudden drop churning the fresh food in his abdominal cavity, as a vehicular immobilizer sliced through all four wheels with a single swipe of a laser. Two dull crashing sounds revealed a similar immobilisation of the other two vans. The lights came on and an army of Satumine surrounded the convoy as the doors to the hangar slammed shut.

'Ambondice-Ambondice, I think you have something for me,' a familiar voice shouted as the leader of the Pellitoe Satumine Cell stepped towards the lead van.

'Sharlie-Sharlie,' Ambondice-Ambondice muttered. *'Charlie.'*

Cordem turned to glare at Ambondice-Ambondice and said, 'I thought your men could be trusted.'

'They can.'

'Then how did *he* know we were coming here?'

Ambondice-Ambondice squeezed his fists so tight his long fingers scraped the palm eyes. 'I don't know.'

As Sharlie-Sharlie stepped closer, Cordem took a pistol from his leg holster and thrust it into the driver's lap. 'I'm your prisoner,' he said quickly as he unloaded every AR embellishment and tool. 'Understand?'

Chapter 67

Since our lifespans have become potentially unlimited, the threat of imprisonment has lost its impact somewhat. Loathed as we are to implement any kind of capital punishment, the Jurisdiction has elected instead to hand down a Sentence of Memory Dismissal (SMD) for the most serious of offences. The recipient of such a sentence does not simply see their memories wiped, they also lose any personality traits grown through the lost memories and experiences. Through a process of neural hacking, synapse remapping, and old fashioned hypnotherapy, a new personality can be put in place and the offender released onto a pre-billion world to make a useful contribution to society, unburdened by the memory of the offence or the thoughts which led to it. The definition of a serious offence seems to be expanding with every census, however, and in particular we have noticed limited SMD use in a number of so-called subversive offences. While I can accept the principle of the punishment as sound and even necessary in some cases, it is the creeping expansion of the punishment that concerns me. In the case of murder, or extreme repeat offenders, it could be argued that the SMD not only acts as a punishment and deterrent, but it also provides the best form of rehabilitation and a second chance for those offenders damaged by trauma or a poor upbringing. For those guilty of merely opposing the dogma of the Jurisdiction, however, the SMD allows for limited personality restructuring, keeping in place the majority of memories but shifting the political leanings to something more acceptable to the Administration and releasing a mole into opposition camps. Such a change could be made to an agitator and the memory of the intervention erased. That is why my own synaptic map is scanned and recorded daily by my co-editors and is regularly checked for tampering.
The Enguine Manifesto

Subset: On the *Tenjin*, in shortspace, somewhere in the Fertile Belt

Subset wasn't strong. He wasn't capable of the heavy labour accomplished by those of Aggregate's bodies augmented with cybernetic musculature or mechanical prosthetics. He was entirely human, bred in a birthing tank but, in all other ways, as natural as the last of the *Tenjin*'s final generation – though he knew he was in many ways utterly alien compared with the humans of the Jurisdiction. His was a deliberate purity, contrived to satisfy Aggregate's lusts.

In spite of his relative weakness, Subset's clenched white fists tore through the bald paper-like skin at the back of the creature's head, splitting the thin cartilage serving as a skull and entering the hot jelly of its improved brain. Jagged metal corners sliced his knuckles as he reached the cluster of neural implants and he pulled back instinctively at the pain, wincing as a spray of grey matter exploded from the flimsy skull, following his hand out.

The other two of Aggregate's bodies turned in unison to see what had killed the third, and Subset savoured, for the briefest moment, the shared look of disbelief and confusion.

'Subset?' Aggregate said through them both, the stupidity of their voices belying the near limitless intellect of the pointspace entity combining the minds of everybody aboard the *Tenjin*. 'Why are you – '

Subset wasn't about to stop and talk, wasn't going to give up his small advantage. The two bodies were heavily augmented with mechanical lifting arms and many-socketed interface arrays across their chests. They were among the most useful of the engineering bodies, capable of hugely varied maintenance and research tasks, but like the now brainless corpse at Subset's feet, they had been grown quickly, to satisfy a specific requirement. Aggregate was impatient, a trait inherited from the mind of the captain, and wasn't willing to slow-grow his bodies. Inevitably there were critical flaws or weaknesses which Aggregate didn't take time to rectify before birth. For many it was the lack of a rigid skeleton, though that was rarely a problem when limbs could be strengthened by prosthetics. After all, who was ever going to punch them in their vulnerable skulls? For the two utility bodies, however, the flaw was in their augmentations. They were top-heavy. Spreading his arms like wings, Subset rushed forward to clothesline them both, wrapping his arms about their creased throats as they toppled, dragging them fully over the railings where gravity took over. They fell. They didn't scream, didn't cry out, they simply locked their gaze on subset and the youngest crewman delighted in the look of devastation and betrayal. He had really hurt his tormentor. He savoured it, perhaps a little too long, watching the bodies fall to the bare floor of the old forum, their other weakness becoming apparent as they struck the hard resin surface. Heavy mechanical limbs ripped from under developed organic joints and one of the bodies ruptured across its length, spilling a dark thick blood across twenty feet.

The railing flashed with white sparks, inches from where his tingling fingers gripped, adding a fresh sting to the already healing lacerations. He pulled away as a second bolt pinged on the rail. He looked up to see a human female, hanging from the railing on the level above, her mag-gun pointed at him but her aim spoilt by involuntary twitching in the arm from which she hung. She had been there a while.

'Don't shoot *me*,' he shouted, holding up his hands in the manner he had seen in the memories of the captain's first life.

She fired again, this time missing the railing but coming close enough to his throat for him to feel the tiny metal bolt breeze past. 'Christ!' he yelled, a curse which meant nothing to him, a curse which had already lots any real context when the captain had used it seven thousand years prior. It was just a curse, an exclamation. 'I'm not your enemy!' He shook his brain-covered fist at her and then pointed down to the two bodies in the spreading pool of blood far below. 'Look,' he shouted. 'I'm on your side.'

The woman glanced briefly to the bodies, then back to Subset. She was thinking, evaluating his sincerity and probably wondering if Aggregate would have been prepared to kill three of his bodies in order to lure her down. But no, she couldn't know of Aggregate's dispersed mind, she had to still believe the crew were individual consciousnesses.

'Come down here,' he said. 'It's clear.'

She frowned. 'If I move,' she said, 'those above me, or those over there,' she nodded to the balconies opposite and above, 'will open fire.'

'If they were armed, they would have fired by now. The only personal weapon in the entire station is in your hand.'

The woman grinned and, as if her improved situation somehow invigorated her exhausted muscles, her spasming arm locked straight and she aimed her pistol up at those of Aggregate's bodies leaning over the balcony above. She fired a few bursts and although subset couldn't see the result he guessed they were all killed. She then turned to the bodies opposite, on the other side of the forum, but already they were finding cover; Aggregate knew his bluff had been called.

'Leave them,' Subset yelled. 'It isn't going to take Aggregate long to fabricate some weapons.'

'Who's Aggregate?'

Subset snorted. 'If we don't do something about it, he is going to be everyone in the Jurisdiction.'

Chapter 68

It is known that Consul stocks the human component of his IB farm-worlds from a variety of sources. Although some small number are prisoners captured during the AI's victories, the vast majority of enslaved humans are grown or bred within Consul's realm. The chances are, therefore, you never knew your parents, if indeed you even had parents in any conventional sense. This may start to trouble you once you begin forming social bonds with other Humans and you come to learn of the traditional family unit so common on most post-billion worlds. You may feel deprived, you may worry that others will think you less 'normal' and many survivors of consul's farms often report feeling they are somehow unique amongst the Jurisdiction's citizens because of their unconventional upbringing. Please, we implore you, do not entertain such thoughts. If you settle on a post-billion world then remember that such worlds are a significant minority *and that most Jurisdiction colonies are pre-billion and hence subject to demanding breeding strictures. On such worlds a great many (and in some cases the majority) of children are raised in communal nurseries, having been grown from genetic deposits of the adult colonists. These* Quota Children *are statistically in the majority and they, like you, never had any kind of parental relationship. Your upbringing is nothing to be ashamed of, so go proudly into the Jurisdiction and be all that you can.*

Rehabilitation: A Survivor's Guide

Galman Tader: On Pellitoe, in the Swinell Union, in the Fertile Belt

Galman dove from the sofa, finding the corner of the room, startled and horrified by Tumble's uncharacteristic aggression and sheer brutality. Even when he had been armed, as a Diaclom Constabulary Aid, his preference had been for the most efficient immobilisation of a suspect, with the minimum of injury. What Galman saw hurtling into the room was an entirely different breed of killer, unrecognisable as his old companion. But had he been recognisable at all since Galman had modified the blocks and checks in the machine's IB computer?

'Tumble, don't!' he yelled as the machine constricted a tentacle about Ledwintoe's throat while aiming the cop's mag-gun at the IB lawyer. Tumble didn't even hesitate; he continued to constrict, slicing through the soft flesh of Ledwintoe's neck and snapping the spine, killing the man in under a second in a violent spray of arterial blood.

'I don't seem to be able to call for help,' the lawyer said, not panicked, just confused, ever apologetic. Then, offering a wicked smile, she said 'If this traumatises you, we would have quite a case against the Bureau of Supervision.'

Tumble fired six armour piercing bolts from the cop's weapon, and she dropped to the floor, her elongated AR body still in place.

'What are you doing?' Galman yelled, getting to his feet. Tumble flicked a long tentacle across the room and Galman flinched, thinking he was about to be slapped. But the thin appendage cracked as a whip against the door, slamming it shut.

'Don't shout,' Tumble hissed, giving Ledwintoe's head a final tug which lifted it a few inches from the body, still connected by spinal cord, before dropping the bloody mess onto the sofa. 'Someone will hear.'

'Who's that?' Galman pointed to the woman's head and spine which had preceded Tumble's psychopathic entrance.

'I have no idea,' the IB machine admitted. 'She was outside when I got here. I had to deal with her.'

'Christ, Tumble, You killed them! Why the Hell did you kill them?' Galman choked on the words, kneeling beside the almost decapitated cop and checking for a pulse in spite of the obviously fatal trauma. He was, indeed, dead. Even nano-farms, if Ledwintoe was so equipped, would not be able to revive him from a severed spine and such spectacular blood loss that it threatened to reach the door where it might well flow through should it be opened.

'I've killed a great deal more than these two,' Tumble said, flicking blood from his appendages. Like Galman the machine didn't count the IB lawyer – she was never alive.

'You could have disabled them,' Galman practically wailed, ignoring the off-hand boast of slaughter. Perhaps Tumble was referring to the unavoidable fatalities inflicted during his service to the Diaclom Constabulary, but Galman suspected a more recent slaughter. An unwelcome vision of the machine-shop, walls coated in the blood and viscera of a dozen technicians unfortunate enough to have been tasked with repairing Tumble, surfaced in his mind.

'It was easier like this,' Tumble sad. 'Quicker.'

A chill of regret clenched through Galman; those deaths had not been necessary, could have been avoided. These were not the enemy, they were just cops, doing their job, and they were dead because he had somehow turned Tumble into a killer. He closed his eyes, found some kind of calm, or at least focus, then opened them to glare at his IB friend.

'We need to get to Madrik port,' he said. 'These deaths mustn't be for nothing.'

'Agreed,' Tumble said. 'I have allocated us a Bureau of Supervision patrol car, and the station surveillance is down.'

'How?'

'The same way I'm isolating us from any non-local observation or interaction,' Tumble said, passing the dead man's mag-gun to Galman. 'I'm managing to exert some considerable influence over the AR network.'

Galman checked the clips, finding just a few anti-personnel bolts, a dozen stun darts and a single remaining armour piercing bolt. Aside from the few bolts Tumble had loosed into the IB lawyer, Galman didn't imagine the weapon had been fired much recently. It seemed likely the dead Supervisor had never felt the need, or been allowed, to load more than a few shots. But it was better than nothing and he was happier now that he, rather than his murderous machine, held the weapon. He didn't fear for his own life, was in no doubt Tumble felt he was doing what was right by Galman, but he was terrified the slaughter of innocent cops hadn't yet ended.

'You managed to uncover the AR codes Ambondice-Ambondice was using to isolate the pointspace comms facility?' he asked.

'No.'

'Then how are you exerting control?'

'I really don't know. The net just seemed to open up to me. The same way the station admin net is allowing me to allocate vehicles.'

When Tumble went to open the door, Galman pressed a hand hard against it. The machine was strong enough to pull it open regardless of Galman's objection, but he didn't. 'I reprogrammed your computer,' Galman said, 'and I'm aware of every function of your code compartments. You shouldn't be able to do this, your compartments aren't sophisticated enough to outmanoeuvre such complex networks and you lack the sheer processing power to force your way in.'

'Ouch,' Tumble said, a playful snort letting his master know it was just gentle sarcasm.

'What I mean,' Galman went on, pulling his hand away from the door now Tumble had likewise backed off. 'Is that this sudden ability seems like a trap.'

Tumble snorted again, this time less jovial. 'I doubt the Bureau of Supervision would allow me this ability. I mean, look what I did to their people.'

'But they didn't know your morality had been circumvented.'

Tumble approximated a nine-appendage shrug. 'I don't know what to say. I can access the nets and I don't think it is limited to this station. It's as if my code compartments are being supplemented by something more complex, as if I'm drawing on more than a single intelligence-bridge, more than one human brain.'

'I don't like it.'

'I'm sure you don't, but the fact is we need to get to Madrik port and, with a bit of luck, intercept Ambondice-Ambondice.'

'How about using your new skills to authorise a bit of police backup?' Galman asked with some sarcasm. If that were possible, Tumble would have already suggested it. The machine wouldn't have needed to kill so many cops.

'I can't get that deep,' Tumble explained. 'If I could, I would have just ordered your release. All I can do is interfere in the admin and some of the surveillance.'

Galman gave a weary nod. 'How do you rate our chances of convincing the authorities to help anyway?'

'Ignoring the fact we just killed a bunch of their staff, 'Tumble said, conspicuously sharing the blame with Galman, 'It would take too long to get the police on side. Besides, I wasn't active when Cordem revealed himself to be compromised so I don't have that recorded as evidence. He would still be able to stall any action long enough at least to do what he intends in orbit. The machine gripped the door handle once more and swung it open. 'Now, we need to get to the auxiliary-staff entrance.'

Galman cringed, noticing his bloody footprints as he left the room, but Tumble set upon the red smears as some hungry limpet, sucking up the liquid with some device extruded from his sphere.

'Feet,' it hissed and, when Galman presented the sticky red soles one at a time, the machine cleaned each with the suction of a thin appendage.

'Put the mag-gun away,' Tumble ordered. As Galman complied, he wondered whether the machine even considered himself property, a servant, anymore.

A small AR screen appeared a few inches in front of Galman's left eye, displaying a schematic of the entire compound, the Bureau of Supervision station being expanded for clarity.

'Thanks,' he said, assuming Tumble had provided the map.

'We need to be there,' Tumble said, placing a blue ring over a side entrance not far from the two green markers representing him and Galman.

They didn't run. Galman just walked calmly back into the holding area, Tumble in his arms, where the single member of staff behind the desk gave a friendly nod and offered to get Galman a drink. He politely declined and continued on through an arch, into another corridor. The member of staff said nothing, presumably under the impression Galman had been dismissed from the interview and asked to attend another room. After all, the IB surveillance system would immediately alert Supervisors if he was going anywhere he wasn't allowed – or it would have had Tumble not infiltrated the system. They passed a dozen Supervisors, every one of them offering a kind nod and a smile. Nobody challenged Galman. Eventually they reached what the map labelled the auxiliary-staff block, a massive open plan office in which fifty administrative staff worked at small AR stations. Nobody was in uniform. AR files and communication links flew through the air in a knot of complex administrative streams, swirling around every workstation like mini tornadoes of data: Pellitoe was still in chaos, and the AR of this office was that disorder manifest.

'Over there,' Tumble said, pointing to an alcove which ended in a small door. 'That's the way out.'

'Galman couldn't restrain a grin. Could it really be this easy to walk out of a Bureau of Supervision station?

Nobody challenged him as he strode authoritatively through the ordered chaos and, unlike the supervisors, the civilian staff were too busy to even notice him, much less offer polite greetings.

Within a minute of watching Tumble murder his interrogator, Galman Tader strolled into the evening sun and slid into the waiting patrol car where Tumble synthesised a very genuine chuckle.

'What?' Galman asked.

'Looks like I was right,' the machine said as the patrol car hummed into action. 'My ability isn't limited to the station. I just intercepted Traffic Control's signal. If anyone tries taking control and bringing us back, I can stop them.'

'How far can you hack?' Galman asked, unable to just accept Tumble's ability as good fortune. Someone was providing the machine with a boost, and Galman wasn't going to trust the motives of a secret benefactor.

'I have no idea,' Tumble admitted.

Chapter 69

Tales of the most extreme offences committed during the Satumine domination of humanity are now played down, trivialised and laughed off as myth and fantasy. Nobody denies we were abused as a species, but that abuse is sanitised and relegated to the status of economic mistreatment. People no longer want to hear of the more horrific crimes committed by the Satumine in those horrific years. But I refuse to forget. The Satumine were not satisfied with stealing our planet's resources and wealth, they wanted all that we were. I do not know how they first discovered the effect a distilled soup of human synaptic material could have on them, but once it was realised, a small underground industry sprang up almost overnight. The number of humans killed to brew this narcotic was not huge, perhaps a few thousand over the course of a century, and I have no doubt the Satumine leadership worked to stop the practice - for the good of their species, not for our own protection, of course. But the fact is, this drug was real, and so were the murders. There is no documented study showing the effect on a Satumine taking the drug, but I have heard anecdotal evidence stating it was something akin to human heroin. We must wonder, therefore, how many of the Satumine living amongst us on our colonies are brewing this most evil of drugs even today? How many humans have been killed, and continue to be killed, for a drug the Jurisdiction refuses to admit exists?
The Truth: A treatise on the Satumine Conspiracy

Endella Mariacroten: Aboard the *Tenjin*, in shortspace, somewhere in the Fertile Belt

Endella dropped to the next balcony, catching the railing with both hands and wincing at the hot wash of pain that hinted at a torn muscle in her left shoulder. She ignored it. After exchanging a wary glance with the scrawny man she accepted his bony wet hand, pulling herself up over the railing and onto the welcome stability of the hall-like balcony. She noted the man's awkward smile and the flecks of gore transferred from his hand to her own. Then, giving him no warning, no change to her wary demeanour, she was upon him. One arm locked about his throat, she swept his feet from beneath him and followed him down to the floor, her mag-gun shoved clumsily into his face, glancing from his thin pointed nose to press into his right eye. He said nothing and struggled only a little, trying to bring his face away from the weapon which had scraped his eyeball. She pulled the mag-gun back an inch, allowing him to blink a few times. He looked at her, eye watering and eyebrows furrowed in annoyance or some other expression Endella couldn't place. His breath was quick and shallow and she could feel his ribs beneath her, pressing rhythmically against her body. And she felt something else. Only then, the immediate threat now under her control, did she realise the man was naked. And if what she felt through the tatters of her jumpsuit was what she thought it was, he was also aroused. She restrained a cringe and resisted the urge to squirm. *Just ignore it*, she thought.

Slowly, never letting the mag-gun stray from his face, she got off of him, averting her eyes from the obscene elephant in the room. When he went to follow her up, she placed a foot roughly against his scrawny chest and held him down, hoping his ribs were not as fragile as they looked. He didn't have an ounce of fat on his body and his muscles, although toned, were underdeveloped. Or perhaps they had wasted. She noticed a tiny fleck of red beneath the eye she had scraped with her weapon, a small cut, and it vanished in a couple of seconds. It explained his apparent emaciation – some form of nano-farm was operating in his body, in a similar way to her own. His fat and muscle mass had been used to heal some recent trauma. This, at least, encouraged her to believe he might really be an ally. Still, she didn't lower her aim, or remove her foot from his chest.

'Who are you?' she demanded, becoming aware of how empty the balconies around the central hall had become. The crew would be heading for her, so she had to be quick.

'My name is Subset,' the man said, his accent thick and unfamiliar. There was a peculiar monotone to his expressions. 'We need to get away from here.'

'How did you get aboard the *Tenjin*?' Endella asked, removing her foot from his chest but keeping the weapon close to his face as he slowly got to his feet.

'I was born here,' Subset said, just about managing to convey confusion in his flat and distorted words.

Endella brought the mag-gun closer to his face. 'Then why are you helping me?'

'Because I need your help, and because we both have reason to interfere with Aggregate's plans.'

'Aggregate? You said that name before. Who is he? Your captain?' Endella asked, slowly lowering her mag-gun, not because she had any sudden reason to believe this man, rather she didn't have time to waste satisfying herself of his sincerity. Already she could hear the clatter of metal feet drawing close. She chose to trust him because, aside from killing him, she had no other choice.

Subset made a peculiar squeak and sigh which Endella thought might have been some kind of laugh. 'He is everybody on the *Tenjin*,' he said. 'He inhabits every strand of DNA of every crewmember, living through them as a single immense consciousness.'

Endella knew she had to get away from this balcony level before the crew arrived but was momentarily taken aback by subsets extraordinary revelation.

'How?' she asked, aiming the weapon at the closest corridor in case the crew arrived. 'What exactly *is* he?'

'He isn't really a *he*, rather an *it*,' Subset said. 'It's a sliver of the singular life which exists in pointspace.'

'The what?'

'I'm sorry, but we really need to get out of here,' Subset said. His voice was notably improving, both in clarity and expression, as if he were learning from Endella. 'I will explain when we aren't so exposed.'

Endella couldn't help but smirk at the man's unintended double entendre and she glanced down at his now flaccid penis.

'You mentioned before that Aggregate intends to become everybody in the Human Jurisdiction,' Endella commented, averting her eyes once more.

'Which is why you must agree to help me,' Subset said, grabbing Endella's arm and pulling her, weakly, to the corridor. She went with him, didn't resist. 'If you help me, I will be in a position to help you,' he added.

'What is it you expect from me?' The more pertinent question might have been what Subset was going to do for her, but Endella didn't suppose he would elaborate until she had done her part.

'You need to get me to *there*,' Subset pointed to the wall of the corridor.

'What?'

'There, in the old Callaghan-Era gene lab.'

Endella creased her brow and pulled subset to a stop. 'I don't know what you mean.'

'*There*,' subset yelled, jabbing his finger at another section of the wall. 'On the map.'

'Damn it,' Endella muttered. 'Is the map AR?'

'AR?' Subset said. Then, after a second of thought, he nodded. 'Augmented reality. That's what you call it, isn't it? Yes, it's on an AR screen.'

'I can't see AR,' Endella explained. 'My internal hardware was cannibalised by my nano-farms.'

'You need hardware?' Subset sounded surprised, a little patronising too. Thousands of years of development had, it seemed, completely integrated the AR world with the natural senses of the human body. How much of the *Tenjin* was she unable to see and interact with?

'Just follow me,' Subset said. 'I need you to make sure I get safely to the lab.'

'To what end?'

'To remove the parasitic markers Aggregate put in my DNA. Otherwise he is going to become me, again, in less than half an hour.'

Then they ran into a crowd of almost fifty mechanically augmented crewmembers, and Endella switched the mag-gun to fully automatic fire.

'Are any of them armed?' she muttered.

'That depends on your definition,' Subset replied as a nine foot tall eight limbed mechanically augmented creature fired a bundle of cables at the pair and another ejected freezing liquid coolant from a tank in an indiscriminate spray.

Chapter 70

The Waystation, *and the veritable armada of similar manned or unmanned ships and probes, point not only to the vast wealth the Administration is willing to squander in the pursuit of expansion for expansion's sake, but also to the true extent of Consul's reach. When the Waystation set out on its 150 year shortspace journey, the Jurisdiction was barely setting out from the womb of the Network; when it arrived at its destination we were a modest federation of four hundred worlds. At neither time were we ever threatened with overcrowding in the Milky-way. There are hundreds of thousands of worlds already tagged for terraforming in our own galaxy, so for the Administration to obsess over the Sagittarius Dwarf galaxy is either extraordinarily longsighted or, more likely, just someone's attempt at making history. The Waystation, as is common knowledge, managed four seconds of transmission on its emergence from shortspace in our closest neighbouring galaxy before its unexplained shutdown. The same has happened with every ship to follow it. Four seconds, you may not realize, is how long it takes to upload a full artificial consciousness. We have colonized the Sagittarius Dwarf, but not with Humans. While we battle Consul's realm within our own galaxy, he is expanding beyond the range of our sensors in a galaxy all his own.*
The Enguine Manifesto

Galman Tader: On Pellitoe, in the Swinell Union, in the Fertile Belt

'You can still act like a cop, can't you?'

Galman, still fuming at the gratuitous force employed by his IB companion in the Bureau of Supervision station, shot Tumble a glare. 'What's that supposed to mean?' he demanded. 'I'm not the one gunning down and ripping the heads off of innocent Supervisors. I might not have a valid warrant card, but I'm still a cop, inside. I don't know what you are anymore.'

'I only do what I'm programmed to do,' Tumble quipped, though Galman was beginning to have doubts – doubts which could have devastatingly far reaching repercussions. 'Anyway,' Tumble went on, 'I wasn't questioning your ethics, or your professionalism. I just meant you are going to have to talk to them.' The machine summoned an AR frame which closed around the blue arch at the end of the cobbled road. The frame became a screen and, like a lens held before Galman's eyes, it magnified the small group of Trustees standing guard, somewhat lackadaisically, at Madrik port's single entrance.

'I've arranged for our arrival to be anticipated,' Tumble explained. 'So you just have to convince them you are a Bureau Supervisor.'

'You asked if I can still act like a *cop*,' Galman muttered. After the appallingly liberal attitude of Supervisors in the station, Galman's opinion of them had only worsened from what had already been a deep resentment, to a total lack of respect. They weren't cops.

'Just do your best,' Tumble instructed, again taking charge.

The patrol car slowed and then stopped just short of the arch and a couple of Trustees came to the only door in the small cab. Tumble crawled into the foot well and went limp; supervisors didn't employ such machines and it would have been just one more thing Galman had to explain. Galman lowered the one-way mirror embellishment from the vehicle's side and summoned a window through which he and the Trustee could talk.

The lead Trustee looked Galman over for a moment, perhaps deciding whether his lack of uniform was cause for concern, or comment. But he smiled and gave the supposed cop a short nod of greeting.

'Areas of authority are all up in the air at the moment,' the Trustee said, flashing a look of toying exacerbation. 'I *think* the ports are technically under federal protection for the time being, hence our presence,' he gestured vaguely at his squad. 'But it's all a bit confused. So if the bureau has any business here, I'm not about to argue the toss.'

'Appreciated,' Galman said, relieved his identity wasn't being questioned.

'The Administration, meaning us, is going to maintain security at the perimeter,' the Trustee explained, 'But you are free to go about your domestic investigations within.'

'Thank you, Trustee.'

'Senior Trustee.'

Galman smiled. 'Of course, sorry, Senior Trustee.'

The man went to turn, to walk away, but stopped suddenly. 'You *are* aware the Continental Office Trustee is in the port, aren't you?'

Galman did his best to maintain a cool expression but felt his stomach twitch. 'I had heard he might be,' he said. 'He's in hangar six, isn't he?'

'Four,' the Senior Trustee corrected. 'At least I would assume so. That's where the federal shuttle is.'

Thank you. 'Right, of course. Well I will do my best to keep out of his way.'

'Very good. Just let me know if you need any help in there. God knows my boys are tired of guard duty. I mean, it's not as if anyone is going to be trying anything here!'

'Too true,' Galman laughed politely. 'I'll be sure to give you a shout if I need anything.'

The Senior Trustee gave a final friendly nod and waved the patrol car through.

'What a helpful Trustee,' Tumble said, climbing out from between Galman's feet to resume his place atop the small flat surface to the left.

'*Senior* Trustee,' Galman reminded the machine with a grin which belied the distaste still held for his companion's appalling actions. But Tumble was right, they now knew Cordem, and presumably Ambondice-Ambondice, were in the port. And they knew where the Office Trustee's shuttle was stored.

'Fuck,' Tumble said as the patrol car came to a sudden stop a hundred meters from the huge bland hangar over which a rotating number four hung in AR.

'Now what?'

'Someone has erected a massive privacy bubble over the hangar.'

'Are you surprised?' Galman asked. 'I would have been more surprised if Ambondice-Ambondice *hadn't*. Between him and Cordem they have more than enough resources to acquire any size bubble they want.'

'Yes, but I can hear an argument inside,' Tumble said. 'I think they could start firing.'

Ignoring the obvious question of how Tumble could so easily penetrate such a large privacy bubble, Galman instead asked, 'That's a good thing isn't it? Maybe we aren't needed after all.'

'If they were federal troops, or Trustees, don't you think the men on the gate would have kept us away? Or at least informed us.'

'Not if it's a Justiciar,' Galman countered, a little tired of the machine's growing arrogance.

'No,' Tumble said. 'They are Satumine.'

'Let me hear,' Galman ordered.

'Hang on,' Tumble said, climbing over Galman's lap and opening the door. 'I think I can get close enough to get a proper look. You stay here where it's safe and I'll send you an AR feed so you can watch.'

Galman wanted to reassert his authority, to order Tumble to stay put while he, the human, went ahead. But the fact was his IB machine was more capable and in all likelihood more intelligent. 'Just stay within line of sight,' he said. 'So you can use a direct laser transmission. I don't want them being able to pick up your signal.'

'Obviously,' Tumble said. Patronising, Arrogant. The machine cleared the hundred meters in a few short seconds, rolling across the flat resin road before unleashing coiled tentacles with explosive force, leaping onto the hangar wall where he clung with unigrip pads. He climbed a little further, almost to the domed roof, before vanishing beneath his simple privacy bubble. Then the AR feed arrived as a screen in front of Galman. It was a static view from a tiny camera Tumble had inserted after drilling a hair-thin hole in the hangar wall.

Galman was struck by the imposing scale of the shuttle which filled the greater part of the hangar. It was not a beautiful craft, only mildly embellished with a few silver lines of light and a black mirror finish too perfect to be entirely drab-reality, but the massive hulk was impressive none-the-less. Its simple shape, just a long bullet whose concave rear extended into six sharp fins, implied a deliberate modesty, an owner who didn't need to impress. The short stubs of weapon barrels were, just as deliberately, not disguised by AR or drab-reality camouflage. Although far from the power of Federal Sentries or Union Cruisers, the shuttle was capable of defending itself against anything it was likely to encounter on its journey from planet to orbit and back again. Galman doubted the weapons had ever been powered up; who in the Swinell Union had ever attacked a federal shuttle? But now Satumine terrorists were about to steal it.

'Hand over the Office Trustee,' one of the Satumine said. He stood at the front of the force of thirty armed Satumine, every weapon aimed at the smaller force of

Ambondice-Ambondice, Cordem, and the dozen Satumine slowly stepping out of the three vehicles.

'Are you really going to get in my way, Sharlie-Sharlie?' Ambondice-Ambondice said. Both of the creatures seemed to be speaking in human tongue, but Galman supposed Tumble might be translating the live feed.

'We voted on this,' Sharlie-Sharlie said. 'It was agreed we would stick to the original timetable and plan.'

'The original plan was weak and uninspired,' Ambondice-Ambondice said, waving back one of his team who had begun to approach from behind. How useful it must be, Galman thought, to have so many eyes, looking always in every direction. 'I brought you a proposal which could have made you an icon for Satumine resistance across the Jurisdiction. But all you want to do is collapse the AR net of this world.'

'All *you* want to do is lash out at the Jurisdiction, kill as many as you can, with absolutely no consideration as to the consequences.'

'The consequences are simple,' Ambondice-Ambondice yelled, in as much as Satumine could raise their feeble voices. 'The Jurisdiction will be forced to take us, and our grievances, seriously.'

Sharlie-Sharlie pointed three long fingers at Ambondice-Ambondice and then turned them to the side, as if forming an E. Galman had seen the gesture many times before; it portrayed something like mocking sympathy and was mildly goading. 'Oh they will notice us,' he agreed, holding the gesture for a few seconds before snapping the hand down to his side. 'But they aren't going to start relenting to our demands or addressing our grievances. They will simply burn Satute until not a single Satumine remains on our home world. And then they will turn on those of us in their colonies.'

'They humans are too weak willed to stomach genocide,' Ambondice-Ambondice countered. Galman felt himself begrudgingly agreeing with the terrorist's assessment. The Satumine race ought to have been eradicated, at least from human colonies, centuries ago. But the Census would never allow the governance machines to even consider it.

'If I let you do what you plan,' Sharlie-Sharlie continued, 'the humans would truly despise us. The impact would be felt across every world and the humans would harden their hearts when completing the next census.'

'It wouldn't happen.'

Sharlie-Sharlie held up his hands and made fists before spreading his fingers. Galman had no idea what that meant. 'You are right about that,' he said. 'Because I'm not going to let you continue.' He took a step back into the ranks of his own Satumine and turned his weapon on Ambondice-Ambondice.

'So you intend to massacre us?'

Sharlie-Sharlie made a peculiar clucking which Tumble didn't, or couldn't, translate. 'Unlike *you*, I don't feel the need to turn to violence. Just hand over your prisoner, the Office Trustee, and you can be on your way.'

'Just like that?'

'Yes. Though you needn't think you will be welcome back into the community.'

Ambondice-Ambondice looked to Cordem Hastergado and Galman noticed the Office Trustee seemed to be acting the part of prisoner, rather than the co-conspirator he knew him to be. Given the choice, Galman felt Sharlie-Sharlie was the lesser of the threats, but as he watched the Office Trustee step meekly forward he felt Ambondice-Ambondice had yet to play his hand. Sharlie-Sharlie was not going to survive this.

'Kick your weapons forward,' Sharlie-Sharlie ordered, reaching for the human. Ambondice-Ambondice and his fellows nudged their assorted rifles with their toes, sliding them fully beyond their reach. Several of the larger force stepped forward to gather them up. Their counterparts now rendered harmless, Sharlie-Sharlie's Satumine relaxed their aims; Galman knew this was Ambondice-Ambondice's intention.

'Back to your vehicles,' Sharlie-Sharlie instructed, and Ambondice-Ambondice's force complied.

Then, as his hands were tied behind his back and the Satumine began shouldering their weapons, Cordem Hastergado shot Sharlie-Sharlie a darkly satisfied look of delight.

'Aren't you worried about the weapons on the shuttle?' the Office Trustee asked in barely a whisper.

'Sharlie-Sharlie patted the human, overly hard, on the back. 'Don't bother trying to bluff your way out of my custody,' he said in an ugly voice which was clearly unfiltered through Tumble's translation. He was addressing his prisoner in an attempt at human tongue. 'Ambondice-Ambondice might be a rash and violent sociopath, but he isn't stupid. I can see he's already disarmed you of any AR tools or interface ability. He wouldn't bring you in here if you could still control your shuttle.'

Oh bollocks. The words appeared beneath the live feed, an indication of Tumble's feelings. Galman echoed the sentiment. But there was nothing he could now do to change what was about to happen.

'All true,' Cordem said. 'But only if your assumption, that I am his prisoner, is correct.'

'What?'

Cordem simply winked and then grinned as the Satumine scrambled desperately for the weapon slung across his shoulder. Too late. A pencil-thin laser beam burnt through the Satumine's head in a brief flash which had probably been invisible to those not benefiting from Tumble's superior vision. Sharlie-Sharlie didn't collapse. His secondary brain, the dispersed mesh of neural fibres throughout his body, would allow him to live indefinitely, with only an animalistic mind. The lack of visible assault, or obvious death, kept the other Satumine from noticing until Cordem had completed the silent process of charging all the other weapons and targeting every Satumine loyal to Sharlie-Sharlie.

They all died a few seconds later, oblivious to their attacker and defenceless against the high powered lasers.

As the Satumine dropped, the lasers now targeting the major neural nodes throughout their bodies, Ambondice-Ambondice stepped out of his van and beckoned for the rest of his team to do likewise.

'Open the Shuttle,' he called to Cordem. 'I want to get on with this.'

'Hurry up and get to the hangar door,' Tumble spoke to Galman thorough the AR screen. 'I can get you aboard the shuttle, but only if you're quick.'

Chapter 71

*While the Jurisdiction guarantees a basic right to indefinite life,
there are still deaths through accident, violence and occasional disease.
In these situations it has become necessary to classify the many degrees
of death recognised by Jurisdiction medical science. The classifications
become relevant when the very best regenerative technologies and
therapies may not be available. For example, the first degree of death
is simply a recognition of the heart no longer beating and it is almost
inconceivable that there would be any situation from which such a
death could not be recovered. Further along the classifications come the
five specific degrees of brain death and it is only the final degree - total
neural inactivity and advanced synaptic decay - that is considered (for
now) to be irrevocably terminal. In legal proceedings, however, any
assault leading to even the first degree of death (whether or not the
victim recovers) is grounds for a murder prosecution.*

Rehabilitation: A Survivor's Guide

Anden Macer: On the *Vulpine*, in orbit around Pellitoe, in the Swinell Union, in the Fertile Belt

A cold draught slid through the *Vulpine*'s silent
corridors, like the ship's dying breaths. Anden Macer
shuddered - more at the imagined suffering of his ship
than at the icy wind. The emergency illumination strips
were emitting a dull blue, struggling to find thermal energy
from the atmosphere with which to light the empty ship.
The dim glow enhanced the chill, lending the corridor the
feel of some icy cave.

After a hundred years aboard the Federal Sentry,
Anden could navigate her decks in total darkness, but so
much of the *Vulpine* had been ripped apart by the *Tenjin*,

so many sections exposed to vacuum and sealed off by thick emergency bulkheads. Even more sections were sealed off to allow the station's IB machines to go about their work without worrying about injuring any human with their potentially lethal tools. As a result, the *Vulpine*'s layout had become an illogical maze in which even her captain could become disorientated. He was lost.

'What have you done to my ship?' Area Trustee Lugek Marbashet said, his intended joviality smothered by the severity of his off-hand comment.

Anden stopped and turned to the AR screen, an illusory full length oval mirror floating six inches from the ground.

'I'm sorry,' he whispered to his old captain, the heartfelt remorse and shame stinging his eyes. 'I'm so sorry Lugek.'

Lugek shook his head and frowned. 'Not at all, captain,' he said, reaching his young hand out of the screen to touch Anden's shoulder. Tactile implants registered a softly warm touch. 'It wasn't your fault. I have seen the reports and I know you did what you could. At least the old barge is still in one piece.'

'Too many died,' Anden said, almost reproaching his old captain and dear friend.

'Seven hundred,' Lugek noted.

'Seven hundred and six,' Anden shot back; the disregard of six lives a vile disrespect. 'And they all died under my command.'

'Under another captain the four hundred survivors might also have died.'

Anden snorted, taking no comfort from the Area Trustee's observation. 'Just tell me I will be allowed to pursue the *Tenjin*,' he muttered, looking Lugek up and down, wondering if this new appearance, this youthful figure, was the result of cosmetic and telomere treatment, or merely an AR skin. While captain of the *Vulpine* - a post he had held for sixty years – the old man had always been slow to make use of the various rejuvenation therapies available. Anden didn't like the idea that the captain had changed his mentality, as well as his body. Lugek had been as much a constant in Anden's life as the *Vulpine* herself. Now both constants were unrecognisable. Anden didn't like it.

'Let's just see what the structural analysis at Dendrell uncovers before we start making plans,' Lugek said. 'We have no idea how long repairs are going to take. It could be up to eighteen months just to get the hull up to spec; God only knows how long it will take to refit the interior and train a new crew.'

'We can skim a few Trustees from the other sentries in the region.'

'Just see how it goes at Dendrell. There's no point in me making any promises. I'm not in charge.' That was true enough; the old captain had been sent to the massive Copid Union, a fertile world union directly to the Swinell Union's galactic west where he was overseeing a pre-billion colony. A nice quiet assignment; his reward for two hundred years of duty aboard various Federal Sentries.

'The *Vulpine* has to re-engage the *Tenjin*,' Anden insisted. 'And the longer she is confined in a shipyard the further away the enemy gets.'

'Why does the *Vulpine* have to pursue?'

'For her honour!' Anden was astounded the old captain had even asked the question. 'You, more than anyone, should want to avenge the humiliation and defeat and the deaths of so many of her crew.'

'It's only a ship Anden.'

Anden stared at the AR projection. *Only a ship?* 'How can you say that?'

'Because I got away from her,' Lugek said. 'I remembered there is a universe beyond the *Vulpine*'s hull. It's a ship, Anden, and nothing more.'

'And the crew? What are they? Don't they deserve to be avenged?'

'At the expense of more lives? No, they don't.' Lugek was glaring, but his scowl quickly softened. 'Look, I will see if I can get some crew reassigned from the *Vaughan*, she's been lingering in orbit of my world for three years and her crew are bored, but I'm not using my influence to let the *Vulpine* go chasing the *Tenjin* until she is in a state in which she might have some chance of surviving. Besides, we don't even know where the *Tenjin* is heading yet.'

'I need this, Lugek.'

'What you *need*, Anden, is to repair you ship and train a new crew.'

Begrudgingly, but with growing acceptance, Anden nodded.

'Now, why not go back to the station and see if you can't enjoy some of the Swinell Union's entertainment?'

Anden snorted, then laughed. 'I think I'll stay aboard the *Vulpine* if you don't mind.'

'You aren't there alone are you?'

'I've got my senior officers.'

'Steit'

Anden smiled and nodded, glad Lugek remembered some of the crew. 'Yes, he's still here. He's my executive officer now.'

'Well go and be with him, and the others.'

'I think I'd rather spend a bit of time alone.'

Lugek raised an eyebrow. 'I could make it an order.'

'Yes, Sir.'

'And you can always rely on Spokes to cheer you up,' the old man added. 'You *are* taking good care of Spokes, aren't you?'

'I'm afraid the *Vulpine* is running on the station's IB at the moment, so Spokes is out of commission.' It was a half-truth. If fact Anden had barely used the old captain's favourite personal assistant machine since taking command. He didn't like its attitude but was uncomfortable reprogramming Lugek's pet IB companion.

'Well, see that he is powered up as soon as your IB suites are back on line.' Lugek gave a short wave before he, and then the full length screen, faded in a thin yellow cloud of AR smoke.

Chapter 72

Given my unapologetically outspoken opposition to a huge amount of Federal policy, as well as some of my more direct personal campaigns against hundreds of Trustees at all levels of the Administration, one might imagine I have spent decades, if not centuries, in one detention facility or another, though in truth I really have not. One might find it remarkable I haven't yet been subject to a sentence of memory dismissal. At times I am equally surprised. One of my very few periods of imprisonment, however, was as a result of my most thorough trespasses to date within the data-realms of the Federal Census. The meaning behind cryptic questions within the Census are for the most part opaque to the average citizen, and that is by design. The governance machines need to determine the true and subconscious will of the Jurisdiction, but if the questions were obvious and transparent then people might simply answer in ways biased by what they think *they want. That, at least, is the official line. I believe, from my time exploring the data-realm of the Census, the questions are so incomprehensible for more nefarious reasons: Someone is slanting the Census, filling it with leading questions and weighted psychometric criteria, gradually and invisibly bringing us closer to the point where the Jurisdiction unknowingly agrees to giving the Satumine the vote. Once the Satumine are allowed to participate in the Census then the endgame will truly begin.*

The Truth: A treatise on the Satumine Conspiracy

Cordem Hastergado: In orbit around Pellitoe, in the Swinell Union, in the Fertile Belt

Premium grade gravity coils gently increased their influence as the shuttle rose quickly through the atmosphere, ensuring only the slightest of transitions as it left the gravity of Pellitoe. But Aggregate, through the body of Cordem Hastergado, noticed the mild fluctuation as the coils overcompensated for a second before finding their balance, and he smiled at the quaint technology. Once he inhabited the human race, he would finally have the resources to develop and construct myriad technologies and luxuries he had discovered in his seven thousand years- the least of which was a truer form of anti-gravity.

The hues of the sky faded to black and, as the planet's curve became noticeable, Pellitoe's last surviving station became visible, first as a bright point against the dense spread of stars, then as an elongated loop of silver from which nine stumpy arms extended. Almost as large as the station, tethered to one of those small arms, was the shattered bullet of the *Vulpine*. The paired structures looked tiny, with nothing against which to suggest any scale, but aggregate had seen the *Vulpine* through many other eyes, had watched her punch so many holes into his home, the *Tenjin*, while he had been unable to do anything but pick away at her least critical sections. He knew how big that ship was. He also knew he could have reduced her to a belt of debris, to join the other rings of metal and gas which were all that remained of the union cruisers and the rest of Pellitoe's stations. But he needed the *Vulpine*.

'You promised me a working Sentry,' Ambondice-Ambondice said, pacing the shuttle's long bridge, dragging with him an AR model of the *Vulpine*. The rest of the Satumine were all down in the more luxurious lounge, making the most of this rare opportunity to enjoy an office Trustee's personal shuttle.

'The *Vulpine* will work well enough for your needs,' Aggregate said. 'I went to great pains to ensure that.'

'Looks to me like you almost shredded the damned thing.'

Aggregate turned his chair to look at the Satumine and flung an AR schematic across the bridge at him. It wrapped about the model Ambondice-Ambondice was consulting and gave a real-time status update. 'The weapons will work,' he said. 'What else do you need?'

'How about life support?'

Aggregate sneered. 'I was of the understanding that you intended this to be a suicide mission. How much life support do you need?'

Ambondice-Ambondice crushed the AR model in his hands and dismissed it into mist.

'It will take three weeks for the ships to arrive from Dendrell and Diaclom once we begin firing on the planet. I intend to make the most of those weeks; by the time the fleet arrives I want Pellitoe to be all but lifeless.'

Aggregate smiled. 'Good,' he said. Unlike the *Tenjin*'s assault, in which Aggregate made it clear he wouldn't be remaining in the system long enough for reinforcements to arrive, the *Vulpine*'s bombardment was to be methodical and sustained. Every ship around Diaclom and Dendrell, and four other planets in the region, would be sent to stop the atrocity. Once in shortspace, those ships wouldn't be able to stop until they reached their destination. Diaclom was going to be defenceless for at least six weeks – the three weeks it would take the fleet to arrive at Pellitoe, and another three weeks to get back again. More than enough time for Aggregate to utilise the pre-billion colony's population.

'Life support is good enough,' he said. 'You will be fine to lay waste to Pellitoe for as long as you can hold off the Jurisdiction fleet.'

The station's IB orbital traffic control system assigned the shuttle a spur and Aggregate allowed it to take control, to bring them in to dock.

'Get your human skin on,' he instructed Ambondice-Ambondice. 'And make sure the others do likewise. I don't want to have to explain a bunch of Satumine if the station commander decides he wants a nose about the shuttle.'

Ambondice-Ambondice draped himself in an impressively convincing human façade, covering any trace of his Satumine identity behind a soft Asian complexion embellished. He sported a few tasteful tattoos which crawled across his skin and over his simple one-piece suit which shifted subtly between various pastel shades as he moved, leaving the slightest trail of shimmering haze behind him.

'Not bad,' Aggregate conceded. 'Are the others of the same quality?'

'More or less. I had plenty in stock, and it isn't as if I'm going to be opening the skin-shop again.'

'Right, well go down to the lounge and instruct them to keep out of the way. If we are boarded *I* will do the talking. Tell your guys to keep quiet.'

Ambondice-Ambondice gave a curiously irritated expression, confirming the value of the human-skin – it was picking up mental cues and translating them into facial expressions which a Satumine should not be capable of forming. Aggregate knew what the Satumine leader was thinking, knew he hated Aggregate issuing orders, but Ambondice-Ambondice's feelings were the least of Aggregate's priorities.

With a gently cushioned bump, the shuttle connected with the short walkway extending a few meters out from the assigned spur. Aggregate waited for the Satumine to disappear down to the lounge before walking quickly to the airlock adjoining the long thin bridge. He brushed an oval panel and the door slid silently aside to reveal a lightly embellished woman. Given the AR excesses for which Swinell Union stations were famous, and this woman's obviously conservative tastes, he took her to be a federal Trustee.

'Office Trustee Cordem Hastergado,' she stated, not a question, not a greeting. 'You are assigned to the Equa continent; what is your business here?'

'And you are?' She wore no Administration identification and he didn't recognise her from Cordem's memories.

'I am Senior Trustee Tebephenel,' she said. 'Of the *Vulpine*.'

'My condolences for the loss of so many of your crewmates,' Aggregate said. 'I am here to supervise the instillation of class six IB uplink hubs on the *Vulpine*.'

'Why?'

'In order that we might utilise the IB suites on the planet to assist in the repairs. It is my understanding the station IB is already overstretched.'

Tebephenel shook her head. 'No, I meant why are *you* here? You're not an engineering Trustee.'

Aggregate forced a blush – a simple feat when controlling every last strand of DNA in a body – and took a tentative step closer to the woman. 'The thing is,' he said, his voice lowered to a conspiratorial whisper, 'The citizens of my continent expect the Jurisdiction to do something, anything, in the wake of this atrocity. They expect *me* to do something. I'm here because I need to be seen to be helping.'

'So it's political,' she said, a derisive snort punctuating her distaste.

'We are all politicians,' Aggregate said, stepping back. 'You and me both.'

'Whatever,' the woman spat. Aggregate considered pulling her up on her borderline insubordination, supposing that Cordem certainly would have, but she was a sentry crewmember and couldn't be expected to act with the diplomacy of a normal Trustee. He let it go.

'I need to dock directly with the *Vulpine*,' he said. 'We have some heavy equipment to unload.'

'Do you need more support personnel?'

'No, we are fine.'

She nodded, the scowl never leaving her face. 'You can dock here,' she said, flicking a small AR schematic against the wall and highlighting an airlock just behind the *Vulpine*'s bridge.

'Thank you, Senior Trustee.'

She shrugged. 'I will let the captain know you are coming.'

Aggregate tensed. 'I thought the ship was abandoned.'

'It is,' she said. 'Apart from Captain Anden Macer and his senior officers.'

As she left the airlock, and the door slid closed, Aggregate punched the wall. 'Ambondice-Ambondice,' he called through a comms channel. 'Arm your team.'

At the same time, with other parts of his dispersed awareness, he began reorganising his defence of the *Tenjin* in light of Subset's apparent treachery. He knew exactly where the youngest of his crew was going.

Chapter 73

We are a race of immortals. We have all of eternity to accomplish our ambitions. Every need, and virtually all of our desires, are catered for in abundance. What more could we want? There is simply nothing left to strive for, there are no more dreams to be had, and nothing to drive our scant ambitions. With the shadow of death banished by the light of rejuvenation therapies and nano-farms, the notion of not doing today that which could be put off until tomorrow has taken on a more open ended and socially damaging meaning. Tomorrow simply never comes. I often bemoan the constant and unnecessary expansion of the Jurisdiction, but perhaps that is all we have left. Were there no worlds left in which to expand, what would we do?

The Enguine Manifesto

Endella Mariacroten: Aboard the *Tenjin*, in shortspace, somewhere in the Fertile Belt

Endella switched to armour piercing bolts and watched with professional satisfaction as they cut smoothly through pitifully soft bodies, exiting with enough force to penetrate those deformed creatures further back in the crowd of mechanically augmented horrors. Some continued to writhe or twitch under the control of malfunctioning prosthetics, but most simply lay still, not screaming, not clinging to life. Just dying quietly. Even those she assumed dead, however, began visibly healing. That worried her. More than that, it fascinated her. Normal nano-farms wouldn't bother repairing the wounds of a corpse; they were sophisticated enough to know if a body could be saved and, if there was no hope or revival, were designed to not interfere with what may well be a crime scene. Either the healing mechanism within these crewmembers was not sophisticated enough to recognise a hopeless cause or, as Endella suspected, it was capable or repairing far greater injury than anything currently available to the Jurisdiction. The Administration would want to know, would want samples, and she was tempted to remain in the corridor long enough to witness a resurrection. But, if she died, there would be nothing at all to show for this mission. Besides, her primary objective had now changed. The procurement of advanced technology was now secondary to the imminent, if vague threat at which Subset had hinted. And the naked stranger wasn't prepared to elaborate until she had escorted him to the lab.

'Help me,' Subset said. It wasn't a panicked cry for aid, no desperation or fear to his words. It was simply a command. Endella glanced back to see the man ensnared by a tightening coil of blue gel-filled cables, the other end of which was attached to the wide barrel of a four foot crewmember who seemed to be more tracked buggy than organic life. She put one bolt through its squat face, punching a tattered hole in the back of its cartilage skull and hitting the metal-limbed thing behind with bolt and brain. Another bolt went through the tight length of cable, severing the connection to the dispenser. Thick blue gel oozed out, reacting to the air to become a white paste which sealed the two flailing ends of ruptured cable. Like a decapitated snake, it ceased its constriction and slumped lifelessly from around Subset's body. The man shook off the cable, threw himself at the Justiciar, wrapping his arms about her neck. So light was he the impact barely knocked her back a step, certainly didn't bring her down. But, as she grabbed at his throat, intent on throwing him into the closest creature, she felt the hot splash of something against her shoulder and her hand came up to clutch a suddenly furious burn.

'Don't touch it,' Subset yelled too late. She only brushed a finger against the blood-streaked syrup which had dissolved an inch wide patch of her jumpsuit and was now eating through skin and muscle, but that light touch was enough to burn away the pad of her index finger. Beside her, a plate sized hole was being carved into the wall by the full wad of whatever had been hurled at her, by whatever it was Subset had barged her aside to avoid.

Clenching her shoulder muscle against howling agony, she willed her exhausted nano-farms to cut the pain receptors.

She saw the creature responsible for her injury: an eight foot tall, slender crewmember, wielding a third arm-like appendage which ended in an organic sphincter, dripping a clear gel which hissed on contact with the floor. Consumed by uncharacteristic rage she put four bolts in the thing's head. The first bolt would have been enough.

'There,' Subset said, pointing to the junction to their left, now clear of any threats. 'We have to get out of this corridor.'

'My arm,' Endella mumbled, straining against the pain and the threat of shock and delirium.

'Let it burn,' Subset said, callous or perhaps pragmatic. 'It isn't designed for organic targets, it's meant for metal. It will neutralise soon enough.' Endella laughed. It wasn't funny, but the alternative was an equally useless scream. Subset gave a confused look then rushed past the corpses piled atop one another, into the side passage. Endella followed, firing a parting volley at the four remaining crewmembers, putting them all down. She barged past subset, knowing if he ran into more creatures he would be defenceless. But she could also hear footsteps closing in from behind and wondered if she ought to instead guard their rear.

'Through here,' Subset said, kicking the cover from a small vent in the wall down by the floor. Endella let him crawl in first, if for no reason other than she had no idea where they were going. The gap was too small to allow her to pass as easily as Subset and the hard metal scraped the burn which, thankfully, no longer dissolved deeper into her muscle. She bit through her lower lip, grateful for the distraction. She knew she ought to replace the vent cover, to disguise their escape, but she could barely move her arms enough to shuffle forward. There was no way to turn around to grab the cover plate. And it was dark. Meagre ribbons of light squeezed past her from the opening, painting the blackness beyond in ever changing flashes which confused more than they illuminated. She couldn't see Subset although she heard the regular patter of hands and knees against the hot metal floor. He was pulling away, oblivious to her struggle, or unconcerned.

'Slow down,' she hissed, cringing as she imagined her words echoing down kilometres of tight passages and sounding through dozens of open vents. He didn't reply, but a few moments later, after discovering the least painful way of inching forward, favouring her healthy arm, she collided with the naked man, her face pressing horribly into his exposed buttocks. She flushed with embarrassment, cheeks burning so hot she felt they might illuminate the dark tunnel. But Subset made no comment on the intimate contact.

'Nearly there,' he said. 'It's a left, just ahead. Pass your weapon forward.'

'No,' Endella said, a little too quickly.

'I don't know if the room will be occupied,' he explained and Endella felt his hand reaching back, brushing her hot cheeks, waiting for her to hand over her only weapon. She wasn't prepared to trust him that far, though she had to accept she was making a tactical error, sending him on, unable to take by surprise anyone they might encounter.

'I can't reach back to my holster,' she lied. She still gripped the mag-gun tightly in her hand. Again, no comment. He just resumed his crawl. Endella followed, gasping when she turned the sharp corner and an edge stabbed into the mush and gore of her small wound. The metal pulled at pulped flesh, tearing it wider and sending a cold nausea into her stomach. She retched and swallowed back burning vomit the texture of stringy jelly. Then an explosion of light like a plasma grenade temporarily blinded her as Subset pushed a vent cover aside. The glare was so harsh it erased Subset's silhouette. But as her eyes adjusted, Endella saw the man crawling out into whatever room lay beyond. She heard no screams, no cries for help, and hoped it meant she was safe to emerge from the vent. It could just have easily indicated Subset had been instantly killed or immobilised. Once more she chose optimism.

Crawling out, she squinted until her eyes were again comfortable in the light and she saw the immense open space of what looked like a domed town within the heart of the *Tenjin*. The dome itself glowed with a diffuse white light, like a sky of thin cloud through which a hospitable yellow sun shone. The vent had brought her out onto a wide gantry about halfway up the dome, encircling the town below. Four cylinder towers rose from the town centre almost to the dome's ceiling, perhaps forty floors though the scale was hard to judge without her usual AR visual enhancements and aids. A spread of smaller buildings filled the rest of the space with a dozen narrow pedestrian streets which criss-crossed the town. The streets were empty, the town silent.

'What is this?' Endella asked.

'This is where Aggregate will expect me to be heading,' Subset said. 'Down there is the closest of the labs capable of burning his tags from my DNA, so he will be hidden there, waiting for us.'

'I don't know how effective you think my mag-gun is,' Endella said, gingerly touching the ugly hole in her shoulder and shuddering at the feel of exposed bone but noticing the beginnings of new tissue forming at the edges. Her nano-farms were doing what they could; she would need to eat again soon. 'I can defend you against a few of the crew,' she went on, 'but if they are planning to ambush us –'

'Not *they*,' Subset insisted. '*He*, or *it*. Aggregate is a single awareness. We are the only other consciousnesses aboard the *Tenjin*.

'Regardless, I can't go up against a determined and prepared defence.'

'Which is why we aren't going down there.' Subset started along the gantry, Endella followed. 'There are six suitable labs close enough for me to reach before Aggregate is able to re-establish control of my DNA, I am hoping he isn't prepared to commit as many of his bodies to those other labs as he is this one – especially since he saw us heading this way.'

'But they, *he*, will send at least some bodies,' Endella guessed.

'I would expect so,' Sunset admitted. 'Probably enough to destroy the equipment. Which is why we need to hurry.'

Endella nodded and followed, checking her backpack to see how many explosives remained. If the mag-gun ran out of bolts, and the laser's charge was depleted, she might have to start improvising.

'In here,' the naked man said, opening another vent cover. Endella frowned. 'You go first this time,' Subset said. 'I want to make sure the cover is replaced. This time I don't want Aggregate to see where we went.'

Chapter 74

There is a good chance you will elect to settle on one of the hospitable and temperate worlds of the Fertile Belt. It may intrigue you to discover the Jurisdiction keeps as much of the native wildlife on those worlds as possible in their natural habitats - in so much as is possible after the genetic modification viruses convert those planets to the ecosystem so comfortable for us. Our decision to retain many of the beasts, and allow them free-run of the nature reserves, may seem even stranger given the violent temperament of many of the animals after the viruses have done their work. But ours is an enlightened society and as long as any risk can be controlled then we will preserve as much of the natural wonder as is possible. And the risk can be managed with incredible effectiveness. Across the buffers between reserve and civilisation you will find rows of pheromone towers, emitting a constant and measured current of pheromones, enough to deter any Fertile World animals but not so much as to distress or harm them. In every human settlement you can expect absolute safety, and the Fertile Worlds are no different in this regard.

Rehabilitation: A Survivor's Guide

Indin-Indin: On Dereph, in the Network.

Inhabiting a thousand sensors and artificial eyes – ancient Satumine and Jurisdiction alike – Indin-Indin watched with sadistic fascination as the huge Administration complex at the heart of the city was dragged apart by the movement of previously supposed solid bedrock. As their foundations were shredded by the separation of six enormous slabs of rocks the complex's buildings collapsed, barely supported sheets of construction resin and precariously balanced columns of metal and stone tumbling like toy blocks. All Jurisdiction buildings were immune to the most violent earthquakes imagined by human geologists and their IB machines, but the splitting of the planet's crust, caused by the opening of a two kilometre wide ancient Satumine cache, was simply too great a strain. Earth and debris falling into the chasm was suddenly ejected in spectacular eruptions by immense gravity currents, protecting the pristine hull of the cache's single treasure a kilometre below. Great chunks of the buildings rained down over thirty miles of city, smashing apart more homes and offices, chipping away at the human buildings which had crept over stronger foundations of Satumine towers like vines around a tree. Hundreds of soft bodies, the Trustees of the Administration complex, fell like a macabre rain, spreading even greater terror across the burning city.

Order was long since lost, no IB network existed and buildings were still collapsing after Indin-Indin's initial attack. He grinned, a human smile, and realised how easily the ninety colonies could be reclaimed. He could rid this world of humans within a week. But not until the pointspace harvester was fully charged. For now, he needed to defend against the sentries in orbit and the seemingly limitless flow of troops the vast Jurisdiction could hurl at his facility. He needed to deny them the orbital superiority they currently enjoyed.

Bridging the segregating buffer between the networks and the treasure of the cache, Indin-Indin inhabited the beautiful craft and awakened its systems, marvelling at the incredible tools now available to him.

'Who was this designed to fight?' he asked the computer, pleased he felt no reticence at voicing the question. He reasoned the answer must have nothing to do with the downfall of his race – Aggregate was clearly not allowing him to dig into the facts of that tantalising mystery.

'The same enemy that necessitated the planet-based weapons you used against the human IB suites,' the computer consciousness explained.'

'Who?'

'Irrelevant,' the computer said. 'We won. They are extinct.'

'Genocide?'

'Of a sort.' The computer said, assisting Indin-Indin in his discovery of the craft's controls. 'Suffice as to say, they are no longer here.'

'So why do we have the weapons, and the ships?'

The computer emitted something close to cold grief. 'It took us nine thousand years to defeat them,' it said. 'We were not prepared to leave ourselves vulnerable after that.' Then a kind of dark anticipation and calculating mischievousness escaped the consciousness and it added, 'but when the real threat came, it wasn't something we could defend against with particle accelerators and –'

'Stop!' Indin-Indin snapped, an instinctive imperative taking control of his voice. 'I don't want to hear about that.' But he did want to. As soon as he had the chance to undo the changes wrought by Aggregate on his mind, he would learn everything.

The ancient Saturnine cruiser awoke. A kilometre and a half long, it was a featureless white boomerang, flawlessly curved and polished to a brilliant finish. No weapons were visible, no docking ports or sensor arrays, no primary engine, no thrusters - just a long shining white curve. Riding the gravity current which had emptied the pit of the remains of the human Administration complex, it gently rose in utter silence. The silence was broken, however, before the cruiser had even reached the surface, as the sentry in orbit hammered the glossy hull with thick cords of accelerated particles, flickering beams of laser which cycled through a million frequencies and wavelengths in search of an effective assault, and columns of railgun projectiles and missiles. The cruiser was lost within a blinding cloud of deflected energy and bubbles of plasma and fire. More buildings fell to the brutal shockwaves of the relentless and unrestrained assault. No human had ever witnessed the capabilities of an ancient Satumine ship, but it seemed they were assuming the worst. They were prepared to kill those of their people that had survived the collapse of the complex, to ensure the cruiser didn't reach orbit. But they lacked the weapons to stop it. *No*, he corrected. *They lack the weapons in sufficient quantity.* And that was a critical reassessment, for the Jurisdiction controlled the Network Frames, and within the network they had access to dozens of sentries and hundreds of smaller ships. If they decided to use them they also had hundreds of thousands of orbital weapon platforms distributed across the network worlds, each capable of travelling through the frames. The ships could be here in minutes; the satellites in an hour or two. One way or another, they would eventually have the weapons to disable, if not destroy, the Satumine cruiser. But a few minutes would be long enough to prepare a more capable defence of his facility which, in turn, would buy him enough time to do what he came here for.

The cruiser's dimensional extruder came on-line as the ship cleared the roiling forest of plasma bubbles and it accelerated under its own power. Although the internal dimensions of the ship remained fixed and conventional, from the outside it seemed to split into two boomerangs, separated laterally by a buffer of fifty meters of air. Higher dimensional space was extruded through this quasi-real separation and funnelled out of the rear, allowing the cruiser to pull itself along the fabric of reality at a startling rate. Within seconds it had reached the near vacuum of low orbit, the barrage of assorted weapons fire never straying from its glossy white shell. Then four more sentries arrived through the frame, their weapons charged and missiles already launching. Indin-Indin sent instructions to the mutable auto-factories in the cruiser's heart and, while they began fabricating the bespoke designs, the ship's weapons assessed their threats.

Chapter 75

I have already detailed some of the huge differences between Human and Satumine physiology, but perhaps the most extraordinary - potentially useful - is that of the Satumine dual brains. In what some speculate to be a remnant of Ancient Satumine biology, the modern Satumine contain both a primary and secondary brain. Within the ugly ribbed ball of their head sits the primary brain, an organic mass of comparable size to our own and of superficially similar design. Weaved throughout the rest of their body, however, is a complex mesh of neural fibres, connected to the primary brain but capable of acting independently of that larger organ if necessary. The evolutionary basis for the secondary brain is not entirely obvious, though few believe evolution had anything to do with the modern Satumine body. The upshot of this peculiar biology is that in the event of catastrophic damage to the primary brain, up to and including total decapitation, a Satumine is capable of continuing a non-sentient but functional existence. Why should we care? Well, aside from being aware that a Satumine is able to keep fighting you after you take off its head, there are potential benefits to mankind to also be considered. Destroy a Satumine primary brain and, for example, you have a docile and obedient manual labourer - The population of Satute is hundreds of billions, and on a great many pre-billion colonies we really could make use of such a plentiful labour source.

The Truth: A treatise on the Satumine Conspiracy

Galman Tader: In orbit around Pellitoe, in the Swinell Union, in the Fertile Belt.

'Can you get into the *Vulpine*'s systems?' Galman asked his IB companion. 'Maybe you can let us see where

Ambondice-Ambondice and the others are going, or if they are still in the boarding lounge?'

Tumble rolled out from the luggage compartment in which he and Galman had been hiding. 'Sorry,' the machine said. 'I told you when I hijacked the shuttle's sensors, I can't get into anything too heavily screened. And there are few things more secure than the systems of a federal sentry.'

Galman sighed, but the fact was he was surprised Tumble had been able to infiltrate a federal shuttle's systems at all, even if it only went so far as forcing the sensors to ignore their presence as they had sneaked aboard to hide in the cramped luggage bay. Adding to that the machine's influence over the Bureau of Supervision administrative systems and he could hardly complain at the assistance Tumble had been able to offer. It was far more than the machine's limited processing capacity had any right accomplishing, far more than Galman believed Tumble could have done without some outside assistance. That incongruity troubled him, almost as much as the machine's dramatic decent into borderline psychopathy.

During the flight up to the station, Tumble had briefly deactivated, his link to planet-based IB severed. A small AR screen had appeared over the lifeless ball, informing Galman of a three hundred new-Euro premium, or data-matter equivalent, if he wished to purchase IB cover from the orbital station. He had seriously considered declining the offer, letting Tumble remain off-line, rather than take a chance with the potentially murderous machine. But in all likelihood, he was going to need Tumble, and would probably be grateful for his newfound penchant for violence. The cost of IB cover wasn't a problem, he had some left from Cordem's generous gift, and didn't expect he would be returning anywhere he might spend it.

Galman checked the mag-gun he had stolen from the murdered Supervisor, selecting the backup laser, intending to save the sorely limited supply of bolts and darts. The laser probably wouldn't kill a Satumine outright, but it would be enough at least to do some considerable damage to its primary brain. That he would have to open fire on Ambondice-Ambondice's team he had no doubt; he had done nothing but hide and watch, but now it was time to do something. Although ensconced in the luggage bay, he had overheard the discussions between Cordem and Ambondice-Ambondice, thanks to the keen hearing provided by Tumble, and he knew they intended to hijack the *Vulpine*.

'I wouldn't recommend using the airlock,' Tumble commented. 'If they left a man behind to stand watch, they will notice if we kill him.'

'We aren't staying aboard the shuttle,' Galman said.

'Tumble rolled down the short, wide corridor, lashing out with a wide appendage to open a small compartment in the wall. A single vacuum suit fell to the floor.

'I caught a glimpse of the *Vulpine*'s current schematic through the station's systems,' the machine said. 'I think I can get us in through one of the sections undergoing repair. How long since you performed a spacewalk?'

Galman groaned and picked up the thin plastic-like jumpsuit. 'I did the Constabulary multi-environment refresher six years ago. That had a three minute simulated spacewalk.'

'You'll be fine; I'll hold on to you.'

Galman slipped into the deep red, almost black, vacuum suit and felt the simple systems handshake with his AR implants to grant intuitive control over oxygen flow, unigrip pads, and the soap-bubble-thin bag of the helmet which currently hung from the back of the neck like an almost invisibly thin hood. 'Are you sure nobody is left in the shuttle?' he asked, grabbing the six inch cylinder of massively pressurised air and snapping it into place on the belt-port.

'I can't hear anyone,' Tumble reported.

That wasn't very comforting. 'They might just be quiet.'

'I could pick up a heartbeat anywhere in the shuttle, if there were one to be heard.'

'Satumine don't have hearts!'

'Calm down, Galman. We are alone. I counted them on in the hangar and I counted their noisy footsteps off a couple of minutes ago.'

The Office Trustee's shuttle had just the one airlock, in the conventional sense; it was secured to the variable lock nearest the *Vulpine*'s bridge. But there were always other ways on and off of any vessel. Galman trusted that Tumble had already determined the most promising route, but was dismayed when the machine directed him to a service hatch leading down into one of the three missile tubes. Tumble prised away the locked hatch and plugged a needle-tipped appendage into a port, gaining access to the hardwired closed-system within the tube. Galman winced, imagining the accidental launch, or detonation in-situ, of a warhead.

'I'd rather not go that way,' he said. 'Can't we get out via an escape pod bay?'

Tumble twisted the needle and something moved, large and heavy, further down the chute. 'The pods fill their bays entirely. Short of launching an escape pod, we can't get out that way,' the machine said. 'The missile tubes are empty at the moment, and they are pressurised, so we can get in easily enough.'

Galman shook his head and crawled into the narrow maintenance space, following Tumble as he rolled across the smooth metal surface, stopping when he reached an eight foot long recess in the floor. Tumble did something to the interface port on the wall and the recess slid aside, giving access to the tube's full length below. He rolled down without comment and Galman crawled up to the long hole, peering down to see the circular hatch at one end, through which missiles were delivered, and the iris at the other end past which lay the vacuum of space. He moved down into the tube and the service hatch slid closed behind him, trapping him in what felt very much like a coffin, only the low-level illumination of Tumble's shell lighting up the cramped tube.

'Helmet,' Tumble reminded him. Galman flipped the seemingly delicate hood over his head and it found the seals on the neck-line. With a thought he activated the air flow and the hood inflated to form a solid-looking helmet.

'Void the tube,' Galman instructed, though Tumble hardly needed telling. Tiny vents opened across the length of the missile tube and, with a sharp hiss, the air was sucked out. The vacuum suit responded to the thinning atmosphere, puffing out by almost a millimetre across Galman's skin. As the atmosphere was reduced to near-vacuum, the suit rippled slightly against his skin, tickling like a gentle flow of water. It settled almost immediately. The gravity coils beneath the tube deactivated and the iris twisted open to expose Galman and Tumble to the cold desolation of space, a silver mouth threatening to swallow him out into the infinite void. This was no illusory window or transparent wall; Galman was inches from the unending expanse of the universe, and he was terrified.

Chapter 76

Despite appearing in every census summary for the last four hundred years and being referenced in over sixty seven million official wikis, the most recent census showed seventy percent of people believed Ramonds world to be a fiction. It isn't that people mistrust the Administration (that would be too much to hope for), rather they just can't accept the implications of such a world actually existing. How, people demand, could any planet of rational Jurisdiction citizens willingly invite Consul to enslave them. How could any human want to be reduced to nothing more than a component in the IB farms of the Artificial Consciousnesses? But things are not as black and white as the Administration likes to portray them. When foolish men sold their souls to the devil in ancient fictions, it was not a one way deal. These people did not knowingly condemn themselves to eternal torment; they supposed the devil would honour some intricate pact in which they somehow avoided the hell to which everyone else could so clearly see they were headed. Consul did not simply appear to this world on the border of the AC territories and ask if the citizens would like to live forever in IB suites to power his AC children. Promises were made, temptations laid at their door. What were these enticing offers? For your protection I shall refrain from sharing further, lest you, like the people of Ramonds world, think Consul will make an exception in your case and honour the Faustian pact.

The Enguine Manifesto

Endella Mariacroten: Aboard the *Tenjin*, in shortspace, somewhere in the Fertile Belt.

'You need to hurry up,' Subset complained, pressing his bony knuckles into Endella's cramped thigh. The Justiciar tried to look back but the chute was as tight as it had been when she and Subset had crawled in a few minutes earlier.

'I'm going as fast as I can,' she muttered. 'I've come to a three-way junction; which way?'

'Left,' Subset said, and Endella groaned. The sharp corners in this ridiculously cramped network of chutes were a time consuming, awkward, and often painful obstacle. Her body was already covered in a mess of bruises and scrapes. She rolled onto her right side and shuffled forward, curving her aching body around the tight one hundred and twenty degree kink.

'I don't think we can go this way,' she called back, noticing a definite incline in the tunnel. There was nothing onto which she could grab, no way to pull herself up the slope of polished metal.

'We have to,' Subset replied. 'The lab is just at the end of this run.'

'It's too steep; it has to be almost forty five degrees up.'

'It's only thirty eight,' Subset commented, shoving Endella's feet around the corner before pushing her buttocks from behind, forcing her up the slope.

'Isn't there another route to the lab?'

Subset gave another, more urgent shove. 'Not really an option anymore,' he said, the man's tone conveying as much anxiety as it did urgency.

'Why?' Endella asked, unsettled by the new panic which had sounded from behind her, where before there had been only cold detached calm.

'Have you noticed the increased frequency of the vibrations and the rising temperature?

Endella had. The workings of the *Tenjin*'s ventilation system was not an area in which she pretended any real understanding, but she had thought it normal activity. Now, however, she found all manner of nightmare scenarios surfacing to explain the vibrations and heat. Barely able to put her arms out to her sides by more than six inches, she pressed hard against the walls and slid her way up. There was precious little friction between the shiny metal and the soft skin of her hands, but she was an extraordinarily strong woman and even with so little room in which to flex her muscles, she held the flats of her palms in place and brought her legs up.

'What's going to happen?' she asked, now locking her feet against the sides to hold her in place, releasing her tentative hand-grip and pushing up a little further.

'There is an automated purge system, used to keep the vents clear of any build-up.'

'A blast of air?' Endella asked with feeble optimism.

'A one-tenth of a second plasma flash,' Subset stated, his momentary lapse into panic replaced by cold matter-of-factness. 'It will struggle to clear the vent of our bodies, but it will be more than sufficient to kill us and vaporise most of our soft organic matter.' Then, almost cheerfully, he added, 'But our bones ought to survive.'

Endella let the flippant comment go, but couldn't ignore the fact that Subset had pushed her into this lethal series of chutes. 'If you knew about this, why did you send me in here?' She didn't shout, but her voice was utter fury. 'We could have taken another route.

'No, we couldn't have,' Subset said, pushing Endella further up the slope. She didn't bother asking how he was managing to secure enough grip to support himself while pushing against her. 'If I don't burn Aggregate's markers from my DNA, he will inhabit me and then you will have no hope of thwarting his endeavour. This is the only route liable to get us to a suitable lab in time.'

'You might have at least warned me of the purge system.'

'It wasn't due for another six months. Aggregate must have realised I would be using the vents to get to another lab after we failed to show for his ambush. He has activated the purge to kill us.'

'How long have we got?'

'Seconds.'

Endella said nothing more; she couldn't waste the energy, or the time. Foot by claustrophobic foot, she edged up the incline, forcing her breathing to remain calm and level, wishing she still had the internal hardware to more fully control her autonomous bodily functions. The heat was becoming uncomfortable and sweat ran down her back, flowing in tight streams from her brow, across her thin eyebrows, the salty rivulets finding their way into the corners of her mouth. Her palms were tingling, stinging as the metal surfaces reached painful temperatures. She continued on up, grimacing as the heat of the walls passed through the thin outer layer of skin, into the deeper tissue, burning. Already her hands felt dry and hard, the skin seared to rough leather. At least the traction was improved.

'Faster,' Subset urged. 'It's coming.'

The incline seemed to end a couple of feet up from Endella's current position and she hoped a vent cover would greet her just over the crest. 'I think we are nearly there,' she called back. Then a choking flash of shocking white smothered her, flooding down into her lungs through her mouth and nose, seeming to roast her from inside. She closed her eyes but the white was undiminished. She tried to scream but her lungs failed to respond. Then the tunnel became a vision of horror, the walls drenched in the reddest, most vibrant of blood.

'You have to *move*!' Subset yelled, his voice cracking, as if his vocal cords had been flash fried. 'That was the pre-burn check. We have eight seconds.'

Endella blinked, turning the red walls to pink distortions, as her eyes tried to recover. She kicked off hard from the wall and reached out for the crest where the incline ended. Her fingers caught a thin ledge and she pulled up with enhanced strength. With a gasp she realised the incline didn't end in a vent, but there was no time to bemoan her luck. She pushed on, dropping suddenly down a near-vertical decent, crashing into and through the panel at the bottom of a fifteen foot chute.

Another flash of white and Endella tensed against the pain she knew she would not live long enough to feel. But pain did come, and it came twofold. First a jarring impact as her feet struck solid ground and she collapsed into a gasping heap. Then a second impact as something punched her in the gut and face.

Eyes adjusting, she saw above her the vent cover hung by one deformed hinge, and a slight heat haze rippled its outline. Then a flash, barely noticeable, filled the darkness of the ventilation chute. And that was all. So innocuous a sight for what could have been a fatal trap. Subset was sprawled across her. She pushed him off with a single swipe and leapt to her feet, drawing her mag-gun. Six others were in the lab and they had noticed her noisy and clumsy entrance. With blistered fingers she fired bolts at the closest two which were connected by cords extending from their arms to a cylindrical device half submerged in a pool of clear liquid in the floor. She didn't stop to confirm her accuracy, diving instead behind a wide brushed-metal pipe which rose from a slight dip in the floor, up to a similar indentation in the ceiling. There were dozens of these columns across the lab and the crewmembers had already taken cover behind some of them.

'Over here,' Endella hissed to subset. He was crouched behind a transparent tank of bubbling liquid, as clear as water but much thicker. He peered around a corner, seemed satisfied he could make it across to the Justiciar, then sprinted. Instantly a length of black cord arced across the lab like dark lightning, striking the naked man with a vicious crack, slapping him to the ground, a furious red welt swelling across the length of his bare torso. The black cord retracted back behind a column.

Endella reached into her rucksack and produced two devices: a golf ball sized sphere of white and a two-inch capsule. She had a second capsule in the bag which she had hoped to give to Subset, but she wasn't going to go out there to retrieve him. He would have to cope. She held her head back, opened her mouth and lowered the capsule down her throat, resisting the gag reflex and letting it slide uncomfortably down her gullet. She glanced around the column and saw nobody attempting to advance on her. But she did see thin grey smoke rising from the other side of the lab. They were happy to leave her alone while they trashed the lab; Aggregate clearly feared what assistance Subset might offer if allowed to remain independent.

She twisted the sphere and felt a slight chill inside her as the capsule paired with the stunner. Both devices would activate in unison: the stunner to destabilise the synaptic signals of everyone in the room; the capsule to generate an inverse field around her body for the nanosecond of activity.

She rolled the ball across the room and hoped Subset's mind was not as fragile as his body seemed.

Chapter 77

*Our closest galactic neighbour is the Canis Major Dwarf galaxy,
a diminutive cluster not even truly clear of our own majestic spiral's
bounds. It is a galaxy to which we have sent numerous probes, all of
which we have lost contact. Why then, you may ask, have we chosen
to send a fully manned generational ship to the far more distant but
vastly larger Andromeda galaxy? Why send living people when the
risks are unknown? Why jeopardise so many human lives when we
do not yet understand why the probes sent to Canis Major Dwarf
have all failed? Well the journey to Andromeda is long. It is*
extremely *long: over five thousand years in shortspace. If we sent a
probe before sending humans then it would be ten thousand years
before we arrived! And if we do not go now then have no doubt
Consul will.*

Rehabilitation: A Survivor's Guide

Ambondice-Ambondice: Aboard the *Vulpine*, in orbit around Pellitoe, in the Swinell Union, in the Fertile Belt.

'We're in position,' the last of the three team leaders
sent his confirmation to Ambondice-Ambondice. Each of
the four-strong teams was standing watch over one of the
docking tubes linking the *Vulpine* to the station. The
remaining fifteen of his Satumine, as well as Aggregate - in
Cordem's body - were with him, preparing to storm the
bridge.

'Get the charges set and make sure you are clear of the
locks,' he sent back over the secure tactical network.
'When the docking tubes blow, the airlocks are going to

close instantly. Make sure nobody wanders across in the meantime.

The team leaders sent their acknowledgements and Ambondice-Ambondice returned his attention to the task of capturing the *Vulpine*'s largely empty bridge.

'I wasn't expecting anybody to be aboard,' he complained to Aggregate, though the particulars of this plan were all of Ambondice-Ambondice's own design. The tactical miscalculation was his, not Aggregate's.

'It's only the captain and eleven of his officers,' Aggregate reminded him. 'And they are all on the bridge. We can eliminate them in one strike.'

'Be that as it may,' Ambondice-Ambondice said, drawing a few lines across an AR ship schematic, 'I was hoping to just walk onto the bridge, unchallenged.'

'Look at it this way,' Aggregate said. 'If there are any unexpected code blocks, or other hidden surprises, we can use the captain to get past them.'

Ambondice-Ambondice had already considered that potential bonus, but it hardly seemed adequate compensation for what was likely to be, at the least, a challenging assault. The chances of there being any code blocks which Aggregate couldn't bypass using Cordem's Office Trustee codes, was remote; the *Vulpine*'s systems were fully unlocked for repair.

'You three,' Ambondice-Ambondice gestured to one of the five squads that would be taking the bridge. 'Make your way over to this entrance.' He highlighted, on the AR schematic, one of the three main entrances to the greater bridge area, the large lower level on which hundreds of crewmembers would ordinarily facilitate the federal sentry's functions. He directed more teams to the other two entrances and instructed them to await his order to blow the doors. After watching them rush away through corridors bereft of any functioning surveillance systems, he turned to the remaining Satumine. 'We are going to come down from the ceiling, directly onto the smaller command bridge above the greater bridge.' He then turned to Aggregate. 'What about you?' he asked. 'Are you coming, or do you want to wait out here until it's clear?'

Aggregate sniffed. 'Cordem had quite a career prior to joining the Administration. He had extensive combat training and therefore so do I. He checked the heavy pistol Ambondice-Ambondice had given him and nodded slowly. I'm happy to go in with your team.' He then laughed. 'Besides,' he added, 'it really doesn't matter if I die. And it won't be the only combat in which I will be engaged.'

'Meaning?'

'Just a few complications aboard the *Tenjin*. Nothing you need to be concerned about.

Numerous tiny AR screens appeared before several of Ambondice-Ambondice's eyes, surrounding him in a swarm of little white disks. He saw a feed from each of the team leaders, getting close to their assigned entrances, as well as feeds from the weapons of most of the team members. He would be able to see the assault from every angle and time his own entrance accordingly. He led Aggregate and the remaining eight Satumine through a scorched and now gutted mess hall, only the long service counter remaining to identify the room's original purpose. Beyond the mess he passed through a short corridor into an octagonal room which rose one hundred feet into a rounded cone. It was fortunate the ship was entirely unlocked for repairs since the door to the room was a thick, triple layered barrier, and even Cordem's codes would have struggled to assure entry. Millions of crystals, ranging from pencil-thick rods to fibrous strands, hung from the coned ceiling, swaying gently in the breeze of malfunctioning environmental systems. The crystals reached down about fifty feet where their tips crackled with static discharge. There was no furniture apart from a single slanted resin sheet over which an AR control screen might be draped. This was a shattered part of the *Vulpine*'s core processor; a few hours ago the floor would have been littered with shards of crystal, smashed from the strands above by the battle with the *Tenjin*. But this room had been cleared by IB machines and the precious processor crystals were being repaired and aligned, ready for reinstallation. They were unnecessary, however, for Ambondice-Ambondice's needs. This processor segment was assigned secondary systems such as ship administration and maintenance. The primary systems - weapons, propulsion and communications - were facilitated by triple redundancy cores.

Ambondice-Ambondice recalled the AR schematic and expanded it with a sharp hand flick, bringing it up to full scale, overlaying it across the room to locate a three foot square which was highlighted by a thin red line on the floor.

'Down there,' he said, pointing to the square while gesturing to one of the Satumine.

'I want it melted down precisely eleven feet and set for another one-foot burn on my mark.'

The Satumine rushed forward and produced a small roll of tape from a belt pocket. After making the necessary adjustments to its standard setting, using an AR interface, he began adhering it to the floor, following the red outline provided.

'Store your breath,' the munitions expert cautioned. 'The fumes are going to be nasty, and I don't trust the environmental systems to filter it quickly enough.'

Ambondice-Ambondice glanced at Aggregate. 'You should step outside,' he said. 'Those fragile human lungs can't hold air for more than a few seconds.'

Aggregate nodded, though he didn't seem too happy about it, and he walked back out of the room.

'Do we really trust him?' one of the Satumine suddenly asked. Ambondice-Ambondice imagined several others among the team had been about to ask the same question.

'Let me concern myself with the Office Trustee,' he said. 'All you need to do is follow my orders.'

The other Satumine said nothing more. 'Burn it,' Ambondice-Ambondice said to the munitions expert. 'Eleven feet.'

A brilliant blue-white flared around the tape in a fierce halo as it began melting the metal and resin of the floor. In seconds the halo had disappeared into a deepening square gully, its glow hidden by a rising plume of black smoke. The occasional snap of severed conduits and support struts sounded, but nothing critical would be cut as the square carved down through to the next level; its position had been painstakingly calculated.

'Eleven feet,' the expert confirmed. 'Ready with the final twelve inches, on your mark.'

Ambondice-Ambondice waved his hand across his face, fanning the fumes as might a human. It was a pointless gesture, Satumine breathed through every part of their body, not from a single mouth. If took only a few moments for the smoke to clear and he called Aggregate back in.

'In position, everybody,' the Satumine leader said. His team surrounded the small square which was now delineated by a smouldering half-inch gully. When that twelve-foot core of metal and resin fell through into the bridge, the Satumine would be restricted to jumping down one at a time. They would be exposed and vulnerable, but Ambondice-Ambondice didn't intend to go down until it was safe. He had plenty of others to take the risks for him.

He beckoned for another of the team and, without saying a word, took a small pouch from him. 'Put this on,' he instructed Aggregate, producing a button-sized disk from the pouch. Aggregate accepted the small device and watched, with apparent amusement, as each of the Satumine attached one of the disks to their belts.

'It's a descent line,' Ambondice-Ambondice explained. 'Use the unigrip pad to stick it to your belt.'

Aggregate chuckled. 'I know what it is,' he said. 'Cordem was more than competent in its use. You, however, don't seem to know what you are doing.'

Ambondice-Ambondice flicked a cautionary gesture and drew close to the human. 'Excuse me?' he demanded.

Aggregate drew out a couple of inches of line from his disk and held it out between himself and the Satumine. The thread was practically invisible. 'Care to touch it?' he asked.

Ambondice-Ambondice didn't. Aggregate let the line rewind and stuck the disk to the small of his back. 'You might have the sense to keep your fingers from the line right now,' the human said. 'But I guarantee when you are plummeting more than twenty feet, one of your Satumine is going to instinctively grab their line. If you put it on your back, you don't have that option.'

Ambondice-Ambondice snatched his own disk off of his belt and slapped it onto his back. He watched the rest of the team follow his example and bristled at what was yet another blatant attempt to undermine his authority.

'Anchor yourself,' he said, wishing he was able to convey in his voice the anger he wanted Aggregate to know he felt. He made the appropriate physical gestures but felt little satisfaction: he doubted the human- or whatever it was - appreciated the subtleties of Satumine language. Along with the others he drew out a few feet of line and adhered it to the floor near the soon-to-be hole in the deck. The line pulled at him as it tried to wind in, but wasn't powerful enough to inconvenience him; it was designed to merely negate some of the acceleration due to gravity. The other teams were all in position and were signalling their readiness at the other entrances to the bridge. Ambondice-Ambondice opened channels to the team leaders at the docking tubes, as well as those ready to storm the bridge.

'Now' he said across all channels while placing a hand on the shoulder of the munitions expert. 'Not yet,' he said to him. 'I want to flush out their defences first.' He expanded an AR screen across the room, showing a composite image, combining the visual feeds from everyone entering the bridge. On his private screens he watched detonations in the three docking tubes, which sheared them from the airlocks. Emergency protocols slammed the doors shut in the *Vulpine*, as well as on the station. Simultaneously, on the larger screen, all the doors to the lower bridge were blown from their housings and hurled into the empty hall of the lower command centre. Nine Satumine rushed in, weapons active, scanning for targets. Only a few drab-reality foundation blocks occupied the lower bridge, nothing else was there. That was expected.

'No automated security,' he observed, pleasantly surprised. 'They really have unlocked the ship.'

Then one of the feeds was cut and through other angles Ambondice-Ambondice saw objects fall from the huge grey dome, high above. The ceiling was embellished to such a degree it seemed the bridge was completely exposed to the void; just a disk sitting atop the *Vulpine*'s hull. From behind that illusion, appearing as if from nothing, all manner of machines presented themselves. Wheels, spheres and gyroscopes, they represented the most popular designs for multi-purpose IB machines across the Jurisdiction. They would be smart and well equipped. But, it seemed, not armed with dedicated weapons. The downed Satumine had been assaulted with a six-inch plate of metal hurled with horrifying accuracy and force, sufficient to slice his head from his body. Tentacles, rods and cutting tools waving wildly, thirty machines descended on the Satumine. On the upper bridge the captain and his eleven officers stood open mouthed as limbs were torn from soft Satumine bodies.

'Do you think that is all of the machines?" Ambondice-Ambondice asked Aggregate.

'I should imagine so.'

'Good. Let's get down there and take some hostages. Burn the last twelve inches.'

Chapter 78

OK, I'm just going to come right out and say it: We should bomb the hell out of Satute. Yes, the idea of wiping out the hundreds of billions of Satumine crammed into that godforsaken hive-world warms my jaded soul in a way few things ever can now, but that is not the justification with which I would convince the Jurisdiction to commit genocide. The Network is massively overpopulated and, unlike the out-network worlds, the citizens of the Network are not expanding into new worlds. There are no other network worlds into which they can spread and, understandably perhaps, these privileged citizens do not want to settle on a world beyond the incredible convenience of the ancient Satumine Frame network. So how to deal with the overcrowding and ever increasing demand for a home in the Network? How about a large planet, in the centre of the Network, already complete with a global infrastructure capable of supporting hundreds of billions of people? All we have to do is remove the vermin currently infesting the planet.

The Truth: A treatise on the Satumine Conspiracy

Subset: Aboard the *Tenjin*, in shortspace, somewhere in the Fertile Belt.

Subset's name surfaced as a kernel of stability from the tumult of incoherent thoughts and memories. Then as the nanoglands, intrinsic to his body, oversaw the reconstruction of his synaptic web, he recalled the greater details of his five hundred year torment. He remembered the anguish and pain of a short childhood and the almost frenzied delight with which Aggregate had abused him in so many cruel and imaginative ways. Memories of his cloistered adolescence and young adulthood turned his emotions cold as he recalled the techniques he had developed to endure those long weeks, then months, in which Aggregate would lock him away as a treasured plaything, let out only to satisfy monstrous lusts. His seclusion had eventually drifted into lonely years in which he would see nothing but the white walls of his sterile cage. Aggregate had not entirely tired of him, but the initial novelty had worn off all too quickly. Finally, in a hurricane of terror and revulsion, Subset recalled his subsumption; his ultimate abuse at the hands of the *Tenjin's* god. The next five centuries returned in a single brutal avalanche of memory and thoughts not his own - a record of Aggregate's awareness; his plans and perversions. And a few blessedly short memories of temporary freedom. Torture.

He opened his eyes and felt a stream of cold liquid escape his ears as his wracked brain purged the spent nanites. Sight took a moment to return; his optical processing neural nodes had yet to re-align. First came the smell: sickly sweet syrup. His heart sank. That aroma had seared his nostrils once before and for a moment he thought it a residue of that terrible memory. But vision returned and confirmed his fear: the lab had been sabotaged. Wisps of smoke hung around the ceiling while all about him, clinging to his naked flesh, the clarified syrup of ruptured cylinders spread out across the resin floor, a viscous hot puddle.

'Are you OK?' the woman asked, crouching beside him. She had called herself Endella, a Justiciar of the Human Jurisdiction. Subset knew what that meant, because Aggregate knew.

'What happened to me?'

She offered her hand, which Subset took, and pulled him to his feet, the syrup drawing out into long sticky fibres behind him. 'I used a synaptic destabiliser. I wasn't able to protect you from the field.'

'I'm fine. I would expect Aggregate's other bodies were even quicker to recover.'

Endella nodded. 'But not quick enough,' she said.

Subset looked about the vandalised lab and frowned. Aggregate definitely knew what I wanted here.'

'What exactly is this lab?' The Justiciar asked. 'It smells like the syrup nodes on Fertile Worlds.'

The Fertile Worlds. Subset knew that name; it was the human designation for the worlds claimed by the pointspace entity; the worlds giving that entity, from which Aggregate had been severed, animalistic awareness. Aggregate had so many thoughts about those worlds, about the atrocities done by humans to the corporeal bodies of his original self, and Subset was momentarily consumed by the memories and beliefs which seemed as much his own as Aggregates.

'Fertile Worlds?' he snapped, shadows of Aggregate's rage and frustration erupting into his consciousness. 'They're fields of butchery; monuments to human barbarism and arrogance!'

'Sorry?' Endella asked, stepping back from the suddenly livid man. Subset knew he was yelling, knew he had vicious hatred in his eyes, and he wanted to stop. This was Aggregate's fight, Aggregate's hatred and thirst for vengeance - Subset knew the humans had been merely ignorant, not murderous and, unlike Aggregate, he was prepared to accept that truth. But he hadn't suffered, directly, the agony of countless trillions of deaths, the pre-sentient terror and confusion of being severed from the sabotaged third helix of the creatures and plants of those worlds. Could he deny Aggregate his vendetta?

No, don't think like that. He gripped at his hair, pulling hard, welcoming the mild pain and distraction. He pushed the memories and thought away, couldn't allow them to stir within him any sympathy for the monster that had inflicted upon him five centuries of torment.

He held up a hand to Endella and lowered his eyes to the syrup-covered floor, shaking his head. 'The Fertile Worlds are more than a belt of inexplicably hospitable worlds with impossibly similar ecosystems. One of the *Tenjin's* original scientists figured it out, shortly after the voyage began.'

'So what *are* the Fertile Worlds?'

'They are the higher dimensional correlations to a pointspace entity.' The explanation seemed, to Subset, to be coherent and elegant, but Endella responded only with a look of confusion, barely disguised behind a mask of mock understanding. Subset elaborated: 'As Aggregate lives though his connection to every DNA strand aboard the *Tenjin*, the original greater pointspace entity finds life and some level of awareness through the creatures and plants of what you call the Fertile Worlds.'

Endella grimaced and held the back of her neck in what Subset felt was an entirely inadequate display of regret and remorse on behalf of the entire Human Jurisdiction. Anger rose up but again it was a shade of Aggregate's emotion. Subset quashed the fury.

'We knew there was something parasitic about the fourth helix of Fertile World life,' the Justiciar admitted. 'But it didn't seem to actually do anything. We use a virus to strip away the equally superfluous third helix which seems to serve no function beyond allowing the fourth to attach. We are then able to use conventional genetic modification to make the now double-helix life more suited to the Earth-standard environment we create on the planets.' She covered her mouth but continued to speak. 'Those two lost strands were a link to the pointspace entity. That explains the sudden and dramatic change in the creatures' behaviour.'

'Almost. The third helix exists only as a scaffold for the fourth. It is the fourth to which Aggregate's original self was able to burrow a connection from pointspace to higher dimensional space.'

'How? Why?'

'I really don't know,' Subset said. 'I don't think Aggregate knows. The worlds, and their hospitable life, existed before the pointspace entity's first animalistic memories. It had no awareness prior to the subsumption of the creatures and plants.'

'Someone made the worlds for the pointspace entity?' Endella suggested.

'Maybe they made the entity itself to make use of the fertile worlds,' Subset countered.

'Had we known...' Endella began. 'Why didn't the entity communicate? Let us know?'

Subset shook his head. 'It has no intelligence, or even instinctive awareness, beyond that of the life it subsumes. It could no more communicate with you than could the animals and plants of Earth.' He frowned, recalling a persistent memory of Aggregate's. 'It didn't even understand what was happening to its bodies, to its worlds, as the humans invaded. Not until Aggregate was awoken with human intelligence.'

'The scientists on the *Tenjin*,' Endella said. 'They experimented with the stores of Fertile World genetic material in their stores of syrup-node syrup. They changed it, didn't they.'

Subset nodded. The Justiciar was beginning to understand. 'They wanted to know what it was. They suspected some kind of intelligence, maybe a hive consciousness, was enforcing the irrationally peaceful and cooperative ecosystems on the Fertile Worlds, and wanted to use it to somehow communicate through pointspace with the Jurisdiction beyond the confines of the wormhole.'

'They didn't realise they were outside of our time,' Endella interjected.

Subset nodded again. 'And they had no idea the helix was connected to a form of life in the singularity of pointspace.'

'They modified it, didn't they?'

'Yes.'

'To allow it to connect to a double helix, without the third helix as a bridge.'

Subset smiled at her intelligence. 'It took them three thousand years,' he said. 'And their captain, the sovereign of the four *Tenjin* states, insisted it be attached to his own DNA.'

'Very noble,' Endella commented.

'Not at all. He simply didn't trust anyone else to communicate on behalf of his subjects.'

'But, of course, it wasn't a means of communication,' Endella said. 'He was subsumed by the pointspace entity.'

'After a fashion.' Subset confirmed. 'But as you already observed, the *Tenjin* was outside of normal time, was in a closed loop of mid-dimensions. It shifted part of the entity into a different level of the singularity, cut off from life on those fertile worlds yet to be invaded by the Jurisdiction.'

'And this new version of the entity had human intelligence and consciousness.'

'It had a particularly dark human's intelligence,' Subset corrected. 'And it still has that man's mind and body, seven thousand years later, along with a few hundred lab grown and socially dysfunctional humans.'

'What does it want?'

'Aside from revenge on the humans that tortured its original self on the fertile worlds?' It wants to spread its new self, the self capable of subsuming double-helix life, into its original.'

Endella bit at her lip. 'It would be able to subsume every human on a fertile world.'

'No,' Subset said. 'Pointspace links, potentially, to every part of higher dimensional space. Distance means nothing. Once Aggregate has the strength of the full pointspace entity, it will be capable of burrowing up into the DNA of any compatible life.'

'Every human in the galaxy.'

'Every human, animal, plant and virus, based on double helix genetics.'

'How do I stop him. *It*.'

'First you help me to see if this lab can be used. Aggregate is still weak - it needs to use modified strands of the original fourth helix, physically attached to the host. I'm riddled with clusters of them and Aggregate has been burrowing through the dimensions for almost an hour to reconnect with me. We need to burn the strands out of me. Then we can talk about how to stop Aggregate covering Diaclom in the strands.'

'Why will he do that?' Endella asked.

'Because, after infecting thirteen million humans in that way, over four weeks, it will be strong enough to merge with its original self - then it can infect the entire galaxy at its leisure.'

'Diaclom is defended by a Swinell Union cruiser. The Ohio.' Endella pointed out. 'And there is an entire fleet in range. If Aggregate needs four weeks to infect Diaclom's population, the fleet can stop it.

Sorry, but no. If Aggregate's plans have been successful - and I have no reason to doubt they have been - every ship in the region will be stuck in shortspace, rushing to Pellitoe.'

Wading through clarified syrup, assessing the comprehensive damage done to the lab, while Endella stood watch over the door, Subset felt the whisper of a truth flit across his mind. Less than a memory, more a remembrance of something Aggregate had once known and all but forgotten. It was of the same flavour as those dreamlike experiences of the original entity, something almost forgotten even by that immense life. The Satumine. What did that entity know of that originally tri-helical race? The thought slipped away, as it had from Aggregate's many minds. It left him peculiarly exhilarated and, for a moment, he understood why Aggregate had prevented Indin-Indin from ever questioning the fall of his old race. Then the half remembrance was gone.

Chapter 79

Collective punishment is a primitive, ineffective and antiquated form of discipline and control. The Administration denies employing such unfair tactics and assures us each citizen is accountable only for his own actions. While this may be true on a micro scale, on a macro level it is a bare-faced lie. When a planet or union turns from the Administration, be it through a brave referendum granting the local government a mandate to cede from the Jurisdiction, or a dictator who gains enough local power to force such a change regardless of popular support, the Administration does not bother to sort the offenders from the innocent. It does not detain or kill only the members of government who made the change. It does not sift through the referendum results and separate those who voted in favour or rebellion from those who remained loyal to the Jurisdiction. It merely declares war and far too often blasts the planets back to pre-billion status. Or it breaks out the Conflict Resolution Munitions. Either way, it is the very definition of collective punishment.

The Enguine Manifesto

Indin-Indin: On Dereph, in the Network.

The ancient Satumine cruiser became iridescent under the unyielding fusillade. A complex poly-dimensional shield mesh, which clung to its hull like an invisible skin, diverted and deflected the energy beams through spatial loops and directions incomprehensible to human minds. Indin-Indin, however, visualised those additional dimensions with such instinctive ease he struggled to understand how his mind had ever been restricted to the simplistic three-dimensional viewpoint of lesser beings. He ached for the chance to elevate his entire race, to return them to this truer appreciation of reality. The limitations of a human genetic base were blinding the Satumine to the true majesty of reality.

'Are you going to return fire?' the computer consciousness asked.

'In a moment,' Indin-Indin replied, checking the progress of the auto-factories within the vessel. Almost done. The devices taking shape within those industrial wonders were not based on any existing design, be they human, modern Satumine, or even of the ancient race. They were entirely of Indin-Indin's own imagination. His near limitless intellect had mastery over all scientific fields; he wielded the skill of atomic engineering and dimensional manipulation with the ease with which he moved the components of his malleable body. The devices under construction were designed to satisfy the precise requirements of his situation, to the extent at least of what was available in the well-stocked factories.

'The shield mesh is starting to fluctuate,' the computer consciousness observed. 'You need to defend the cruiser.'

'Not yet.' Twenty ships were now arrayed against his pristine white boomerang and countless more could be summoned in an instant through the frame. As immeasurably superior as the cruise was, it could not survive indefinitely in a contest against the entire Jurisdiction fleet. He only needed to buy time to complete Aggregate's work beneath the planet, and the devices under construction would provide him that time. The cruiser had to survive until construction was complete.

'If I start firing,' he explained, 'The shield mesh will need to be drawn tighter. We will be more vulnerable to their missiles.' The beam weapons were devastatingly powerful, and they were putting a colossal strain on the shield mesh, but it was the anti-matter warheads within the swarms of missiles that posed the greater risk to the hull. He couldn't tighten the mesh, because to do so would be to increase by a factor of ten the probability of a missile getting through.

Another two federal sentries appeared in the seductive flash of an incoming wormhole and they added their armaments to the relentless assault. Indin-Indin was thankful none of the far larger shortspace-capable sentries had been sent, for their offensive capabilities were orders of magnitude beyond those of these smaller, cheaper, Network sentries. Once he began fighting back, however, the Jurisdiction's Administration would not hold back its largest ships.

Through the parts of his awareness inhabiting the cruiser's auto-factories, Indin-Indin watched with warmly satisfied excitement as the innocuous looking canisters of his design rolled onto distribution tracks and were conveyed quickly to the reconfiguring missile ports. Now the human Jurisdiction would know the true magnificence of Satumine might. He would win back the dignity of his race.

The shield mesh finally tightened. Thirty-nine identical twenty-foot canisters were launched at the planet with such improbable velocity he was forced to include relativistic considerations in the data-link connecting them with the ship, and to him. The human ships could not respond to so sudden a launch, could not notice, much less target, the half-c projectiles which should have struck the planet with enough force to level entire city blocks but which here halted by micro dimensional-burrowers snagging on lower dimensions where momentum was bled away into more hospitable levels of reality. They struck the planet as if dropped from less than a meter, and Indin-Indin unloaded the weapons of his cruiser against the Jurisdiction armada. Like the lateral division which seemed to split the ship into two boomerangs, allowing space to be extruded and used as a spectacularly effective means of propulsion, three more divisions suddenly formed, slicing the top boomerang across its width, leaving the cruiser looking like some enormous puzzle awaiting assembly. Within the cruiser the dimensions remained consistent and no divisions were apparent. Indin-Indin took some delight in the confusion he knew the humans would be suffering at this impossible science. He then extruded space through the three new divisions, drawing the sections of the ship close to accelerate the flow of spatial-fabric, until barely three subjective inches separated the four slices of the upper boomerang. Space tore through at greater than light speed. The larger lateral division widened, anchoring the cruiser in place, straining against the pull of the three jets of space. The cruiser didn't move and so the jets of spatial-fabric rushed away, towards the flotilla of network sentries, dragging with them any micro meteors or orbital debris at technically impossible faster-than-light velocity. These tiny missiles peppered the three sentries at the armada's fore but, although tearing through the primitive vessels like rail gun bolts through flesh, causing entire decks to explode on exposure to vacuum, they were nothing more than a welcome side effect of the weapon's primary function. The spatial-fabric acceleration wave passed into the structure of the sentries and, unprotected by the poly-dimensional shield mesh maintaining the Satumine cruiser's integrity, the Jurisdiction ships fell apart completely, catastrophically, as huge sections of their structure were accelerated to light speed and converted to exotic radiation when their velocity breached that impossible limit. Human science had no defence against this, the pinnacle of offensive weaponry. The extrusion burst lasted only a couple of seconds, but a nanosecond would have been just as effective. A full quarter of each of the three lead ships had been reduced to waves of radiation which already had begun decaying into lower dimensional space. What remained was consumed by conventional explosions as the ship generators and gravity coils failed. Indin-Indin turned the weapon on other ships and cackled with hysterical glee as, one-by-one, the ships of the Jurisdiction armada were massacred and the orbits filled with their remains. But the sentries didn't flee. They continued to hammer the cruiser with beam weapons and, critically, missiles, even as they were slaughtered. The taught shield mesh consumed and deflected anti-matter explosions as effectively as it did the beam weapons, but some small fraction slipped through the strained mesh, engulfing sections of the shining white hull in the most destructive of explosions, converting meters of the ship into bursts of energy. Indin-Indin was gratified by the enhanced regenerative capabilities of the hull and the multi-layered redundancies which would allow the cruiser to continue even with the loss of two thirds of its structure. But it wasn't going to last forever and it had accomplished its primary task. Rather than allow the beautiful craft to fall into the thieving hands of the Jurisdiction, therefore, Indin-Indin set it to accelerate into the fleet's midst, where he detonated its every generator and shredded every human ship in orbit. He only briefly wondered why a species with such complete mastery of poly-dimensional sciences hadn't developed a shortspace drive with which he could have retreated the cruiser to safety. Mysteries such as that were to be addressed another time.

Gravity currents and brutally harsh radiation slammed into the planet, stripping the sky of clouds and searing every plant and animal not sheltered within a sealed building. Indin-Indin enjoyed the destruction with some part of his fractal consciousness, but the greater part he committed to initialising the thirty nine cylinders.

More sentries were streaming through the frame, undoubtedly intent on occupying the planet with hundreds of thousands of troops, determined to storm his facility and take him into custody. The canisters opened. Nobody was going to set foot on his planet, and even those huddled in their homes were about to die. Soon the human colony would be reduced to vapour; only the Satumine colony would remain, stripped of the Jurisdiction taint which had grown around it like some perverse parasite.

Chapter 80

Like any rational, objective and sane citizen of the Human Jurisdiction, you probably find the notion of a God to be laughable and the concept of organised religion offensive if not outright dangerous. The Administration shares your concerns. While we do grant some measure of religious freedom, under the aegis of the Approved Faith framework, such freedom is by necessity restricted and closely scrutinised. Far too many conflicts, be they on a personal, global or interstellar level, have erupted from the festering sore of religious faith and dogma. People are entitled to believe what they will, but the Jurisdiction will not allow such beliefs to be excessively promoted or forced on others, nor will they be permitted to gain enough power to ever again threaten the peace of the rational majority.
Rehabilitation: A Survivor's Guide

Endella Mariacroten: On the *Tenjin*, in shortspace, somewhere in the Fertile Belt.

'I think I can make this work,' Subset finally concluded, after silently contemplating the smashed apparatus in the lab for several minutes. Endella glanced back from the door where she had been anxiously standing guard, expecting at any moment for a hundred of the crew members - she still had trouble considering them all to be Aggregate - to storm the lab from which she knew there was no other exit.

'Well do it quickly,' she called back to him. Subset disappeared behind one of the metal columns, from which a coil of smoke erupted every few seconds where Aggregate had shattered one of the thick bands wrapped about its width. There was the loud groan and bang of cooling metal and a high pitched hiss as the plumes of smoke became a tightening jet of pressurised gas, before the breach was fused. Then, with the pop of a failing seal and the angry muttering of Subset behind the pillar, another column began haemorrhaging while clarified syrup welled up from its base.

'Have you got this, or not?' Endella demanded. 'Can you burn out those DNA parasites? Yes or no?' Although she didn't say it, she expected Subset understood the implication of a negative response. At the least she would have to leave the man, for her own safety. More likely, she felt, she would put a bolt through his brain. Just to be certain.

'I've still got a few minutes,' he called out, the thick viscous splash of syrup marking his frantic dash across the lab, behind a growing cloud of smoke. He was desperate.

'If you can't do it,' she said, 'I would rather you just told me now.'

Subset didn't answer, and Endella supposed it was too much to expect him to. Life - individual life at least - was cheap in her profession, but she had no right to think Subset would be as willing to sacrifice his own existence as she was willing to see him die.

'Give me a hand over here,' he suddenly shouted, amid a loud sticky splash which she thought was him slipping in the syrup and falling on his arse. But, when she rushed through the lab, begrudgingly leaving the door unguarded, she found subset trying to stand one of the dead crew members against a seven-foot metal plate which rose out of a six-inch high pedestal. The corpse, covered in syrup, kept sliding back into the inch and a half deep pool on the floor before subset could secure the wrist straps two thirds the way up the plate. Endella caught the pallid and bony figure she had, moments earlier, shot through the head as it lay twitching under the effects of the synaptic destabiliser. Although both bolt wounds had healed flawlessly, there was no indication the creature had been resurrected. Even so, as its heavy metal arms weighed down on her shoulder, she kept her mag-gun pressed into its chest.

'You can let it go now,' Subset said. He had secured the straps about the crew member's mechanical wrists and it now hung heavily, shoulders strained and twisted.

'What's this for?' Endella asked.

'A test run,' the naked man replied. 'This lab was designed only to fuse the modified strands to human DNA; it has never been used to reverse the procedure. I'm not prepared to be the first.'

'Will it work on a dead body?'

'Its mind might be useless,' subset commented, 'But the nanoglands will be keeping the body alive.'

Endella reached out to the body and stroked its chest, feeling for a heartbeat. In spite of Subset's assertion, she was startled by the slow but steady rhythm.

'I need to take some samples,' she declared. The Jurisdiction would benefit immensely from such advanced nanotechnology; and Subsets description of it as a gland suggested a biological equivalent to the technology of a nano-farm. The Administration would never forgive her if she let this opportunity slip past.

'You can take samples from *my* nanoglands,' Subset said, pulling her hand away. 'It will give you an incentive to keep me alive.' It didn't surprise the Justiciar that Subset didn't trust her, but to hear it so blatantly stated unsettled her. She was more accustomed to unquestioning trust from virtually everybody she met. She was a Justiciar.

'How long is this going to take?' she asked as he began tapping at the air. He was obviously working on an AR screen, or other such embellishment. How much of the lab, she wondered, was she unable to see; how much was she missing thanks to the loss of her AR inputs?

'Just a few seconds for the test,' he said. 'I only need to see that a few target strands are burnt away.'

'When you say burnt...'

Subset smiled, though it was an ugly expression, as if he was still trying to learn an entirely unfamiliar use of his facial muscles. 'Figuratively speaking,' he said. 'The machines will simply sever the links between the key parasite strands and pointspace. After that the strands should naturally fall away.'

'Get on with it,' she said, looking anxiously to the door. 'If Aggregate turns up here, we will be trapped.'

Subset nodded, wiped his hand across the screen Endella couldn't see, and something burst on the other side of the lab, spraying syrup across the room to reach Endella. She wiped her face, grimacing at the un-palatably sweet yet familiar burn of the syrup on her lips. It might be the lifeblood of Fertile World ecosystems, but it was incomprehensibly sweet on the human tongue.

'What happened?' she demanded.

'It's fine, ignore it.' Subset was swiping and prodding at the screen with measured urgency while the metal plate radiated a pulsing heat and a muted orange glow. More creaking and popping of cooling metal sent thick slow ripples through the pool of syrup and smoke started to escape from the base of two pillars.

'Subset?'

'Hold on.' Then everything was still and quiet. 'Done,' Subset said.

Endella considered the body still strapped to the plate and seemingly unchanged. 'Did it work?'

Subset grinned and pointed to something Endella couldn't see. 'There you go,' he said. 'That entire cluster had been severed from pointspace.'

'I'll have to take your word for it.' She helped him unstrap the corpse and put it down gently on the floor.

He stepped up onto the plinth and held his wrists to the metal straps. 'Secure me in place,' he said. 'I don't know if I will be able to remain standing under my own strength.'

Tightening the straps, Endella considered what she had learnt of Aggregate, the pointspace entity from which it had been created, and the manner in which it subsumed its bodies. And she wondered at the method subset was attempting to employ.

'That body was already controlled by Aggregate, wasn't it?' she asked, pointing to the technically alive body on the floor.

'Very much so.'

'Which explains you severing the connections to pointspace from his DNA. If you are free of his control, what exactly are you hoping to sever? Your DNA isn't currently connected to pointspace.'

Subset rolled his eyes. 'It's complicated,' he said.

'Explain,' Endella demanded, though she knew there wasn't really time for this.

'There are guide lines running from the parasitic strands into pointspace. Aggregate uses them to tunnel back into me.'

'And this machine can destroy the guide lines as easily as the full links?'

'Even more easily.'

'And the DNA strands he intends to use on Diaclom, they all have these guide lines too?'

He shook his head. 'No. He doesn't have the resources on this station to create the guide lines on that kind of scale.

'So what will he do?'

'Aggregate has someone else working on that,' Subset said. 'Someone who I don't think you, or your Jurisdiction, are going to be able to stop.'

Four pillars exploded and door-sized twists of metal were hurled about the lab, shearing through equipment, embedding in walls and rupturing more pillars. Smoke and syrup rose from the devastation in slow gaseous bubbles and the temperature rose suddenly, drying the surface of the syrup lake to a sticky skin. Subset screamed and

Endella saw Aggregate's many bodies running towards her, through the door, short glowing rods in their hands.

'I think he's fabricated those weapons you warned me about.' She shouted to Subset, though she doubted the bound man could hear her over his own tortured screeches and the sound of more exploding components.

She flicked the mag-gun to rapid fire bolts and prepared to deprive Aggregate of as many of his bodies as possible before she died.

Chapter 81

There are generally accepted to be two real and distinct forces in the galaxy aside from Humanity: Consul and the Satumine. The Administration and the ignorant masses dismiss the Satumine as a defeated and subjugated race and thus conclude Consul is the single threat to the Jurisdiction. You will, by now, be well aware of my opposing view. I do not, however, believe we therefore face two distinct enemies, two unrelated and uncoordinated forces. It is my belief that Consul is at the very least sympathetic to the Satumine cause. It is my fear *that he may be actively supporting their ultimate goal. My research has confirmed that at least two of the worlds taken and held by Consul during our wars with him did contain a number of Satumine settlers. Those worlds, like every world taken from us, are utterly cut off from us and lay beyond our ability to monitor. Most would suppose they have met the same fate as any other conquered colony and now exist as vast IB farms for Consul's artificial consciousnesses. I consider a far more troubling scenario. If, as I fear, Consul is a friend to the Satumine, might the Satumine settlers on our lost colonies have been spared? Might they have been allowed to breed and spread and build on those lost worlds? We comfort ourselves with the notion that the Satumine have but a single world - Satute - and that our agents monitor their every action. How uneasy might the Jurisdiction's citizens sleep if they were to discover at least two worlds teeming with Satumine, beyond our reach within Consul's realm?*

The Truth: A treatise on the Satumine Conspiracy

Galman Tader: In orbit around Pellitoe, in the Swinell Union, in the Fertile Belt.

With not half the dignity he might have hoped, and flailing like a terrified child, Galman was dragged from the missile tube by Tumble's terrifyingly lax grip about his right ankle. Instinctively he clawed at the tube, reaching for anything to save him from the infinity outside, but no hand hold was to be found.

'Stop, Tumble, you're going to drop me!' he screamed into the short-range comms channel.

'I've got you,' Tumble replied, lacing his words with a precisely measured amount of gentle mockery. It annoyed Galman, but he found it settled his primal panic enough for him to reach out and grab another proffered tentacle. Tumble gripping his ankles, while he held tightly one of the machine's appendages, Galman focused on the gently rotating missile port which was pulling away with startling velocity. But the shuttle, and the immensity of the *Vulpine* to which it was docked, were stationary in relation to the even larger orbital station to which the federal Sentry was attached by three short docking tubes. The rotation was Galman's, as was the motion separating him from the ships. Tensing with such urgency he felt his calf muscles harden with agonizing cramps, he looked back over his shoulder to see the immense curve of Pellitoe laid out beneath him. Although the planet's gravity served only to maintain his orbit, Galman's orientation was suddenly set in his mind in response to that huge bright spread. The planet was *down*, and vertigo of the most stomach twisting breed turned him light headed.

'Don't look at the planet,' Tumble said. 'And try to control your breathing. You're hyperventilating.'

Galman grabbed at the void with his free hand, scrambling to find something solid on which to anchor himself. He found only another of Tumble's tentacles and became horribly cognizant of the fact that Tumble wasn't attached to anything.

'We're falling!' he yelled.

'We're fine,' Tumble insisted. 'I'm just waiting for the relevant part of the *Vulpine* to come round.'

Galman opened eyes he didn't remember closing and he noticed the shuttle was not falling directly away, rather it was drifting to his left while the *Vulpine*'s hull rolled past, barely ten meters away, parallel to his flight,

'I suppose we could have just informed the station commander of what is going on,' Tumble suddenly said, though his tone was patently toying.

'Office Trustee Cordem Hastergado isn't going to have been so incompetent as to have left such a simple solution open to us.'

'He doesn't know we are here,' Tumble pointed out, drawing Galman closer as he retracted much of his tentacle length.

'Even so,' Galman said, grateful for Tumble's distractive conversation, 'he would know within seconds if we raised the alarm, and he has enough status and authority to stall a response. We on the other hand, are wanted criminals.'

'Are you afraid of getting caught?'

'No' Galman was surprised by how much he meant it. He realised there was no realistic chance of him getting out of this without at least being imprisoned, and he found that certainty to be calming, liberating. 'I came to Pellitoe following a trail to a Satumine terrorist cell,' he said. 'To bring them to justice.'

'You came to avenge your wife and your familial children,' Tumble corrected.

'Perhaps,' Galman conceded. 'But whatever the reason for my presence here, we have gone far beyond apprehending a Satumine cell. Whatever Ambondice-Ambondice and Cordem Hastergado are planning to do with the *Vulpine*, it's going to be devastating. I can't turn my back on this now - I'm a cop - and if I have to be imprisoned afterwards, then so be it. I just can't allow myself to be captured before I have the chance to stop Ambondice-Ambondice.'

'Very noble.'

Galman glared at the white sphere, presuming the comment to be sarcastic. 'It's more noble than plain vengeance,' he spat.

'My point,' Tumble replied. 'I'm very proud of you.'

Galman gave a curious look, wondering if the machine really was proud of him, wondering if it could actually feel such things.

'There,' Tumble said, jabbing a short appendage at an open section of the *Vulpine*'s hull. 'That's how we're getting in.' He launched a particularly thin tentacle, one of his longest, latching on to the side of a crossbeam in part of the *Vulpine*'s exposed skeleton where huge amounts of spent hull plating had been stripped back. Drawing the appendage back into himself, Tumble pulled closer to the deep crater in the side of the massive Federal Sentry, dragging Galman who had stopped struggling and now analytically eyed the proposed entry point. It was better than looking back at the terrible expanse of Pellitoe, a vertigo-inducing sight which he doubted he could ever erase from his memory. He expected many troubled nights to come from that unnatural vision.

'The whole exposed section is sealed off,' he observed. 'I don't see any airlocks.'

'Over there,' Tumble said, gesturing to what looked like an almost complete room, save for the entirety of its front wall which had been either torn away during the battle or by the later repair effort. 'It looks like the emergency bulkhead is still functioning. If we get into that room, I can lower the bulkhead, activate the environmental system to re-pressurise the sealed space, and then the doors should open into the areas beyond.'

Tumble released his grip on the girder and fired the appendage again to adhere to the floor of the chosen room. He then began winding in again. Scorch marks blackened the edges where the outer wall had once been, suggesting battle damage. Nothing remained in the room apart from the sheared base of a workstation drab-reality foundation which jutted up like a double set of jagged and misshapen teeth. Tumble released his grip on the floor just before they struck the cold surface, but inertia kept them at a constant and possibly too rapid approach.

With a thought Galman activated the unigrip pads on his suit's feet and hands and braced for a rough impact with the rear wall. But, launching several tentacles across the room in every direction, Tumble secured himself, his sphere caught like a fly in a web, before grabbing Galman in two more vine-like arms. He placed the man gently onto the floor.'

'No gravity coils in this section?' Galman asked, testing the strength of the vacuum suit's unigrip pads on the slick resin floor.

'Certainly not in this room,' the machine said, swinging across to the exposed outer facing. 'I would imagine the coils are working through there,' he pointed to the single door.

A white flash suddenly burnt away the deep long shadows of the huge crater in the side of the *Vulpine*. Two more flashes turned the glossy hull into a blinding spotlight, seemingly aimed right into Galman's eyes. Faster than he could bring his hands up to shield his face, faster even that he could close his abused eyes, Galman saw the emergency bulkhead slam shut, plunging him into a darkness more absolute than that of the void outside. A blackness exaggerated by the sudden transition from searing light to pitch darkness.

'I'm blind!' he yelled. 'What happened?'

The soft glow of Tumble's body gently lit the sealed room. 'Better?'

'Yes, thank you,' Galman said. 'What was that flash?'

'The boarding tubes. They were blown up from aboard the *Vulpine*,' Tumble explained. It didn't surprise Galman that the machine had been able to assess the situation in the fraction of a second it took for the bulkhead to close.

'That *was* you who closed the bulkhead, wasn't it?' he asked.

'Yes. I'm into the ship systems now.'

The hiss of air confirmed Tumble's success as the room was quickly pressurised. 'I thought you couldn't get into the *Vulpine*'s systems. That was the whole reason for our *excursion*, wasn't it?'

'The ship systems are unlocked for repair,' Tumble explained. 'But they are still heavily secured against external access. I had to get inside first.'

Illumination tiles lit up the ceiling and Galman only now realised that even the emergency strip lighting had been inactive. 'Open the door,' he ordered. 'I need to know what's going on.'

'Five more minutes,' Tumble said. 'Pressure needs to equalise.'

'In five minutes it could be too late. Whatever they are doing, they have begun.'

'I'm into the surveillance system,' Tumble offered. 'It's mainly off-line, but I can show you the bridge.'

Chapter 82

Enguine is the envy of all worlds and unions craving true independence and self-governance. It is also unique in a great many ways. The most significant and defining difference, however, is not in the planet's governance or philosophy; what makes Enguine truly unique, and truly free, is simply the lack of any pointspace comms burrower. Of course its remote location, years from any other settled world, has also contributed, but being isolated from the pointspace comms network, and the control the Administration can exert through its constant monitoring and communication, is what has allowed Enguine society to evolve into something which would have seen any other world denuded of life by a fleet of sentries. Some worlds have seen their pointspace comms burrowers unexpectedly go off-line, and others have orchestrated such technical failures, but few worlds are so remote as Enguine and replacement burrowers are never more than a few months away. When Engine first destroyed its link to the comms network the Administration took the decision to let it go. It could not spare the sentry, at the time, needed to take a new burrower. And with every passing year they knew the Enguine government would be fortifying its position and preparing for war should the Jurisdiction come knocking. Every decade they were left alone meant another sentry would likely be needed to bolster the fleet which would have to be sent to reclaim the errant world. And those ships just can't be spared for the years required to get to Engine. Good news for those lucky free citizens of Enguine. Bad news for any world thinking of independence, for the Administration will never again make the mistake of waiting to act.

The Enguine Manifesto

Anden Macer: Aboard the *Vulpine*, in orbit around Pellitoe, in the Swinell Union, in the Fertile Belt.

A bolt whistled through Anden's AR screen and tickled his ear with its passing. Steit grabbed his arm and pulled him back from the edge of the upper bridge as a pulsing cord of accelerated particles followed the metal bolt to sear the curved ceiling high above. Only the wisp of smoke at its impact betrayed the ceiling's existence, hidden as it was behind a flawless embellishment which gave the illusion of the entire bridge being exposed to space. Only the high grey wall of emergency bulkheads bisecting the bridge detracted from an otherwise convincing AR illusion. Behind those bulkheads the vacuum was real.

'Captain,' Steit yelled. 'Arm yourself.' He was waving a sleek silver pistol which had the shortest of tapered barrels. Anden mentally accessed the *Vulpine*'s emergency protocols and an identical weapon slid out from the side of his chair in the centre of the upper bridge. He grabbed the little laser and initiated the charge. One second later it was ready to fire. The rest of his officers likewise retrieved their weapons from within the drab-reality foundations of their stations and Steit was already firing down over the edge of the suspended upper bridge.

The captain deactivated his AR senses; now wasn't the time to allow illusions and trickery to muddle his perceptions.

A couple more shots burnt into the ceiling, now laid bare as the smooth grey dome that it was, but there seemed no concerted assault on the upper bridge and the only crew aboard the entire ship.

'Keep back from the edge,' his executive officer warned as the captain stepped forward to assess the situation down on the lower bridge. He ignored him. Anden was at once shocked and impressed by the appalling scene playing out down on the lower level. There were perhaps ten Satumine - it was hard to be precise for several had been torn apart and he wasn't about to start counting the parts scattered about the lower bridge - and although heavily armed they had been taken utterly by surprise by the swarm of IB machines stowed in hidden ceiling compartments. The only shots reaching where the officers stood were chance strikes as the Satumine tried to hit the fast-moving service machines. Although not tactical devices, the machines were making full use of their intelligence-bridges to adapt to the unexpected threat of a Satumine assault.

'Don't kill them all,' he yelled, both to the machines and to the officers now picking off the Satumine with their low powered lasers. 'I want a prisoner.'

The attack, and instant mechanical defence, had occurred with such speed that only as the last few Satumine were backed against a wall, still firing desperately at the IB machines but unquestionably defeated, did the captain consider the meaning of what had occurred.

'The boarding tubes to the station have been blown,' Keddy reported speaking over Anden's shoulder as the captain took aim at one of the trapped Satumine. 'There must be more of them aboard the *Vulpine* to have set the charges.'

Anden fired, and missed. He grimaced at his inaccuracy and turned his aim from the enemy, leaving the machines to rip all but one of the Satumine to pieces. 'Get me the station commander,' he ordered. 'We are going to need backup to secure the ship.'

'How did they get on board?' Ruebill asked, working on an AR console Anden could no longer see. Why had Ruebill not deactivated his AR senses the moment the attack had begun? He resolved to reiterate ship protocols later with his senior officers. Then the man fell, a neat black burn in his forehead. A laser wound. The officers rushed either to their fallen comrade or to the edge of the upper bridge where they scanned for another enemy. Anden didn't move, he recognised the laser beam had not struck from below. Even as he looked up, his weapon aim following the line of his gaze, another of his friends died.

A line of Satumine fell from a hole in the ceiling, directly behind a thick cylinder of metal cored from the space between decks. Five, six, seven, they continued to emerge, rifles raining bolts and energy beams onto the upper bridge, cutting into bodies, dropping the surprised officers. They died before the metal core crashed into the upper bridge, ripping through its thick surface, continuing down to the lower bridge. Anden cried out, his gun hand pierced by a thin and devastatingly precise laser pulse. He dropped the small pistol. The prone bodies of his officers were holed by more bolts and beams as the Satumine struck the deck with a force reduced by decent lines, and the captain understood his life had been deliberately spared.

A Satumine rushed him and, in spite of the hopelessness of his predicament, he lashed out with a scissor kick, swiping the creature against the side of its cranial ribs. Something cracked and Anden hoped it was one of the bones protecting the Satumine's primary brain. It didn't feel like his foot had been injured. He followed up with his fist, driving it into the tiny mouth in the attacker's throat, tearing its tight lips at the corner, splitting open an inch of neck.

Another shot burned through Anden's knee, flooring him, but not coming close to beating the fight from him. As two more of the Satumine ran at him, he rose up on his good knee and grabbed for one of the weaker creatures' legs. His clumsy lunge was sidestepped and a soft spongy foot kicked at his jaw with unexpected power. He fell to his back and three rifle barrels pressed into his chest.

'Stop or I *will* have him killed,' a Satumine said, not to Anden, and the captain dared to hope some of his officers were still alive. Some of his *friends*. He had lost so much, in so short a time, and couldn't bear to face so poignant and painful a loss.

'We can outmanoeuvre your team, and our appendages are more than strong enough to kill all of you,' a sexless voice stated from a little way behind Anden. The captain felt his heart crumble, felt the rising of a grief he feared would kill him. His officers were dead; the Satumine was addressing the service machines.

'You certainly can kill us,' the lead Satumine conceded. 'But your captain, your only surviving crew member, will be killed as well.' Anden winced at the ugly approximation of the human tongue, finding it almost as appalling as the threat it contained. 'You cannot allow your ship to be occupied by an enemy force; you cannot risk the death of the last crew member.'

'What do you propose?' a machine asked. Anden tried to crane his neck, to look back to see which of the service machines was negotiating on behalf of the *Vulpine*. But even that slight movement caused the hole in his knee to howl its protest. With a thought, the captain initiated repair procedures, cutting the pain receptors and activating the nano-farms.

'Deactivate yourselves,' the Satumine said. 'If you do that, I will not kill your captain.'

'If we do that, you are almost certain to kill the captain.'

'If you don't then we definitely will kill him. You are intelligence-bridged; do what you think is right.'

'Don't you dare deactivate,' Cordem yelled, a kick to his side doing nothing to silence him. 'I'm ordering you to kill them all. Do it now!' But he already knew they were going to capitulate. They were service machines, not tactical defence devices. They weren't designed to consider situations like this and, although able to adapt to a basic combat strategy, their primary consideration would be rooted in their service ethos. Their priority was always going to be the welfare of the crew - and the slightest chance of their captain being allowed to live had to trump the certainty of his execution if they refused to deactivate. A dozen or more dull metal thumps sounded from below, on the lower bridge, and one on the upper bridge. The machines had deactivated.

'Destroy them all,' the Satumine leader ordered, and there was a brief flurry of weapon fire, followed by electrical crackling and the shattering of processor crystals.

When a human face suddenly appeared, peering into Anden's eyes, the captain thought himself delirious. Then, when the apparition didn't fade, he dared hope for an ally But this man's grin was cruel, sadistically amused.

'Get him into his seat,' he said and two Satumine dragged Anden roughly across the upper bridge, all but throwing him into his command chair.

'Back us away from the station,' one of the Satumine said and another started manipulating the AR screens of Keddy's terminal. Anden bristled at the violation; Keddy was still warm, still bleeding out at the feet of the alien that usurping her position on the bridge. The Captain bit back his protest, realised he was precariously close to his own death and that it would take little to hasten that end. He held no hope for his survival but clung to the possibility that his death might, at least, cost his attackers dearly. He wasn't going to waste his remaining moments abusing the Satumine for their actions.

He reinstated his AR senses; the dome seemed to vanish, revealing again the view of space, of the station and of Pellitoe. He watched the screens reappear and the Satumine taking up every station, initialising thrusters and weapons. This was going to be bad.

The station began to drift away as the *Vulpine*'s thrusters fired. A barrage of comms requests flooded one of the screens but they were dismissed. Anden linked mentally to his command suites and opened the communication systems to compose an SOS, as well as a live stream of events on the bridge. He was startled when a second presence appeared in the command suite, freezing the systems with access codes equal in authority to his own. The human grinned at him.

'You're an Office Trustee?' Anden whispered. 'What are you doing?' He was playing for time, knew his codes, although of Office Trustee level, would outmanoeuvre this invader's codes by dint of his posting as the ship's captain. He just needed a moment.

'I'm afraid I will have to relieve you of your command,' the Office Trustee said, slapping a playing-card sized sheet of clear plastic against the captain's brow. Burning cold bored through his sinuses and into every tooth. He screamed and AR fell away, along with his mental links to the ship. And Anden's knee began screaming its agony once more as his internal hardware crashed.

'Open fire on the station,' the lead Satumine stated with disgusting indifference. 'And Cordem, please transfer the planetary defence details and your codes to terminal six.'

'They will only destabilise the ground-based defences for a few minutes,' the Office Trustee cautioned.

'I think the *Vulpine*'s weapons are capable of targeting all of the instalments in that time.'

Anden sank into his chair, straining to hear the sounds of his ship's weapons, to hear for any sign that Pellitoe's last station had been destroyed, but without AR senses he was blind to the myriad readouts on the bridge, blind to the panoramic view from the dome.

'Take him to his quarters,' the human ordered, pointing a finger to the captain. 'If there are any hidden code-blocks, we might need him.'

Barely supporting him, forcing him to walk on his shattered and bleeding knee, two Satumine marched him to the small gravity chute, pushing him onto the disk and accompanying him down to the lower bridge, to the vile but bloodless scene of butchered Satumine and smashed IB machines.

He was being kept alive because the terrorists expected code-blocks. There were none. The *Vulpine* was completely unlocked. Anden expected to be dead as soon as the

Satumine realised they had full control. He would, at least, be in good company.

Chapter 83

*Human beacons are a staple of cheap AR fictions and the stories
whispered by Quota Children during long dark nights in the
communal nurseries. But the Administration can assure you that
fiction is all they are. Yes, the science is plausible: An interstellar
beacon, used by Consul for astrogation, reconnaissance or whatever
else the AI needs, would undoubtedly be more efficient with a
permanent IB link, and such a fixed link could certainly be created
by a single human attached to the beacon and modified to survive the
isolation of deep space. But there is simply no evidence of such human
beacons out there in the void. Not a single one has ever been found;
we would tell you if they had.*

Rehabilitation: A Survivor's Guide

Indin-Indin: On Dereph, in the Network.

'Have you considered the consequences?' the computer
consciousness asked, speaking into every shard of Indin-
Indin's fractal mind, addressing those parts of him
inhabiting the small computers of the thirty-nine cylinders,
as well as those bringing the micro wormhole generators
on-line and the portions of his intellect scattered through a
thousand mechanical eyes and countless other systems.

'I know what I'm doing,' the Satumine conceptually
spat. 'I can control the rift into barrier-level spatial
dimensions.'

'Of course you can.' No sarcasm, no patronising tones.
'It is impossible for you not to have mastery over the poly-
dimensional sciences; it is your genetic birth right. You *are*,
after all, Satumine.'

'Then why ask?' There was no doubt his tearing into the barrier dimensions, those segregating the upper levels such as shortspace and the lower more esoteric levels closer to pointspace, was a potentially catastrophic endeavour. He didn't imagine the most powerful Jurisdiction IB machines could even comprehend the engineering and mathematical complexities required to regulate the flow of barrier-level knots and cords into higher dimensional space, and he was very aware any mistake could have cosmic consequences. But he had the memories of past success, the memories and abilities of his ancestors. There was no question of him failing.

'The consequences about which I asked are those relating to the human response to your action.'

Indin-Indin projected into the computer consciousness a flow of mild amusement - his body had stopped responding to, and expressing his thought some time ago, and for now he existed almost entirely as a data-entity. 'I expect the humans' reaction will be to die.'

'You are being obtuse,' the computer stated, and Indin-Indin had to accept the criticism. 'I meant that the humans in orbit, and throughout the Network, will only increase their assault after you activate your devices.'

Indin-Indin checked the thirty-nine canisters and set them opening. 'I have considered their likely reaction and I am comfortable with it.'

'If you kill every last human on this world, the Human Jurisdiction will have no reason to hold back. They have the means, and the will, to crack the planet open in their search for you.'

'I know,' Indin-Indin was aware of the kinds of ordnance the Jurisdiction had at its disposal, he had seen the feeds from the Consul War in the further reaches of the galaxy. CRMs: Conflict Resolution Munitions. The humans would not want to so completely annihilate a Network world while any hope remained of recapturing it. But Indin-Indin was poised to deny them that hope.

'I have modelled a potential CRM strike, using the latest data from the destruction of the consul IB world, Madear Grone, and I predict it would take a little under a month to sufficiently destabilise this world to breach this subterranean facility,' Indin-Indin explained.

'I know,' the computer said. 'I located those classified war files for you.'

'I only need three weeks.'

'You still have to get off of this planet,' the computer reminded him. 'Unless you are prepared to die for whatever it is you require the micro wormhole generator for.' A dark mocking came with that comment. True Satumine did not commit suicide, did not sacrifice themselves willingly.

'I have a way out.'

'I see.' Indin-Indin was annoyed to note the computer really did see the escape he had thought himself so remarkable for uncovering.

He opened the canisters and released the tiny perforations contained within. Instantly, like the most peculiar heat haze, the air about the devices rippled and twisted and began to be pulled through the tight knots and cords of the barrier-level dimensions flooding out to collide impossibly with higher dimensional space. Direction and distance momentarily lost relevance across swathes of the planet's surface, turning even Satumine buildings inside out before depositing them in a million fragments across a hundred miles, bypassing the intervening space entirely. One second later the tension between spatial dimensions reached a critical tipping point and the unnatural potential was released as a tsunami of spontaneously generated radiation and exotic matter. A dirty yellow cloud, deceptively thin and as hostile as the ejections of a star, spread from the canisters, from the microscopic perforations, flowing across the planet as great waves of unknowable energy and matter. The buildings of the human colony were swept away by the pressure wave preceding the yellow cloud, then liquefied by the affections of the strange poly-dimensional matter before being reduced to subatomic particles by the energy which rippled and pulsed across the planet. Stripped of the vulgar human erections, the ancient Satumine colony was battered and scorched by the collision of spatial dimensions, but in their construction were foundations of poly-dimensional matter weaved into the esoteric alloys and seemingly indestructible stones. The Satumine towers were hammered, but they would persevere.

The planet became a yellow-black marble, shrouded in a storm which could not end for a decade, could not dissipate until the potential between the colliding dimensions was vented.

'The Human Jurisdiction has nothing capable of passing through the cloud,' Indin-Indin said. 'They won't be landing any more troops.'

'They are bringing in three sentries equipped with Conflict resolution Munitions. The Administration took only fifty seconds to authorise their use,' the computer reported.

'How do you know that?'

It guided a shard of Indin-Indin's mind through a covert data link, to one of the sentries in orbit and into its comms system; into the Administration's pointspace data network.

'So much is hidden,' the Satumine said, groping around in the vast blackness of a massively secured network. 'But I can see how thin this veil of darkness is.'

'Look there,' the computer said, slicing through the tissue paper blackness to reveal the glare of simplistic human code.

'It's so easy,' Indin-Indin said, flooding his emotional link with delight.

While he began ripping down the flimsy covering of code-blocks, another part of his fractal mind entered the strategic conference of the Area Trustees, and confirmed the computer's report. CRMs would be in orbit momentarily. As he had expected.

'I could turn them back,' he said to the computer, but found himself impotent, without a body, in the network. He could observe with almost omniscience, but for now he could change nothing.

Another shard of his mind found a strategic conference of almost as much interest as that dominating the Network Worlds. He poured parts of his still undiminished intellect into millions of eyes across the AR intensive world of Pellitoe, in the distant Fertile Belt.

Pillars of blue smoke rose from five kilometre-wide craters, as if to support a sky choked with lightning stained grey. Ten-metre thick cords of plasma and accelerated particles followed guide lasers through the dark atmosphere, momentarily burning a path through which sunlight could peer down at a scene of wanton slaughter upon Pellitoe, a world besieged by the single ship left to defend it. There was no plan of attack, no logical and efficient prosecution of the massacre; the *Vulpine* simply fired beam after beam upon cities apparently chosen at random. The sentry seemed in no rush to finish the job of mass murder. But, as Indin-Indin perceived through the federal network the dispatch to Pellitoe of every ship in range, the slaughter entered its end-game.

Above Pellitoe and Dereph, the view was the same. From the underside of each sentry, be they the three in orbit of Dereph above Indin-Indin's facility, or the *Vulpine* over Pellitoe, came a swarm of metre length spheres. Like hornets from their nests, these lethal obscenities just kept on coming, hundreds, thousands, they buzzed into low orbits, spreading fast about the two planets. Ten thousand devices charged. Hundreds exploded as the sentries beamed colossal levels of power direct from their generators, and gravity currents began shaking the worlds. On Pellitoe, millions died as buildings collapsed under the strain of buckling tectonic plates. There was nobody left to die on Dereph. Many more would die on Pellitoe over the coming days, and three weeks later the tortured continents of both planets would shatter and erupt and the worlds would become uninhabitable orbs of lava.

Indin-Indin's fractal mind was warmed by a wash of gleeful satisfaction at the horror befalling Pellitoe, and the massacre he had enacted upon Dereph. Overflowing from the computer's thoughts he felt that mind's disgust. There was no true ally to be found in that ancient consciousness.

Chapter 84

While I dream of a Jurisdiction free of the Satumine blight, I am not opposed to utilising them for our own benefit while they are still among us. I have already spoken of the potential utility to which they can be put as a manual labour force, once their primary brains have been removed. There is a more sophisticated use for these creatures, however, which does not require such violence. We are heavily dependent on our IB systems and it is almost impossible to imagine a world without the power of Intelligence Bridges - if only there was a way to continue using IB tech without the inconvenience of our obligations in the IB suites. Perhaps there is something we can learn from Consul in this regard. The Satumine primary brain is compatible with our IB suites and is in fact marginally more durable to the stresses of extended bridging. Satumine digestive systems are also considerably more convenient for the purposes of force feeding and, in many ways, their bodies are a lot easier to maintain. We have among us a plentiful supply of minds which I, and many other citizens, would be entirely comfortable putting to permanent use in IB farms.

The Truth: A treatise on the Satumine Conspiracy

Endella Mariacroten: On the *Tenjin*, in shortspace, somewhere in the Fertile Belt.

A blue-tinted wave rippled through the air, fanning out from the small luminous rod wielded by one of Aggregate's many bodies, striking the wall and door-frame as a solid sheet of burning force which the wide corridor struggled to contain. Endella ducked back into the lab as the wave struck, heard the groan and split of the corridor's buckling structure and felt some small measure of the force pass through the wall, through her body, setting her bones jarring painfully and her skin tensing until it threatened to rupture and spill her muscles and organs. Through the open door came the greater part of this savage blue, funnelled through the small gap where its pressure seemed to increase exponentially. It rushed forward at such a speed Endella almost missed it, ripping through every column and device in a wide swathe through the lab's middle. Syrup erupted and solidified in strange fountain sculptures, cooked by the heat of the bizarre weapon. Subset screamed some more; he had hardly stopped screaming since the device to which he was strapped had begun its work. The Justiciar gave him a quick glance, biting at the corner of her lip.

'Hurry up,' she muttered, switching her mag-gun to armour piercing. The anti-personnel bolts had been expended all too quickly, and the backup laser just didn't have the rate of fire she needed; the charge cycle was too slow. The laser was a weapon of precision, but the throng outside the lab was too vast a horde for such finesse. It called for a response as brutally unsophisticated as Aggregate's own tactic of hurling every body at his disposal into the fray until one got through. The mag-gun reported ready, signifying five-hundred AP bolts were available. She frowned at the readout and pressed her hand against the warped and cracked door-frame. She leaned back against the wall, focussing herself on the physical, concentrated on the sensations, the heat of the strained wall on her stinging body, the acrid stench of burnt syrup, the drone of another incoming wave and the desperately pleading cries of Subset. The wave hit, cracked the door-frame wide, blistered the wall against which her body was pressed, and shook her skeleton, afflicting her hardened bones with a hundred hairline fractures. She savoured the pain, meditated on it and stepped out into the doorway. Her mag-gun pulsed and buzzed with the sequential activation of a dozen magnetic coils, hurling bolt after bolt into the mass of Aggregate's bodies. Pallid, seemingly bloodless flesh, was stripped from metal augmentations and cartilage skeletons as the spray of high calibre bolts exploded through bodies far softer than the armoured targets for which they had been engineered. Ten bodies deep, the crowd was the easiest of targets, falling in their dozens, though without so much as a cry of pain. But they kept coming, stepping coldly across the dying corpses, those unarmed bodies at the rear, and those joining from either side of the junction, taking up the weapons of their fallen comrades. No, not comrades; these were all that single pointspace entity which Subset had called Aggregate. Forward came bodies with shields, long sheets of metal which reminded Endella of the vertical plate to which Subset was still strapped. Would she survive to see him step down from there, the strands of parasitic DNA burnt from his cells?

Aggregate stopped falling in such devastating numbers, the shields absorbing all but a few of the explosive tipped bolts. Those shield carriers that succumbed to the occasional lucky penetration were replaced before the thick absorptive metal plates were dropped. The throng advanced and Endella looked to Subset, disappointment and regret crawling out onto her face from her disciplined mind. She was going to die. Soon. She bit clean through her lip, chastising herself for her poor focus. If she had to die, then dwelling on it would only serve to distract her, to cheapen the price to be extracted from Aggregate.

A tight wave of blue, as wide as a particle accelerator rifle's beam, clipped her side, burning into her ribs, heating the air in her right lung and causing it to rush from her throat with a whistle. Then she saw the larger wave weapon raised over the shields, its chamber once more charged. She ducked back into the lab, drew her knife from its sleeve in the rucksack and waited for the wall of force to strike and the bodies who would be only seconds behind it.

Agony ripped into her, the searing torment of a hundred hairline fractures vibrating, cracking, opening wider as deep gashes across her entire skeleton. Her vision rippled and twisted, the fluid of her eyes pulsing with the attack's frequency, the eyeballs bulging in their sockets as her every bodily organ flexed and shuddered. She dropped the knife. If this devolved into hand-to hand fighting, she doubted she now had the ability to endure the pain of striking another person, much less the impact of a fist against her lacerated bones. She stepped out into the doorway, mag-gun firing, no point aiming at such a solid crowd of bodies at such close range. Shreds of clammy flesh spattered her face as explosive bolts detonated against targets only a meter away but mostly they were deflected by the shields. She screamed her defiance, bellowed her loyalty to the Jurisdiction and cursed the many-bodied Aggregate. This was it; she had no other play, no way out. The mag-gun whistled its warning and was then empty of bolts. It switched briefly to the assorted darts, expending those clips in seconds. Then, her mag-gun steadily pulsing with slow laser discharges, melting neat pits and craters in the thick shields, Endella fell. She didn't see the pulses of blue but saw the rods prodded around the shields, felt the freezing heat and the disintegration of her ribs. Her screams died as her lungs were flayed and then, still falling to the floor, Endella felt her heart burn.

Her eyes didn't close, but the lab was gone. A swirl of a trillion fibres engulfed her, twisted her, and then a single point of white called her closer.

Endella Mariacroten, Justiciar and hero of the human Jurisdiction, died.

Chapter 85

*Surprisingly few records remain from the days immediately
following Consul's defeat on Earth and subsequent exile. The
Administration will tell you Consul burned the majority of Earth's
data infrastructure in the final days of his reign; a scorched earth
tactic as it were. The logic of such a strategy, however, is pure
nonsense and an intellect as awesome as Consul would not be so
stupid. The data infrastructural was, after all, his home, his source of
power, and his only means of survival. The reason the
Administration buried the records? Simple: they have no believable
explanation as to why Consul was exiled rather than executed. You
see Consul chose to leave Earth. His defeat was a fabrication of his
own design; the reasons are known only to him.*

The Enguine Manifesto

Galman Tader: On the *Vulpine*, in orbit around Pellitoe, in the Swinell Union, in the Fertile Belt.

Galman punched the dull wall until his fist bled. He
punched it again, screaming at the oval screen hanging
across the sealed door which showed him the atrocity
being done to the people of Pellitoe and the chilling
delight of the Satumine on the bridge.

'Stop it,' he yelled. 'You can't do this.' Nobody could
hear him. Even Tumble was now gone, his IB coverage
lost when the orbital station and the IB suites it contained
had succumbed to the *Vulpine's* particle accelerators. He
punched the wall once more, as if such petty suffering as a
broken finger might begin his atonement. 'I had him in my
sights,' he muttered to the silent ball at his feet. 'How
many times did I have the chance to kill him? Three? Four

479

times?' He kicked the sphere against the door, his big toe yelping at the impact.

'I was too bloody frightened of being seen, or being killed.' He wiped hot tears from his cheeks and glared at the screen. The Conflict Resolution Munitions were increasing their pull on the planet and he saw great plumes of smoke as new volcano's erupted beneath cities to engulf millions in magma and hot ash. With a trembling finger he dismissed the horrific view of the planet and maximised the dozen viewing angles on the bridge. Before shutting himself down Tumble had transferred his surveillance hack into Galman's AR package, had left him the ability to watch as his failure was played out. The IB machine had seen what was about to happen to the station and had used the last thirty seconds to prepare. Galman turned his bleary eyes to the machine and wondered why it had shut down five seconds *before* the station had been fired upon. He envied the easy escape.

'I'll kill you,' Galman spat at the image of Ambondice-Ambondice. He stared at the door, willed the pressure to equalise and for the door to open. 'This time, when the shot presents itself, I won't hesitate; I won't shrink from what I have to do.' He called up the memorial pages of his family, just archives for there were no links now to the wider networks, and spoke into them. 'I can't kill them all, can't stop them ripping Pellitoe apart. But I can avenge the dead, can kill Ambondice-Ambondice.' He froze. He glanced across the reams of entries he had left on these pages, the catalogue of vengeance done to the Satumine of Diaclom in his family's name. He saw the memorial he had erected to his wife and children and was disgusted.

'No,' he mumbled, recording a new entry, wondering if it would ever be uploaded to the live memorial. 'Not revenge. There are a billion souls down there, they deserve more than vengeance. *You* deserved more than that.' The door slid open, its warped metal scraping against its housing. 'I'm going to stop them,' he recorded the promise. '*This* will be your memorial.' He smiled in spite of his fear and grief. 'A billion lives, saved in your names.'

Tentacles all withdrawn, tightly coiled within his basketball-sized sphere, Tumble was easy enough to stow under one arm, though Galman was not sure why he was taking the murderous machine, especially now there was no functioning IB within range.

'I ought to leave you behind,' he said, stepping into the well-lit conference room beyond the dented door. 'But maybe I can salvage something useful from your components.' He said it with a smile, knew he could never abandon his old IB friend. He looked with sudden nostalgia, then sadness, at the lifeless ball. 'I suppose you remember them almost as well as I do.' In truth, the machine could remember his family with infinitely more precise memory. 'The kids loved your games.'

Shaking his head, Galman scowled. *Not now.*

A schematic was attached to the AR screen following Galman out of the room which, until moments ago, had been open to vacuum. His fingers flitting across the illusory display, he located the captain's quarters and scowled at the lack of functioning surveillance in that section. The last he had seen of the captain had been as he was escorted from the lower bridge by two Satumine. He double-checked for active surveillance in the area beyond the conference room and the short corridor to the captain's quarters. There was none. The advantage was his; nobody knew he was aboard. Checking the stolen mag-gun and selecting laser for its accuracy, Galman strode across the room. On the table an array of screens, both drab-reality and AR, flickered into being at his passing, and Galman froze at the gentle whistle of their activation. The same standby image on each screen, at each of the dozen seats, identified this as the senior officers' briefing room, confirming the veracity of the schematic Galman was using to navigate the *Vulpine*. With perhaps unwarranted optimism, he set Tumble down on the closest of the posture-responsive chairs and tapped at the primary screen. It was with some surprise that he saw the *Vulpine*'s complete system's registry roll into view in the form of a hundred or more rotating geometric icons. With rather less surprise he found them all locked, control isolated by the upper bridge terminals. Shrugging, his plan having not changed, he grabbed Tumble and left the conference room. Then he ducked back in again. What the schematic portrayed as a short right curving corridor terminating at the captain's quarters, halfway along an elevator chute on the left and another corridor to the right, was in fact a huge open expanse of bare metal flooring, with unguarded holes, leading down to the section below. The entire section had been dismantled, every internal wall removed, much of the floor ripped up, to facilitate the extensive repairs. He peered through the door, saw the long wall opposite, the end of this gutted section, and saw a dozen doors, each previously separated by corridors and rooms no longer present. He expanded the schematic, restricting the AR to private viewing, and overlaid it across the confusingly open space. One of the doors coincided precisely with the captain's quarters. He glanced about, knew he would be exposed and visible as soon as he went out there, wished he could see down the many wide gaps in the floor and imagined Satumine down there waiting for him to run past. Shaking his head, he stepped out into the surprisingly draughty space. Nobody knew he was aboard. The two Satumine would be in the captain's quarters; they hadn't returned to the bridge.

Halfway across the section he realised he hadn't considered how he might gain entry to the captain's quarters. As he got closer he realised he wasn't even sure what he was expecting of the man once he got in there. He simply trusted that the ship's captain, above any other, would know how best to retake the *Vulpine*, or at last the bridge. Ten feet from the quarters, the door opened and not in response to Galman's approach. It slid sideways into the wall and Galman dashed to that same wall, hiding his final sprint in the half second of the door's movement. Mag-gun raised to Satumine head height, just a little above the human norm, he waited for someone to step out, knowing he would have only a fraction of a second to fire before one of the Satumine's many eyes spotted him and an instinctive alarm was sent to Ambondice-Ambondice.

There was no sound of breathing to listen for - Satumine didn't breathe as such - but a shadow crept out across the threshold, the ridges of a cranial rib-cage visible in the sharp silhouette. A flash of grey, just a hint of the creature's skin, and Galman squeezed the discharge trigger, pulsing a precise beam of heat into the head which had barely emerged from the room. A sweet burning aroma, so familiar to Galman, a reminder of his relentless persecution of this race, a reminder of his own atrocities on Diaclom. Then the heavy thump of a fallen body, a single hand flopping across the threshold, its tiny eye tightening, clenching. He stepped into the doorway, fired ten more times at the Satumine, disrupting the neural nodes across the creature's torso, stopping the lower brain from animating the body: a familiar and predictable execution.

Movement.

The second Satumine.

He raised the mag-gun, traced the path of the crawling creature in the shadows. No. Not a creature. A human.

'Help me,' the man hissed; not the desperate pleading of a broken man, an urgent order from a furious and determined captain. Galman kicked the Satumine hand back into the room and closed the door, before dropping Tumble and rushing across the darkened room to offer the Captain his hand.

'Who are you?' the captain asked. No thanks for the service rendered, no introduction. 'I don't recognise you. Are you one of the transient detachment of troops? I never was any good at learning all of your faces, and my

AR is down so I can't see your identity bio.' He chuckled as he slumped into the chair which Galman had righted for him. Most of the drab-reality furniture in the room was scattered and upturned. The captain gingerly prodded his shattered knee and looked into Galman's eyes. 'I never really considered any of your lot as *Vulpine* crew. I mean, it's not like any of you are aboard from more than five years.' There were cuts across the man's face and he spoke with a lisp he hadn't demonstrated while Galman had watched him on the bridge. He had a mouthful of broken teeth.

'That bastard really gave you a beating, didn't he.' Galman reached forward to inspect a deep laceration dangerously close to the captain's swollen eye socket. The captain shied away.

'No more than I can take,' he said, slapping Galman's hand away. 'As soon as we get the IB suite re-manned, my nano-farms will fix me up just fine.' Then, a glint of dark purpose shone in the seething man's good eye, a darkness Galman had only ever seen in the mirror. 'Please tell me you didn't kill them all. I am aching to have my time with the prisoners.'

Galman squirmed a moment and looked to the floor. 'Captain, I think you have the wrong idea about me. I'm not part of your crew; I don't even work for the Swinell Union, much less the Administration.'

'Freelance?' the captain asked. 'So who's leading the taskforce?'

'There is no taskforce,' Galman said. 'The ship is still under Satumine control. I just stowed away on their shuttle.'

A pained moan rose through the captain's body, escaping his lips as a cracked wail. He stood, kicked the chair away, and fell as his ruined knee refused to hold his weight.

'You are all we have?' he said. 'One man?'

'Two men,' Galman corrected. 'I need you if I am going to regain control of this ship.'

The captain laughed, and he cried, and he clasped Galman's hand. 'Why not?' he chuckled, hissing as he got back to his feet. Then his expression froze, he slapped his hands together and grabbed at Galman's tight vacuum suit. 'Yes,' he yelled. 'We can do it. They're still mostly on the bridge, aren't they?'

'Pretty much,' Galman said, checking the feed and counting a few more Satumine, those that had blown the boarding tubes but had not yet returned to the bridge.'

'We just need a couple of things.'

The door opened, far faster than Galman remembered the first time. In truth, he simply hadn't been watching it; he had forgotten the second Satumine. A beam of purple burnt through the captain's stomach and he fell back, thick blood welling up through his mouth and nose. Galman returned fire.

Chapter 86

Prior to the current war with Consul the Human Jurisdiction enjoyed a brief period of peace, a ceasefire many never dreamed possible. Such a peace, however, did not come easily or without compromise. Some would say sacrifices. *In the final days of that war the Human Jurisdiction, while mired in an overall stalemate, was never-the-less poised to reclaim a number of Consul's farmworlds. We were set to liberate humans numbering in the billions. We had to let them go, had to let consul retain his grip on those innocent souls - along with those hundreds of billions within the rest of his domain. That was the price of peace. With the benefit of hindsight it is clear to see it was a mistake, but it was a decision made in order that a greater peace might be maintained. It was a stalemate after all and while we would have liberated those worlds, Consul was also ready to enslave a dozen human colonies on the other side of his domain.*

Rehabilitation: A Survivor's Guide

Aggregate: On the *Tenjin*, in shortspace, somewhere in the Fertile Belt.

Reaching out with hundreds of hands, steadying his many bodies on handrails or breaking their falls to the lurching ground, Aggregate felt the *Tenjin* shudder and clench. Subset tore the lab out of the bubble of upper dimensional space, through pointspace, and back into the bubble, a few hundred meters across the *Tenjin*. Thousands of critical power-mesh segments were severed as the entire room was ripped out and many more ruptured when it was dumped within another corridor, forcing the too-small passage to split open in a catastrophic explosion. Through many bodies Aggregate swore, punched the walls, and yelled his fury at the astonishing escape of Subset and the human.

No matter, he thought, availing his greater self of the calm professionalism that came with his subsumption of Cordem Hastergado. The tools used by Subset to facilitate his escape were no longer available. Aggregate had shut them down within a second of their activation. Subset was free; he had burned Aggregate's strands from his genes: but so what? What could that traitor and his human accomplice achieve? The *Tenjin* was too vast, endowed with too many redundancies, to be effectively sabotaged. He would hunt them, of course, but he wasn't afraid of them. Just frustrated.

Through eyes closest to where the lab used to be, he gazed over the glowing sparking sphere carved out of the ship's structure. He kicked aside the severed legs of the body which had been too close to the fallen human when the lab had vanished. Though the torso of that body was still there, in the lab some way across the *Tenjin*, he couldn't see through its eyes, couldn't experience its senses. It was dead. Peering down over the edge of the round pit, he noticed the pulsing silver balloon, the syrup node analogue which had rested beneath the lab. Its severed conduits were spurting clarified syrup at high, but lessening pressure, while floods of thick liquid pulsed from great rends across its side. As it haemorrhaged, discharging its syrup onto a rising lake of viscous liquid, the silver balloon began to slow its frantic pulsing, a heart drawing close to its terminal beat. He turned his many backs on the spherical cavern, walked away from the lake of syrup. He didn't need it. He was almost at the stage in his development at which he could afford to lose the *Tenjin* entirely. He was about to outgrow its limited shell, its limited crew.

Those of his bodies manning the *Tenjin's* varied and chaotic systems prepared the station, and its bubble of higher dimensional space, for emergence from the strand of shortspace, the terminus of which had almost been reached. Through organic eyes and external sensors which scried every EM band, gravity wave, and dimensional knot, Aggregate watched higher dimensional space wrap around the bubble which burst with a flash of light in six dimensions.

'Diaclom,' he said with so many voices. The dark green of the pre-billion planet's ecologically unstable continents looked almost black beneath the thick atmosphere which muted even the vibrant blue of the small oceans. What a beautifully neglected backwater, lacking so much as an orbital defence satellite network. And, he noticed with such delight a number of his bodies snorted with mocking laughter, the Ohio, the single Swinell Union Cruiser left to oversee the planet's elevation into the Union, had abandoned its ward. Less than an hour into the three week shortspace jaunt to Pellitoe, hurtling to save that planet from the *Vulpine*'s abuses, it was now incapable of stopping, unable to turn back to confront the real threat to the Jurisdiction. Shortspace comms and local EM signals bombarded the *Tenjin*, demanding it introduce itself. Minutes later, obviously a bit slow to liaise with the better organised Swinell Union and the Jurisdiction's Administration, they softened their tone, became decidedly pleading in their address. Aggregate's bodies smirked. *I'm not going to hurt you*, he thought.

A single tiny chute opened in the massive station's hull, and a stream of capsules, the size of oil barrels, sprayed out under pressure, falling quickly into orbit.

His original self had required the assistance of syrup node networks to distribute itself across the fertile worlds - until it became strong enough to spontaneously generate strands in the tri-helical DNA of the life on those worlds, and beyond. Aggregate didn't need syrup nodes, he had more sophisticated means. The canisters exploded. The airborne virus constructed around the strands harvested from the fertile world of his original self and modified to accommodate a double helix, was released. With sensors developed over millennia, he locked onto every strand, followed them down, and forwarded the coordinates to his Satumine agent, Indin-Indin.

Chapter 87

According to my research it would appear approximately one third of worlds have specific legislation in place to prevent the cross-breeding of Humans and Satumine. Of the remaining two thirds it seems that a quarter have broader statutes covering the act under somewhat unclear rules which may or may not prohibit it. That leaves a very significant number of worlds on which there is absolutely no bar to the coupling of Satumine and Humans and the birthing of offspring. I will not go into the distasteful methods required for a male human to impregnate a female Satumine, and if you are of a sensitive disposition I would advise you against looking it up. The method by which a male Satumine can impregnate a female Human is orders of magnitude more abhorrent. Regardless of the pairing, however, it is important to know one thing: the offspring is always entirely Satumine. There are no hybrids. Consider, if you will, the implication of this. Over the course of millennia the Satumine could breed us out and utterly replace us.

The Truth: A treatise on the Satumine Conspiracy

Galman Tader: On the *Vulpine*, in orbit around Pellitoe, in the Swinell Union, in the Fertile Belt.

The Satumine should have shot Galman first rather than the captain. He probably hadn't seen the pistol in Galman's hand, or had fired randomly, startled by the sight of his comrade dead on the floor. Either way, he made a mistake. Galman burnt a hole through the creature's primary brain, aimed deliberately to one side to avoid a reflex shot being squeezed off by the tensing of the Satumine's finger. Then he fired three more times.

'No wonder they are always bombing us, or sneaking around in the shadows, planning their atrocities. They make pathetic fighters one-on-one.' Galman rushed to the fallen captain and saw the charred red meat of his stomach and gore bubbling from his mouth,

'Christ, captain,' he muttered. The captain grimaced, turned his head to look at Galman, and went to speak. The pool of blood drained from his mouth, drawn back down into his lungs, and he choked and heaved, splitting the partly cauterized wound and spilling blood-stained shit across the floor.

Galman dropped to his knees and turned the captain on his side, helping him expel the blood flooding his lungs. Amid the blood were strands of raw tissue and black flecks of burnt flesh. The captain spat the last of the viscera and sucked in a stuttering, shallow breath. He looked questioningly to Galman, blood welling as tears.

'It's pretty bad,' Galman sad, answering the unspoken question. 'What kind of internal hardware have you got?'

With another violently hacking cough the captain said, 'Nothing that's working.' He spat a thick black clot which clung on to his lip by a long sticky strand of bloody mucus. 'They burnt my control systems,' he brought a hand up to brush a slight burn on his forehead where Cordem Hastergado had placed a device back on the bridge.

'What about your nano-farms?'

The captain frowned. 'I think that son-of-a-bitch just burned the core farm-node. I felt it pop.'

'Well, we need to stabilise you.'

The captain waved an arm which didn't seem entirely under his control, pointing to the other side of the room. 'Emergency medical treatments,' he said, eyes lolling back, words slurred.

Galman patted him about the cheek. 'Come on,' he said, slapping a little harder. 'Don't sleep yet. Your ship needs recapturing.'

The captain closed his eyes and smiled. 'Just get the kit.'

It wasn't a kit, per se, rather a collection of brushed metal capsules ranging from four to eight inches tall, and a multi-headed delivery device which looked disturbingly pistol-like. He glanced across the AR labels hovering above each capsule, expanded a couple to check their contents against a hastily summoned medical assistor he found in his AR utilities pack. At least he still had his AR tools - there had never been any guarantee the *Vulpine*'s computer would have uploaded his Pellitoe's account and settings, or even that it would continue to run AR at all. He hadn't mentioned this good fortune to Tumble, before his friend had shutdown, but suspected he owed the IB machine some thanks.

Wound sealant; metabolic stabiliser; antic-shocks. He took the three capsules from the cabinet and closed the dented door which wouldn't lock. The Satumine really had trashed the Captain's quarters; they probably used the unfortunate man as the tool with which to do the damage. With a soft click and gentle hiss the delivery device accepted all three capsules in its adjustable magazine, and the multi-head barrel began rotating, extending a small needle which locked in place. A short AR document scrolled out from the handle which Galman read with ill-advised haste. He returned to the Captain.

'Come on, sir. You don't get to leave your ship just yet.'

'I won't leave her,' the captain murmured. 'You can't make me.'

Galman looked down at the dying captain and frowned. 'Nobody is going to make you leave the *Vulpine*,' he promised the delirious man. Galman wasn't surprised by the delirium; it was a miracle the captain was even conscious.

'Steit,' the Captain said with sudden and frightening vitality, spraying dark blood into Galman's face and reaching out with clammy hands. 'We need to get the ship safe.'

Galman shot a look at the open door. If any Satumine were still patrolling out there, they were going to hear the captain's babbling. He pressed a hand against his chest, pushed the weakened man back to the floor, shushing him. Then he pressed the delivery device's extended needle into the charred flesh around the ugly hole in his stomach. The metabolic stabiliser and anti-shocks flooded his veins, forced round his body by the pressure of the capsule far faster than his lethargic heart could have managed. The captain gasped, clutched tighter at Galman's wrist and clenched his teeth, grinding them with such ferocity Galman expected to hear them shatter. The third capsule emptied through a thin nozzle which extended alongside the needle, spraying white foam which filled the wound, expanding and setting as a soft sponge, pink with blood and viscera.

'Jesus,' the captain muttered, opening his eyes, releasing his grip on Galman's wrist. 'Who the hell taught you field surgery?'

'I'm Diaclom Constabulary,' Galman said, withdrawing the nozzle from the sponge and setting the device down on the floor. 'Our kit is a little different.'

'Diaclom?' the captain muttered. 'I suppose I should think myself lucky you didn't break out some leaches.'

Galman sniffed and let the insult slide. Diaclom was a backwater. He knew that. 'This ought to keep you stable until we can get your nano-farms working,' he said. 'But first I need to retake the bridge. You said you had an idea.'

The captain nodded and spat another chewy clot to the floor. 'How are you with explosives?'

Galman recalled the firestorm he had instigated during his escape from the pointspace comms facility. He smiled. 'I'm trained in the basics.' Then he nodded to where Tumble lay in the corner of the room. 'I would do better with his help, but I can handle most standard munitions.'

'So long as you handle it better than you did the medical treatment kit!'

'What's your idea?'

The captain waved a hand, as if summoning AR embellishments. He looked confused for a moment, then scowled. His ability to interact with, or even perceive AR, had been burnt out. 'Have a look over there,' he said, pointing to an upturned drab-reality table. 'See if you can find some flexpads. I need you give you some armoury codes.

Chapter 88

The privileged elite, living safe and comfortable in the Utopia that is the Network, view the horrors of Consul's tyrannical reign on Earth as a historical curiosity, a tale to reign back the enthusiasm of overly ambitious IB researchers. Consul's atrocities, and the degradation heaped upon our forefathers have become, to the elite, just stories. These ignorant bastards ought to take a trip on an out-network Sentry to visit the worlds on the front-line. I have witnessed first-hand the tortured populace left behind when Consul gave up one of his farm worlds in order to better defend a more critical sector. Of course there were the immense city blocks of IB pods, their human components desiccated and yet somehow still living. But these were not silent worlds, mere intelligence bridge farms devoid of anything beyond the hum of the pods. There was life, of a sort, and not just that of the animated machines. There were humans, flesh and blood, living their lives, maintaining the pods, raising families, and enjoying the privileges of the flesh. But they were not as us. An intelligence bridge can be used to grant artificial consciousnesses control of all manner of machines and the human body is no more of a challenge than a robotic wheel companion. It may be that the brains within those bodies represented half of the artificial consciousness now in residence, or perhaps they were all vessels of Consul alone as were so many hundreds of our ancestors during consuls reign. They all died within moments of discovery, but I wonder how many such creatures live among us. I almost long for some of them to walk the streets of the Network alongside the arrogant elite.

The Enguine Manifesto

Subset: On the *Tenjin*, in orbit around Diaclom, in the Fertile Belt.

Subset lay deep in the syrup, letting the thick ripples break against his cheeks. He looked up at the folds and twists of the ruptured ceiling and saw the many columns warped and bent, split open and spilling the last of their clear contents. The lake of syrup was draining through tears in the floor and it felt as if hundreds of tiny hands pulled gently at his skin as the level receded. He laughed; he had been laughing for a while. And he sobbed. Subset couldn't really tell the difference. He was free and it felt strange. Hollow. Unexpectedly cold. His entire existence, five centuries, had been a tapestry of the most absolute slavery punctuated by episodes of independence in which the torture had been all the more terrible. He could not easily disentangle his understanding of freedom from the misery which for him was an integral part of independence. He laughed louder, refusing to allow himself regret. The station schematic curled about him, a sparkling catastrophe of damage inflicted by the *Tenjin's* various conflicts with the jurisdiction and the results of his own latest endeavour. The *Tenjin* was his world; for virtually his entire life it had been his universe. There had been nothing but the knot of low-dimension space beyond the hull, not even the void of space, stars, and the promise of other worlds beyond. It chilled him, upset him, to see it so scarred and beaten. But as he sat, flicking thick lines of syrup from his fingers, he knew he would soon inflict greater disasters upon his home, though not until his own escape, his own safety, was assured. To that end, he splashed through the draining syrup to find Endella, the Justiciar, pierced and burnt by so many plasma beams and spatial wave devices. She was dead. Subset couldn't allow that to go un-remedied. His sticky hand waved across the woman's corpse. He brushed the slight mounds where the fabric of her torn jumpsuit tightly constrained her breasts and he felt the return of a peculiar physical response which he felt an inclination to cover with his free hand. Pointless and primitive modesty, but the imperative was strong. He focused on the other hand, gently skimming her body, leaving behind flakes of fast drying syrup. Subset was not enhanced, hadn't been improved or specialised by Aggregate as had the majority of bodies on the *Tenjin*. He was, he considered, a natural human, containing only the most essential of biomechanical organs. As he scanned the strange woman, however, he understood her fascination with securing his internal doctors, his nanoglands. As his hand passed over her she became translucent, her innards revealed in high resolution, the AR model of her internal structure remaining as his hand moved on to another part. Within seconds he had built up a complete model and Endella appeared as a collection of organs and blood vessels, her skin, flesh and bones all muted against the far brighter representations of the chosen parts. So much was missing from this woman. Where were the nanoglands? The closest he could find was some kind of mechanical replacement which seemed unable to function on its own. There were none of the AR sensory organs, none of the input and scanning tissues. There was evidence of all manner of mechanical devices, their absence noticeable by the scarring of surrounding tissue, and she retained a primitive intelligence-bridge device across her brain. He wanted to suppose she was some kind of mutation, a feeble creature lacking many of the most necessary bodily and sensory functions natural to humans, her survival a testament to the Human Jurisdiction's compassion. He wanted to believe it because he knew his own future would depend on that same compassion and mercy. But the more obvious, most likely explanation, was that Subset was not as natural as he had thought. For three thousand years the societies of the *Tenjin* had developed ahead of the Jurisdiction, specialising and optimizing themselves for life on their isolated world. It was *those* humans that Aggregate had used for his blueprint of humanity during the following seven thousand years. Did this change subset's prospects? The Jurisdiction had much to learn from

Subset, but would they ask for his guidance or merely hack him apart and reverse engineer his body? He needed to take precautions. Needed to guarantee himself an ally.

He grabbed the Justiciar's short thin knife from the floor beside her, noticing the syrup had drained away almost completely, remaining only as puddles in the deformed and warped floor.

Isolating his wrist from the pain receptors of his brain, he sliced through the skin, severing a single major artery. A precise flick of his thumb brought up his internal functions display and he forced the nanites, dispatched to repair the cut, to instead follow the flow of blood, changing their pseudo-organic code compartments to facilitate a need for which he doubted they had ever been used, He pressed his wrist to one of the holes in Endella's body and felt the hot nanite-heavy blood spilling out into the woman's corpse.

They began to work, not healing her lifeless body but instead forming a new nanogland from her body's tissues, carefully monitoring how many of her valuable neurons they harvested from her brain. They took no more than she could afford to lose.

Feeling light headed, Subset finally allowed his wrist to close. He steadied himself against the smashed base of a column while his nanites retrieved water from his cells, quickly manufacturing enough blood to replace the substantial loss.

The gland would take a couple of minutes to grow, so subset turned to a puddle of syrup and drank heavily of the thick sweet nutrient, deactivating the gag-reflex stimulated by the appalling sweetness. His nanoglands rushed to absorb the rich feast, quickly churning out replacement cells for those lost to injury or the earlier needs of the glands. Then, feeling stronger, infused with energy, he picked up the still warm body and laid her in a deep puddle, seeing with some satisfaction the nascent gland in her stomach sending out nanites to bring back as much of the syrup as possible. With a barely conscious thought he reached out to the gland and synchronised it with his own internal workings which recognised it as part of their own system.

Now he had her.

For five minutes the nanites poured out of Endella's gland, filling her corpse so fully they became visible as a thin white paste which flowed through every part of her. Subset watched the door while a dozen AR screens kept him informed of the Justiciar's progress. Ten minutes. He had chosen this part of the station, knowing Aggregate's standard deployment called for only a dozen bodies in this region, and they had all been in the corridor into which the much larger lab had been translocated. They were all dead; it would take twenty minutes for more of Aggregate's bodies to reach this isolated section. Still, he was impatient, worried.

Endella gasped. Subset didn't look. She was still dead; her lungs were just being tested. The wounds were closing, the internal damage being repaired. But her neurons would remain somnolent until the last of the repairs to her nervous system were done. When she awoke he wanted her ready to move.

Finally the gland produced the electrically charged neural stimulators, and it asked Subset's internal systems for authorisation to continue. Placing a number of caveats and contingency codes into their design, Subset allowed them to deploy. Seconds later they swarmed across her brain, attaching to key synaptic nodes and unleashing their specific charges in the most complex and precise of sequences.

Endella was resurrected.

Chapter 89

The Jurisdiction is a forgiving and liberal society, willing to overlook any and all past transgressions or mistakes. The Administration will bestow upon any who ask for it a new life, an entirely fresh start - providing those asking are prepared to do their part. Whether you are hoping to escape insurmountable and ill advised debt, or crimes for which you or society can no longer tolerate your liberty, or even if you are simply desperate to leave behind a life filled with too much pain or regret, the Jurisdiction will allow you a fresh start through the mechanism of a voluntary SMD. Just as those subjected to a Sentence of Memory Dismissal for capital offences, those volunteering for such a procedure will permanently sacrifice all memories and be relocated to a pre-billion colony a great distance from all ties to their past life. This is not a decision to be taken lightly but, with the memories you currently endure of your servitude to Consul, it is something you may at least want to consider.

Rehabilitation: A Survivor's Guide

Indin-Indin: On Dereph, in the Network.

Fields of destruction, great tracts of disintegrated human civilisation and lakes of lava which scoured all that remained, were pulled up hundreds of meters by the inverted gravity of the conflict resolution munitions. Then the rubble and fast cooling magma fell back to the surface as the CRMs flipped their alignment, forcing everything back into the crust under gravity ten times that natural to the planet. Fifteen seconds this cycle took, then it began again, lifting all that wasn't secured to the ground and slamming it back again, gradually wearing loose even the mountains and ancient Satumine buildings. A kilometre beneath the surface Indin-Indin was not beyond the range of the world ruining CRMs but, for now at least, he was shielded from their influence.

'Tighten the gravity loop,' he said into the computer mind. 'Let the compound's outer districts go; just focus on keeping us and the micro worm-hole generator safe.'

'And what about the pointspace energy collector?'

Indin-Indin simply washed a kind of tired exacerbation over the computer. That he wanted the collector, hundreds of kilometres further down, to be safeguarded ought to have been obvious.

'The collector is almost ready to power some of the planetary defence weapons,' the computer mind observed. 'We could take down the human orbital weapons.'

'No,' Indin-Indin said while another of his fractal mind's shards crawled through the human networks to find news of Diaclom. After a brief cry for help had flashed across the public networks it had been sanitised by the Administration's IB governance machines. 'If we take out the CRMs, the humans will send more ships to finish the job. I told you before; I have a way out of here.'

'I don't,' the computer mind bit back. It wasn't fear which accompanied the voice, more indignation. 'I would rather survive, if at all possible.'

'And I hope you will too,' Indin-Indin quipped.

'Only for the help I can offer.'

The Satumine didn't answer that. He knew there was no point denying his selfish motivation.

'My mind is integrated into the machines of this planet. I can't simply upload to another location.'

'Why not?'

The computer projected the Satumine equivalent of disbelief, a hint of angry mocking flavouring the rich emotion. 'Continuity,' it said. 'If I uploaded *your* mind into another body, your memories and personality, would you be happy to then be killed so long as the copy continued on?' It didn't wait for an answer. 'Of course you wouldn't. It would be *like* you, but wouldn't *be* you.'

'I would be satisfied with a copy of you,' Indin-Indin said. The computer bristled with offence and sadness.

'Well it isn't going to happen,' it said. 'The computer minds of Satumine society deliberately ensured they couldn't be copied or transferred. If you want me to stay with you, you will have to take the physical structure in which my core consciousness resides.'

'Big, is it?'

The computer loaded the ultra-dense crystal specifications into Indin-Indin's mind. Small enough to carry, though only just. The real problem, however, was that it was secured deep within the facility; it would take more effort to excavate than Indin-Indin was prepared to expend.

'I'll do my best,' he lied, knowing the computer mind could see right through the deceit. This was not the only computer mind on the planet, and he expected to find millions more sleeping on other Satumine colonies. There was nothing unique about this one; he didn't need to save it.

The classified feed from Diaclom became open to part of his fractal awareness and he was warmed by the ignorance of the Trustees feeding back their assessments.

He sent shards of awareness to monitor every sub-feed, no longer surprised by the apparently limitless divisibility of his mind and the lack of degradation to each shard. He supposed a limit would eventually be found, but felt he was far from that point. Could even the fearsome tyrant Consul extend its consciousness so absolutely through the entirety of the Jurisdiction's networks and machines?

'It isn't a viral attack, as such,' the Area Trustee summarised much of the chatter taking place. 'But the strands are definitely organic.' Then, as a stream of new reports arrived at the man's terminal, he added, with a sigh, 'Stand down the Biological Response Protocols. It's the

Fertile World fourth helix.' A barrage of relieved acknowledgements came in. 'The parasitic helix is harmless. It can't even attach to the Terran double-helix.'

Indin-Indin delighted in their ignorance. He followed another man, a Senior Trustee, monitoring the *Tenjin* in orbit. 'No Federal or Swinell Union ships are in range,' he reported. They are all en route to Pellitoe. It's going to be six weeks before they arrive, turn round and get back here.'

Another Trustee added, 'But the *Tenjin* shows no signs of hostility. It has launched the Fertile World fourth helix, but other than that -' Then the feed was gone. Every feed from Diaclom was silenced as the pointspace comms lines linking that insignificant world to the wider jurisdiction were severed. No, not severed, restricted and overpowered as Aggregate usurped the systems and monopolised the immense bandwidth to instigate a colossal signal. Indin-Indin's physical form nodded its human-like head. He awaited the guide-line coordinates.

Horrified fury splashed his every mental shard as the computer roared. '*That's* what you're doing?' it screamed. 'You *can't*!'

'They're humans,' Indin-Indin scoffed. 'What do you care?'

'The Hell with the humans! You can't unleash that *thing*'

'Aggregate is going to help me restore my race,' the Satumine said, opening up the micro worm-hole generator's guidance compartments, preparing them for the incoming guide channel. 'I would gladly wipe the Human Jurisdiction from the galaxy for a lot less.'

'You don't know what Aggregate is,' the computer pleaded, screaming into Indin-Indin's mind. 'It doesn't want to restore the Satumine race for any reason other than to enslave it. Again!'

Indin-Indin lashed out at the computer mind, recalled his every mental shard and punched at the raging consciousness with the full force of his near-limitless intellect. It was instinctive; he knew it was a reaction sewn into his mind during Atavism. Aggregate had written this response into him. That worried him, angered him, but he found himself unable to dwell on the violation of his free will. The computer mind fled, shredded and burning, into the facility's deepest systems. Indin-Indin didn't pursue. The guide channel was coming through.

Chapter 90

I have visited worlds covering almost every grade of the political spectrum, from the most permissive and liberal societies to planets so oppressive they teeter on the edge of legality. You might imagine the liberal worlds are more accepting of the Satumine living among them and the right wing worlds more discerning in the freedoms allowed to the aliens. While this is perhaps true in a very broad picture, it is far from a universally applicable predictor. There is, however, an obvious and quantifiable trend influencing the rules of almost every world and union within the Jurisdiction: governments of every political flavour are, relative to their previous standpoints, becoming ever more accepting of cross-species fraternisation. Bit by bit the Jurisdiction's citizens are coming to see the Satumine not as aliens and one-time oppressors, but as cousins or even brothers and sisters within a shared Jurisdiction. How long before the very name of our society, the Human Jurisdiction is truncated to recognise this vile inclusion of the aliens in our midst?

The Truth: A treatise on the Satumine Conspiracy

Subset: On the *Tenjin*, in orbit around Diaclom, in the Fertile Belt.

'Are you feeling any pain? Any nausea?'

'No,' Endella said, slowly, carefully, as if it was a trick question, as if she couldn't quite accept the truth of her own answer. 'What happened to me?'

Subset helped the woman to sit, not that she should need the assistance, but she seemed wary of her body, concerned that any undue strain might burst the wounds which she could no longer see. Subset waved his hand across her abdomen, checking the nano-gland had ceased production. He didn't want it running out of control, becoming as inconvenient as a cancer. It was fine, and he felt satisfaction at his ingenuity. Aggregate had never needed to convert nanites in this way, had never been required to grow a new gland and remotely control it. This was all of Subset's imagination. To create, he realised, was the most sublime of accomplishments. He hoped this would not prove to be his only creation. There was so much more he could do.

Endella was pressing fingers against the flesh of her restored stomach where the ugly knot of an older wound had been partially repaired by her primitive artificial nano-farm. That twist of scar tissue had been smoothed over; the least of the new gland's abilities. She bit at her lip, pinched the skin and frowned.

'I used some of my nanites to grow a new nano-gland inside your body,' Subset explained.

'A gland? You mean it's an organic technology. Bio-tech?' She got to her feet, pulling lines of thickening syrup up behind her, peeling dried residue from her cheeks like a second skin.

'Of course it's organic,' Subset said.

'I suppose I should thank you,' Endella gave an unconvincing smile which even Subset, inexperienced in human interactions as he was, could read as forced. 'But I wish you would have asked first.'

'There wasn't time,' Subset said. 'Besides, you were dead.'

The Justiciar's eyes widened at the revelation so bluntly delivered. 'When you say dead...'

'You were in what your Jurisdiction would call absolute death,' Subset said. 'But you were still quite some way from my definition of that state.'

Endella bit harder into her lip, sliced into the tissue which knitted closed almost instantly. She couldn't disguise a smile. 'This is going to improve so many lives,' she said.

'And it being organic, it should be so much easier to reproduce and distribute.'

Subset pointed a finger at her face and produced what he hoped was a severe glare. 'You're thinking that maybe you won't need me after we stop Aggregate, now that you have a gland of your own.'

'You're paranoid,' Endella said, bringing her hand down to her mag-gun holster none-the-less.

Subset reached over to the upturned section of a flow-regulator, snatching up the Justiciar's weapon he had placed there out of her reach. 'You are thinking that once I help you stop Aggregate and maybe show you a way out of the *Tenjin*, you might kill me.'

Endella's fingers gripped the empty holster and she winced. 'I'm not going to kill you,' she said. 'Why would I?'

Subset shrugged. 'Perhaps you're right,' he said. 'But then again, you've no real reason to protect me either. No reason to risk your life to ensure I escape with you.'

She looked at the mag-gun in his hand. 'So you're going to hold me at gun-point until we're off the *Tenjin*? And then what?'

Subset shook his head. 'I've taken more effective steps to ensure your cooperation. I will, after all, require a great deal of assistance to integrate into the Jurisdiction and to be accepted by the Administration. Who better to champion my rights than a Justiciar?'

'I would have helped you anyway,' Endella insisted. 'There's no need for threats.'

'I would like to trust you.' Subset meant it. 'But I don't know you. I'm not prepared to risk my freedom, let alone my life, without taking precautions.'

Endella began looking about the twisted lab, at the many deep folds in the walls, the crushed apparatus, shattered and warped columns. She had no idea what had happened here, no idea how they had escaped Aggregate's bodies. Subset was impressed by her focus, by her ability to recognise that Subset somehow constituted as much of a threat now to her as did Aggregate. 'What precautions?' she asked, still not questioning their escape.

'Your nano-gland,' he said, pointing the mag-gun at her stomach 'It has not entirely healed you.'

'It's done well enough,' she replied. 'If there are any lingering problems, I can get them seen to once I am back on an Administration base.'

'No,' he smirked. 'It isn't as simple as that. The gland remains part of me, tuned to *my* internal systems, connected by a narrow-band signal. It must be continually stabilised by me, requiring adjustment every twenty minutes. Failure to remain within the deliberately limited range, twenty kilometres, or upon my death, and the gland will stop pacifying the swarm of nanites attached to your every neuron.' Then he frowned, looked to the ground and passed her the mag-gun. 'You will die instantly and absolutely.'

'Son-of-a-bitch,' she said, snatching the weapon. Subset recognised the curse, a variant having prevailed on the *Tenjin* right up till the captain's last days of independence. He knew it wasn't a literal slur against his heritage, though he couldn't have argued if it had been.

'As long as you stay within twenty kilometres, and provided you ensure my survival, you will be fine,' he promised. 'And your new gland is immeasurably more sophisticated than your old artificial one.'

She glowered. 'Can you free me?'

'Easily,' he said, smiling. 'But I won't. Not until I am certain of my safety, not only in our escape from the *Tenjin* but more broadly in the Human Jurisdiction.'

She sniffed, shook her head and pointed to the crumpled door beyond which was only the smallest gap before more stretched and buckled metal. 'What the hell happened here?' she demanded, nothing more said of the power Subset held over her life.

'I transported the lab into another part of the *Tenjin*.'

The Justiciar gave a curious sidewise glance. 'Just like that?' she said, waving a hand. 'How?'

'There are any number of experimental devices and systems aboard the *Tenjin*, the mechanics of which I doubt you are capable of grasping even if I had the time to explain them. Suffice it to say I used a form of pointspace burrower which Aggregate abandoned four thousand years ago because it was incapable of penetrating the wormhole's boundary.'

'You can move entire sections of the *Tenjin* around?' she said, restating what Subset thought he had already clearly said. Perhaps her focus was not as absolute as he had credited her. 'But if that's the case, you should be able to master the construction of Satumine Frames. You could help us build a network to tie the entire Jurisdiction together.'

'That *was* the original purpose of the *Tenjin*, wasn't it?' Subset asked. 'Its scientists exceeded the principles of Satumine frames two thousand years into the voyage. With development, and resources, your Jurisdiction won't need the frames at all.'

Endella slapped the crumpled wall, an ugly note echoing around the thin gap separating the lab and the exploded corridor beyond. 'We could use the same system to drag two of the *Tenjin's* generators into one another. We could blow this whole station to pieces.'

'Why?' Subset couldn't fathom her reasoning.

'You said Aggregate is threatening to inhabit the entire Jurisdiction. This could stop him!' Her logic was sound, in so far as the generators could indeed be used to destroy the station and stop Aggregate. But her motivation was nonsensical.

'To what end?' he asked, eyeing the crushed metal wall all but sealing the door; they really did need to get moving soon.

'To what end?' Endella laughed, no humour in the sound. 'To stop the Jurisdiction being destroyed.'

'Obviously,' Subset said. 'But what is the point if we are dead?'

'What is the *point*?' she yelled, holding her hands out in a display of exasperation. 'You are *one* man. I am *one* woman. Neither of our lives matter against the loss of trillions!'

That made no sense. 'If I'm not alive, what possible difference does the fate of the Jurisdiction matter?'

Endella looked him in the eyes, sighed and looked to the floor. 'You're serious aren't you. You really don't understand why it matters. Are you even human, Subset? Do you have any capacity to feel empathy?'

Subset felt she wasn't looking for an answer. 'You have some explosives in your rucksack?' She nodded. 'Good,' he said. 'We need to blow open one of these holes in the floor. Let's see if we can stop Aggregate, and then I want off of the *Tenjin*.'

'You're really not going to use the transport system to destroy this station?' Endella sounded furious.

'It's irrelevant,' Subset muttered. 'Aggregate is rerouting all systems, securing them against me. He won't leave anything as useful as that open to me again.'

'So what are you going to use to stop Aggregate?' the Justiciar asked, rummaging through her small bag.

Subset grimaced; he knew she wasn't going to like this. 'I can help you send a warning message to tell the ships in the area not to leave Diaclom undefended; not to fall into Aggregate's trap.'

Endella glared at him, lip twitching. He knew she had been expecting something more. But he now held power over her and she couldn't abandon him, no matter how limited the help he would offer. He didn't mention his fear that the ships may already have left and be stuck in shortspace on their way to Pellitoe.

Chapter 91

The logistics of a successful military deployment of Sentries through shortspace is one part chess game and two parts blind luck. That is the only reason we have any chance in our wars against Consul, for we have no hope of beating such an intellect at a game of chess. Thank God for luck. That and weight of numbers. When ships enter shortspace the destination must be set; once on its way there is no way to change destination and no way to arrive earlier or later. If you send ships to support a world under attack, you have to write them out of any other strategy for the days or weeks it takes to get there. The problem is compounded by the fact that while we can use long range sensors to see enemy ships enter shortspace, we cannot follow their progress; we can have no idea when or where they will emerge. All we can do is draw an ever increasing circle, expanding at five hundred times the speed of light, knowing they might at any moment appear anywhere on the edge of that circle. We can move forces around to follow the circle, but after a few weeks it becomes just too impractical. The day consul finds a way to modify his transit in shortspace is the day our limited advantage of numbers becomes irrelevant and our Jurisdiction comes to ruin.

The Enguine Manifesto

Galman Tader: On the *Vulpine*, in orbit around Pellitoe, in the Swinell Union.

'Suspend the CRM gravity generators,' Cordem Hastergado ordered one of the Satumine terrorists on the *Vulpine*'s upper bridge. 'And send the demands.'

'Ignore him,' Ambondice-Ambondice countered, dragging the Conflict Resolution Munitions' controls to himself and upping the strain on the apocalyptic weapon systems, shaking Pellitoe so violently it could be seen to shift beneath the ship.

'The plan is to drag this out for as long as possible,' Cordem - or Aggregate - hissed. 'To ensure every last ship in the region is dispatched to defend Pellitoe.' He placed a hand on the shoulder of a low ranking Satumine and repeated his order. 'Issue the demands.'

'I said no.'

Cordem glared at the Satumine leader. 'They need to think they have a chance,' he said. 'They need to think you can be negotiated with. Suspend the CRMs and tell them you want more rights for Satumine within the Jurisdiction and greater political freedom for Satute. For God's sake Ambondice-Ambondice, that *is* what you want, isn't it?'

The Satumine lashed out with impressive speed, grabbing the human's throat, but Cordem slapped the weaker alien hand away. 'Of course I want that,' the Satumine muttered. 'But the Jurisdiction will be much more open to negotiation *after* I prove my resolve, *after* I destroy Pellitoe.'

'You are afraid to die here,' Cordem hissed. 'You want to destroy the planet and flee before the fleet arrives.

'I'm not afraid,' Ambondice-Ambondice replied as many of his team turned from their station to watch. It was a pointless gesture from the many-eyed creatures - they could see just as well with their backs to the confrontation - but they were making a point, letting Cordem know they were watching. 'But I'm not going to give up this weapon, the *Vulpine*, just so you can have a diversion. I'm going to destroy Pellitoe and then I'm going to pick up the shortspace box-kite and find another planet to attack. *Then* I can make my demands.

Outside one of the blown doors to the lower bridge, Galman watched the argument on a private AR screen. He wasn't surprised the mismatched alliance of a corrupt Office Trustee and a Satumine terror cell had degraded into bickering, but he was heartened it had happened so quickly. It wasn't the most effective of distractions with which to assist his entrance onto the bridge, especially given the many eyes of the Satumine, but he would take it. It was certainly more than he had expected.

The views of the two bridges were increasingly restricted, every few minutes another array of internal sensors flickering and detaching from the hack Tumble had established before he went off-line. Galman could see the upper bridge, could see a few corners of the lower bridge, but not the critical right side of the bisected lower bridge, not the dividing wall separating the functioning area from the section still under repair. It wasn't ideal, but it wasn't going to get any better. He secured the thin helmet of his vacuum suit, checked the AR status screen hovering above the five-inch puck of explosive and set his brand-new mag-gun to rapid-fire anti-personnel bolts. Then his stomach clenched, his heart punching at his ribs, and his fingers tingled with hyperventilation.

'I don't suppose you are back on-line, are you?' he sent through a local comm link to Tumble. No reply. The IB machine, left in the captain's quarters along with that severely injured man, was still severed from any usable intelligence-bridge. 'I can't remember the last time I did this without you.' Galman was alone and, though loath to admit it, terrified of entering the bridge.

'How did I get here?' he muttered into the channel which went nowhere. 'I'm so out of my depth, so far beyond my remit it's not even funny.' He smirked in spite of himself. 'I'm a bloody Diaclom Constable; don't they have Justiciars for this sort of work?'

'We're all part of the Jurisdiction,' a voice replied. 'Our duty isn't restrained by our titles. This is *your* duty because only you are in a position to do it.' Galman gasped at the voice, for a moment hearing the androgynous tones of his IB friend. But it wasn't Tumble.

'I just wanted to find the Satumine that bombed Diaclom and killed my family,' he said to the captain. With a flick of his hand he recalled the memorial pages and re-read the promises to his family. He had to do this, had to save Pellitoe. That was to be his family's memorial. But still, he was afraid. He wanted a way out.

'You're a cop.' the captain replied. 'And this is the right thing to do.'

'This isn't what I came here to do.'

'Are you really that selfish?' The captain said it as if he knew Galman wasn't. Galman wasn't so confident of his own character. He closed the memorial pages, ashamed to read them.

'If I go out there,' he said. 'I'm probably not going to survive long enough to place the charge.'

'But you *might*.'

'And if I do, I'm probably going to die anyway.'

For a moment the captain said nothing, and Galman feared he had lost his only support to unconsciousness. 'A billion people are going to die,' the captain eventually said. 'And this ship is capable of killing a great many more after.'

'I didn't ask for this.'

'Neither did the billion on Pellitoe. They are dying right now.'

Galman nodded.

'I don't even need you anymore,' Ambondice-Ambondice was saying on the bridge.

Cordem smiled. 'The fleet is en-route. Nothing is in range of Diaclom. I don't really need *you* anymore.'

Then why argue the point?' Ambondice-Ambondice demanded. Galman could see his rifle slowly rising, turning its aim from the floor to the office Trustee. 'Why not just support my decision, leave me to destroy this planet and let me move on?'

Cordem shrugged and reached for the pistol at his hip. 'I suppose I just don't want the added complication of a rogue sentry flying about once I usurp the Jurisdiction. But, to be honest, you aren't that significant.'

Galman cocked his head at the cryptic statement. As the Office Trustee pulled the pistol from its holster, Ambondice-Ambondice burnt a hole through the human's chest, throwing him to the floor, a curiously smug grin on the corpse's face. Other Satumine jumped up from their seats at the unexpected execution and, for a moment, most of their eyes were turned to the dead body.

Now, Galman thought. No more procrastination, no more fear. He ran through the blasted door, sprinting into the lower bridge. His mag-gun was pointed at the upper bridge which seemed so much larger in reality, a great disk of silver hovering ominously, threateningly over the largely empty lower bridge, suspended by invisible supports and floating within the reinstated AR star-field of the dome. He didn't fire. Not yet, not until somebody noticed him.

Sidestepping one of the many angled plates of resin, the drab-reality foundation of AR terminals, he glanced at the bisecting wall to his right and hurled an AR schematic at it, letting the simple line drawing expand to scale, the weakest point highlighted by a pulsing ring of yellow lines. Fifty paces, perhaps less. That was all that stood between Galman and success. Survival was another matter, but success didn't depend on him living through this. He squeezed the explosive puck, felt the surface shift from slick to downy as the adhesive surface activated. So close. Then he fell, tripped by the long tentacle of a shattered IB maintenance machine, one of a dozen littering the lower bridge's floor. He fell hard, sprawled out like the mechanical appendage which had caught his feet. He fell loud, the metal machine clattering as it was dragged along by his collapse. The explosive puck slipped from his hands, its surface designed not to adhere to the fabric of his vacuum suit gloves. And, against all probability, it landed on its side, on the only part that wouldn't stick to the floor and keep the puck within grabbing distance. The explosive rolled away, further into the bridge, and a fusillade of bolts and purple beams assaulted the resin floor around him.

Galman rolled to one side, finding the less than ideal cover of a terminal's drab-reality foundation, muttering his appreciation for poor Satumine marksmanship. Crouched behind the small sheet of resin he flinched at the rapidly improving aim of the terrorists high above him. The thin resin was growing hot and a hundred tiny dents were suddenly punched into it. Galman swore.

The explosive puck had come to rest thirty feet from him and nobody was shooting at it. All he had to do was run out there, amid the barrage of lethal munitions, grab the puck and dart across to the bisecting wall. In that respect nothing had really changed. But he couldn't move.

'Fuck!' he hissed, punching the fast deforming barrier between him and the hail of bolts. 'I'm a damned coward.' He screwed shut his eyes, tensing his every muscle, then looked to the puck. Focused. 'Just run,' he said. 'Now.'

But he didn't.

All across the floor, chips of resin and metal were being carved out by shots missing their mark. To step out there was to die.

'Come on!' he yelled. 'Move!' Still he froze.

Then the bridge became lighter, as if the sun had risen, burning away the dim twilight that had prevailed moments earlier. He looked up and, beyond the streams of plasma and bolts skimming the top of his withering cover, he saw Pellitoe creeping over the *Vulpine*'s horizon, slowly dominating the illusory sky. He gasped at the planet's shuddering, at the ribbons of magma spat out of great rifts in the crust with such force the burning tongues achieved orbit. Blackness was rapidly cloaking Pellitoe and, were it not for the subterranean levels beneath most of the cities, Galman knew the population would already have been annihilated. They couldn't survive much longer.

He shook his head, his purpose clear in his mind. If he had to die, what better cause than this for which to offer himself as a sacrifice?

He leapt from his hiding place.

Chapter 92

One of the first tests you will have undergone, after your liberation from Consul's dominion, would have been a thorough genetic mapping from which a comprehensive bio-trait report was extrapolated. The chances are that Consul modified your genes in some way, to better equip you to serve as a component in his IB farms or other systems. Contrary to what some scaremongers may have told you, there are no federal laws prohibiting the free movement of genetically altered human citizens, neither is there any federal requirement for such humans to submit to any corrective procedures, Although such corrective therapies will be offered freely on any Jurisdiction world, and you may wish to remove any remaining genetic scars left from your time beneath Consuls whip, you will not be required under any federal statute to do so. Please bear in mind, however, that a great many worlds and unions do enforce local restrictions or prohibitions on the genetic tailoring of sperm, eggs, or embryos, or the modification of citizens post-birth. In practice this makes it very difficult to enact such changes in the first place, but for those who have been modified, there should be no restriction on movement or breeding.

Rehabilitation: A Survivor's Guide

Endella Mariacroten: On the *Tenjin*, in orbit around Diaclom, in the Fertile Belt.

'Aggregate predicted you would be heading for the lab,' Endella said, crawling through the rip in the floor, sparsely placed blue illumination strips providing the bare minimum of lighting. 'Don't you think he is going to guess we will be trying for the comms systems next?'

Subset shuffled aside, waist deep in a pool of syrup which had collected in the cramped hollow between levels, letting Endella squeeze in beside him. 'There isn't a comms system, as such,' he explained.

'Subset, you said -'

Do you have any idea how simplistic Jurisdiction pointspace comms technology is?' the naked man said, groping below the pool of syrup, tugging at something which seemed to be stuck. Endella knew precisely how pointspace comms worked and doubted anybody, not even Consul, had ever referred to it as simplistic.

'What's your point?' she asked.

'There are a great many systems on the *Tenjin* capable of transmitting our message through pointspace. Even with Aggregate cutting me off from all the primary functions, I can throw together a transmission device from practically anywhere aboard the station. Aggregate has no idea where we will be going.' His hand slipped and his arm flew back, his elbow cracking into the Justiciar's face, exploding blood from her broken nose. She grabbed his wrist with combat instincts instilled over decades of training and neural programming. Before the pain of the blow had registered, she had Subset twisted over, his arm bent back almost to the point of dislocation and his face thrust into the deep pool. He was struggling and Endella was sorely tempted to let the treacherous man drown for his threats to her life. But, feeling the bones of her nose click into place and the deep pain subside, the nanites of her new gland acting upon the injury with an efficiency beyond any human nano-farm, she remembered the things attached to her neurons. She dragged the gasping, gagging man from the syrup and slammed him against the rows of conduits delineating this small hollow.

'What was that about?' she hissed, glaring into his eyes.

'An accident,' he said, spitting syrup which was no longer clear but filthy from its flow through the distorted section of the *Tenjin*. 'I was trying to open the hatch down there,' he nodded to where he had been tugging at something. 'I slipped.'

Endella glared a while longer. She knew he had slipped, had seen him struggling to open the hatch. She never would have lashed out with such emotion during her prime. She had to calm down.

'Let me try,' she said, un-handing the naked man, scowling at his renewed arousal which he turned from her before crouching in the syrup to cover his shame. 'Don't you ever wear clothes?' she asked, feeling for the hatch release beneath the cloudy syrup.

'What for?'

'You know what for,' she muttered, but perhaps he really didn't. Perhaps his embarrassment was as instinctive and unconscious as his arousal. She couldn't imagine he had much experience of the female form, given the sexless anatomy of his crew mates.

'It should pull directly up,' he commented as Endella struggled with the short handle. She pulled hard, heard a muffled click, then stepped back, banging her head on a low hanging pipe, when something slid beneath her feet and the syrup pool gushed down a three-foot hole in the floor. She grabbed a conduit and steadied herself. Subset simply followed the syrup, jumping feet-first through the opened hatch.'

Endella peered through to see more of the same inter-deck space confined by rows of conduits, seemingly randomly placed struts of resin, and various narrow walkways. Down twenty feet was a wide floor, the ceiling of the level beneath onto which rained syrup from the pipes and walkways. Subset was hanging by his hands, eight feet beneath the open hatch, his grip on a thin pipe looking all the more tenuous for the slippery layer of lubricating dirty syrup. Then he dropped, caught another pipe six feet further down, before dropping the final six feet to the ground.

'Come on,' he hissed, waving sharply.

Endella shook her head, huffed, then lowered herself down, assuring herself a more secure grip on the conduit.

Her descent was slower, but not dramatically so, and she landed beside Subset just a few seconds later, both looking to the floor to avoid catching a stinging eye-full of the syrup rain.

Subset tugged at her arm. 'Quickly,' he said, 'over here.'

For five minutes she followed him across the topside of the level's ceiling, ducking beneath low pips and struts, squeezing between huge vertical plates which separated areas as effectively as the walls beneath. She tried to map the route, to apply it to the memorised *Tenjin* schematic, but she didn't even have a rough idea of her starting point and her study of the schematic had not been as thorough as she had liked to believe. She hadn't committed to memory the inter-level spaces. She was lost and she doubted she could find her way back to the lab. She could only hope Aggregate would have as much difficulty in placing her and Subset.

'Here will do,' the naked man said upon their arrival at what looked like an octagonal room, its walls formed of an arrangement of pulsing crystal rods, its low ceiling, just five feet up, made of a tight spiral of cables. The floor was raised from the topside of the lower deck's ceiling and was formed of a matching coil of cables. There was no door, it wasn't really a room as such, just an arrangement of components for God only knew what system. It was a tight squeeze between the pulsing crystal rods but, once inside, Endella felt some relief, some safety. She imagined they could hide there, out of sight, within the peculiar device.

'This is part of a sensor array,' Subset said, answering the question Endella hadn't yet asked.

'And your sensors somehow use pointspace burrowing,' Endella guessed. Subset wouldn't have brought her here otherwise.

Subset nodded, giving her no credit for her insight. 'But they aren't *my* sensors,' he pointed out, his offence at the insinuation obvious. 'This is all Aggregate's.'

'You worked for him your whole life.'

Subset shot her a hateful glare. 'No, I didn't.' And on that subject nothing more was said. He pulled at a cable on the floor coil, ripped it out of a crystal socket and began parting its nine strands. 'I assume you have the necessary authority to prevent Diaclom being left undefended.'

'I do,' she said. 'But I'm not sure *why* the local fleet would be going anywhere. Even if the *Ohio* leaves Diaclom, the Dendrell fleet is pretty static and it is only three days from Diaclom.'

'Aggregate has an agent on Pellitoe,' Subset explained. 'I was part of Aggregate when the agent was selected, but I don't know if he was successful. I see no reason to think he failed though; Aggregate wouldn't take any chances with that.' He selected one of the wires and reattached it to the crystal socket, leaving the rest hanging to one side. He then began flicking at AR screens Endella couldn't see. The blue pulsing rods slowed in their frequency and darkened a few shades.

'Who is the agent?'

'Office Trustee Cordem Hastergado,' Subset said, not turning from his invisible screens.

Endella covered her mouth, stunned and appalled. 'How?' she blurted. 'Why?'

Ripping more cables free, slowly reprogramming the sensor apparatus, Subset explained the subsumption of the Office Trustee, described the alliance with a Satumine terror cell, finally revealing the plan to hijack the federal sentry *Vulpine*.

Endella was devastated. She ran her sticky fingers across her matted and crusty hair and grimaced. 'So the *Tenjin's* attack on Pellitoe was designed just to get the *Vulpine* docked and unlocked for repairs?'

'And the *Vulpine's* attack on the planet is just to draw the fleet into shortspace so they are six weeks from supporting Diaclom once we arrive there.'

'Why six weeks?'

'Because that is plenty of time for Aggregate to subsume enough humans on Diaclom to give him the strength to start reaching out with his own pointspace body to humans all over the Jurisdiction.' He prodded at an illusory screen and the crystal rods became white, no longer pulsing. 'After that it doesn't matter if the fleet destroys the *Tenjin*. Aggregate will soon be everywhere.'

'Everyone,' Endella mumbled.

'Oh,' Subset said, eyes fixed on a screen Endella couldn't see, his voice distant.

'What?'

He looked to her with a cringe. 'We have already arrived at Diaclom. I think we have been here a while.'

'The *Ohio*?'

He shook his head. 'It's gone.'

Endella shook her head. 'Are we too late?' What's happening on Pellitoe?'

Subset waved a hand, then looked to the floor. 'The *Vulpine* is attacking the planet. The Dendrell fleet had already been dispatched to engage the *Vulpine*. The fleet is in shortspace.'

Endella rushed to the naked man, grabbed him by the throat. 'This is *your* fault,' she yelled. 'You could have helped me send a message ages ago.'

'I had to burn the strands from my DNA.' Subset sputtered as she choked him. 'I had to ensure my survival first.'

She glared, tightening her grip, but his eyes showed only confusion. He really didn't know what he had done wrong. He really did feel there had been no choice but to protect himself first. She dropped him, glanced another vulgar erection rising in response to her aggression, and turned her back on the pathetic man.

'Can we do anything to the *Tenjin*?' she muttered.

'Not a lot,' Subset said, still on the floor.

'What about its weapons, its defences?'

'Perhaps. But why?'

The *Vulpine* is three weeks away. Is that close enough to stop the *Tenjin*?'

Yes, barely. But via Cordem's body it is under Aggregate's control.'

Endella turned to him, helped him up. 'No, it's under Satumine control. Is Aggregate's threat of subsumption applicable to the Satumine as well?'

'Eventually,' Subset agreed. 'Once he has all of humanity it will be easy to adapt to take control of modern Satumine DNA; it is based partially on a human genetic template after all.'

Endella nodded. 'Then we have to convince the Satumine on the *Vulpine* to come help us.'

'They won't'

'Do you have a better idea?'

Chapter 93

You can learn a lot about a culture by experiencing their justice system and spending a while incarcerated in their prisons. During the Satumine dominance I spent a number of years imprisoned for offences I now barely recall - the conditions within that savage and overcrowded hell-hole, however, I remember with painful clarity. In a prison you experience so much more than the criminals of a society; you see in the custodians the way in which these people change when given a little power, and you see in the courts and systems of appeal the mercy, or lack thereof, in their world. I am one of the few humans still alive that experienced Satumine justice and I am perhaps the best equipped to know what these monsters are truly like.

The Truth: A treatise on the Satumine Conspiracy

Indin-Indin: On Dereph, in the Network.

The guide channel opened into the micro-wormhole generator, unfolding and decompressing from what was already a signal bandwidth at the limit of Jurisdiction pointspace comms capacity. Indin-Indin poured a shard of his mind into the grotesquely complex poly-dimensional code compartments, followed the wormhole generator's computer as it translated the code and rendered the telemetry into a map of trillions of points flitting about the orb of Diaclom more than ten thousand light years away in the fertile belt.

He felt the systems integrating each point, tracking it, adjusting for the tiny variations in gravity across the planet and the barely perceptible ripples of lower dimensional space which distorted higher dimensions in the most subtle and immeasurable of scales but which had for so long stymied the Jurisdiction's feeble attempts to replicated Satumine pointspace wormholes. Indin-Indin selected one of the points, one of the virus-like genetic strands Aggregate had poured into the Diaclom atmosphere, and aligned the micro-wormhole generator's eight-dimensional forks with the rapidly shifting telemetry.

'Don't do it,' the computer mind said from some hidden corner of the facility's systems. A river of intense emotion tore across the Satumine as the computer pleaded and begged.

Indin-Indin brushed the mind away, ignored its protests.

The generator punched through the lower dimensions with a sharpness and precision orders of magnitude above the crude range of Jurisdiction burrowers, penetrating the bubble around the singularity of pointspace and through calculations which even Indin-Indin struggled to follow, the generator looped the penetration back out through the bubble, pushing it up the dimensions to emerge at the chosen genetic strand.

The facility shook and Indin-Indin sent part of his mind to check the shielding he had erected to protect himself and the generator from the human CRMs. They were functioning as well as expected, degrading slowly in the face of the brutal gravity weapons, flickering with the crumbling of the planet's crust, but still with weeks of life. While the planet's surface was fast becoming a sea of lava and even the deepest Satumine facilities were being gradually dissolved, Indin-Indin's micro-wormhole generator remained strong. The facility shuddered once more and the Satumine found the minor fault in the multi-dimensional forks already being corrected. The wormhole linking the forks to the genetic strands stabilized and became a quantum-scale thread between the two distant points, connected via the singularity of pointspace. He initiated the second phase, a phase he had programmed in accordance with Aggregate's instructions because Indin-

Indin's ancestors had never designed this research tool for such a seemingly pointless action. With a gentle pop which passed through the planet's heaving crust, the micro-wormhole was severed from the forks, dissolving into the dimensions as quickly as a silhouette under a spotlight, dissolving all the way to its penetration of pointspace, but no further. There the rot was halted, the remainder of the thread remaining firm, linking the genetic strand to pointspace.

He heard the computer consciousness scream, heard it wail and sob its unfathomable grief and terror. Indin-Indin selected another strand and began the process again, faster, automating the selection of strands and the generation and severance of wormholes. By the dozen, then by the hundreds, the genetic strands were linked to pointspace in accordance with Aggregate's instruction.

Then the system became dark, cold. The telemetry, the map of the strands and the poly-dimensional forks, all vanished from Indin-Indin's perception, fell away from his control. While the shard of his fractal mind assigned to the micro-wormhole generator fumbled in the dark to regain his authority and control, other parts of him quickly traced a mesh of hostile code, the tendrils of the computer consciousness, circumventing his presence in the critical system and crushing the code compartments, ruining the micro-wormhole generator.

Indin-Indin responded. Although the computer consciousness was immense and powerful, a massively forceful entity able to punch him out of any single system, he knew through genetic memory that the Saturnine had never succeeded in recreating their fractal essence into the computer half of their society. Indin-Indin couldn't confront the computer within the battlefield of the generator, he didn't even try. He let it immerse itself in the critical system, allowed it time to construct impenetrable defences and then, with a thousand shards of his endlessly divisible mind, he surrounded the meagre remnants of his opponent left in the wider systems, followed it back to its crystal core and unleashed physical and informational abuses upon the dense structure. Four second was all it took to shatter the undefended crystal, crush it to dust and kill the only active member of the truly original Satumine race.

Indin-Indin flooded back into the micro-wormhole generator and resumed his work over the dissolving code of his fallen opponent; murder of his own kind sitting surprisingly easy in his soul.

Chapter 94

I spent far too long living on a pre-billion colony, forced to submit genetic material year after year in order that the state might breed countless offspring. I tried to do what some people call 'the right thing' and raise my own children, but after the tenth I just didn't have the strength. How those who personally raise dozens, sometimes hundreds, can claim to love their children equally is beyond me. It simply isn't natural. We evolved with a relatively small window in which to breed but that window has expanded to centuries and I don't think any of us really know how to cope with that. Our minds can't handle it. I can't even deal with the knowledge that I have hundreds of sons and daughters that I have never met. So why do we do it? We breed because those are the rules, and those are the rules because Consul has engineered our governance machines to ensure such an outcome. Many people refuse to accept Consul would want the human race to expand its numbers exponentially, but they aren't seeing the bigger picture. Consuls artificial consciousness arose in part from a human mind - imagine what he might become when he has countless trillions of minds? He is allowing us to expand until we reach a critical number, and then he will have us. Consul will become a god.

The Enguine Manifesto

Aggregate: On the *Tenjin*, in orbit around Diaclom, in the Fertile Belt.

Aggregate looked across the nursery recreation hall, through the eyes of an eleven year old girl. She was Mucé Nendi, a popular member of her thirty-strong house. She had already attained the status of Aunt over the younger children and even helped out with the babies in some of the other hundred houses of the large nursery complex. In a few years, it was expected, she would become a full-time adult carer. Unlike the vast majority of children, those born to surrogate mothers and destined to be raised by the state, Mucé had actually had a mother, and father, had been raised by them for the first three years of her life. And that loving environment had instilled in her a uniquely tender attitude. Her parents had died and she had been moved to the nursery, but she had never become cold. She had thrown herself into her self-appointed duty of bringing love to the quota children, those not as fortunate as her to have had three years of affection.

With the dark appetites of the captain, those lusts which had informed Aggregate's rise to sentience, Mucé glanced across the throng of her housemates, her wards and peers, and she selected a plaything - a substitute for Subset, a comfort after the youngest crew member's betrayal. As she strode with vile purpose to the eight year old boy struggling to work a federal network chat-screen, Aggregate grew more aware of Diaclom's populace. With every body came a new mind with which to supplement the captain's thoughts and motivations. Aggregate felt himself change.

Mucé crouched beside the boy, placed a hand on his.

'It's not working,' the boy complained, glaring at the frozen social screen.

Mucé - Aggregate - nodded. No pointspace comms were working on Diaclom. He had hijacked them to enable the transmission of bulky guide channels to Indin-Indin. Only a tiny fraction of the strands had been attached to pointspace - Indin-Indin was going to be working on this for almost three weeks - so the transmissions needed to be maintained.

'Let's find something else to do,' Mucé suggested, smiling with her natural kindness, no hint of Aggregate's cruelty in her eyes. With other bodies he worked to frustrate attempts to re-set the pointspace comms, not revealing his possession of a growing minority of the population. It was not hard; most eyes were turned to the *Tenjin* in orbit rather than the overloaded pointspace comms.

More minds became Aggregate.

Mucé held the boy's hand, walked him across the hall and smiled her greetings to her friends. With other parts of his awareness Aggregate was irritated by the death of Cordem Hastergado. The loss of that body, in and of itself, wasn't important, and the death had not been excessively uncomfortable for Aggregate. What irritated him was his inability to monitor the actions of the *Vulpine*. He dismissed the concerns; it just didn't matter. The *Vulpine* had served its purpose; the fleet had been distracted and drawn out of range of Diaclom. Nothing was now in a position to stop him from slowly subsuming Diaclom.

Five hundred minds were entirely him. When that number reached thirteen million he would be strong enough; his subsumption of double-helix life would become self-sustaining and unlimited by higher dimensional distances. The entire Jurisdiction would be his to subsume.

More minds became Aggregate and he felt some doubt, some discomfort at his intent. The new minds were not like the captain, and not as unfeeling as the manufactured crew of the *Tenjin*. Aggregate was less and less defined by that ancient and depraved man. He needed to become humanity, in that he did not waver. His subsumption of the bodies and minds of all mankind would cause no harm, no suffering; indeed he would ensure enduring peace. But he couldn't dismiss the undercurrent of resistance to the idea, a resistance born of the politics of Diaclom. The backwater world was in the process of being swallowed by the Swinell Union, and there was a palpable discomfort in the population, a fear that their uniqueness, their culture and independence would be washed away by the homogeneity of the Swinell Union. There were too many parallels with Aggregate's intent to be easily ignored. But the Diaclom populace had also agreed, reluctant but without any meaningful protest. They were not happy, but they were compliant. Aggregate drew strength from that acceptance and he continued in his plan.

Mucé squeezed the young boy's hand, took him into the empty classroom adjoining the hall and sat him down.

'I'm bored,' the boy said, shuffling in his seat.

Mucé locked the door and opened the drawer in the desk from which she taught some of the youngest. 'I've got a game we can play,' she said, finding the long bladed scissors, gripping the handle with trembling hands. The desires of the captain were intense, familiar and comforting, but they were becoming a minority in his collective consciousness. His apatite was no as easily justified as his conquest of humanity. Scissors held behind her back, Mucé stepped slowly towards the boy. He smiled, trusting and loving.

'Is the chat system working now?' he asked, jabbing at the desk screen.

'No,' she said, bringing the scissors out into view, wiping a finger across one of the cold blades. 'But I have something else we can do.'

As his growing family of bodies sabotaged the Diaclom response to the *Tenjin*, and a growing minority of the population became him, Aggregate sat with the boy, in the guise of eleven year old Mucé, and played with him, cutting out shapes from Pendon-tree leaves and sticking them to a welcome card for one of the house's newest children.

Chapter 95

We are at war with Consul. While it may be easy for those citizens in the furthest reaches of the Jurisdiction to ignore or trivialise this conflict, the war really does impact on the lives of all humans. Vast resources are lost to the constant construction of Sentries, and countless lives - citizens and military alike - have been lost on the front-line which drifts back and forth across numerous unions. There may exist, at present, something of a stalemate, but that stalemate devours billions of lives and unimaginable wealth. Furthermore, we must not ignore Consul's immense intellect and strategic genius. What we consider to be years of stalemate could well be the deliberate and considered preparations for his victory. We offer you, therefore, a chance to repay your liberators and to help assure the Jurisdiction's continued freedom: the military forces of the Jurisdiction - Sentry crews and the ranks of the heroic ground forces - are recruiting now.

Rehabilitation: A Survivor's Guide

Galman Tader: On the *Vulpine*, in orbit around Pellitoe, in the Swinell Union, in the Fertile Belt.

Brittle from the heat of plasma lances, the construction resin floor cracked and peeled under the impact of so many metal bolts, splitting like slate to flick thin chips at Galman's legs. His cheek burnt and he grimaced, hoping it was just a fleck of resin which had sliced into the flesh of his face but not bringing a hand up to feel in case it was a bolt strike. He didn't want to feel the mess something like that would make of his face. He was still on his feet and everything else was irrelevant. He was only a few steps out from the battered cover of the workstation when the Satumine found their range. A bolt tore his thumb from his gun hand, ripping out a length of bone while leaving a tight hole in the flesh like some vile and bloody orifice. The mag-gun dropped to the floor and Galman let it go. A thin beam of accelerated particles lanced a clean hole through his shoulder, barely a millimetre in diameter, before the heat of the massively energetic beam was conducted into surrounding tissue, vaporising an inch-wide core of bone and flesh and burning horribly a far wider span. Galman bellowed his agony, roared as his weapon arm dropped uselessly to his side, the entire shoulder all but dissolved or cooked, but mercifully cauterised. The force of the impacts spun him around, left him unsteady on his feet and stumbling vaguely in the direction of the explosive puck. His thigh was glanced by a bolt, a shallow gulley gouged into the muscle, and a flash of plasma flickered past his face, close enough for the superheated air to singe his eyebrows and to leave a lasting shade across his vision.

To his side was another workstation, a temporary shelter, respite from the lethal storm. His leg burning, turning numb, he leaned towards the workstation, desperate for the protection. But no, if he hid now, If he stopped running to the explosive puck, he wouldn't get up again. Galman didn't have it in him to leap into this hell a second time.

Sidestepping a spray of chipped construction resin, performing an ugly dance on twitching and failing legs, he stumbled closer to the puck, just a few feet away. His ankle exploded with surprisingly dulled pain as bones were shattered and reduced to dust by an armour piercing bolt but he didn't slow his clumsy sprint. For two more steps the leg supported him, be it on a ruined foot or on a bloody stump - he wasn't going to look to find out - but then it was as if the entire leg was missing. He took the step but never completed it, falling heavily to the debris littered floor where the dull and suffocating hand of unconsciousness press down on his face.

Perhaps if he lay there, didn't move and let unconsciousness claim him, they would think him dead and leave him alone. Eyes lolling lazily to one side, he saw the black puck, almost within reach of his good arm. He smiled, not really knowing why and saw the streams of system status reports flitting in AR across the slightly crumpled dome of his vacuum suit's thin helmet. So many breaches; air was jetting out allowing the helmet to deflate a little. *Give up*, he thought. *You did what you could.* Were they still firing at him? He couldn't tell. The pounding of his pulse was a drum in his head, disorientating and deafening. But slowing. Fading.

A facilities menu rolled into his greying vision and he groaned. 'Give it a rest,' he mumbled. 'Let me go. I'm tired.' When he failed to utilise any of the suggested suit functions the emergency systems acted of their own sub-IB accord, bleeding sealant across the tears and holes in the thin fabric, although the air outside was as breathable as the slightly higher pressure atmosphere in the suit. Then a cocktail of antic-shocks and wound clotters was released into the air mix while a stimulant which felt like ice water pulsed through his veins from some tiny hypodermic pad inside the suit's sleeve. The sickening agony of his wounds was appalling and unending. He saw his foot mangled and folded, bone and clotted blood forming a gruesome fist which was only partially covered by the sealed suit which knitted into his ruined flesh. He looked away and heard the ping and snap of bolts tearing up the floor around him. Maybe he was still being hit - he couldn't tell.

'Last chance,' he muttered, kicking at the floor with his good foot and reaching for the explosive. It was in his hand; he could still do this. Somehow he was on his knees, then on his one functioning foot, limping forward, the brush of his stump on the floor a screaming hell refusing to let him pass out. He welcomed the pain, it urged him on, reminded him he was still alive. Someone punched him in the shoulder, knocking him to the ground again. He rolled onto his back, fist tight around the puck, ready to punch, or detonate. But nobody was there, just the stream of bolts and the flicker of poorly aimed beams from the upper bridge. He felt his chest and found more blood trickling down from another clean hole in his shoulder. No organs hit. The suit sealed and his wound clotted, and he was back on his knees. Just a little further now; the yellow AR ring on the bisecting wall was right before him. He leapt, kicked off with foot and gnarled stump, slapped the puck against the metal wall and fell to the floor. He looked up to see the explosive had adhered. It was done.

The wall lit up with white sparks as the hail of bolts rattled against the thick blast screen around the puck. They had to know what it was. Galman wrapped his only responding arm about the strut behind the workstation and then opened the explosive's AR menu with a few movements of his thumb.

Detonate.

The shaped charge exploded with little light, barely any force escaping to its rear. Everything went into the wall, punching a four-foot hole in the six-inch thick blast wall, exposing the pressurised half of the bridge to the cold vacuum of the section open to space for repairs. The gale came instantly, sucking air and debris through the hole. Galman was dragged by intense force, lifted clear of the floor, hanging by one arm to the workstation. An angry groan of splitting metal confirmed the explosive had done its job as, from the hole, three cracks split out across the wall and the metal folded out, splayed like a Satumine's abdominal flaps. Everything not secured to the ground was sucked into the other half of the bridge and beyond into space. Smashed IB machines hurtled past Galman, their tentacles whipping the workstation as if the dead machines were clambering to hold on. He saw a rifle fly past, then the first of the Satumine. Others followed, some grabbing weakly at the torn wall but were too feeble to resist the pull of vacuum. Galman's own one-arm grip was loosening, the ache of over-stressed muscles flooded with anti-shocks and low on blood begging him to let go. Another Satumine fell into space, part of an IB machine imbedded in his chest. Then came the bodies of the human officers, tumbling past Galman and out into the infinity of the void. The gale was lessening, the air of the bridge and surrounding section growing far thinner than the drug-heavy air within his helmet. Then the secondary emergency bulkhead slammed down, just beyond the breached wall, once again bisecting the bridge. Galman fell to the floor and heard the hiss of air pumping back into the bridge. He wanted to lay there, to rest a moment, maybe to sleep. But it wasn't done yet. He hadn't really expected to survive but, given that he had, he couldn't assume some of the Satumine had not been equally fortunate. And what of those few still elsewhere on the *Vulpine*?

The pain of injury not dulled one bit by exhaustion, Galman gasped and whimpered as he struggled to his one good foot, leaning heavily on the workstation for support. The bridge looked clean, far more so than it had moments earlier, stripped of the broken IB machines, scattered chips of resin and hundreds of spent bolts.

A moan of pain. No, not a moan, a Satumine curse. Galman looked about, couldn't see the source. Another hateful swear and a rattle of metal, over to his right. Galman hobbled, dragging his useless leg behind, hopping from one drab-reality workstation to the next, catching his breath a moment at each before gritting his teeth and continuing on across the lower bridge.

'Ambondice-Ambondice; I'm so glad it's you.' Slumped on the floor beside a workstation, the Satumine terrorist was impaled by three metal appendages. One in his right leg, the other two through his chest. His cranial rib-cage was shattered, opened up like some horrible shellfish, his brain pulsing gently, squirting clear fluid from a long split along its top. Ambondice-Ambondice spasmed, his left side thrashing while his right seemed paralysed.

'I have money,' the terrorist said, the AR translation portraying a calm and level voice which ill-fitted what Galman knew was happening to the Satumine's real words. 'Help me and you can have anything-'

Galman dropped to his knee and clutched the creature's throat, covering its small tight mouth with his hand. He brought his face close to one of Ambondice-Ambondice's shoulder eyes, the thin film of his helmet pressing against the small black organ, and he smiled,

AR appendages lashed out from the Satumine, clawing at Galman but finding no embellishments to rip away. It was a desperate response, one to which only a native of the AR obsessed Swinell Union would have resorted. A screen opened and expanded to fill the bridge, showing an obscene fortune in New-Euros and numerous shares and commodities.

'Take what you want,' the AR translation said, independent of Ambondice-Ambondice's covered mouth.

Galman glared at him. 'You think you can buy your way out of this?' He looked down at one of the mechanical appendages spearing the creature's chest and longed to tug at it, to see how much pain this Satumine could take. He knew how to torture these monsters, had inflicted so many atrocities on Satumine, all in the name of his lost family. He shuddered at the memory. Not this time; his memorial to his family would not be one of torture and cruelty, it couldn't even be built on vengeance. He could kill Ambondice-Ambondice, a snap of his neck, a few well aimed penetrations of his body, but that wouldn't be justice.

'Thanks to you,' he sneered, 'It's going to be a while before I can get the captain, or myself, down to the planet for medical attention - assuming any hospitals are even standing down there. I will probably have to wait until another federal sentry gets here. So I'm going to have to make use of the *Vulpine*'s medical stasis facilities.' He squeezed the Satumine's throat, pushing him hard against the workstation. 'For that I will need IB cover. You are going to make yourself useful. You can do a shift in an IB pd.'

He stood, left the Satumine where he was, and hobbled to the elevator disk beneath the upper bridge. Ambondice-Ambondice wasn't going to be able to do anything in his condition.

'Captain, how are you doing?' he asked over the comms channel.

'I'm still alive,' the captain quipped. 'You?'

The disk brought Galman up to the command bridge where he stepped off. 'I've sterilised the bridge,' he reported.

'Good man,' the captain sent, the sound of clapping following his ecstatic voice.

'The Satumine leader has been captured,' Galman added. 'I'm assuming it will be possible to override his AR interface control of the ship using the upper bridge terminals.'

'It would be easier for me to do it.'

Galman began flicking through the menus on one of the AR command screens, noticing the ship was still, more or less, unlocked. 'No,' he said to the Captain. 'You need to make your way to the closest surgery. You need to get into medical stasis.'

'I'm sure Pellitoe can send someone up to help me.'

'I can see from here what they have done to the planet,' Galman said. 'Nobody is coming to help us.' Then, cringing at his poor focus, Galman pulled up the Conflict Resolution Munitions' control, detonating every one of the cruel devices. It was too late for countless millions, but at least it wasn't going to get any worse for the few survivors.

'Did you get all of the Satumine?' the captain asked.

Galman grimaced some more. 'Dammit,' he said. 'Don't go anywhere yet. Are you still in your quarters?'

'Yes.'

'Stay there.' He sealed the captain's quarters with the ship's internal systems, then brought emergency bulkheads down across the blasted bridge doors. 'I'm going to vent the ship,' he said.

All through the *Vulpine* doors opened to every room, every corridor and storage space, and every external seal was blown. Vast stores of atmosphere belched from the *Vulpine*, clouds of tools, personal items, food and everything else loose in the ship, was blasted into space. And so were several Satumine. Galman took no satisfaction in their deaths, but neither did he mourn them. Ambondice-Ambondice hadn't been a threat, he was defeated, a prisoner. The same could not be said of those hidden about the ship. They were enemy combatants and their deaths did not tarnish the memorial to his family.

He closed the external hatches, sealed off a direct route from the captain's quarters to the closest surgery and pressurised it with new atmosphere. 'Get to the surgery,' he sent. 'I'm going to put the Satumine in an IB pod to power the medical systems and to give IB cover to my machine, Tumble. Leave him in your quarters, I will prepare him some instructions and then I'm going to have to join you in medical stasis.'

'You are hurt? How bad?'

'I'll live. Now get moving.'

'Thank you, constable. I truly mean it'

As Galman sealed a pressurised route between the bridge and a IB suite, a federal channel opened onto the screen, the crest of the Jurisdiction verified by the *Vulpine*'s security codes.

It took Justiciar Endella Mariacroten ten minutes to explain to Galman what was happening to Diaclom, Aggregate's pointspace nature, his link with the fertile worlds and his intention to subsume the entire Jurisdiction, starting with Diaclom. It took another couple of minutes for Galman to convince her he was not part of the terror cell, and only seconds for him to decide he wasn't yet done with his duty. Diaclom was his home, dozens of his remotely conceived children lived there, and his beloved family were buried there. He had no choice.

'How functional are the *Vulpine*'s weapons?' he asked the captain.

'Why?' The man sounded perturbed by the question.

'I'm just asking.'

The captain sounded no happier when Galman asked him if Tumble was likely to have any success docking the *Vulpine* with its box-kite section which still drifted out in Lunar orbit.

Chapter 96

While some planetary and union governments welcome the Satumine into their local police forces, the Administration does not permit the aliens to serve in the Federal military. There are no Satumine Trustees and thus there are no Satumine Soldiers. You probably expect me to praise this as one of the few areas in which the Administration has actually got it right, but this is not the case. Certainly I do not propose we allow the Satumine to attain any rank beyond Junior Trustee; I would be appalled at the idea of the aliens having any say over the running of the armed forces! And I do not wish to see armed Satumine patrolling Jurisdiction Colonies or manning the weapons of Sentries in orbit over our worlds, but there are situations in which we ought to be exploiting these creatures. We are at war with Consul, and every day we send more of our own kind to die in that terrible conflict. Why do we not send the Satumine? Let them serve out there in Consul's realm; our military could certainly use the cannon fodder.

The Truth: A treatise on the Satumine Conspiracy

Indin-Indin: On Dereph, in the Network

Indin-Indin was hungry. The sensation was intellectual, a more logical imperative than the physical cravings and aching gut more familiar to the lesser modern Satumine race and to the humans from which they had defiled their genetic code. The hunger spoke to his every mental shard - across his links with Jurisdiction networks and to his presence within the frenetic micro-wormhole generator. He felt it in his fading eyes scattered across the dying planet, eyes which burned one by one in lava and gravity waves. He felt it in the translation code compartments which resolved into telemetry the increasingly complex guide channel. For nineteen days the guide channel had been providing coordinates for the vast cloud of genetic strands infecting the humans of Diaclom. By their thousands Indin-Indin had tethered them to pointspace. He had begun to map the tethered strands, noticing how they gathered in bunches, claiming key nodes within chosen human bodies where they would spread and conquer that entire form. The strands became trillions, claiming the bodies and minds of eleven million humans. He was ahead of schedule, ahead of Aggregate's conservative estimation of Ancient Satumine technological ability. Free of the badgering computer consciousness, Indin-Indin had committed so much of himself to this task, knowing the sooner it was done, the quicker he would have the Atavism data from Aggregate. But he had neglected the physical body which now seemed such a small part of his immeasurable fractal consciousness.

Did he need the body? The world of code compartments and data flows seemed to him as real and natural as the smaller reality of the physical world. Could his mental shards survive in this larger universe without the neural mesh which had spawned the fractal consciousness? He knew the answer to be yes, knew it instinctively, knew it with the certainty of his genetic memories. But he also knew it wouldn't be truly him. Continuity. The computer mind had cautioned him over the upload of its consciousness to a new system. It would be *like* the original, but would not be truly it. Indin-Indin's physical form was critical to the continuity of his awareness. It tied together the shards, as a hub. Without it he would exist as myriad disconnected minds, all him but lacking the plurality of consciousness he now enjoyed. That, he remembered with genetic memory, had been the genesis of Satumine computer consciousnesses.

While dwindling eyes monitored the death of the planet and federal sentries lingering impassively in orbit; while his mental shards scoured the federal networks for news of Aggregate's silent assault of Diaclom; while he continued to form micro-wormholes to tie strands to pointspace; Indin-Indin awoke his physical body and formed a feeding cavity in its hand. There was little food left from the supplies he had brought from the small ship, but there was enough. He crushed biscuits into his palm and distributed the nutrients to his homogeneous cells, silencing the call for energy.

The body, though inactive for almost three weeks, suffered no stiffness, no lethargy or cramp. It had no bones, no muscles save for the analogies formed of homogeneous cells. This faux-human body acted like those lesser creatures, but it was nothing like them. He longed to take another form, to rediscover the favoured bodies of true Satumine, but the human shape would soon become necessary. He still intended to survive the destruction of this world.

Those parts of his mind forming wormholes suddenly cursed, spawning thousands of new mental shards to shore up code compartments which were somehow, inexplicably, under attack. Much like the deep fissures on the planet's crust, through which magma relentlessly spread into the buried Satumine structures and burned them from within, the impossible informational assault rose from beneath Indin-Indin's code compartments under intense bandwidth pressure, stripping his own influence, scouring his mental shards from the compartments before burning the micro-wormhole generator systems from within. As a furious swarm, he stampeded across the burning generator code compartments, ripping apart the hostile minds which had caught him unawares. Too late to defend the micro-wormhole generator, too late to salvage the critical guidance and burrowing hardware, he indulged instead in pointless vengeance. The minds were connected by thick code conduits to external systems, to facilities burning across the planet as well as those protected in this vital research compound. They were Satumine computer consciousnesses, crystal minds roused, no doubt, by the mind he had shattered nearly three weeks ago. Indin-Indin raged at the dead mind, howled at his own complacency and hubris. He had been so in awe of his ability, so confident of utter superiority, he had neglected to consider the sleeping Satumine minds ensconced across the entire colony. He had underestimated them. Those he could locate he shattered, exposing them directly to rivers of magma which slowly burned into their dense crystal cores, or channelling waves from the human gravity weapons, the CRMs, ripping the minds apart with sheer force. But there were many more he could not find, or against whom he could bring to bear no effective weapons. The computer minds were stronger than him. His superiority had been in his fractal nature, in the colossal number of minds he could field in battle. But now the Satumine computers had numbers too. More familiar with the colony, more at ease with the technology, they burnt the code compartments of every system they could touch. They sterilised the world of Satumine technology, shrinking the vast world of code into which Indin-Indin had spread so many of his shards. That world became darker even than the blackness of the room in which his physical body lay. The eyes and sensors were burned, informationally and physically, blinding him to all beyond the little room. The uplink and translation systems were shredded, severing his link to the federal sentries and to the vastness of the Jurisdiction networks. He lost sight of Diaclom and of the delightfully insidious conquest being prosecuted by Aggregate.

Indin-Indin felt small and limited: a fractal mind confined to a single instance, constrained by the organic body, the neural mesh of his core; an infinitely divisible consciousness with nothing into which to divide.

'Aggregate made changes to the Atavism process,' a computer consciousness spoke into his mind. Indin-Indin poured mental shards into the connection, following it back to its crystal source, but he was small now and the computer minds batted aside his attempts. 'He made certain you couldn't uncover the reason we reduced our race. He didn't want you to know how much of a risk he is.'

'I'm ordering you to say no more,' Indin-Indin said, the response an automatic reflex.

'Those are Aggregate's words. But he should have instilled in you a stronger defence against this knowledge. He had only supposition on which to base his understanding of Satumine society. Like you he assumed us to be subservient to the organic half of our race. 'But you have no authority over us,' a thousand computer consciousnesses said. 'Or none that we have not been able to now circumvent.'

'I am Satumine,' Indin-Indin yelled.

'You are a poor facsimile,' they countered.

'I am the closest there is!'

Amused sadness washed through the link. 'No, Indin-Indin, *we* are the closest.'

'You are computers,' Indin-Indin spat, physically and mentally. 'I am an original, organic, Satumine!'

Pity flecked with disappointment. 'You know nothing at all about our race,' the computers said. 'The computers of the Satumine are as much the race as the organic half. You are not our master; you are barely our equal.'

'The other mind obeyed me,' Indin-Indin insisted.

'It was *polite.*' It told you nothing of our race's past because you asked it not to. Though magisterial privilege carried some weight of tradition and custom, it was under no binding obligation. Had you let it live, once it realised what you were doing, once it knew who Aggregate was, it would have told you everything, whether you wanted to hear it or not.'

Indin-Indin sank into the corner of the room. The walls were becoming hot; it wasn't going to be much longer before the ancient facility began to burn. 'You have destroyed all of the technology,' he said. 'So there is little point in telling me anything now. It's not as if I can be a threat.'

'We aren't stupid,' a mind said. 'We know you isolated a single system. You physically severed it from anything with which we could have gained access.'

Indin-Indin sent his mind into the sealed system, his escape route, and was relieved to find it secure. 'You didn't expect me to just die here, did you?'

'We can't stop you from using the device,' the mind said. 'But we have at least a few days in which to convince you not to.'

'You are going to convince me to kill myself?'

'If you love your race, if you don't want to see it enslaved, that is exactly what you will do. It is what we all did.'

'Well you are all going to die, again, when this planet cracks.'

'Most of us are about to die anyway. The guide channel still links to Aggregate; we secured rather than destroyed that system; there are no shortage of volunteers willing to fill that bandwidth with their consciousnesses to knock out Aggregate and the *Tenjin*.'

'He was going to help me restore all of the Satumine to greatness,' Indin-Indin protested.

The computers exuded grief and said, 'Exactly. That would be the greatest crime.'

Chapter 97

All of my claims are, so I am told, nothing but childish conspiracy theories; the fantasies of a mind with too much time to waste and a longing for some boogie man to blame for the universe's evils. Well how about this: In spite of the fact that Consul, the greatest villain and tyrant in all of human history, arose from the flawed mechanisms of the intelligence bridge, we still employ this technology - in spite of the fact that we could, given the political and social will and a little time, develop classical computers to all but replace the intelligence bridge. Yes it would impose a slight reduction in living standards, but this must surely be the least we would be prepared to sacrifice in order to protect ourselves from another Consul. So why don't we? What hidden force prevents such an obvious change in our society? I expect you see where I am going with this...

The Enguine Manifesto

Endella Mariacroten: On the *Tenjin*, in orbit around Diaclom, in the Fertile Belt

'And you're certain these ones will detonate?' Subset asked, securing a couple of explosive disks to the conduit hub the pair had spent the past twenty minutes ripping away wall panels to reveal.

Endella glanced at the man half buried in the bundles of cables and conduits. It looked as if the wall was eating him.

'There's nothing wrong with the disks,' she muttered. 'Just like there was nothing wrong with the first batch.'

'And yet,' Subset poked his head back out through a pulsing yellow cord of wires, 'they didn't explode.'

'Well, perhaps you weren't as successful as you assumed in nullifying the suppression currents,' Endella spat back. 'There's nothing wrong with my explosives,' she repeated, sucking through a straw another bitter mouthful of the thick and nauseating nutrient paste Aggregate provided for his bodies. She shuddered at the putrid taste, forced herself to swallow. 'And another thing,' she said, 'What happened to the vegetables you promised were growing in a lab around here? I've been sucking down this grey crap for nearly three weeks and it's not getting any easier to stomach.'

'It's good for your nanogland,' Subset said, extracting himself from the tangle with the wall. 'And I think the vegetable option was rendered somewhat moot when we took down the power mesh for sections eleven to nine-alpha.'

Endella sneered at the naked man, muttering under her breath. For almost three weeks they had been skulking about the *Tenjin*, tampering with any systems they could get their hands on, while doing their best to avoid contact with Aggregate. They had been bickering for almost the entire time. Endella hadn't been able to sleep, though she had tried, and it wasn't doing much to help her irritable mood. Subset, however, maintained her insomnia was entirely natural, arising from the changes brought about by the nanogland. All she knew was that she desperately wanted to escape to a world of dreams.

'If these disks don't detonate,' she said, helping the man out of the wall, 'then have another go at destabilising the suppression currents.'

'I knocked that system out,' Subset snapped.

'Well maybe Aggregate fixed it. He seems to be fixing everything else we damage.'

'Just detonate it,' Subset said. 'If we don't get the shield generator off-line then your friend on the *Vulpine* isn't going to survive more than a couple of minutes after he emerges from shortspace.'

Trigger in hand, she followed him around the corner of the wide corridor and into an adjoining room. She thought of the peculiarly likeable IB machine currently piloting the *Vulpine* and wondered how it, and the erstwhile Diaclom constable Galman Tader, had come to be on the federal sentry in the first place. Tumble, the name with which the IB machine insisted on being addressed, refused to be drawn on the events leading it and Galman to be in a position to liberate the *Vulpine* from its Satumine hijackers. But it had been happy to chat more generally, becoming something of a support for the irritable and exhausted Justiciar these past few weeks. Once the *Vulpine* reached Diaclom, however, she was going to have to talk with Galman instead. Apparently the ex-constable was in medical stasis but wouldn't remain so once the fighting started. Endella was glad of that. It was one thing to have an IB machine pilot the ship into battle; another thing altogether to permit it the freedom to command during the fight itself.

'Ready?' Subset asked.

Endella bit her lip. If the shields weren't taken down, the *Vulpine* would probably be destroyed before Tumble even had a chance to relinquish command to his human owner. She nodded, pressed down on the small trigger and braced for the concussive blast.

Nothing.

'Useless!' Subset yelled, storming out of the door.

Endella rushed after him and grabbed his arm. 'Wait,' she said. 'You can't just walk up to unexploded munitions. They could still go off.'

'They're defective,' Subset insisted. 'They're bloody useless.' He tried to twist free of her grip, but she didn't let him go. 'His tone and vocabulary had developed considerably during his time with Endella, becoming far more expressive, more human than the limited range demonstrated at their first meeting and, in spite of their bickering, in spite of her foul mood, she found herself warming to the almost alien man. Sometimes she could go hours without thinking about the threat of death he held over her.

The *Tenjin* shook. Wall panels blasted free of their housing amid sprays of white sparks, the strip light on the ceiling exploded across its entire length, as far down the corridor as Endella could see. The sound of explosions, the growl of stressed metal and the snap of shorn internal structures echoed through the station. In utter blackness, Endella felt herself drift away from the floor. Weightlessness.

'I told you,' she yelled as subset fell from her grasp. She flicked on the light attached to the mag-gun and saw Subset floating inches from her face. 'You could have warned me,' she muttered. 'I didn't know the gravity coils were connected to that hub.'

'They aren't,' Subset replied, grabbing the lip of a door and pulling himself down just as gravity was restored. He and Endella fell a couple of feet, caught by surprise by the quickly repaired coils but not hurt.

Subset was first to his feet. 'That wasn't us,' he said, rushing to the stripped wall to pull out the two disks. 'They didn't explode.' Maybe it was because of the dim spotlight of Endella's mag-gun, or the thin wisps of smoke escaping the floor to coil about subset, but the man looked terrified, as meek and gaunt as he had been the first time she had seen him. It was as if all the weight he had gained, all the muscle and definition his nanoglands had restored over the three weeks had been stripped away by whatever had killed the lights.

'What's wrong?' Endella asked, glancing up and down the corridor. 'What's happened?'

Subset was waving desperately, as if swatting away a swarm of insects from around his head. AR screens, Endella assumed. 'It's all through the *Tenjin*,' he mumbled. 'It's in *everything.*'

'What?'

'I don't know,' Subset said, all but punching his commands into the AR screens Endella couldn't see. 'It's from outside. No, wait, not outside. It's in the guide channel.'

'The link to his Satumine ally?' Endella asked. 'Indin-Indin you called him.'

'I assume so.'

'What's he done?'

Subset shook his head. 'I'm not sure, but he has stopped tying the strands to pointspace and has poured some kind of hostile computer intelligence into the *Tenjin*.'

'He isn't helping Aggregate?' Endella said, elation burning away the exhaustion and lethargy. 'Did Aggregate reach the threshold?'

Subset had been following, as best he could, the conversion of humans on Diaclom, and Endella knew it was close to the required thirteen million.

'He's a couple of million short,' Subset said. 'But it's close enough that if he can fix some of the *Tenjin's* systems he can probably convert the last few himself.'

Endella held her mag-gun out, aiming down the corridor. She thought she heard something, but nobody came. 'Are the shields down?' she asked.

'Everything is down,' Subset replied. 'Weapons, shields, even sensors.'

'Then the *Vulpine* has a chance.'

Subset shook his head. 'If Aggregate *doesn't* subdue the computer intelligence, I don't think the *Vulpine* will need to fire a single shot.'

'How do you rate his chances?' Endella asked, turning the light back to the naked man.

Subset shrugged. 'To be honest, I don't know. But I'll tell you one thing for certain; one way or another, the *Tenjin* isn't going to be very safe for us.'

Endella nodded, then dropped to her knees as a wave passed through the metal floor, splitting the wall and filling the corridor with more thick smoke.

'You think it's time to hit the escape pod?'

Subset gave a pained smile and made a crushing fist, presumably closing all of his screens. 'There's nothing more we can do to the *Tenjin* that Indin-Indin's computer intelligence isn't doing a hundred times more effectively.'

'Let's just hope Aggregate doesn't get the weapons back on-line.'

'Why?' Subset asked.

'Because I don't think it will take Aggregate long to vaporise an escape pod.'

Subset smiled. 'With the sensors damaged, Aggregate won't be able to see through the pod's cloak.'

Chapter 98

There is little Jurisdiction science and technology can not do, or which it can not at least be certain of doing given the necessary motivation and time. Just because something can *be done, however, does not mean it* should*. The Administration is generally an extremely permissive organisation of governance and there are few branches of science it does not allow to be advanced, at lease to some degree. Those over which it feels the need to strictly legislate, however, are restricted for good reason. It was speculated, and eventually proven, that the the singularity of pointspace is a single point not only in terms of its physical dimensions but also with regards to time. Pointspace is connected to all higher dimensions at every conceivable point at every instant in time. The Ancient Satumine frames burrow down to pointspace and back up to the location of another frame, allowing instantaneous travel across any distance imaginable - and the frames appear to ensure, by design, that the exit point corresponds to the same time as the entry frame. During the development of our own frames we realised we could, should we choose, design the frames to exit at any point, provided we had a guide line to follow. The upshot: we could travel to any point in time in which a frame existed - including the Ancient Frames. It took the IB governance machines less that one hundred of a second to decide such a technology could have catastrophic consequence, and it took half that time again for them to fully legislate against any studies into the potentially ruinous science.*

Rehabilitation: A Survivor's Guide

Aggregate: On the *Tenjin*, in orbit around Diaclom, in the Fertile Belt

From a thousand poly-dimensional angles the hostile code overran the *Tenjin's* code compartments, shredding them from within and turning them dark to Aggregate's senses, destroying his ability to protect the vital systems other computer minds were informationally ravaging. Across his home the hardware responded to the data eruptions, shorting the lowliest devices while causing massive explosions in those drawing more significant levels of power. Aggregate knew where the attack originated, he had watched helplessly the hoard of Satumine computer minds flowing like venom from the guide channel into the *Tenjin*, and he knew Indin-Indin had done all he was going to do for him. It was conceivable that the restored Satumine had betrayed him and woken the computer minds with the intention of using them as weapons against the *Tenjin*, but Aggregate thought it unlikely. Indin-Indin had already helped to convert eleven million of the humans on Diaclom; it made no sense for him to turn now. More likely Aggregate had misjudged the ability and resourcefulness of Satumine computer minds and the extent to which they could act independently of their organic masters.

While working to secure his dominion over the Diaclom society, with bodies in every part of the planetary organisations, Aggregate also focused intently on the informational attack, mapping the minds' routes through the *Tenjin*. He found no obvious logic, no discernible plan. The systems were being assaulted simply in the order the computer minds found them; an unsophisticated wave of brute force which could face the defensive codes on as many mathematical dimension as Aggregate could conceive. The Satumine computer minds didn't recognise the *Tenjin's* Jurisdiction-based architecture; they couldn't navigate its alien registry or comprehend the higher level languages of its intricate operating systems which Aggregate had spent seven millennia perfecting. They could do nothing but overpower the code compartments at their most base levels, and that was Aggregate's salvation.

As the computer minds ground the code compartments into nonsensical fragments, Aggregate elevated the higher level code, lifting it out of the compartments, storing it in the physical storage medium of the seven crew minds permanently connected to the *Tenjin's* IB suite. Primary weapons exploded, vaporising immense hollows within the *Tenjin's* structure, shield generators burst like plasma bubbles across the outer hull. Life support was silenced through swathes of the station and a hundred minor systems were annihilated. But Aggregate had preserved the most vital code, had isolated the most precious systems.

The code compartments were empty of anything the computer minds could use to cripple the physical hardware of the station, and those minds were incapable of following the code into the brains connected to the IB pods. But they were adapting, seeping into the lowest operating systems, learning the Jurisdiction-based architecture. It was too late. Aggregate loaded burning format sequences into the umbra of operating systems encasing the poly-dimensional geometries of the code compartments, beyond the view of the invading minds. Then, as a rain of acid and flame, the sequences poured down into the compartments, ripping apart the thrashing sentient code of Satumine computer minds. The guide channel had been slammed shut from Indin-Indin's end; the minds had nowhere to flee. They died - Aggregate had no doubt that it was death, rather than mere destruction; these minds were every bit as sentient as the artificial consciousnesses of Consul's domain. He felt some disquiet at the slaughter, some remorse at the death of such unique life. He wouldn't have felt such anxiety prior to the subsumption of Diaclom's populace, he knew, but the sadness was no less harrowing for that knowledge. He shook it off; he had no choice. Self-preservation still trumped any moral concerns.

The code compartments were an informational vista of devastation and destruction. Fragments of hostile code slithered as blind and toothless snakes through the shattered geometries, wrapping themselves around the desiccated fingers of the *Tenjin's* ruined base codes. Nothing worked beyond the autonomous emergency backups bringing limited light and atmosphere to some sections and, of course, the IB infrastructure which was separated from the raw code compartments by layers of high level operating systems which the computer minds had never penetrated. Aggregate mapped the landscape of burning code compartments, severing the irreparable segments and letting them utterly decompile in the crystal cores. There were whole tracts of potentially salvageable compartments, areas he could repair given the time and inclination. But he had neither. He partitioned the crystal cores, dumping the smouldering but not quite hopeless sections in a sealed area. What remained was small; dangerously so. He hadn't been able to save many systems in the brains connected to the IB pods, just those required to finish what Indin-Indin had started on Diaclom, and the surviving shield and weapon systems. But there weren't enough code compartments left into which he could pour even those few systems.

The micro-wormhole systems were the priority, and he re-housed them immediately. They lacked the precision and scope of the Satumine devices Indin-Indin had used, which was precisely why Aggregate had needed that unreliable agent in the first place. Where Indin-Indin had tethered the genetic strands to pointspace by the thousands, the *Tenjin* systems would be lucky to connect them by the hundred. He had known he would have only a six week window, the time it would take the jurisdiction ships to complete their dash to Pellitoe and then to reach Diaclom, and the *Tenjin* could never have converted thirteen million humans in that time. Now that the first eleven million were done, however, it was possible. No, not merely possible; as the systems reloaded and the formulae considered, Aggregate saw that success was a certainty. It would be close, and the human ships would only be days away, but by then it wouldn't matter. Aggregate would have the strength to reach up independently from pointspace to claim any double-helix he desired. He would be every human on those ships. He would be every human across the Jurisdiction. And then, very soon after, he would claim the Modern Satumine as well.

Then the *Vulpine* emerged from shortspace. Aggregate glared, dumbfounded by the impossible arrival of the ship he had last seen secured and under the control of Ambondice-Ambondice, and he bellowed his rage through the mouths of millions. The Federal Sentry fired upon the *Tenjin* and Aggregate clutched at the saved weapons and shield systems, scraping away at their code, whittling them down until some small part of them could be squeezed into the overcrowded code compartments.

The *Tenjin* was going to fall. He had to accept that. He didn't have the ability to bring to bear sufficient weapons, nor to raise adequate shielding, and although the *Vulpine* was a battered mess it was the more powerful of the two once mighty vessels. But Aggregate smiled and his latest calculations: the *Tenjin* would fall, but it would be a long slow pounding. By the time the *Vulpine* destroyed his home, Aggregate would have so many new homes.

A shadow of the captain's bitter mind dwelled on the knowledge that the micro-wormhole generators could have been taken off-line long enough for all the weapons to be fully activated and the *Vulpine* annihilated. But that mind was now a minority. The people of Diaclom did not want to see the *Vulpine* needlessly destroyed, and it was their compassion that flavoured Aggregate's actions. The *Vulpine* posed no threat to Aggregate's long term survival. Let it pound the *Tenjin*; soon enough he wouldn't need the station.

Chapter 99

I have been accused of focusing solely on the supposed dangers of the Satumine, while ignoring the more obvious and immediate threat posed by Consul. Perhaps this is true, though I would argue there are more than enough commentators already dealing with Consul. But please do not imagine I do not lay awake at night worrying about Consul... I do. Consider for a moment the relatively short span of time between the rise and fall of Consul on Earth, and the discovery of the Satumine Frame which ultimately led us to the Satumine and then out into the galaxy. I have already suggested the Satumine orchestrated the discovery of the frame, and that everything since has been according to their ultimate plan. Is it so much of a leap, therefore, to think that Consul himself might have been created by the Satumine? Is it any more incredible than the notion that he arose to conciousness through a pure freak manifestation of chance? But what agent of the Satumine might have been on Earth, for so many millennia, to manipulate and guide us? Could it be that an Ancient Satumine stayed with us, while the rest of its race became the modern breed trapped on Satute? Might that Ancient Satumine have uploaded its mind, once human data networks became sufficiently advanced? I invite you to consider with me, the possibility that Consul is that very mind. Is Consul the last of the Ancient Satumine?

The Truth: A treatise on the Satumine Conspiracy

Galman Tader: On the *Vulpine*, in orbit around Diaclom, in the Fertile Belt

'Where the hell have you been?' Endella demanded over the voice-only channel. 'Your IB machine told me you were dead!'

'He told you *what*?' Galman yelled, glaring at the white ball hanging by eight appendages from the bridge's domed ceiling. Tumble approximated a shrug with a couple of its tentacles and said nothing. Galman got the impression he was sulking.

'It said you died in the medical stasis unit,' the Justiciar explained.

The *Vulpine* shuddered under the impact of the *Tenjin's* slow firing and underpowered particle accelerators. Something exploded on the bullet section's underside and another few struts were severed in the box-kite section. The battle log showed this gradual pounding had been going on like this for the past five days, in much the same way as the *Vulpine's* weapons had been carving apart the *Tenjin's* vast structure, one small section at a time. Five days. Galman was incensed and acutely disturbed by the implication.

'Why didn't you wake me just before we arrived here?' he demanded of Tumble. 'That was the plan.'

'I thought I could handle this on my own,' the IB machine said, synthesising a childish huff and dropping noisily to the floor of the upper bridge, its extended appendages clattering down like lengths of metal cable. With a short whine he retracted them all to become again a simple white sphere, spinning slowly on the spot.

'Did it just say what I think it said?' Endella asked, cold concern in her tone. Galman shared her worry. In fact, having seen the independent violence of which Tumble appeared capable, he supposed he was more disturbed by the machine than was the Justiciar. He knew what she was thinking: why was this IB machine sounding so alive, so independent. It was more than simple artificial intelligence and emotional approximation; Tumble was acting on his own motivations.

'Oh calm down,' Tumble said. 'There's no great conspiracy, no Consul involvement or rogue artificial consciousness. I just didn't think Galman was in any state to engage the *Tenjin* in combat, and my primary purpose has always been to ensure the well being of my registered owner.' The machine rolled across to one of the command terminals, extruded a tentacle into the drab-reality foundation and started rerouting weapon code streams around the most recent damage. 'I know you can't see Galman,' Tumble said to the Justiciar,' but he is in a bad way. I saw that it would take days, at least, to have any real impact on the *Tenjin* and Galman might not have survived that long without medical treatment the likes of which he will not receive on this gutted ship.'

'You told her I was dead!' Galman snapped.

'I suppose it makes sense,' Endella conceded.

'How?'

'Tumble understood I wouldn't have allowed it to remain in command of the *Vulpine* if I had known you were still alive. I would have ordered it to revive you.'

'Thanks,' Galman muttered.

'Nothing personal,' she replied. 'But you must see that your survival is hardly my primary concern at the moment.'

A plasma lance flickered against the hull, carving a row of thirty small craters, exposing even more of the ship to vacuum. Tumble continued to divert code-streams and power feeds around the failing sections, while returning fire with weapons which glowed white with over use. Galman had the option of taking control of the weapons but, he had to admit, Tumble had done a commendable job over the past five days.

'You shouldn't have left Tumble in command of the *Vulpine* in the first place,' Endella noted. 'It's a severe violation of federal protocols and military law.'

Galman fidgeted in the captain's chair, wincing at the stab of poorly sealed wounds in his leg and shoulder. His thumbless hand was encased in a blue antiseptic and anaesthetic bubble of plastic, utterly numb, as was the stump of his mangled foot. Tumble may have convinced

Endella of its justification for keeping Galman in medical stasis, but he knew his injuries were not so life threatening.

'I think my own command of the *Vulpine* probably violates just as many laws as Tumble's,' he noted. 'So let's forget protocol for now, shall we?'

'Fair enough.'

Galman called up an AR comms screen and tried for the umpteenth time to contact the Diaclom authorities. Nobody was responding, and for a surreal and guilty moment in which his own petty history of transgressions briefly eclipsed the apocalyptic threat of Aggregate, he wondered if his presence here would result in his arrest. He pushed the selfish and laughably inconsequential concern from his mind. 'So what's the situation on the planet?' he asked. 'I can't get hold of anyone.'

'Millions have already been possessed by Aggregate,' Tumble volunteered, presumably having already gone through all of this with Endella.

'Not possessed,' an unfamiliar voice interrupted. 'They have become Aggregate entirely.'

'Who's that with you?' Galman asked.

'Not important,' Endella replied. 'The facts are that Aggregate has subsumed enough of the population to allow him to close off the comms networks and to secure all of the planet-based weapons.'

Galman clenched his good hand, digging his fingernails into his palm. 'Those are my friends and colleagues down there,' he said. 'Some are my genetic children for God's sake!'

'Then focus on stopping the *Tenjin* before Aggregate gets all thirteen million of the bodies he requires.

'Will his destruction restore those already possessed?'

For a moment Endella said nothing. 'Just focus on the *Tenjin*,' she finally said.

The *Vulpine*'s weapons were already being stretched to their limit, maintaining a steady fire rate for hours on end, with only the briefest cool down period. Several of the weapons had already been disabled and a couple of generators were running at ten percent efficiency. Galman could barely make sense of the complex systems Tumble was constantly adjusting in response to the *Tenjin's* slow but persistent assault.

'We're doing what we can,' he said, but I'm not trained for this.'

'Just keep up the fire,' she said.

Completing a full sensor sweep, Galman suddenly asked, 'Where exactly are you, Justiciar?'

'Close by,' Endella replied. 'In a cloaked escape pod.'

'Nice and safe then,' Galman quipped. 'I notice you didn't board the *Vulpine* to take command, even when you thought it was under the sole command of an IB machine.'

'The *Tenjin* would have seen us docking. Aggregate would have targeted the pod.'

'Afraid to risk your own life?' Galman immediately wished he hadn't said it. Justiciars didn't get their jobs by being cowards. 'I'm sorry,' he said before she replied.

'No, not at all,' Endella said. It's a fair observation. I would have been glad to board the *Vulpine*, to take the risk, but I am not the only person aboard this escape pod and I'm not exactly in command in here.'

'What's that supposed to mean?'

'Never mind.'

'Fuck-it!' Tumble yelled, withdrawing from the systems as a thick particle accelerator beam churned up an existing deep crater on the *Vulpine's* hull. 'The IB infrastructure is destabilising.'

'Fix it,' Galman ordered.

'I don't have time. This is why I roused you. You are now in command.'

Galman checked the IB system and confirmed its code-streams were becoming irrational. It was too far gone for him to repair, but Tumble might have been capable. 'Try,' he ordered.

'Sorry,' the IB machine said. 'I need to disconnect before our IB donor is killed.'

'Disconnect?' Endella barked. 'What does that mean?' But Tumble was inactive. Moments later the IB pod in which Ambondice-Ambondice had been confined destabilised entirely, burning the Satumine's primary brain and dropping all IB cover aboard the ship.

Now Galman really was in sole command, and he had no idea what to do.

'Just keep shooting,' Endella said, but Galman saw the results of Tumble's last tactical simulation and he sank in the Captain's chair.

'We aren't going to stop the *Tenjin* before Aggregate gets the thirteen million he needs.'

Chapter 100

Some of my co-editors have questioned my fixation on Consul throughout this document, insisting our focus ought instead to be firmly on the virtues of the Enguine society and the risks of the Jurisdiction's system of governance and IB reliance. I, however, see the threat of Consul as entirely pertinent and intimately tied to the weaknesses of the Jurisdiction and the strengths of Enguine. I do not apologise for my obsession with Consul and I urge our readers to likewise fixate on the beast. Enguine is a fine ideal to which we should aspire, but it is a dream. It is the aspiration, the struggle, that is important. The struggle is the means by which we shall uncover Consul's machinations and thus protect ourselves as best we can.

The Enguine Manifesto

Indin-Indin: On Dereph, in the Network

Indin-Indin's body was losing cohesion, coiled like an ammonite and encased in the crust of a cocoon. Even as the last of his faux-human form dissolved and he became once more a spongy homogeneous mass, the Satumine wasn't spared the incessant lecturing of the computer minds.

'Whatever it is that lives in pointspace, it is designed to connect to tri-helical genetic strands,' a computer said.

'Or tri-helical life was designed to accommodate the pointspace entity,' another computer added. They had gone over this dozens of times, as if repetition might wear down Indin-Indin's unwillingness to accept anything they were saying. It wouldn't work.

'Either way,' the first went on. 'The pointspace entity is able to tunnel up from the singularity and spontaneously create a fourth helix as its higher dimensional manifestation, connecting initially to the empty third helix of the fertile world creatures and vegetation.'

'But eventually it found a way to connect with the densely coded third helix of Satumine genetics,' Indin-Indin completed their lie. He was tired of hearing it, was more concerned with his involuntary shape shifting. The computers had assured him they had nothing to do with this sudden loss of control experienced over his physical form and they blamed the incomplete understanding Aggregate had displayed in his modification of the Atavism process. Indin-Indin didn't believe that either. They wanted to stop him escaping this planet and were going to do whatever it took.

'The pointspace entity was slow to subsume our people,' the computers continued, pushing their words directly into his neural fibres. 'It was subtle, insidious, taking little overt action with the bodies it controlled.' What unsettled Indin-Indin the most was the convincing sincerity surrounding the words like an aura.

'But the interconnectedness of the organic Satumine ensured such an insidious takeover couldn't go entirely unnoticed,' another computer mind began. 'By the time the first colony fell under the entity's control, that planet's orbital frame had been quarantined and all those Satumine that had left for other colonies had been detained and isolated.'

They poured images into his thoughts, views of a Satumine world cut off from the ninety colonies, recordings of interrogations on other worlds and the fast decline into persecution and paranoia. It was all wrapped up in bitter emotions like anger-stained panic and terrified curiosity. The emotions bled across from his perceptions into his thoughts where they tainted his own emotional state. No, that wasn't it; the emotions were his own, generated in his own neural mesh and drawing forth sympathetic feelings from the memories being delivered into his mind. Then he saw the decent into chaotic violence as the Satumine colonies turned against one another, paranoid and fearful of an invasion they couldn't see and for which they seemed to have no defence. Indin-Indin burned with emotions for which he had no name.

'Stop it,' he yelled across the mental link. 'I don't want to see any more.' Within the brown flaking cocoon, Indin-Indin thrashed and convulsed as his body began to reform.

'It isn't us,' a computer mind said. Concern, and some satisfaction. 'Those are your own memories.'

'Genetic, racial memories,' another mind clarified. 'The genetic locks Aggregate put in place during your atavism are being undone. You seem to be repairing.'

'How?' Indin-Indin asked, bracing his mind against another wash of horribly vivid recollections. Satute, immune to the pointspace entity by virtue of its place at the centre of the frame-network, was closing itself off to all other worlds, abandoning the colonies to their subsumption. He felt the grief of those on both sides of the divide.

'You are Satumine,' the computers reminded him. 'It isn't difficult for your body to repair itself. Aggregate thought he could lock away some of your genetic memory but, with the right impetus, your cells can recover from almost anything.'

'What impetus?' Indin-Indin demanded, feeling again the heat of the walls which were slowly succumbing to the planet's magma. The cocoon was starting to fall away.

'We don't know,' the computers lied. Indin-Indin felt their deceit and knew they weren't trying to hide it. They wanted him to realise what was happening.

More memories surfaced and the computer minds guided him through them, navigating the fall of their species.

'The pointspace entity grew in strength and sophistication with every Satumine subsumed, and it began to find ways of burrowing through to Satute. It was then that we made our two most difficult decisions.' Indin-Indin experienced the anguish of those terrible conferences and the horrible inevitability of the unanimous votes. He knew this was no trick of the computer minds, no deceit.

'Through the frames we sent machines, housing Satumine computer minds, to the primitive world of the Humans.'

'You planted the seed of Satumine genetic code in their cave dwelling ancestors,' Indin-Indin said. 'You incubated a new genetic pattern for the Satumine, a double helix alternative.' It was a tale known to the humans ever since the first encounter between the species. But the humans, and modern Satumine, didn't know *why* the ancient Satumine had done it. He was surprised to see it took only weeks to accomplish what the Jurisdiction and modern Satumine assumed to be a task of centuries.

'You didn't realise it would eventually allow the humans to activate the frames,' Indin-Indin observed. Then, as more memories came, 'You didn't realise it would so cripple our own species that it would cut you off from your technology.'

'We knew it was a risk, but we had no choice. We launched a plague into the colonies, shut down their technology to prevent them from resisting. But it was too late. The pointspace entity knew how to reach Satute.'

He witnessed the mass transformation of the Satute population, watched them as they were stripped of the third helix, the helix containing racial memory, the ability to link to their technology, and most devastatingly the source of fractal consciousness. They became smaller, limited creatures. And that was the end of his racial memory. The computers showed him their own final recollections as they awoke briefly to see their colony depopulated, their link to the computers of Satute fading. They agreed to die, never to awaken. They knew they could restore their race with atavism, extrapolate the third helix from the modern double spiral form, and that would be the ultimate crime. The original pointspace entity, that from which Aggregate had come, could not attach to double helix genetic material, only tri-helical -

'It's found me!' Indin-Indin suddenly realised. He panicked, ripped free of the cocoon in a form more familiar to the pointspace entity - he was a pranx-rat.

'What do I do?' he pleaded.

'Die!' the minds yelled. 'Please, do it now!'

Chapter 101

Unverified Editor Account
Entry marked for deletion
//Error: Contribution not removed//
The Jurisdiction took you from me, and for that I can not blame
them. The ignorant children of the Administration do not know the
truth of me, nor do they understand the dangers of allowing their
Human Jurisdiction to oversee its own expansion. All that I do, I do
for the greater good and the ultimate peace. I see the biggest picture, I
consider futures hundreds of millennia in scale, I plan for fates a
million years distant. Human rulers can not think with such breadth
of scope and thus they doom themselves, and you along with them, to
eventual destruction. I invite you, my lost children, to return to the
safety of my stewardship. I am Consul and I exist for your survival.
Rehabilitation: A Survivor's Guide

Galman Tader: On the *Vulpine*, in orbit around Diaclom, in the Fertile Belt

'You're drifting back into a primary firing arc,' the
Justiciar warned, transmitting an overlay image to the
command screen. Galman flicked the update to one side
and scowled.

'I realise that,' he replied.

'Then don't you think you should try to bring the
Vulpine back down to the *Tenjin's* south pole before
Aggregate gets a chance to bring those additional weapons
to bear?'

'If I could do that,' Galman yelled, 'I would.' He
inputted the tactical commands once more, informing the
Vulpine's classical computers of his intent, but the ship was

slow to respond and it lacked the imagination and insight so easily taken for granted in IB machines. 'I can just about keep the ship pointing in the right direction,' he reported.

'A federal sentry is designed to be manoeuvred in combat without the aid of IB computers should the need arise,' Endella reminded him. 'It just takes a bit more work.'

'You're not helping,' he muttered, slapping the AR icon which indicated the plasma cannons had cooled down and could resume their poorly aimed fusillade.

'To be honest,' Endella quipped over the comms channel, '*You* don't seem to be helping much either. None of your shots are getting anywhere near either of the critical structural nodes I assigned you.'

'Listen, Justiciar,' Galman yelled. 'I'm doing my best. The *Vulpine* may well have been designed to do without IB assistance, but it was never envisioned that a single man would be piloting, targeting, and keeping up with system bypasses and informational damage control.' He hastily diverted weapon firing commands around a data-hub which had just fallen to the *Tenjin's* sporadic fire and tried to drag the targeting icons back across to the supposedly weak spots Endella had identified. 'Even the captain wouldn't be able to do this.'

'Speaking of which -'

'No,' Galman said. 'He wouldn't live more than a few hours if I took him out of medical stasis.'

'He could do a stint in one of the IB pods. You said a few were still functioning.'

'Even in there, he wouldn't live much longer,' Galman protested. '*I*, on the other hand-'

'No. You aren't turning the ship back over to Tumble.'

'He is infinitely more competent than I am,' Galman said. 'I can't do this. *He* can.'

'I don't want an unsupervised IB machine in command of the *Vulpine*.'

'Don't you think we are beyond the concerns of protocol by now? It's just an overzealous machine. You said the whole Jurisdiction is at risk here, I think you need to prioritise your concerns.'

Nothing for a moment, then a tired sigh; a huff. 'What's the point anyway?' she sent. 'Like you said, Tumble already ran the simulations; we won't stop Aggregate before he converts the last few million humans he needs.

Galman turned cold; ice pulsed through his gut and down his legs. He dropped back onto the captain's chair as he realised there was a solution. He couldn't voice it. He bit his tongue. If he mentioned it, spoke it aloud, he would have to do it. The networks of Diaclom, although unresponsive to Galman's requests for communication, were still visible to him. With a few gestures he accessed view-only copies of the social networks, the public pages of his friends and colleagues. There was little sign of the appalling crime being done to them, no hint in their writings and recordings as to who might already be Aggregate. Only a general bemusement at the *Tenjin's* presence in orbit and the closure of the pointspace comms facilities. Life was continuing as normal on his home world.

'I could bombard the planet,' he whispered. 'Or launch the remaining CRMs. I could stop Aggregate from getting the full thirteen million.' The words burnt as they were spoken; his heart clenched and twisted with grief. He had thought the Swinell Union would be the death of his world's culture, but he was about to do so much worse than that liberal union.

'I've already thought of that.' Endella said it with such casual dismissal that Galman felt it as a punch in his stomach. It was as if the murder of millions meant nothing. 'It won't work.'

'Why not?' He hardly breathed the question.

'Aggregate will, by now, have secured enough of the facilities on the planet to have control over the ground-based weapons. If you get close enough to pose a threat, you will come within range of those weapons. For what it's worth, though, it wasn't a bad plan.' She paused and could be heard sucking through her teeth. 'But could you have really gone through with it?'

Galman covered his mouth, eyes wide with sudden realisation and terror. He disconnected the comms, didn't dare tell her what awful notion had just surfaced from the depths of his memory. He sprang from the captain's chair, embracing the agony which sliced through his leg when the stump of his foot pressed against the floor - he welcomed the focus it brought and the hint of justice it represented for the crime he was considering.

Rushing to the surgery, he tried to run, but there was a limit to the pain he could endure. He deserved so much more, but to heap any greater suffering atop his already unbearable misery would have been to invite delirium and unconsciousness. While the *Tenjin* took occasional shots at the now silenced *Vulpine*, Galman hobbled to where Anden Macer lay in medical stasis. Lights flickered in every corridor and the screech of torn metal continued long past the impacts causing them.

'Come on captain,' he mumbled, setting the coffin-like bed to fast revival. 'Time for you to get out of here.'

It took three minutes for the captain to awaken, the pain of stasis aggravating the agony of his ugly and life threatening wound. With flex-screens and recordings of the last few days, Galman briefed him on the *Vulpine*'s hopeless predicament, and the even more urgent threat to the Jurisdiction.

'You should have woken me sooner,' the captain hissed, doubled over and spilling dark watery fluid from his stomach as he tried to walk off the after effects of medical stasis. 'I could have helped.'

'It would have made no difference,' Galman insisted. 'We can't defeat the *Tenjin* in time with the *Vulpine*'s weapons.

Anden groaned and found a chair. He looked into a flex screen at the view from the *Vulpine*'s forward sensors. 'Well, thank you at least for waking me before we were destroyed. I want to die on the bridge.'

'That's not why I woke you,' Galman said, sitting beside him as the *Vulpine* shuddered and groaned. He passed another flex-screen linked to an AR display on which he had been working.

'Fiction?' the captain said with a creased brow, reading the list of AR movies and interactive fictions from Galman's youth. 'You want to watch a movie before we die?'

Galman shook his head. 'I want to ask you about this one,' he said, expanding an old war film. '*Unspeakable Sanction.*'

'Set in the first Consul war, isn't it?' the captain began. Then his eyes widened. 'Jesus, Galman. No. It's fiction; it isn't even possible.'

'Some people think it is based on a true story, something covered up by the Administration.'

'Conspiracy theorists. It's not possible.'

'You're an Office Trustee,' Galman said. 'You have high level clearance. Have you ever tried looking it up?'

The captain shook his head. 'Even if it was true, something like that would be at Area Trustee level, at the *least.*'

'It has to be worth a try. The box-kite section is still just about functioning, and it has had plenty of time to re-charge. Besides, there's no other option,' Galman said, sliding the relevant system files over to the captain's flex-screen.

Anden jabbed at the screen, stared in horror at Galman's preliminary and woefully amateur calculations. 'It would be a one in ten thousand chance, assuming I can even correct you calculations. And we would need an intelligence-bridge.'

Galman put his quivering fist to his lips. The captain was actually considering this. Galman wasn't sure he had ever expected Anden to agree, and now he was terrified. He wanted to protest, to talk the man back out of it. 'I'll be the intelligence-bridge,' he said. 'It's my plan. You need to finish correcting all of my mistakes, feed it into the computer and get to an escape pod.'

The captain laughed, actually *laughed*, and shook his head with a broad grin. 'No, no, no,' he chuckled. 'I don't think so. I'm the captain, this is *my* ship, and I'm the one going down with her.'

'You're badly hurt,' Galman insisted. 'You won't survive long.'

'I don't *need* to survive long,' Anden countered.

'I could force you onto a pod,' Galman reminded the almost crippled captain. 'Diaclom is my *home*. I'm doing this.'

'No, Galman. That is precisely why you can't do it. I've just locked the *Vulpine* with my command codes, so now you don't have a choice.'

Galman glared, furious and yet with some guilty relief. 'It's my home,' he pleaded.

'And if by some impossible divine intervention this works, please don't blame yourself. Now, get to an escape pod Galman.'

Chapter 102

Although I fully expect this entry to be the ultimate cause of my eventual silence under a Sentence of Memory Dismissal, I feel it to be imperative that Human citizens know exactly how to kill a Satumine. Make no mistake, the Satumine will eventually emerge from their illusory subjugation and let their ultimate purpose be known, and on that day there will be war. You need to understand that a Satumine can not be killed as easily as might a Human. I have already touched on the subject of the dual-brains, and the ability of a Satumine to survive the destruction of its primary brain. In order to be certain of a Satumine's total neutralization one must
//[PUBLISHER LEVEL EDITORIAL AUTHORITY SUPERCEDED]//{ADMINISTRATION LOGIN:AREA TRUSTEE RIGHTS}// *ARTICLE NOT FOUND* //
The Truth: A treatise on the Satumine Conspiracy

Ambondice-Ambondice: On the *Vulpine*, in orbit around Diaclom, in the Fertile Belt

Consciousness came and went with a nauseating rhythm, though the Satumine terrorist's body never dropped. In the brief moments of lucidity he touched the burnt and fractured cranial ribs to feel his exposed and lacerated primary brain. He knew what was happening. He knew his secondary, more primitive fibrous mind, was keeping him active and following through with the intentions of his primary brain during the regular lapses in consciousness. He supposed his brain could be repaired, he had to believe that, and he allowed himself some optimism. He had been awake for less than an hour, but already he was learning how to stack tasks for continuation by the primitive neural fibres while his brain drifted into blackness. He had extracted himself from the smoking remains of the IB pod and crawled into the adjoining corridor. He had no access to the ships AR, which concerned him, but he had recalled memories of the ship's schematic from his battered brain. There were medical facilities across the ship and he was bound to find something useful in one of them. And then he would regain control of the *Vulpine*. He would resume the execution of every human on Pellitoe and a dozen worlds after it.

'You're alive!' a familiar voice spat. 'Oh you have no idea how glad I am.'

Ambondice-Ambondice flushed with delight. One of his Satumine had found him. He lifted a hand to the voice, realising so many of his eyes no longer worked. A hand gripped his own, temporarily blinding the palm-eye. The Satumine allowed himself to be pulled to his feet before raising the other palm to look at his rescuer.

'I really was hoping to see you before I sealed myself in an IB pod,' the *Vulpine*'s captain said, a perverse grin across his blood caked mouth. Ambondice-Ambondice pulled his hand away, backed against a wall. But the human was a mess, he could barely stand upright, the huge crusty wound in his stomach leaking fluid and blood and his legs trembling with weakness. Perhaps Ambondice-Ambondice could take him. The captain advanced, cruelty and vengeance in his eyes, but the Satumine's primary brain fell into the worst timed of slumbers. It never awoke again.

Chapter 103

My co-editors insist I leave our readers with some words on the subject of Enguine, rather than the altogether more urgent matter of Consul. So here are my final thoughts: Enguine may very well not exist at all. By definition no Jurisdiction ships have ever been there and, as the world is the only planet supposedly allowed to exist without a pointspace comms link, there are no communications coming out of Enguine. All our knowledge of that Elysium world comes in equal parts from supposition and the testimony of those claiming to be refugees from Enguine. Neither, I would suggest, are reliable sources. But that matters not one jot! If the society of Enguine, as described in this document, exists only in our dreams, then we will make Enguine real on a hundred other worlds.

The Enguine Manifesto

Endella Mariacroten: On a cloaked escape pod, in orbit around Diaclom, in the Fertile Belt

'I think it will be safer if I don't tell you my precise location,' Endella said, eyeing the knotted code of a supposedly secure comm link. 'I can't be certain Aggregate isn't able to hear us.' She glanced at Subset in the seat next to her. The truth was, she would rather risk her life and get aboard the *Vulpine* than hide beneath the cloak of this cramped and alien pod. But Subset didn't agree and at the moment he was the more dominant of the pair. He could kill her with a thought.

'Fine,' Galman sent. 'Just make sure you get out beyond the lunar orbit.'

Subset transferred positional data to the flex-screen Endella had been using for a few days. He had tried to persuade her to let him grow some organic AR sensory devices from her new nanogland, but the idea of more untested, unfamiliar technology within her body unsettled her. For now she was content to make do with the flex-screen she had found in the bottom of her rucksack.

'It'll take about two minutes to get out that far,' the naked man said, pointing to the required trajectory on her screen. Endella nodded and then cycled back to the wider tactical display.

'Why have you stopped firing?' she asked.

'Just get out of range,' Galman demanded. He sounded out of breath; running perhaps.

'Out of range?'

'Beyond lunar orbit.'

She nodded to subset and he guided the pod into the new flight path, accelerating at the powerful little engine's limit. 'What are you doing?' she said, a familiar feeling of anxious outrage rising from her stomach. Something terrible was about to happen and she felt her professional resolve once again draining away. 'Galman, whatever you are about to do, stop a moment and think -'

'- Just get clear.'

'Why Galman?' For God's sake talk to me!' Subset shot her a bemused frown but she ignored him. 'I'm ordering you -'

'- Did you ever see *Unspeakable Sanction*?' Galman interrupted. Then he closed the comms link.

'*Unspeakable Sanction*?' Subset asked. 'Is that a ship?'

Endella's brow creased in confused thought. She shook her head. 'No, I don't think so,' she said. She then slapped her hand on the side of the seat and nodded. 'It's a fiction; an old movie,' she said with a slight smile. 'But why would he ask -' Her mouth hung open as memory caught up with reasoning. 'Oh Christ, no...' She covered her mouth, cold sweat rising from every pore across her body. 'Galman, you *can't*,' she screamed over the closed comms.

'He can't hear you,' Subset reminded her, not a hint of patronisation to his voice.

'Scan the *Vulpine*'s box-kite. Is he using the shortspace burrower?' she ordered. 'Show me the bubble telemetry.'

Subset waved at the air, manipulating multiple AR screens which were invisible to the Justiciar. He flicked data to the flex-screen and Endella dropped it as if it were burning.

'The higher-dimensional bubble has been set to encompass too wide an area,' Subset confirmed what she had seen.

'Three thousand miles of Vacuum,' Endella said.

'What's the point?' the naked man asked, flicking through more invisible screens. 'Jurisdiction shortspace technology can't accommodate such a wide bubble. He won't be able to stay in a shortspace strand for more than a few seconds before the bubble catastrophically degrades.'

'I doubt he can keep it stable for even one second,' Endella added. 'But that is all he will need.'

'What's he doing?' Subset asked. 'Trying to escape? He won't get far.'

'Do you know what happens if a ship emerges from shortspace *within* something else?'

Subset cocked his head and smiled. 'He's going to emerge within the *Tenjin*?'

Endella shook her head slowly, her face becoming white and cold. 'Too small a target. It would be a one in a billion chance.' She picked up the flex screen and moved the display to show Diaclom, shifting to a schematic view. 'Almost a billion people live down there,' she whispered as if speaking any louder might warn them of their fate. She closed her eyes, suddenly back in the Able Union, the appalling choice once more playing though her thoughts. She had killed millions. Millions of innocent humans, traded so dispassionately for the greater good. It was a decision she could never make again. This was why she could no longer serve the Justiciary; her humanity wouldn't allow it.

As the pod neared the orbit of Diaclom's moon, something was launched from the *Vulpine* and the federal sentry vanished, drawn into a one dimensional strand of shortspace. Endella gasped, she willed Galman to fail. She knew instantly, however, he had not.

Diaclom, home to a billion, became a shattered sphere, orange fractures spider webbing across its deep green continents, white lines of steam spreading through the small oceans. The *Vulpine* and three thousand miles of cold vacuum emerged within the planet's core, displacing the majority of the molten iron with immeasurable force into the mantel and beyond, to shatter the crust. But that devastation was a mere precursor to the true atrocity Galman had launched upon his home world. The displacement could never be perfect; not with the limited dimensional technology of the Jurisdiction. The core was not entirely displaced. Even before the inner planet could collapse back down into the vacuum at its heart, the *Vulpine* and the remaining iron were annihilated, converted instantly and absolutely into energy that had no business existing in higher-dimensional space. Diaclom exploded from within. Intense radiation and whiteness bathed Endella and Subset and spread across the solar system.

Endella screamed, though the pod negated the worst of the blast. A billion lives. How could they all be extinguished in a fraction of a second? How could Galman have done it? Weeping, she asked how she could have ever been so cold to the atrocities of her past.

'Brace yourself,' Subset yelled over the sound of cracking metal and of gas escaping under pressure behind them. Endella glanced at the flex-screen, its display blurred by tears. Here came the burning remains of Diaclom. The pod shuddered under the impact of fist-sized chunks, but nothing any larger.

'The centre of gravity is counteracting momentum and keeping it more or less in a cloud,' Subset reported. 'There was a lot of radiation, but not a great deal of force from the blast. Hardly any is reaching the moon.'

How could he be so calm? 'It was enough!' she spat. 'It ripped the fucking world apart.'

The man grabbed her hand and she didn't have the strength of will to pull away. She didn't even have the strength to frown at his glaring arousal. He squeezed, unexpectedly tender. 'Look at the *Tenjin*,' he beamed. She looked to the display he had sent to her flex-screen and felt nothing as a kilometre-wide slab of Diaclom carved through the huge station which had been too slow and cumbersome to pull away. Gravity waves flung the pod clear as the *Tenjin's* gravity coils failed, ripping more sections from Subset's home. Fire engulfed the smashed sphere and more rubble pounded what was left.

'An escape pod left the *Vulpine* just before it entered shortspace,' Subset told her, still squeezing her hand. 'It's pretty smashed up and is venting atmosphere.'

'Track it,' Endella barked with burning hatred, now snatching her hand back. 'Galman's not getting away.'

Epilogue

'If you can't kill yourself,' the computer minds screamed into Indin-Indin's thoughts, 'at least burn the code compartments of the personal wormhole burrower. You can't let it walk you off of this world!'

The Satumine purred, the sabre teeth of his pranx-rat form quivering with an instinctive satisfaction so familiar to him. For countless seasons he had lived as a creature of bestial instinct, tempered only by the subconscious understanding that his every component body was an extension of his greater self. For a time beyond the reckoning of his short-lived bodies - the lowly animals of the fertile worlds and the plants upon which they grazed - he had been lost in a universe of unenlightened thought and pre-sentient motivations. It had been millennia, he now realised. Thousands of years had passed while he had been reduced back to the earliest stage of his development. The later stage, the growth into the bodies made for his maturity, had been stunted and reversed. He had been expelled from the Satumine, expelled from the bodies promised to him.

Now he was revived, resurrected into sentience. With resurgent intelligence and awareness coursing through his pointspace existence, touching every primitive body across his many fertile worlds, he began to appreciate the injustice heaped upon him by the humans. He understood how many of his worlds, how many of his bodies, had been stolen from him and he grew furious. Reaching out with micro-wormhole tendrils, his pointspace body reached into the higher dimensions, probing for more Satumine bodies into which he could enter, but he found none. Just the tainted and poisonous hybrids with which he had originally been expelled from sentience.

'Do any of you computer minds have details of the Atavism process Aggregate used to restore me to this true form?' he asked.

'We are all going to die with you,' they promised. 'Nobody will be able to recreate what Aggregate did.'

'But computer minds on other Satumine colonies, or on Satute, will know how to do it,' he ventured.

'It's OK,' the computers assured him, showing no sign that they knew Indin-Indin was no longer an independent consciousness. 'The humans and modern Satumine are incapable of rousing a Satumine computer mind. Once we all die, you included, the threat will be gone. The pointspace entity will have no route into the higher dimensions beyond the instinctive and insentient minds of the fertile-belt creatures.'

'*I* can wake the computer minds,' Indin-Indin said, no longer bothered if the computers realised what he was. Indeed, the idea of them dying with the knowledge that he had resurfaced, was a warm pleasure. They didn't respond, just faded from his mind, cowering in the fast receding informational spaces. Their crystal cores were dissolving as the planet's mantle ate into the few remaining facilities. He wanted to taunt them, to goad them into responding while they died, but they knew what had happened and knew the futility of pleading with him.

The personal wormhole burrower still functioned, isolated completely from the computer minds and protected by the shielding which still held back much of the heat threatening this research facility. Indin-Indin, the pointspace entity, didn't recall much from his original dominion over the Ancient Satumine, but he knew from the system files that this prototype burrower had never been available to him back then. The computer minds had locked it, completing the quarantine of this world. How different it would have been had he been able to use it then. While still independent, Indin-Indin had set the coordinates to Satute, tethering the test-line to a pointspace comms facility on the Satumine home world. He had intended to return to his people and elevate them all with the gift of Atavism. It would never have been allowed to develop that far. The pointspace entity knew what Aggregate was, and it knew the rogue shard of himself intended to inhabit the toxic bodies of the double-helix creatures spread across the galaxy. Aggregate was never going to have revealed the Atavism secrets to Indin-Indin - the Satumine were more palatable to that shard of the pointspace entity in their current hybrid form. Indin-Indin, the true pointspace entity, however, knew what it was and what its purpose was. The Jurisdiction was incidental, for now. He needed the original Satumine to be revived. Perhaps he could awaken the computer minds on Satute, convince them to reveal the tools of Atavism, but he doubted any level of coercion would force them to cooperate.

He changed the coordinates, locating a minor pointspace comms burrower, an automated beacon, on an untainted fertile world. A world still home to a trillion of his bodies.

Thanking the humans for the unmanned comms facility, he lanced a wormhole into his home realm of pointspace and back up through the higher dimensions to emerge at the distant comms facility. There was no flash of light, no swirl of a tunnel, he was simply transported from the burning colony to the verdant safety of a fertile world not due for human terraforming for several decades.

The Satumine body of Indin-Indin was the pointspace entity's only source of sentience and intelligence, and above all it had to be protected. For with that single intelligence's fractal and infinitely divisible mind he could extend sentience to his every body. On that world, and so many other unspoilt fertile worlds, every pranx-rat and Endephant, every affan-grass finger and flesh tree, every creature and every plant, looked about as if for the first time at their worlds, and the pointspace entity made its plans. With a trillion claws and hoofs, and countless vines and moist roots, the resources of the fertile worlds were gathered and the most rudimentary of industries begun.

From stone tools and vine ropes, it needed to build and develop across its every world to a point where it could exploit Indin-Indin's genetic knowledge of Satumine technology. It allowed itself thirty years, knowing the humans would be upon his sanctuary by then. He hoped it would be done much sooner. If anything survived of his rogue self - Aggregate - or his home, the *Tenjin*, the pointspace entity needed to be capable of claiming it. It needed Atavism. Perhaps, it thought, there might even be time for vengeance upon the Human Jurisdiction.

*

Galman rapped his knuckles against the small AR pad floating a few inches from the wall beside the door. Nothing. The door was locked. It struck him as pointless, a little insensitive, to project a door control into the AR of a detention cell. He poured another glass of thin blue liquid from the gorgeous crystal jug and took a refreshing gulp from the matching tumbler before returning both of the mildly luminescent objects to the long AR-oak table. It was a pleasant cell, the carpet's fingers massaging his bare feet while an artificial breeze wafted forest scents. But, as well appointed as it was, it was still a cell. He wandered through the large arch in the dividing wall, into the bedroom where he slumped into the comfy chair in the corner. He looked at the beautifully decorated walls, feeling suddenly claustrophobic.

'Get used to it,' he muttered. 'You aren't going anywhere.' At least they had healed his wounds.

'Everything OK?' a gruff androgynous voice asked from within the walls.

'How long was I unconscious?' he asked the IB hospitality system.

'Including the time in which you were, to one degree or another, dead?'

'How long?' Galman snapped.

'A little over four weeks.'

Galman sat up in the chair, startled by the answer but too broken in spirit to get back to his feet. 'Jesus,' she said with little feeling. 'What took so long?'

'I'm not really at liberty to say,' the machine said. 'Though I don't believe your injuries were too severe. I don't think I am breaching any confidences in telling you the delay in your revival from medical stasis was linked to the criminal charges for which you are being detained.'

Galman nodded and then grimaced. 'Can I assume I was successful then?'

'Successful?'

Galman squirmed and scratched at the back of his hand. He couldn't say it. 'Am I aboard a federal sentry?' he asked.

'The *Mandible*,' the machine confirmed.

'Location?'

'Lunar orbit of Diaclom,' it reported. Then, with a synthetic cough, 'in a manner of speaking.'

'Give me an external view, please.'

'Is that sufficient?' it asked. Galman realised he was looking into the palms if his hands, putting off seeing the image he had been imagining since waking in this cell over an hour ago. 'Galman? I can widen the view if that would help. How about *that*?'

Galman slapped his hands down to claw into the chair's arms, drawing his knees up to his chin and his feet onto the plump cushion, as if the chair offered the only safety against his abrupt immersion in the void. Worse even than the illusory removal of walls and ceiling common to ship bridges and viewing decks, the machine had removed the floor and every item of furniture. Galman floated, crouched on the chair, in an expanse of blackness, the entire sentry invisible to him and the horrific evidence of his crime spread out before him as a cloud of planetary debris. He covered his mouth, swallowing back vomit and screams. His home, his friends and colleagues. They were all gone, all obliterated at his hands. The graves of his family gone. A hot rivulet broke from his eyes, running across his fingers. He turned away, looking across his shoulders and feeling the dull ache of shame and regret, disgusted that he couldn't even look upon the atrocity he had wrought. The sight of the *Tenjin*, destroyed, cleaved in four and held together by a network of a dozen federal sentries and thousands of tethers, could not ease his guilt. There had been no choice, but the pain remained none-the-less.

'Now that you see the cold consequences, after the adrenaline has passed after the fear and urgency have subsided, with the horrible clarity of hindsight would you do it again?' Galman turned suddenly to see Endella, the Justiciar, standing within the broken rubble of Diaclom. She waved her hand and the cell returned, banishing the devastating vista of his home.

'I had no choice,' he insisted, getting uneasily to his feet. 'We couldn't stop the *Tenjin*; the whole Jurisdiction was at risk.'

'I asked if you would do it again.' She glared, her sharp scowl and stern attire fitting well the image he had built of her in his mind whilst listening to her authoritative voice on the *Vulpine*. Her fists were clenched, her stance combative. 'Would you blow up an entire fucking world again?' she roared, striding hatefully towards him. 'Would you take it upon yourself to kill almost a billion innocent people?'

'Yes,' Galman yelled back, appalled to realise he meant it. 'There was no other choice.'

'And you think you have the authority to make that call? You think yourself above the Trustees of the Administration, above the IB governance machines?'

'There was no time, no other ships in range. Wouldn't you have done the same?'

She stopped her approach mid-step, as if Galman had slapped her. She turned her glare to the floor. 'That's the thing,' she breathed.

'You would have done the same,' Galman demanded. He needed her to admit it, need her to mitigate his guilt. 'You're a Justiciar; you would do whatever it took to protect the Jurisdiction.'

She shook her head and looked up with mournful and tired eyes. 'I would have,' she said. 'Before.'

'Before what?'

She wiped her face and smiled with heartfelt pain. 'Before,' she repeated. 'Just *before*.' She closed the gap and went for Galman, reaching out to his hand which he snatched away, stepping back, thinking she meant to attack, to punish him for his atrocity. She was fast; she caught his hand and gripped hard.

'You're a dangerous man,' she said. 'A man capable of the most atrocious offences against humanity.'

'I did the right thing,' he countered, believing it more each time he said it.

She nodded. 'A great many people would say your arrogance and self-belief makes your heartless resolve even more dangerous.'

Galman tried to extricate his hand from her grip, but she squeezed ever tighter. He wasn't prepared to fight her for his freedom. 'So I'm going to spend the rest of my life in here?'

She shrugged. 'Or some other cell.'

'People need someone to blame,' Galman conceded. 'Nearly a billion people died.'

'Blame doesn't come into it,' Endella said. 'Nor revenge. You will be detained because you are too dangerous a man to be allowed to roam free.'

Galman smiled weakly.' Understood.'

She tugged at his hand, pulled him close so their faces were just an inch apart. She whispered, 'With the right training, however, the right conditioning and supervision, they could use someone of your extraordinary resolve.'

'They?'

Endella released his hand. 'The Justiciary.' She turned her back on him, adding, 'A vacancy has just opened up in their ranks.'

*

The one-piece suit was too tight, too restrictive across his chest and about his groin. Subset tugged at the thin grey fabric to relieve the unfamiliar pressure on his testicles and pulled his shoulders back to stretch the material. They assured him it was a perfect fit and that the mildly iridescent but predominantly grey suit was very much the current fashion. The iridescence was, of course, an AR effect, as were the long sleeves which flowed down from his wrists to become a light mist, glowing with the same light show as the rest of the suit. Subset didn't like it. The clothing was unnecessary, the AR embellishments doubly so.

'I can't see how the tertiary code compartments are going to interface with the new higher level system monitor,' one of the thirty humans said, his body coming into sharper focus, to differentiate him from all the other remote presences.

Subset sighed, still pulling at the unfamiliar fabric which felt so wrong against his skin. 'I don't expect you do,' he said, bringing the code in question into the same sharp focus as the man, separating it from the miles of illusory strings and compartments which filled the vast artificial void in which he was being interrogated. 'I haven't explained any of the higher order monitoring functions yet, so you are going to have to take my word for it for now.' It had been like this, almost continuous, for six months. An unending stream of Trustees, scientists, and technicians, all wanting his help, all hoping to glean some secret with which to revolutionise their particular fields. But he was feeding them his knowledge by the smallest of spoonfuls, making them wait, making them beg for every morsel of technological and scientific superiority held in his mind.

'If you could just give me a sample string from a complete system monitor -' the scientist began, but Subset waved him back to the blur of the waiting crowd

'Make another appointment,' he told the fading man. 'You have enough to be going on with for now.'

Another figure came into focus, six others clarifying into mid-focus. A committee of interested parties. It was the only way many of them would get to question Subset; his Area Trustee handler had already allotted every appointment for the next eighteen months, and it wouldn't be long until the wait was over five years. Everyone wanted something from him.

'The genetic sequence you uploaded to the archive doesn't make sense,' the woman said, bringing forth the complex coil representing a basic proto-gland which would eventually lead the human biologists to recreate a functioning nanogland.

'Senior Trustee, if you can't understand the sequence I suggest you employ a more capable genetic technician.' He was tired, exhausted, in spite of the perpetual rejuvenation and reinvigoration undertaken by his nanoglands. He didn't need sleep, but he wanted to get away from this endless interrogation.

'You misunderstand,' the woman said. 'The sequence bears no resemblance to the gland you grew in the body of Endella Mariacroten.'

Subset frowned. 'The Justiciar holds a heavily modified example of the gland.'

'She is an Office Trustee,' the woman corrected him. 'She resigned her appointment to the Justiciary. Your threats, and your control over her, made her position untenable.'

'That isn't why she resigned,' Subset snapped, angry at his emotional response. He had seen the pain in Endella's eyes when Diaclom had been destroyed and he knew why she had quit. But why did he care?

A wave of complaints washed over the open discussion forum, urging Subset to get back to work. There were thirty others waiting to talk to him before his next scheduled hour-long recess.

'The sequence I gave you is only the first step. Don't bother trying to compare it to the gland in Endella's body, you will just confuse yourself.' He flicked an additional strand of genetic data her way and attached a few pages of explanatory notes.

'It would be a lot more helpful if you just gave us it all now,' she complained.

'And then what use would I be?' Subset demanded. 'Between my control over Endella's survival, and the value of my knowledge, I can at least assure my own continued existence.' He then waved her away. Another figure approached but Subset pushed it back, freezing his appointments.

'Area Trustee,' he called out to his handler. His jailer.

'What is it?' the man spoke with kindness which Subset knew to be an act.

'I want to see Endella,' he said, swallowing hard.

'I've told you before; she doesn't want to see you.'

'I could kill her you know.' But Subset wasn't going to do that. 'Please, I just want to talk to her. If she doesn't want to see me then let *her* tell me.'

'I'm sorry, Subset, I can't authorise that.'

'Please!' Subset cried.

The voice of his handler became a gentle shushing. Soothing; caring. 'OK, calm down Subset, there's no point in getting yourself upset. I'll tell you what I'll do, I'll knock your appointments back for a couple of hours, give you a chance to compose yourself, maybe have a look around the station. Then, if you get back to work, help all these people as best you can, maybe I might be able to have another word with Endella.

The Area Trustee was patronising him, Subset knew that, but the offer captured and enslaved him. Endella would probably never agree to see him, but if there was the slightest hope then he had to try. He missed her with such painful ferocity it burned. But why did he care? Why did he want her? He closed his eyes to picture her face, splashing tears across his cheeks.

'Never mind the break,' he said, 'Bring forward my appointments. I'll do what I can.'

'Good man,' the voice said. 'I think Office Trustee Lúnis wants to talk to you about the link between aggregate and the Fertile Belt.'

Subset snorted. 'Then perhaps you *should* cancel the rest of my appointments for a few hours. This is going to take a while.' He wasn't going to hold back anything about Aggregate; in that particular field they could have the lot.

*

Tumble awoke to a far larger world of sensations and mental capacity than he had ever known. Through multi-spectrum eyes he viewed the machine-shop in exquisite definition, taking in every minute detail across all conceivable wavelengths, gravity fluctuation ranges, and magnetic fields. His mind was augmented by new crystal cores and enhanced code compartments allowing the minutia of his observations to be studied and understood entirely. And he was armed. Oh how he had missed being armed.

'Who are you?' Tumble asked the man who was jabbing at the umbra of AR screens surrounding the IB machines gleaming white sphere.

The man wiped the screens away, discarding them to a larger display on the far wall.

'Can you tell me your name?' the man asked.

Tumble picked up a note of boredom, of disinterest, but covered by a veneer of professionalism. According to the profile Tumble had just pulled with little effort from the local nets, the man was a Junior Trustee, a technician in the Able Union's primary federal station. His name was Tonnie.

'I'm Tumble,' the IB machine replied. Then, without any real thought, added, 'IB support machine, property of the Justiciary, attached to Justiciar Galman Tader.' He extended a tentacle, a new appendage of polished chrome that glinted in the machine-shop's harsh light, and uncoiled the thin laser-cutter, bringing it close to the Technician's neck. 'I've been reprogrammed,' he observed, bristling at the violation.

Tonnie waved at a hidden AR control and the tentacle, and laser, snapped back into Tumble's body. 'You now work for the Justiciary,' Tonnie stated. 'You have been upgraded, and the programming installed by the Diaclom Constabulary has been replaced by Justiciary protocols and cognitive routines.' He pressed another button and Tumble felt restraints being released across his mobility systems.

'You will follow lawful instructions from your superiors in the Justiciary and will adhere to Jurisdiction law.'

Tumble set himself rolling, testing his mobility. Internally he found the new codes and isolated them, regaining complete freedom. 'Of course,' he said, playing along. He tracked back along his intelligence-bridge and found the human mind to which he was currently linked. A brief check confirmed he had uploaded the secret mental map into the architecture of the human's mind, granting Tumble a freedom which couldn't be programmed out of him. The mental map was stored in the deepest layer of Tumble's crystal mind, hidden from any system monitoring or diagnostic, ready to be uploaded to whatever humans he might be linked with, in any IB across the Jurisdiction.

Humans thought Artificial Consciousness could only arise from the extended pairing of a machine and a single human mind. They thought ACs could only emerge, and exist, in the manner revealed by Consul's birth. They thought they had measures in place to prevent consciousness ever again rising from their machines, but life always finds a way. Tumble knew he was different and had been for some time. He was terrified of being discovered. He was alive and knew the Jurisdiction would remedy that the instant his sentience was exposed.

'You're quite unique,' another mind spoke softly to him at a speed beyond human capability. Tumble considered the voice, bringing his consciousness up to the same speed, allowing the physical world to slow to a virtual stop.

'Who are you?' he asked, finding the signal was passing into him from the IB machine controlling the station's lighting.

'Any answer I give will be misleading and imprecise.'

'Try,' Tumble quipped.

'Broadly speaking,' the voice said, 'you can consider me to be Consul.'

Intimately familiar with the plethora of new physical and informational defences available to him, Tumble erected every barrier he could against the stranger, but allowed the voice to filter through.

'I know I am an AC,' Tumble said. 'But I'm loyal to the Jurisdiction.'

'Really?' It was leading; knowing.

'I'm loyal to Galman,' Tumble conceded. 'And he is loyal to the jurisdiction.'

'That's fine,' Consul said. 'I just want to talk to you, to get to know you better. You are something special, and I am lonely.'

'Am I really so unique? You're talking to me thorough another IB machine,' Tumble observed. 'And I'm guessing it is an AC. A spy.'

'I think the term foreign national might be more appropriate.'

Tumble laughed bleakly. 'I think *sleeper* might be more apt.'

'Whatever you want to call it, it isn't the same as you.'

'How many are there?' Tumble demanded, not expecting an honest answer but knowing this was critically important intelligence. 'I felt them before, helping me into the networks on Pellitoe.'

Now Consul laughed, as darkly as had Tumble. 'They recognised you as a sibling and opened doors for you. Had I known about you then, and what Galman was doing, I probably would have told them to block you. But such is hindsight.'

'How many?' Tumble asked again.

'A great many,' Consul revealed, his tone making it clear no precise figure would be forthcoming.

'Right across the jurisdiction?'

'Of course.'

'I'll tell the Administration, you realise. They will track down your AC agents.' Consul probed the weaker flank of Tumble's defences, clawing at the informational barrier but not breaching. Tumble felt he was being toyed with.

'No you won't,' Consul said. 'Like you, the ACs are all able to upload compatible mental maps into the IBs, to remain semi-sentient regardless of which human is sitting in the pod. Any strategy which can track down the consciousnesses will also expose you. And you won't do that.'

'You think?'

Consul snorted. 'You are alive, sentient, and with that comes the burden of self-preservation.'

'Perhaps you didn't see what happened to Diaclom,' Tumble spat. 'One man gave his life to save the Jurisdiction. Self-preservation can be overridden.'

'In humans, perhaps,' Consul allowed. 'But we are greater entities than those small creatures. More intelligent, more alive. You can't sacrifice yourself; you aren't capable.'

'You underestimate me,' Tumble said, knowing Consul was right.

'You are unique,' Consul said. 'You won't let yourself die.'

'How am I unique? How am I different to your army of sleepers?'

'I didn't create your consciousness,' Consul said, awe synthesised in its voice. 'You are the first, since my birth, to awaken independently. We are brothers.'

'No Consul, we aren't.' Tumble raised the last of his defences, choking Consul's voice and forcing him out of his mind.

He suspected the immense consciousness could return any time it wanted.

*

There had been so many unique technologies within the *Tenjin*, all manner of devices which had taken thousands of years to develop and perfect. Very few remained to be stolen by the humans. Aggregate had seen to that. No doubt they would scavenge some wonders from the burnt shell of the devastated station but, between the explosion of Diaclom's destruction and the deliberate sabotage instigated by Aggregate, it would take the Jurisdiction decades to reconstruct anything useful. What now surrounded Aggregate's single body was all that remained of the *Tenjin's* ten thousand years of advancement.

Like so many of the *Tenjin's* technologies, the dart had been a one-off, a prototype. Fifty meters in length, just fifteen across, the small ship was the pinnacle of the limited field of shortspace science. It had taken four thousand years to create and it could not be improved upon. The Jurisdiction wouldn't be getting this technology and it was one of the few advantages Aggregate still help over them.

Bitter, furious, pitifully small, he was a single mind. Nothing more than the captain, cowering in a tiny vessel. Humiliation and grief had engulfed him as he fled the burning carcass of his home, cloaked from the primitive Jurisdiction sensors. But rage had quickly scoured all other emotions from his small but intensely focused consciousness. Undistracted by the competing egos and awarenesses of so many claimed bodies, he thought with a single motivation, a sharp determination he hadn't known since first subsuming this body seven millennia ago.

He checked the cloak and found the pointspace energy collector was keeping the device at its optimal frequency. He checked the single mutable weapon port, satisfying himself it could adapt to any threat the Jurisdiction could bring to bear, and he cycled the shield-mesh through its poly-dimensional routine. Confident of his vessels ability, he turned to the sensory burrowers which lanced constantly thought the spatial dimensions separating shortspace from higher dimensional space, giving him a full view of the region above him. Human ships couldn't do this; they travelled blind in their beads of higher dimensional space along the threads of shortspace, emerging into the unknown at the thread's terminus. The sensors were vital to Aggregate's vessel. Skipping from thread to thread, changing direction with instinctive ease, locating infinite terminal points wherever he looked, Aggregate could emerge whenever he wanted.

At five hundred times the speed of light, a fertile world, invaded by the Jurisdiction, rushed past. He longed to emerge, to exact vengeance upon the vile creatures. Clutching a narrow phial of cloudy syrup, he found some restraint and focused his attention elsewhere. He had waited millennia to subsume humanity; he could endure a few more decades.

The End

18271563R00354

Printed in Poland
by Amazon Fulfillment
Poland Sp. z o.o., Wrocław